Goodnight, My Angel

'Kate felt the chill creep over her . . . It's not Melanie, she told herself. This isn't my child. It's some kind of sadistic game . . .'

It is nearly five months since eleven-year-old Melanie Pearson disappeared while walking home from school – since her mother was asked to identify her battered, lifeless body.

Kate Pearson is only just beginning to come to terms with her daughter's murder when a sinister message appears on her computer screen at work:

Why did you let him hurt me, Mummy?

As more horrifying messages follow, Kate realizes there is only one person who could be doing this to her – Melanie's murderer.

Leading the hunt for the killer, Chief Inspector Harmon focuses his inquiries on Kate's abusive ex-husband David and her colleague, Internet whiz-kid Adam Shepherd. Both men certainly have shadowy pasts – but could either be capable of such evil?

For it soon becomes clear that the killer is not content merely to hack into Kate's computer. He is out to infiltrate her life and destroy her completely. But Kate has already lost the one thing that gave her life meaning. So instead she turns his evil back on itself and unmasks the killer . . .

MARGARET MURPHY

Goodnight, My Angel

MACMILLAN

First published 1996 by Macmillan

an imprint of Macmillan Publishers Ltd
25 Eccleston Place, London SW1W 9NF
and Basingstoke

Associated companies throughout the world

ISBN 0 333 66948 7

1 3 5 7 9 8 6 4 2

A CIP catalogue record for this book is available from
the British Library

Phototypeset by Intype London Ltd
Printed by Mackays of Chatham PLC, Chatham, Kent

The line from *Neuromancer* by William Gibson (reprinted on page 271)
is reproduced by permission of William Gibson,
Martha Millard Literary Agency and HarperCollins Publishers Limited.

With thanks to Murf for the laughter,
and to Dr R. C. Bucknall, who keeps
the Wolf from the door

Acknowledgements

My thanks for technical help and advice on the Internet and e-mail to Pete Elms and Dr Martin Mortimer. Tribute must also be paid to the insights into the hacker mentality provided by the excellent book *Cyberpunk* by Katie Hafner and John Markoff.

MELANIE SLAIN

Melanie Pearson has been found battered to death and dumped by the side of a path in woodland 10 miles from her home in Manchester. There were no signs of sexual assault, but articles of clothing had been removed.

Dark-haired Melanie, who disappeared a week ago, should have been celebrating her twelfth birthday today. Her distraught mother was supported by a police escort as she left the mortuary after identifying the body.

Melanie's disappearance sparked a nationwide hunt. Police described the public response as 'overwhelming', and officers are said to be shattered by today's grim discovery. Experienced policemen and women are said to have been sickened by the viciousness of the attack on the little girl.

The officer leading the investigation, Detective Chief Inspector Harmon, said, 'Until the murderer of Melanie Pearson is caught, no parent can feel complacent about their children's safety.

We are looking for a very dangerous killer. I would urge anyone who has any information to come forward. A husband or a son who has been acting strangely, or who may have come home yesterday with blood on his hands or his clothing. Any information will be treated as confidential.'

Few girls at Melanie's school, Trafford High, are being allowed to walk home alone; parents have set up a rota and groups of girls are walked home by at least one adult. Teachers have been seen patrolling the perimeter of the grounds at three thirty and are supervising children catching buses. Melanie was seen leaving the school grounds with a tall, slim man, who wore a dark, anorak-type coat with the hood up.

One parent summed up the feeling of everyone when she said, 'You can't feel safe with a nutter like that about. We're making sure he doesn't snatch one of our kids on the way home from school. But you can't watch them all the time. You can't keep them prisoner in the house, can you?'

Chapter One

A murmur of voices, subdued and soothing, melded with the soft, rapid click of the computer keyboards in a pleasing harmony. November sunshine slanted into the office. Golden, still warm. Somebody had opened a window, and the steady hum of afternoon traffic in Albert Square created its own static noise.

Kate Pearson sighed. It was not a discontented sigh, and she smiled, half bemused and half amused by her mood. Something was missing. She realized with considerable surprise that she felt as mellow as the afternoon light. For the first time in nearly five months she was relatively content. So this is what it feels like, she thought, letting her gaze drift to the window and out over the little square of garden at the back of the office building. I had forgotten what it is like to be— She stopped. Not happy. She felt she would never be happy again. Not truly happy. But sanguine. Perhaps that was the word. The trees, flushed with late autumn sunlight, some now quite bare in the lowering sun, flared red as if in one last mutinous surge against the oncoming winter, and a draught of cool, scented air followed, buffeting her face. She closed her eyes for a moment and breathed deeply, then returned to her proof-reading, lightly tapping the 'page down' key.

Eight horrifying words filled the screen.

Kate gasped, snatching her hands away from the keyboard. Her breath came in short gasps.

Everyone was working quietly. Sam was going over some paperwork with Emma, and their voices could be heard above the keyboard clack and the soft swish of traffic.

Kate forced herself to look again at the monitor. At the bottom of the screen, another line of text.

She pushed her chair away from her work-station and stared, appalled, at the screen.

There was a murmur of disquiet. Glances were exchanged. The staff, mainly women, grew more uneasy as Kate's agitation increased. She wanted to get out, to run from the terrible words on the monitor, from the prying eyes of the others, but she did not trust her legs to carry her, so she sat, looking from the monitor to the anxious faces of her co-workers and back to the monitor.

Her view was blocked. She felt a confused mixture of relief and irritation. She was staring at somebody's midriff. Her eyes tracked upwards to his face. Adam. He, of them all, was the only person it could have been. She didn't have many friends at the office. She didn't blame them. She'd given them good reason over the last few months to dislike her.

'Kate?'

She stood, hardly knowing what she was doing, and he put out a hand to support her.

'Kate, what is it? What's wrong?'

She was staring over his shoulder and he turned, following the line of her gaze.

'Christ!' he whispered. In the silence of the room the word carried like a shout.

Curiosity overcame the wariness of the rest of the staff, and they edged towards Kate's station. It was placed fairly centrally, and several people had already leaned forward or across and exclaimed at the lines of text.

Why did you let him hurt me, Mummy?

and below:

I love you, Mummy. I want to come home.

Adam highlighted the messages with quick, almost automatic movements and deleted them. He saved the report that Kate had been working on and then switched off her machine.

Kate had not moved. She was deathly pale. He was still holding her just above the left elbow, and now he led her from the office.

The mumble of questions exploded into an excited babble before the door closed behind them.

Melanie was laughing at one of her terrible jokes and Kate felt a warm rush of love for her. She slipped her arm around her daughter's shoulder and gave her a fierce hug. Melanie shrieked with laughter, answering with a squeeze of her mother's waist. She looked up and her silky, brown hair fell away from her face; her eyes were wide, sensing fear. They were in a wood by a stream. It was growing dark, and Kate was anxious that they should return home.

'Are we lost?' Melanie asked, suddenly frightened.

Kate smiled down into her daughter's eyes, trying to draw the fear from her, to take the burden for the two of them. Melanie's eyes, as green as her own, shone back at her, round and showing too much of the whites.

'No, love, we're not lost,' she said, calmly, but she didn't finish with the usual line, 'I just don't know where we are.' Melanie, aware of the omission, huddled closer to her mother.

The woods became darker, more tangled and wild. Brambles scratched their legs and snatched at their clothing.

'Mum . . .'

Kate gripped her daughter's hand tightly. 'It's all right. We'll be all right if we stay together. We just have to stay together. Stay with me, Mel. Don't let go of my hand.'

'Melanie!'

Kate was alone now. Standing in a clearing. Standing in the darkness. Her voice, shrill and panicky, seemed to stop, carrying no further than the edge of the trees that circled the rough patch of grass and bracken where she stood. She could hear running water. Not the stream they had walked by earlier, but a river, bubbling and grumbling over rocks. It was dark, so dark, and she could not find Melanie.

She screamed again, 'Melanie!' and ran towards the sound of the river. A gun boomed. It seemed to be above her head. Dull, damped by the strangely heavy air of this place.

'MELANIE!'

Kate woke with tears streaming down her face. It was dark, so dark. She blinked in the darkness around her. The dull pounding began again. Her neighbour, Mrs Wilson, was banging to complain of the noise.

She was in Melanie's room, holding her daughter's favourite teddy bear in her arms. Melanie had told her she'd thrown it away when she started at the big school, and Kate had protested that you were never too old for your teddy. Melanie, aloof and disdainful, had said, 'Well, I am. That's kids' stuff.' Kate had found it in the bottom drawer of Melanie's dresser during one of her restless all-night prowlings in the early days.

She could just make out the luminous dial of the Mickey Mouse clock on the dresser. Melanie had insisted on placing it on the windowsill, facing the sunlight, every morning –

4

'To pump up its energy pack,' she said. Kate kept the curtains closed now, and the glow of Mickey's gloved hands and the markers on the dial were dimmed. Ten thirty.

Gradually the sobbing became less painful, the tears abated, and she regained control. The numbness she had felt all afternoon and evening had gone, but she felt a terrible yearning for Melanie. She had thought that the aching emptiness she suffered in the first few weeks could never be so debilitating again, but she felt it now, as intense and as real as in those stumbling half-mad moments when they told her Melanie was dead.

She thought that she must make an effort to move. Adam had brought her home from work, leaving her reluctantly on the doorstep – she had refused his offer to make her a cup of tea. She had tried to watch TV, to break the suffocating silence of the flat, but she couldn't follow the dialogue; it made no sense to her. She remembered little of what followed, only that eventually, exhausted, she had crawled into bed in her own room: she was sure of that much. She had, in fact, avoided Melanie's room because she hadn't wanted to unleash the storm of emotion that would rage through her body and mind, leaving her feeling weak and ill. As she felt now. She realized with a sigh that she had only held off the storm a little longer.

The telephone rang and Kate jumped. Clutching Melanie's teddy bear more tightly to her, she walked to the door and turned the handle, standing for some moments, her eyes fixed on the telephone. She felt the same unbearable tension that had stretched her nerves to breaking point every time the phone rang in that first week after Mel had disappeared. Who would telephone her? And at this hour? She glanced at her watch. Seven thirty. Puzzled, she half turned as though to go back into the room. *But the clock on Melanie's dresser said ten thirty* . . . Kate shook her head tiredly. Melanie's clock must have stopped. She had forgotten to rewind it.

She felt a stab of guilt, like a sharp pain below her heart; she had never forgotten to rewind the clock before. This morning, when she had gone to work, she had been the nearest to happy she felt she could ever be. And she had forgotten to rewind the clock. Melanie's clock. She had, in a way, forgotten Melanie.

A pounding from above made Kate shudder violently. Thud, thud, thud. Three times in rapid succession. Mrs Wilson was irritated that she had left the phone ringing. She fumbled the receiver from the cradle and held it away from her ear.

'Kate?'

A juddering sigh, and then Kate got a grip of herself. She answered calmly enough: 'Adam.'

'Are you . . . feeling better?'

'Much. Thanks,' she added as an afterthought.

There was a pause, and then Adam said, apparently choosing his words carefully: 'I know you'd rather not have someone from work round, but perhaps I could contact a friend for you – ask them to come over?'

'No. I— No.'

'Well . . .' He seemed embarrassed. 'What about your mother?'

'No!' Kate winced at the urgency in her voice and repeated more quietly, 'No. Really, I'm fine. I just— It was just a shock, that's all. I'll be back at work tomorrow.'

'Mr Owen said to tell you that you can have the rest of the week off.' Adam sounded apologetic.

Kate groaned. 'Jesus. Who told him?'

'I'm sorry, Kate. It was all round the office when I got back.' The hesitation that followed lengthened to a pause, and

Kate realized that Adam was preparing to tell her something unpleasant. 'Kate, they're saying you did it yourself.'

Kate frowned.

Alarmed by her silence, Adam spoke her name again.

'Maybe I did,' she said in angry defiance.

'Kate . . .'

'I'll be in first thing.' She hung up. Let them think what they want. I don't give a toss.

'Maybe I did,' she said defiantly to the wall. 'Maybe I did . . .' Fear had crept, uninvited, into her voice. She had been typing before those words appeared on the screen. Proof-reading, correcting and day-dreaming. Could she have typed them in herself without knowing it? As she had gone into Melanie's room without knowing it? The second line, 'I love you, Mummy. I want to come home': had that been on the monitor before? She could touch-type; had she typed the messages herself to punish herself for having forgotten? For being, if not happy, at least less tormented by Melanie's death for a few short hours?

Chapter Two

Kate lit a second cigarette with trembling hands.

'You should go to the police.'

She leaned back against the wall and closed her eyes, inhaling deeply. She had bought the cigarettes on the way in, thinking she might need them if Mr Owen forced her into an argument over her fitness to work. It was remarkable how quickly she had got used to smoking again. How easily the old mannerisms had returned. And how *good* it tasted, even after five years. She ignored Adam's suggestion.

'I gave up for Melanie's sake, you know,' she said.

'Gave up what?'

'Smoking. Melanie came home from school upset. She'd been crying. They'd been shown some health-promotion film.'

Adam was silent.

Kate could see her so clearly. Standing in their little kitchen, wearing her blue raincoat with the hood. Mel had chosen it herself. Her hair lying against the red silk lining like a skein of silky brown thread. Her long socks were pushed down round her ankles – *everyone* wore them that way, she insisted. The back door stood open while Kate cooked dinner. It was windy, and she had pushed a kitchen chair against the door to stop it blowing shut. Melanie had climbed up on to the chair so that she could talk to her mother without getting under her feet.

'I don't want you to die, Mummy,' she said, earnestly. Seven years old and already worrying about her Mummy dying.

Kate had told her not to be silly, that lots of people smoked and didn't get cancer, but Melanie had been well tutored. She quoted *stisticks* at Kate, firm evidence that her mother would fall prey to this terrible thing she did not understand but which, in her childish mind, was equivalent in malevolence and power to the devil or the bogeyman.

'Miss Unsworth said if you smoke a cigarette, it takes five minutes off your life.' Melanie, whose concept of time was still a little shaky, took this as proof that Kate had little time left. 'That's an hour and a quarter just for today!'

Kate, who smoked about fifteen a day at that time, was impressed by her daughter's mathematical skill and couldn't resist asking if anybody had helped her with the calculation. But Melanie had burst into tears of frustration and fear, wailing, *'Please,* Mummy!'

Kate had soothed and cajoled and threatened by turns, but Melanie was inconsolable. In the end Kate had conceded defeat.

'Okay, okay.'

'Okay what?' Melanie snuffled, uncertainly.

'Okay, I'll give up.'

Melanie's eyes narrowed suspiciously. 'You've got to say it,' she insisted.

'Miserable toad! D'you think your own mother would lie to you?'

Melanie's mouth was set in a stubborn line.

'Don't look at me like that. You look like your father,' Kate remarked, with a grimace. Melanie had lifted her chin and frowned even more furiously.

'I promise I'll give up smoking,' she said, with a sigh.

'Now? Today?'

Kate hesitated. 'Tomorrow. I've got to prepare myself, Mel,' she protested, as Melanie's brows gathered, ready for another storm. 'Tomorrow morning.'

'Promise?'

'Promise.'

'Cross your heart?'

'Don't push it, kid.'

Melanie had watched her mother with that steady, knowing look, well beyond her years, and then she had subsided, sniffing.

'You'll be stuck with me for a while yet, I'm afraid,' Kate said.

Melanie grinned tearfully.

'Anyway, we can't really afford it. And since you're so concerned for my health, there's something you can do for me.'

'Ye-es?' Melanie answered, instantly wary.

'You can tidy your bag and your Forever Friends lunch box *and* your coat off the hall floor so I don't break my precious neck on them.' She threw Melanie a pert smile, and the girl chuckled, wiping her nose with the back of her hand, and was out of the door in a moment.

'And you might blow your nose while you're at it!' Kate yelled through the open door.

Kate sighed. Melanie had been seven years old then. She had gone missing a week before her twelfth birthday. 'Mum was right about one thing,' she said: 'A mother shouldn't outlive her child.' She pulled nervily on her cigarette.

Adam stole a glance at her. She was wearing brown woollen trousers and ankle-length boots. A long, dark-oatmeal polo-neck sweater hid the looseness at the waist of her trousers. She flicked the ash from her cigarette and raised it to her mouth, inhaling deeply. Her small, rather delicate nostrils flared as she exhaled. Her skin was unnaturally pale, the pallor the more apparent set against the rich chestnut curls of her hair. She kept it tied back, tightly plaited. When they had first met, he had been bewitched by the way she had let her hair tumble loose, catching the sunlight and glowing with teasing highlights of subtle auburn. Silky and sensuous, it had caressed her shoulders and curled softly at the neck in a way that made him want to reach out and touch it.

Looking at her now, with her hair pulled back severely from that taut, watchful face, Adam reflected that Kate kept the rest of herself pretty tightly bound up these days, too. She's afraid to ease off because she's so close to hysteria so much of the time, he thought. It'd be easy to unravel the threads of her careful constraint.

Her green eyes flashed back at him. She had the dangerous air of an animal in pain. Needing help, but trusting nobody to give it.

'D'you know the bloke who—?' He broke off. His finger went to his eyebrow in a nervous, jerky movement. He had embarked upon a difficult subject.

He felt Kate tense beside him, but dared not look at her. What man? What was he going to say? She had come outside to get *away* from that. Another message. A note had been left on her e-mail:

Help me, Mummy! Make him stop!

What was Adam going to say? That the filthy animal – the monster who had murdered her daughter – was back?

'The inspector— What's his name?'

Kate exhaled, almost laughing with relief. '*Chief* Inspector,' she corrected. 'Harmon.'

'Do you trust him?'

Kate frowned, as though the idea of trusting someone was in some way alien to her. After considering a moment, she said, 'Yes, I suppose I did – I mean I do.'

'Shouldn't you tell him?'

'Why?'

It was Adam's turn to look puzzled. 'Why? Because he's a policeman. Because he dealt with your c—'

'My what? My "case"? Is that what you were going to say?'

'What I'm trying to say is that he knows about you and about—'

'My "case".'

'About what happened to Melanie,' Adam persevered. 'If you tell him about this crank stuff, he might be able to do something about them – him. Whoever.'

'Like what? The Pearson *case* is investigative history. They've scaled down the inquiry – it's old news. Old hat. Didn't you know?' Kate's face took on that stony, unreachable expression he had seen so many times in the last few months.

'Kate—' He hesitated. 'What if it's *him*?' Meaning Melanie's murderer. Unable to say the word.

'No!'

He tried once more: 'Kate, you can't let this guy get away with it—'

'Lay off, Adam,' she warned. 'You said yourself it's probably a crank.' She waved down his objection that cranks could be dangerous and added, 'I didn't ask for your advice. I didn't ask you to follow me out here. When I need a shoulder to cry on, I'll let you know. Now sod off and let me enjoy my fag.'

She felt a stab of regret at his hurt look, but affected unconcern, and Adam walked slowly back into the building.

The office was buzzing when he returned.

'What's up with her now?'

Adam shrugged.

Moira's lips pressed together into a narrow line. She hated to be obstructed when trawling for gossip.

'Mr Owen's looking for her,' she said, her voice prickly with spite. 'And you. You left your terminal logged on.'

Adam looked at her. She was a big woman with a physical presence that would not be ignored. Hers was a pleasant face, made for a kinder disposition. Only her eyes betrayed her. Dark and round, they darted about too eagerly for friendly interest and too intently for mild curiosity.

Her eyes dropped under his hard stare. 'I wouldn't want her to get into trouble,' she muttered.

'Really, Moira? I'd've thought that Kate getting into trouble would be enough to make you wet yourself with excitement.'

A ripple of laughter went round the room. Moira reddened. 'I'm not one to spread gossip.'

Andrew threw back his head and laughed. 'That's rich.'

'Meaning?'

'Meaning you're a nosy, interfering, nasty bitch who gets off on poking into other people's business—'

'Is there any danger of a bit of work getting done in here today?'

The staff moved as one body to look at Owen. He stood at the door of the aquarium, his shirt sleeves rolled up, exposing a mat of black hair on each forearm. The staff dispersed, spilling away from Adam and Moira likes beads of quicksilver.

We've some unfinished business to settle, Adam thought, throwing Moira a venomous look. It was mirrored in the pupils of her eyes and reflected back, magnified and full of malicious intent.

When Kate returned to the office some minutes later, it

was silent save for the clack of the keyboards and the faint exhalation of laser printers.

Owen scowled at her from his office, and she stared back with innocent unconcern. She noticed Moira writing something in her ridiculous notebook and had to quell an urge to snatch it away from her and throw it across the office.

She sat at her desk and lifted the telephone receiver; her hand was steady as she punched two digits on the pad. A moment later she spoke: 'John? Kate Pearson. Listen, someone's messing about with my files. Can I come down for a chat?'

Adam's face registered surprise and then embarrassment at his own surprise. He recalled having seen the tall, black policeman on *News at Ten* on the day they had found Melanie. He was standing behind Kate, a steadying hand on her shoulder.

There had been a surge of reporters as Kate appeared on the steps, and Adam distinctly remembered thinking that the sound of their shoes slipping on the smooth stone, dry and cold in the early morning air, was unpleasant, insinuating, too eager.

A reporter had shoved a microphone in Kate's face and shouted above the others, asking her to comment on speculation that Melanie had been 'home alone' when she was abducted. There had been a few scandals that summer about mothers leaving their children unsupervised. One of them had even been prosecuted after a campaign by one 'caring' tabloid.

Kate, her lips almost blue with shock, had not responded at first, seeing past the reporter, still gazing in horror at her daughter's pale and battered face, then she stuttered, 'N-no, she— She should have been with her friend – Jenny, her friend. They were going to have tea together—'

She looked up bewildered and desperate, at Harmon. He had put his arm round her shoulders, in a protective gesture that was warm and natural, and hurried her to a car saying quietly, but firmly:

'No more questions.'

He had ducked to follow Kate into the car, then seemed to change his mind. He said something to the driver and backed out, closing the door after him. The clamour of questions rose again from the reporters. They shouted. Some waved notebooks at him. He looked gravely at them, his hands relaxed at his sides. If he felt any distaste for them, he didn't show it. One by one, the reporters fell silent.

He began talking slowly and quietly, but his voice carried nevertheless. 'Mrs Pearson is deeply distressed, ladies and gentleman, as we all are. I know that she appreciates the support you have given in trying to find Melanie. I am sure you will respect her need for privacy right now. I promise you that your questions will be answered at a press conference later today.'

There was a murmur from the media crowd, but before the tumult could erupt, Harmon got into the car and they were gone.

Chief Inspector Harmon noted Adam's surprise and embarrassment. He was used, by now, to the various reactions of people to a black senior police officer and accepted the situation with equanimity. He regarded the young man with mild curiosity.

Adam blushed.

'You wanted to speak to me about Melanie Pearson, Mr Shepherd.' His accent was cultured but retained a suggestion of his native West Indian.

'The case – yes.' Adam winced. He'd used that bloody word again.

'I find the application of the term "case" particularly distasteful when referring to the taking of a little girl's life, Mr Shepherd. Melanie Pearson was a little girl, not a "case".'

'Yes, of course, I didn't mean—' Adam stammered. 'What I meant was that it isn't directly to do with Melanie. More Mrs Pearson.'

'Not *directly*.' Chief Inspector Harmon remained placid, still. His dark eyes studied the young man thoughtfully. It seemed that Mr Shepherd was extremely nervous. His hand kept going to his eyebrow, stroking it with a jerky, restless movement, and a light sweat had produced a sheen on his forehead.

'Is something wrong, Mr Shepherd?'

Adam's hand strayed to his eyebrow. 'Wrong? No. What could be wrong?'

'I don't know.' Harmon paused, and again Shepherd stroked his eyebrow. 'You seem agitated.'

'Oh. Well, she doesn't know I'm here, you see.'

'Who?'

'Kate – Katherine.' He laughed shakily. 'Mrs Pearson.'

Again the thoughtful look.

Again the nervous gesture.

A light tap at the office door distracted them. Both glanced at the door, Harmon with irritation and Shepherd with relief. The detective took in the situation immediately and was backing out of the room, making his apologies, when Harmon said, 'Come in, Bill. You might be interested in what Mr Shepherd has to say. Sergeant Wainwright is assisting in the investigation into Melanie's murder,' he explained to Adam.

The man paused, his thin, rather bony hand resting on the door handle, and Adam felt himself once more under scrutiny, assessed, labelled, pigeon-holed, all in less time than it took for the man to come into the room. The sergeant closed the door and leaned with his back to it, an action which produced momentary panic in Adam.

'I take it Mrs Pearson would not approve of your coming here?' Harmon asked.

'She – she told me not to come. Said I shouldn't bother you. She said you were busy enough.'

Amusement flickered momentarily in the chief inspector's eyes. 'But still you came.' He stood. He was taller than Adam remembered from the television pictures, at least six foot four, and, though slim, he looked solid, strong.

Adam felt intimidated. 'Yes,' he said, but it came out as a croak, and he had to cough to clear his throat. His hand went up and, suddenly aware of the gesture, and the fact that Harmon had noticed it too, he managed to keep his finger away from his eyebrow by an effort of will. He lifted his head and looked Harmon in the eye. 'She's trying to deny it, but she needs help. Something should be done about it.'

'About what? You haven't told me yet why you're here.'

'She's been getting messages. Weird stuff. On her e-mail. And her files have been altered – reports she's writing, letters, that sort of thing. I don't know if she's had any phone calls – she's not said. It's sick. I don't know why anyone would want to— She was just beginning to get over it – well, over the worst of it anyway, and then this sick bastard starts—'

'Messages on her e-mail, you say.'

'And sends on mail as she's writing it.'

'I take it that's some sort of computer jargon?' Wainwright asked.

'Sends?' Adam blushed. 'I suppose so.'

'Are we allowed the secret of this arcane word?' This time it was Harmon who spoke.

The young man shrugged. His eyes were fixed firmly on the floor.

'It's a way of sending e-mail so that it interrupts what a person is doing on their PC. You hear a bleep, and then the message comes up on screen. Actually, it's bad manners.'

'Etiquette on the Internet?'

Adam looked up, frowning. 'If you like.'

'Can that be done easily? I mean could the average office worker, do it, or . . . would it take a computer whiz, such as yourself?'

Adam blinked. 'I don't get you.'

'I use e-mail myself. It's simple enough to send a message to someone you want to reach: all you need is an address, isn't it? But reports, files – wouldn't you need a password to gain access to them?'

'I'm not a computer whiz. I'm just an operator,' Adam protested, rather too late.

Inspector Harmon inclined his head. 'Even so, would it take somebody with expertise to hack into reports and files?'

'That's what worries me,' Adam said, relaxing a fraction. 'Don't get me wrong. Technicomm's security's not brilliant, but we do have basic measures in place.'

'You'd know about that, would you?' Wainwright asked.

Adam stopped. 'About what?'

'Computer security.'

Instantly wary again, he shrugged. 'No more than anyone else at the office.'

'So you're not in charge of computer security.' It was a statement, and Adam got the unpleasant feeling Harmon knew more than he was saying.

'As I said, I'm an operator, that's all.'

'No need for false modesty here, Mr Shepherd,' Harmon said. 'If you know that security has been breached—'

'You don't have to be Bill bloody Gates to work that one

out. It's obvious. Otherwise how could he have fu—?' Adam stopped himself in time. They had rattled him with their tennis game of back-and-forth questioning and he was reacting, just as they intended – like a prize bloody pillock. He gave himself a moment to regain control, then began again: 'Otherwise how could he have *fiddled with* Kate's files?'

'How indeed?' Inspector Harmon turned to the window and watched the traffic below for a few minutes. Wainwright watched him, his grey eyes unblinking, his face shadowed by worry. When Adam began to fidget Harmon said:

'Why did you say "he"?'

'What?'

'You referred to the hacker as "he". "Otherwise how could 'he' have fiddled with Kate's files," ' he quoted verbatim.

'Figure of speech. Anyway, hackers usually are men – or boys.'

Harmon turned back to watch Shepherd's reaction. 'Could the security breach have been within the firm? I mean, notwithstanding your relative ignorance of the subject, in your *layman's* opinion, could somebody within the firm be tampering with the files?'

Adam flushed again. He answered cautiously: 'It's possible, of course. But who would want to—' Something in Harmon's expression made him stop.

'What did these messages say?' Harmon asked abruptly.

'Crazy stuff. Like it was her daughter.'

Harmon's head raised a fraction. 'Melanie,' he breathed.

Adam nodded. 'Stuff about how she let him hurt Melanie. The last one said she wanted to come home.'

The silence lasted several minutes. At length, Adam rose to leave. Wainwright remained with his back to the door. Immobile. Immovable.

'You will do something, won't you?' he asked of Harmon.

'Why did you come here, Mr Shepherd?'

'Because I don't want to see Kate hurt any more. Because she trusts you.' He shrugged. 'Because I don't know what else to do.'

Harmon watched Shepherd out of the room. The door swung shut.

Chapter Three

He worked quietly and with painstaking care, composing his bulletins at leisure on an off-line Network Simulator. Purchased some months ago to make his network communications less expensive in phone bills, it had, he discovered, other benefits: clarity of expression aligned with speed of transmission that had made him virtually untraceable.

Daylight faded to darkness, but he kept the lights off. He liked the darkness to creep into his room and wrap him in folds of chill comfort. He felt the night press in, and smiled.

The computer glow seemed to gain power. Its light sharpened, casting a blue tinge on his skin, giving his eyes a metallic cast, like scales of mica.

My work is almost an act of love, he thought, then hesitated, frowning, uncertain that anyone could be worthy of his love. Without conscious thought, intuitively, the answer presented itself: since giving his love to another was so unsafe, so hurtful, he recalled it, turning it inward, admiring with lavish sentiment the cleverness of his own art and skill. The quick, precise movements of his fingers over the keyboard; his careful layout of the text; his apt phrasing – just the right word and perfect restraint in expression. He flushed momentarily with pleasure, resuming his work with renewed purpose.

> **Mummy**
> **Mummy, help me . . .**

Two hits of the return key, then two tab indents, and:

> **It's so DARK out here, so . . . COLD.**

A little *frisson* of pleasure trickled down his spine, and he sighed with exquisite satisfaction. Things were going perfectly to plan.

Chapter Four

It was as well that Adam kept his meeting with Inspector Harmon secret; Kate, as the inspector had surmised, would certainly not have approved. Her fierce independence resented any perceived interference in her private affairs, but, more than this, to turn to Inspector Harmon would be to return to a state of helplessness she could not countenance.

She had nothing against Harmon as a man; his kindness had seemed no imposition during those awful weeks following the discovery of Melanie's poor abused body. Kate knew that he had sheltered her from the worst of the press inquiries. He had accepted her hasty and rather violent refusal of his offer to contact her mother in order to arrange for Kate to stay with her for a while, only resting his grave, gentle eyes on her for some moments before giving instructions that a room be reserved for Kate and a friend at the Grand Midland Hotel, in the centre of Manchester and barely five minutes walk from the town hall and the offices where she worked. Kate was doubtful as to the wisdom of his choice. He had quieted her edgy protests with the wry observation that sometimes it's easier to be invisible in the thick of things. He added, with a look of sympathy that somehow did not arouse her irritable sensitivity, that he could arrange for a WPC to keep her company, if she would prefer.

In the event, Kate had asked Mary Marchant. Mary arranged for her sister to look after Jenny for a few days, and they had shared a suite. They were still on good terms then. It had helped, being away from the flat for a short time, and in company. But she had ached to return and had stayed for less than a week.

Even now, when her reaction to most people and their treatment of her had changed from gratitude in the early days to bridling hostility at their officious interference, she still held Chief Inspector Harmon in high regard for his tact and his protection at a time when she was least able to stand her own corner.

But it had fallen to him to tell Kate that Melanie had been found dead. Not wanting her to hear it from somebody she did not know, he had come to the door of her flat, and she had known, *had known*. Before he opened the door. Before he spoke. Known and not wanted to know. Harmon had prepared her for the terrible injuries that had been inflicted on her little girl. Harmon himself had taken Kate to the mortuary to identify Melanie, and it was Harmon who had supported her when she had collapsed because nothing, after all, could prepare a mother to see her daughter, her little baby, pale and cold and so terribly injured, lying on a pathologist's slab.

For this Kate would always be grateful and would never forgive him. She knew in her rational mind – and she could be rational now, nearly five months later – that the inspector had done all of these things out of a delicacy of feeling she would scarcely have thought possible in a man of his rank and profession. He had shown respect and real sympathy for her dreadful loss. But Chief Inspector Harmon would for ever be the man who had told her in that calm, reasonable voice that Melanie would never come home, that she had died at the hands of a brutal murderer, had died in pain and terror. And she, Kate, had not been there to save her.

She could not forgive Harmon in her deepest being, any more than she could forgive the monster that had stolen her baby from her. Could not forgive that the last, the most powerful memory she would carry for ever of her little girl was of that sad, grey, lifeless thing that was not her Melanie in that cold, cold place.

'Oh, this is futile!' Kate got up and walked impatiently to the window, causing a flutter of glances around the office. Its open-plan design precluded any hope of privacy.

'All right, love?' Said almost as a warning. Moira. Meddling Moira. Fussy, fastidious, officious Moira Jones – *Corporal* Jones, she and Melanie had called her, after the character in *Dad's Army* – always willing to listen and more than willing to spread the news of a crisis. Moira had ambitions towards good-heartedness, but lacked discretion and showed little understanding or even interest beyond the basic facts. Kate knew she would be watching her with those bright, bird-like eyes that tried to look solicitous but succeeded only in look- ing curious.

'Fine,' Kate answered, without turning round. She stood at the window, looking out at Albert Square, and watched the leaves falling like teardrops in slow succession from the trees on to the cobblestones and benches. The square seemed empty and forlorn despite the constant drone of traffic.

She sighed and turned to face the room. Some of her colleagues were a little slow and were caught watching her. The more sensitive let their gaze drift away from her, day-dreaming out of the window. Others dropped their eyes abruptly and set to work with atypical industriousness. A few continued to stare with casual defiance, as if daring her to speak.

Kate took all of this in, yet it had no significance for her.

She was too absorbed in her own thoughts to speculate about theirs.

'Futile,' she murmured, and then made herself concentrate on the rest of the report.

The phone on her desk rang. She picked it up calmly enough, although her heart was racing.

'Where the hell is the Furnley file?'

'I'm working on it, Mr Owen.'

'What? I need it *now*. I've got a meeting in an hour with Furnley himself, for Christ's sake.'

Mr Owen was bald. Baldness had happened suddenly, catching him off guard in his mid-thirties. He had never quite got over it, and he had never permitted himself to be caught off guard since then. He had built up Technicomm from a two-man team designing computer games to a company that employed sixty staff, including security, and a turnover approaching £1 million per annum. He had remortgaged his home to finance the venture, and when the big firms had gained a stranglehold on the games market, he had adapted, widening Technicomm's remit to providing hardware and ready-made office-software bundles to businesses throughout the north-west. But his real interest remained software design, so when his partner and software designer defected to IBM in the late Eighties for a fat salary and a company pension, he had refused to capitulate. Instead he had employed a couple of teenage computer freaks who had produced what he considered to be some of the best custom-designed software on the market.

The bigger firms had largely ignored the potential of his programs, preferring to struggle with inappropriate software because it had been made by one of the American giants and therefore *must* be good. He had continued, somewhat embittered but with dogged determination, and now, six years after his partner left him in the lurch, he had a thriving business.

True, they bundled software from the big software houses and used it as an enticement to new clients, but his back-up team were known for giving good advice to businesses struggling to make sense of their software, and he prided himself on the fact that without Technicomm's help, more than a few firms might have gone under, suffocated by a mass of data they didn't know how to organize or utilize. His team were able to offer advice and practical help on a range of subjects, from file management to the use of spreadsheets in targeting mail-shots, from databases to diary systems, and the bigger companies were now asking about networking, video-conferencing and the efficient use of e-mail. A few had even begun to trust him enough to inquire into Technicomm's own software applications. He was on the way up, and he wasn't about to let inefficient office staff ruin the reputation which had cost him so much to build.

'I'm sorry . . .'

'What the hell have you been doing all day? I asked for that report to be given priority. I expected it by lunchtime at the very latest.' The Pearson woman was becoming a liability.

Kate checked the big clock at the far end of the office. Half-past two. 'I didn't realize—'

'I left a message on your e-mail. For God's sake, Kate, get a grip! D'you mean you haven't read your memos all day?' Furnley's was a potentially lucrative new deal. A furniture company with outlets all over the north-west ('Furnley's for Fine Furniture') and a venerable computer network that was more eccentric than efficient. If he clinched this deal . . . But it was a cautious old establishment, and the senior partners had yet to be convinced that a new system was, in fact, economically expedient.

'Of course,' Kate lied easily, 'I must have overlooked it, that's all. Look, I've just about finished. I haven't proof-read it, but if you'd like to call up the file, you could read it over while I check it and print it.'

'I suppose I've got no bloody choice.' He deliberated briefly. 'Get it to me as soon as it's done.'

'Twenty minutes, no, half an hour,' Kate estimated, but Owen had already slammed down the receiver.

The report delivered, Kate resigned herself to checking her e-mail. She found Mr Owen's memo immediately. It had been logged at seven p.m., the previous evening – Mr Owen did a lot of work from home. Most of the rest she had dealt with during the course of the day, but there were two requests for information from restricted files; she would have to vet those before she went home. She flicked on through the mail list, finding the anonymous entry listed as number twenty-two in her mail box, the date – yesterday's – and, instead of the sender's name:

Name withheld on request

She reached across, lifting the receiver and punching the keys with the same hand. 'John? Anything?' A pause. 'No . . . No, I'm sure you did your best.' Another pause. 'No!' she exclaimed. 'Don't do that. Let all the calls through . . .' She thanked the systems manager and then hung up, staring at the screen.

Kate clicked the cursor down to the anonymous listing, took a deep breath and hit the return key. And there it was. Like a cry from the darkness:

so . . . COLD.

Kate felt a chill creep over her, too. Her hands were bone-white, and her skin broke out in a rash of goose pimples.

It's not Melanie, she told herself. This isn't my child. *It's some kind of sadistic game to him. He's gloating because the police haven't caught him — can't and never will catch him.*

Anger bubbled to the surface, taking the edge off her pain. She quelled it, telling herself to check the header, the return address.

Kate glanced surreptitiously around the office. It's quiet activity continued, unconscious of her turmoil, somnolent in the afternoon sunshine that promised a night frost. Adam stood next to Lynn at the coffee machine, sharing a joke, their laughter subdued, polite. She looked back at the machine. The header read:

Return-Path <vox@vox.xs4all.nl>

An anonymous posting service.

Well, she told herself, it would be rude not to reply. She typed a few words and then sent the message.

Why are you hiding behind a dead child?

She stole another look at Adam. He seemed to be watching her, but then he checked his watch, said a word or two to Lynn and gulped down his drink before ambling out of the office without a backward glance.

Kate turned her attention again to the bulletin on screen and selected the print option. The printer panel flashed briefly, then hummed into life, turning out the page in a matter of seconds. Kate folded it hastily and slipped it into her handbag. She finished going through her mail before allowing herself to leave.

She fought the impulse to run, making herself walk through

29

the fire door on to the concrete steps of the fire escape. She was two flights down before she heard a door swing to with a soft boom that echoed upwards. Kate's eyes followed the sound involuntarily, and she thought she saw a movement in the shadows above. The darkness seemed to crowd down on her and she fled, running down the stairs and bursting through the door at basement level. A woman stepped back in alarm at her sudden and wild appearance. Kate managed to whisper a breathless apology and, gathering what little composure she had left, walked to a steel door on the right of the stairwell. The basement housed Technicomm's office server and John James, the systems manager. She had no doubt that she could get more cooperation from John through a personal visit than a telephone call. To the right of the wide steel door, at about waist height, was a wall-mounted card-swipe and, above that, an intercom. Kate pressed the call button and waited. After a few seconds the intercom hissed at her, and she assumed someone had spoken. She pressed the 'talk' button and said, 'Kate Pearson to see John.' The intercom hissed again, like water in an old plumbing system, and then the door buzzed. Kate marvelled that Owen, who insisted on having the most powerful, the most up-to-date computer hardware, couldn't bring himself to accept the expense of an intercom system that would convey intelligible messages. She put her shoulder to the door and heaved. It gave without noise but with a reluctance that bordered on bad grace, and she stepped inside.

It was like stepping into a vault. The room was at least twenty feet in height. It was well lit and spacious, but with a hermetic quality that she found slightly claustrophobic. Several tones of air movement could be heard: the gentle exhalation of laser printers; the quiet fans of the PCs that were dotted about the room on miraculously clear desks, and the deeper, more insistent hum of the air-conditioning. The server stood on Marley tiles that were carefully cleaned each night. Stacks of magnetic tapes and floppy disks were ranged around the walls in boxes on slatted wooden shelves, and a mezzanine had been built to provide extra storage space at the far end of the room. The vault – for that's what it felt like to Kate – was too cool to be comfortable and too antiseptic to be welcoming.

John James, Technicomm's systems manager and part-time programmer, was sitting at his bench, working on one of the office PCs. The CPU cover lay to one side, exposing a swarm of microchips resembling an infestation of armoured bugs. John was absorbed in his work, and Kate, reluctant to disturb him, did not speak. She took out a cigarette without thinking. There was no identifiable movement, no eye contact, but John managed to emanate such a strong aura of disapproval that she thought better of it and slipped it back into the pack. She waited politely while he removed one chip and replaced it with another.

John James was a small man of slight build. He sported a white goatee beard and a strawberry-blond ponytail. The effect was startling; he looked rather like a roan-coloured Aberdeen Angus, she had thought when she first met him. Except that he was from Edinburgh, not Aberdeen, and was by no means shaggy in appearance. His hair had begun to recede, but it was carefully groomed. There were two things he wore constantly: a clean lab coat and an expression of surprised amusement.

He spoke, at last, in his fastidious Edinburgh tones. 'I should have a technician to do this bloody dog's-bodying, but Owen's such a mean bloody Welshman he won't give me the technical support I need.'

Kate recognized this as a warning that he was far too busy to talk to her, but she was not to be so easily deterred. 'I thought he was from Liverpool originally.' John was never quite sure how to deal with obtuseness in women; if a man had made the same comment, he would have dismissed him with a few words, direct and to the point. But he had been brought up to be polite to the ladies – added to which, Kate knew, as a father of three girls he had great sympathy for her. She reproached herself for playing on the man's feelings, but she intended to find Melanie's murderer, and she couldn't do that without help.

John cocked a suspicious eye at her, and said, 'His origins are Welsh. It's in his blood, and there's a bloody mean streak a mile wide in the Welsh.'

Kate's mouth twitched in amusement. Now she wasn't sure if she was being teased. 'Isn't that supposed to be a Scottish trait?' she asked. 'Anyway, I thought you had a whole hatful of technicians attending to your every whim.'

John sighed. 'And d'ye see a one of them?' He gazed about the room in astonishment, screwdriver in hand. 'Either doing on-site repairs or hand-holding folk who think the Superhighway is an extension of the M6. Or,' he said, warming to his theme, 'more likely trying to impress on Furnley and his old fogies that the age of the valve-powered number-cruncher is past.'

Kate winced at the reference. Owen had been less than delighted with her performance on the Furnley file, and he wasn't a man to keep his feelings secret.

John took her grimace as a gesture of sympathy and shrugged, positioning and tightening the screws of the processing unit with a casual dexterity born of practice. Finally, he put down the screwdriver and said, 'Okay, let's see it.'

Kate handed him the note.

'Bloody bastard!' The vehemence of his words was somewhat diminished by his habitually mild, amused expression.

'Yeah,' said Kate. Then, 'You mean you didn't read it when it came in?'

The amiable expression flickered, faltered and all but vanished. 'Why would I want to read your private mail?' he asked severely. 'You asked me to try to trace it. I did, and I'm sorry to say, without success. But you did not ask me to read it. Your e-mail is private. I'm not a Peeping Tom.'

Kate saw that she had offended him. John had a Presbyterian streak every inch as wide as Owen's mean one, and she had affronted his delicate sense of morality and good conduct. 'I thought you have to check on e-mail as part of your job,' she said, trying to placate him. 'For security. Guarding against misuse of the system.'

Kate felt herself colour under his stare. She was on the point of telling him to forget it when he nodded. 'On a strictly random basis,' he said, carefully. 'The computer decides on the sample, and I check the accounts it suggests. Anything else would hardly be moral, Kate,' he said, with gentle reproof.

'No,' she agreed solemnly, 'of course not.'

John remained silent for some minutes, tinkering with the server, checking tapes and binning print jobs according to a code system on to a rack of shelves at the back of the room. The printing of tests and trials for programming purposes was done on continuous printer paper here in the basement. Some of the programmers worked on their PCs upstairs in the main building, but one or two preferred the atmosphere of the server room. She couldn't see why; she was finding the room, with its artificial light and air, depressing. Her courage almost failed her. If John had balked at reading her mail when she had asked him to check it, he wasn't going to like what she was about to suggest.

'I think he's dangerous.' She paused, watchful. John's fixed expression of good humour rarely altered, and that could be confusing, but his lack of readable facial clues was more than made up for by the eloquence of his body language. He agreed with her, she was sure of it. The note had shocked him, as it had shocked her. 'John, I think the man who took Melanie sent me the e-mail.'

He looked up at her, troubled, still with the suggestion of a smile on his face, but her eyes betraying a deeper emotion.

'I want to find him.'

'Aye . . . I expect you would.' He sighed, waiting for her inevitable request.

'Maybe— I was wondering whether—'

He watched her keenly.

'. . . whether you could dip into a few files for me.'

John stiffened.

'Only to establish if they sent the e-mail.' She hurried on, 'I mean, can't you check for specific data using a search string or something?'

'I *can*,' John said, in a tone that implied *but I've no intention of doing so.*

'If you could just see if my name came up, it wouldn't be like reading their files.' She was losing ground, she could sense it from John's increasingly disapproving stare. 'Or,' – she thrust the printout of the e-mail into his hand – 'you could see if anyone has this message stored on their files.'

He read the message again, staring at it as though for the first time.

'John, I *have* to find him. If I don't, he'll never stop.'

His shoulders sagged, and she knew she had won him over. 'I'll see what I can do,' he promised.

Chapter Five

Lynn felt a warm rush of blood to her cheeks as Adam leaned over her, one hand on the back of her chair and the other reaching across to guide the mouse. He smelled faintly of cologne: Versace, something like that. Classy. She leaned back in her chair, unable to concentrate on his instructions, feeling her hair make contact with his shirt. She allowed her eyes to stray from the screen to the side of his face. Lean but strong. His dark hair, clean but carelessly combed, curled over his shirt collar. The other girls were right – he was wasted on Kate Pearson.

'Pardon?'

'Give it a go,' Adam repeated. 'You try it.'

'I'm so dense.' She giggled. 'Can you go over it just once more?'

'When you've finished over there, I'm having some trouble getting this table layout right.' Moira's voice crackled with irritation. She had watched the erotic game being played out for some minutes, and it made her feel ill.

'RTFM, Moira,' Adam replied cheerfully.

'Oh? And what's that supposed to mean?'

Adam smiled. Moira walked right into them, 'Read the Flaming Manual.'

Moira arched an eyebrow, ignoring the snickers of amusement around her. 'You might have said that to Tilly Mint,' she said, nodding at Lynn.

'Give it a week or two, I will. But since she's new—' He shrugged, 'I thought you'd approve – extending the hand of friendship, all that guff.'

Moira snorted, refusing to be baited any further, and Adam returned to his desk a few minutes later. He was stationed at the back of the room. It had taken some time to acquire this favourable position, which made it difficult for anyone to look over his shoulder and gave him ample warning when Owen was on the prowl. Owen had not blocked the move but had exacted a small revenge: a framed poster on the wall behind Adam read:

> # A tidy desk
> ## and
> # a tidy mind!

Adam logged on, clearing the loosely organized mess of memos and computer printouts to one side of his desk. Taped to his monitor was a neatly bordered oblong card, laser-printed, bearing the maxim

> # A tidy desk
> ## and
> a tiny **mind!**

'Owen'll have a fit if he sees that.'

Adam didn't bother to look up. 'Anything I can do for you, John?'

'I just came to say thanks. The reprogramming you recommended winkled out the bug. The file manager's running as smooth as silk now.'

'As long as it doesn't chew up my files.'

John chuckled, turning to go.

'You could've mailed me.'

'Thought you might like the personal touch.'

'I'm gratified.'

'If there's anything I can do in return—'

'You might put in a good word with Owen for me.' Adam tapped the card. 'He's already seen it, and you're right – he did have a fit.'

John laughed. 'Leave it to me.'

Adam watched the systems manager weave his way through the maze of desks towards Owen's office, pausing only to speak briefly to Kate and hand her something. When he was at a safe distance, Adam hit a function key, replacing the accounts spreadsheet he had called up to hide the screen he had actually been working on. It was filled with numbers and symbols. He continued typing, keeping one eye on the office. Owen was glaring out at him whilst John extolled his virtues. Owen looked extremely pissed off, which made Adam more than content.

An hour later he strolled over to Kate with his hands in his pockets.

'All right?' he asked, more in the manner of saying 'How do you do?' than as an inquiry after her state of mind, which, she could have told him, was good: John had searched every file on the system and discovered no trace of the e-mail she had received. She should have been disappointed – after all, it brought her no closer to the anonymous mailer – but it meant that she hadn't been working with Melanie's murderer for the past five months. It also meant that Adam was in the clear, and that was important to her; she needed someone she could trust.

She dazzled him with a smile. 'Never better.'

'Oh . . .' He seemed at a loss for something to say, and his finger went to his eyebrow.

Kate felt a rush of warmth for him, and she smiled again. 'Fancy a bit of something to eat?'

'Sounds mouth-watering.'

He grinned. 'You're on form today.'

'Like I said—'

'Never better. I know. I thought maybe a pasta at the Italian opposite Waterstone's. I'm paying,' he offered, taking her silence for hesitation.

'We'll go Dutch,' Kate said, firmly. I can afford to treat myself, now, she thought, gaining no satisfaction from the realization.

Adam was disconcerted by the sudden shadow that crossed her face. 'Are you—?'

'Ready?' she said. This time the smile was forced. 'Yeah. Let's go.'

Watching him across the table, listening to his efforts to make her laugh, noting his solicitous concern for her, noting also the occasional nervous smoothing of his eyebrow, Kate thought, Adam is what we used to call a *good bloke*. 'We' had been the girls of the Upper Sixth at Manchester High School for Girls. Miss Mottersham would have been appalled to hear it, but somehow it conveyed so much more than the descriptions of which the Head of Sixth Form and Examiner for the English Speaking Board would approve. A *true gentleman* didn't say it. A *good bloke* did.

Why was it, she wondered, since she knew the difference

between a *good bloke* and a *right bastard*, that she had ended up marrying one in the latter category?

Her mother had a lot to do with that particular mystery. Kate was never good enough, clever enough, industrious enough, for her mother. It had taken some time before she really understood the odd wording of her mother's favourite phrase, 'You're no better than you should be', but she'd got the gist of it well enough. And, to banish all doubt, her mother had a number of more direct criticisms. She had said often enough that Kate would come to no good, and in the end Kate had believed her. During five long years of marriage she had accepted that she really didn't deserve any better, had believed it with the same unquestioning belief a child has that whatever its parents say is true, holding fast to the idea that it was all her fault. If only she could get it right – gauge his moods, say the right thing instead of messing everything up – then he would be happy and everything would be just fine.

Even as she left him, she blamed herself for failing as a wife. But she had left him for Melanie's sake because she feared for her little girl. And this small defiance had allowed the possibility that although she was lousy at practically everything else, she was perhaps a good mother, or at least a caring one. Kate would never know it, but her belief in her own commonplace competence had set her on the way to recovery. It wasn't until later – years later – that she came to think that perhaps David should share some of the blame. If this conviction had turned to bitter recrimination, then it was understandable. She half-smiled to herself. Who am I kidding? she thought. *Share the blame?* I hate his bloody guts. The only thing I did wrong was to stay with him for so long.

'You're very quiet,' Adam remarked, fingering the stem of his wine glass.

Kate shrugged, smiling. The restaurant was almost full

now. Christmas trade, attracted by the Italian trappings, the unassuming layout: wooden chairs, electric 'oil' lamps glowing warmly on the plain brick walls, tablecloths in green-and-white or red-and-white check. The place had carefully cultured nostalgic charm aimed at people who had in all probability never travelled to Italy, offered an idealized, sanitized interpretation of what an Italian restaurant ought to look like.

'Have you had another bulletin?'

'Not since the last one.' Kate looked into his earnest, open face and regretted for the hundredth time the sharpness of her tongue. Adam was so aware of her feelings, so sensitive to her needs, that he suppressed his own, betraying them only by little signs, his nervous gestures, the stroking of his eyebrow, the occasional drumming of his fingers on the check tablecloth. With the other women in the office he adopted an easy insouciance they found engaging, all except Moira, of course – but even her spiteful remarks appeared barely to touch him. It was, it seemed, only she who brought out this nervousness in him. And perhaps Mr Harmon. His friendship with Sims had something to do with that, she suspected, but Adam had been uncharacteristically close about how he and Sims had met.

Adam genuinely was a *good bloke*, and he didn't deserve to be punished because her ex-husband had been a bastard. He was trying to be kind and she was beating him off as usual.

'Sorry,' she said.

'What for?' He seemed genuinely perplexed.

She smiled again. He reminded her of herself at twenty-five. Insults had rolled off her because people generally lacked David's expertise in cutting her down – his phrase: he claimed he wasn't *putting* her down but *cutting*, as in down to size, since she was too full of herself. Also Kate tended to expect a certain off-handedness in people. She was, after all, a bit of a mess. She couldn't blame people for being impatient with her. If anyone had been interested enough to ask her to describe herself at the time, she would have summed herself up in one word: hopeless.

'At least you're smiling,' he said.

'I've got good reason to.'

He frowned. 'Aren't you worried?'

Her smile became puzzled. 'No. Odd, isn't it? It never occurred to me that I should worry. I'm angry – incensed. But in a way I'm relieved too.'

He raised his eyebrows. 'Now that is bloody odd. Kate, you don't know who this guy is. What he might do.'

I know who he *isn't*, thought Kate, but, of course, she couldn't tell Adam that, and not only because it would be a betrayal of John James's trust. How could she explain to Adam that she was relieved because she now knew she had nothing to fear from him? As for not knowing the man who was sending the mail . . .

'I think I know who he is,' she said, almost to herself.

The nervous drumming of Adam's fingers was stilled, and he gripped the table top. His fingers whitened. Kate took this in and looked curiously into his face. She was startled by the intense colour of his eyes, a blue that seemed to shimmer at the surface but beyond which was a darkness like ocean water.

'Oh!' she exclaimed, suddenly understanding the inference he had made. 'No. No, I don't know his name. Not yet. But I *do* know who he is – what he is,' she corrected, her voice becoming hard. 'And I do know what he's capable of.'

Adam relaxed slowly. He was watching her in a way she found unnerving, as though he was half afraid of her.

'Then,' he said, speaking slowly, carefully, 'you've got to go to the police.'

'I went to the police in July. It didn't do much good then, and I don't see that it'll do much good now.'

'Kate, believe me, I know how you feel about the police, but—'

Kate sat back, stunned momentarily by the naïveté of the statement. 'Do you, Adam?' she asked. 'Do you know how I feel?'

She was surprised that Adam showed no embarrassment. The tense movements had stopped, and he held her angry glare, aware of her rising irritation but not intimidated by it.

'You'd be surprised,' he said.

Kate laughed. 'Yes, I should think I would be surprised if you had the tiniest inkling of how I feel. About the police or anything else.'

She saw a flash of anger, rare in Adam, and he said: 'Oh, so I'm just some kid, still wet behind the ears, am I?'

'I didn't say that, but you could never understand what I've been through, Adam.'

'Have I ever said I did? I've a bit more sensitivity than that, I hope. But at least I'm *trying*, aren't I? At least I'm making some kind of effort. I'm not bloody sneering at you – and laughing when you're trying to be sincere, trying to help.'

'Adam—'

'It's not as if you've shown any particular interest. You've let me prattle on the whole of lunchtime, but you've not been listening. D'you know what? I don't think you've heard a single word I've said – I'd lay odds you haven't. I know you've been through it, Kate. But we all have our personal tragedies, you know.'

Kate felt a pang of guilt. She'd never really said anything about Sims. Not since that day. She reached across the table, but Adam snatched his hand away.

'I thought we understood each other. But you're so boxed in by your own situation, you've got no time for anyone else.'

Kate's eyes sparked green fire. 'Yes, I suppose I have been rather preoccupied. How bloody boring of me. I really should have had more regard for your feelings, your sensitive male pride. Christ! You men make me sick. You show a little consideration, and you expect us to fall at your feet in gratitude. My daughter was murdered, Adam. That tends to make you a bit introspective, maybe even a bit selfish. If you can't deal with that, I suggest you go fuck yourself.'

Adam stood up quickly, catching the tops of his legs on the table and nearly overturning it. Kate steadied the table with both hands.

'Adam, I'm sorry.'

'Forget it. I wouldn't want to intrude on your private grief. What right have I got to express any feelings in all this?' He threw some money on to the table and left.

After the row with Adam the previous afternoon, she had developed a headache. The type that started with a dull, pulsing pain in her right temple and grew to a pounding, incapacitating, ugly throb that made the right side of her face feel swollen and tender, finally overcoming her with waves of nausea. She had made it home – just – having gone to the wild expense of a taxi, crawled on to her bed, unable even to undress. She had expected to sleep badly, had expected to dream. She had dreamed. Of the first day Melanie had worn her roller boots. It was her tenth birthday, a hot July day, and Melanie had begged to be taken to the park to practise.

'Aunty Mary's going to take us to the roller rink for Jenny's birthday and I want to be able to skate then.'

This gave her precisely two weeks, but Kate had no doubt

that Melanie would master the skill in that time. She was fearless, confident and determined at ten as Kate had been fearful, diffident and hesitant at the same age.

'D'you mind not having a party, Mel?'

Melanie gave her a long-suffering look, tilting her head, letting her hair swing luxuriously over one shoulder and resting a hand on her hip. Kate recognized these as reflections of her own mannerisms. 'Mum, can we afford it?'

'Well, not this year, but—'

'Then there's no point mooning over it, is there?'

'Isn't that what *I'm* supposed to say?'

Melanie laughed. 'Can we, Mum?'

'Can we what?'

'Go to Longford Park.'

'What's wrong with Victoria Park? It's a heck of a lot nearer, and we could visit Aunty Mary on the way home.'

'Victoria Park's too small. Anyway, Longford's got this fantastic Tarmac. It's brilliant for skating on.'

'It's seven o'clock in the morning, Mel!' But Kate was relieved that her daughter looked like a ten-year-old again, and not a mirror image of herself.

'So it'll be empty, won't it?'

'Except for a few dirty old men and the odd sprinkling of drunks and dossers.' Kate laughed. 'That's good. I like that. A sprinkling of drunks.'

Melanie's forehead wrinkled. 'Why?'

'You'll understand when you're older,' Kate said, using what Melanie called a 'Family Phrase'.

'I hate it when you say that. I won't *remember* when I'm older.'

'Then write it down. No better still, I'll remind you.'

'*Mum!*'

Kate slipped into the hallway, then poked her head around the door a moment later. 'Aren't you coming?'

'You mean we can go?'

'Well, I've only the Big Shop to do, and the flat to clean, and your uniform to iron, and the beds to change, but so what?' She grinned, looking like a teenager. 'It's Saturday, and besides, you're only ten once, you know.' She touched the side of her nose, knowingly, and Melanie perched both hands, knuckles in, on her hips.

'Oh, very deep, Mum.'

'As deep as a pan pizza?'

Melanie deliberated for a moment. 'Only not quite as tasty.'

The bus ride was quiet and pleasant. Melanie insisted on sitting at the back, in her favourite seat next to the window, but Kate sat nearer the front. The morning was already hot, and the lurch of the bus and the faint smell of diesel fumes would, she knew, make her sick.

Melanie sidled up to her ten minutes into the journey, slipping her hand through the crook of Kate's arm.

'What's up, tuppence? Did you not like it back there?'

Melanie turned a pale and rather nauseated face up to her. 'Not so very much.'

'It's all gone Horribly Wrong,' said Kate in her newsreader's voice. Melanie grinned and elbowed her. 'They thought it was going to be the Perfect Birthday, then – Disaster Struck. Who would have guessed, when they set out on that glorious July morning, that Miss Pearson would fall prey to . . . Car Sickness?'

'Bus Sickness,' Melanie corrected. Kate put her arm round her daughter, catching her hilarity, and they giggled together.

The park was, as predicted, empty except for one sad old man who arrived just after them. He scuffed along the pathway, choosing the first bench that the sun had dried the dew off. Depositing his carrier bag under his seat with a musical *clunk*, he immediately started on his first can, then sat back, enjoying the sunshine and slowly working his way through the beer.

Kate could see why Melanie was so keen; the ornamental gardens presented a maze of Tarmac walkways bordered by wider arcs around the central flower beds. 'We'll stay on the main path,' Kate suggested. 'We don't want to knock anyone down on these narrow bits.'

On the bus home, Melanie complained that her legs felt all wobbly, and Kate explained in a Captain Bird's-Eye voice that she had to get her land-legs back. Melanie was convulsed with laughter at the thought of swapping one pair of legs for another. She subsided after a few minutes, hiccuping, and sat in silence.

Then: 'It takes you back, doesn't it?' she asked, wistfully.

'What?' said Kate.

'A return ticket.'

Kate slapped her forehead.

'Gotcha!' squealed Melanie.

'Fell for it hook, line and stinker, kid.'

'Sinker.'

'What?'

'It's sinker. Hook, line and *sinker*.'

'Not this time. That was a real stinker.'

They argued amiably all the way home.

Kate had woken in the dark, smiling. Her migraine was gone, but she felt shaky, both sick and hungry at the same time. She'd had nothing to eat since lunchtime. It was nine thirty. She rummaged around the kitchen and managed to scrounge some dried pasta from one of the cupboards and a jar of pesto sauce from the fridge. She cooked the pasta and thought she had never tasted anything so good.

She had come in to work that morning expecting more

anonymous mail. She had checked her e-mail as soon as she got in and it was clear. The anonymous mail had vanished from her computer mailbox. Technicomm's system assumed that important mail would be printed out or else saved to floppy disk, and the office file-management policy was that unread mail remained in the records for thirty days, but files that had been read were deleted after fourteen. The message should still be in her mailbox. Kate tried undeleting the file, but it had gone. There was no record of the file ever having been there except for the printout John had passed back to her the day before. It rested in her handbag, the only remaining evidence that the bizarre haunting had ever taken place.

Kate felt curiously relieved. She was even tempted to shred the printout, feeling that perhaps the contact had been a brief and nasty bit of fun for some crank and now he would leave her alone. She could sense Adam watching her from his work-station, and once she turned and threw him a smile.

When the phone on her desk rang, she reached for it, untroubled by any premonition of what was to come.

'What can I do for you, John?' In the silence that followed, she imagined the systems manager raising his eyebrows and smiling in his mild, amused way and, without him having to say a word, she knew that there was very little she could do for him; their relationship was rather one-sided, but John was too gallant to point it out.

'Have you read your e-mail?' he asked.

Kate's heart skipped a beat, then she remembered, 'Nine o'clock this morning.'

'Not since then?'

'Has something come in?' Kate reached for her mouse.

'Don't!' John warned and, startled, Kate let go of the mouse. 'Don't look at it up there. Come and see me. I'll be waiting.' The line went dead.

In contrast to the previous occasion, two days before, when she had come to ask for John's help, the server room was busy. Three technicians sat at the workbench, tinkering with the disgorged contents of PCs and modems. A couple of programmers worked at their own terminals, staring with rapt concentration at screens of slowly scrolling symbols and text. Systems operators moved about with apparent purpose, checking tapes, binning printouts, filing, faxing, consulting. The programmers looked younger than the technicians; Owen believed that only the newly qualified and totally obsessed were of any real use to him.

Kate's presence went unmarked, and as she watched them, feeling like an intruder in their world, she had the passing notion that they looked like worker insects nurturing a huge and grotesque termite queen – even the subterranean setting was right for it.

'Kate?' John had been observing her, curious, wondering at her disorientation and the expression of distaste on her face.

Kate shuddered with sudden violence and moved with grateful alacrity towards the one white-coated figure in the lab. Others disdained wearing lab coats, regarding them as badges of conformity; John wore his as an emblem of superiority and a mark of efficiency. He guided Kate to his own PC, tucked away in a corner of the room. Owen had offered to build him an office like his own, a glass-fronted box, but John had scorned it. 'A box within a box?' he had said, a lopsided smile on his face. 'Like a wee terrarium . . . I'm not such a hot-house flower that I need my own microclimate – thanks all the same.' Although Owen knew he was being insulted, John's bland expression foxed him and he was unable to justify taking offence.

John drew up a chair for Kate and then, working rapidly, called up her account.

'Do you have everyone's password?' She had been unable to follow the quick, sure movements of his fingers over the keyboard.

'We do keep a record,' he said, 'but I don't need your password: I've got superuser status. That gives me access to whatever files I want to get into. Here—' Her mailbox had appeared on screen. Kate scanned the entries. There were half a dozen new mailings. She frowned, leaning closer to the screen.

'*Moira?*' She glanced at John. 'Why would Moira send me an e-mail?'

'Or Adam, for that matter,' John commented.

Kate smiled faintly. In the past Adam had sometimes sent her joke messages. Once he'd mailed her a send during a telephone conversation with Owen. Her terminal had bleeped rudely at her and then the message came up: 'Tell the old fart to can it. It's after five and the Lion King waits for no man.' Adam had booked tickets to take her and Melanie to the six o'clock showing of the latest Disney.

John was talking and Kate forced her attention back to him. 'You'll notice there's one from me and one from Owen as well.' He studied her closely. 'They're all the same,' he said, fidgeting uncomfortably. Kate took this to signify his embarrassment over reading her mail, but he went on, 'I'm not sure it's a good idea that you read it.'

Kate listened to the quiet hum of the machines and the murmur of voices. John didn't want her to read her own mail. Why? Perhaps she had done the wrong thing in trying to deal with this herself. Had she provoked a response she could not deal with? Perhaps Adam was right: she should have turned the whole thing over to the police.

'Tell me what it says, then I'll read it.'

John hesitated and Kate flashed him a look in an agony

of expectation. He sighed, 'It says, "Corpses make good shields." ' He reached across and squeezed Kate's hand.

Kate swivelled in her chair and watched the tranquil, unhurried work of the men for several minutes. She had stung him with a simple question, sent to his anonymous address: 'Why are you hiding behind a dead child?' she had asked. And this was a direct reply to her message. No pretence. His hatred unmasked. 'Corpses make good shields.' What did that mean? *If I make you focus on the idea that Melanie sent the messages, you won't focus on the real sender.* Is that what it meant? Then the real sender must be known to her. It must be someone she should be able to identify. The killer had told her a lot in those few words. She swung her chair back to face the screen.

'He got into four accounts,' John told her. 'Mine, Moira's, Adam's and Owen's. He sent the e-mail to you via those accounts. The message on all of them is the same. What does it mean, Kate? This message is not like the others. It's like he's answering a question.'

Kate frowned. 'To an anonymous e-mail? Is that possible?'

For the second time in a matter of days, John's mask of benign unrufflability failed him, and Kate thought she could detect sadness in his face. 'Ach, it's your own business, I suppose,' he said, 'but if you've entered into correspondence with this crank, you're taking a big risk.'

Kate lowered her eyes, ashamed of her dishonesty.

'This kind of hacker is like a malignancy – out of control, invasive, destructive – and if he feels he's having an effect, he'll do it all the more. It gives him a sense of power, d'ye see?'

Kate raised her head. 'Yes,' she said. 'I see that he has the freedom to send me these vile messages. He can implicate my friends and colleagues, and I'm supposed to do nothing.

Well, you may be right, John. Maybe the more I react, the more he enjoys it. But there's another possibility.' David flashed into her mind as she spoke: 'If I don't react, he'll push it further and further until he gets the reaction he wants.'

Chapter Six

'I don't know why you're asking me.' Angie Harmon continued lacing her son's trainer. 'See,' she demonstrated. 'It has to cross over.'

'Because you have a sixth sense about these things.'

Angie glanced up, her eyes sparkling with amusement. 'Just as well you didn't say "intuition", or you wouldn't've got one more word out of me.'

'Let me try, Mummy.' Angie handed the trainer to her son and watched as he threaded the next eyelet, his tongue clenched between his teeth and his brows knitted in concentration.

'Trevor, I'm a clinical psychologist, not a psychiatrist. I deal mainly with people who've suffered head injuries or strokes. I'm not some soap-opera psych who can diagnose schizophrenia by the way a guy smokes his cigarette. Anyway, how am I supposed to make any sort of judgement without having even met the woman?'

'Come on, Angie, I'm not going to quote you on this. But you know more about these things than I do.'

'Because I'm a woman?' she teased.

'Because you're a blood—' He stopped, responding to his wife's disapproving look. 'You're a *very* good psychologist,' he corrected, 'and I'm asking your opinion.'

'What do you think, Mummy?' Michael held up his shoe for inspection.

'Now *this* I can express an opinion on with no qualms at all,' Angie said, smiling. 'It's a masterpiece, Michael.'

Michael grinned with pleasure, jamming his foot into the trainer and tying the lace haphazardly.

'You can go and play outside for five minutes, but tell Joseph breakfast won't wait for ever. And stay out of my flowerbeds. Clear?'

'Crystal,' Michael replied, hopping down from the kitchen stool and tearing outside, shouting.

Angie watched him go, letting the smile melt from her face. She caught her husband's eye and pursed her lips. 'You're serious?'

'Deadly.'

'You really want my opinion?'

His look was answer enough.

She sliced bread thoughtfully while Harmon set the table.

'A lot of grieving parents go through a period of denial,' she began. 'Their child isn't dead. The hospital made a mistake. They got the wrong person. Usually it's at the beginning of the grieving process, but I suppose if she's been in shock, on medication, whatever, it could have been delayed.' She was silent for some time. 'I'm trying to imagine how I would feel if one of the boys – God forbid . . .' This time the silence was prolonged. Harmon did not prompt her. He waited, watching the emotions chase across her face.

'Perhaps Kate Pearson is reincarnating her daughter. She doesn't want Melanie to be dead, so she imagines that Melanie is alive. She blames herself for Melanie's death, so Melanie blames her in her messages.'

'It's possible.'

'But you don't think it likely? You know her, Trevor, I don't. What do you think?'

'It's anyone's guess. She's keeping it between herself and the guy who came to see me.'

'Boyfriend?'

He frowned. 'Not sure. It seems a fairly platonic relation-ship, but before all this happened—'

'When your child is murdered, you're liable to go off men for a bit,' Angie observed, with the hint of a smile. 'If he's started putting on pressure to get the relationship going again—'

'It could be a reaction?'

'If she's not ready . . .' She shrugged. 'Who knows?'

'And if it's the other way round, if he seems to be losing interest, could she be making up all of this to get his attention?'

'It's a thought.' She watched Michael kicking a football to his older brother. Michael adored Joseph. There was four years' difference in their age, and Joseph was everything that Michael aspired to be. He was tall, like his father, and darker than Michael, who had her own, lighter skin tones. A skilful football player and captain of the under-thirteens cricket team, Joseph was something of a hero among his peers at Manchester Grammar. He tolerated Michael in his easy, somewhat patronizing way, and Michael was more than happy to go along with it.

'You say he was alone, this friend?'

Harmon nodded.

'Mrs Pearson didn't feel up to coming to the police station?'

'She didn't know he'd come to see me.'

'Ah . . .' Angie knocked on the window. The boys gave their attention reluctantly.

'What do you mean, "Ah"?'

Angie beckoned the boys in, and they mouthed 'five more minutes' at her. She shook her head vigorously.

'She doesn't want you to know. Is that because she doesn't

want to be reminded of what happened to her little girl? It would be natural enough – God knows, she wouldn't go looking for that sort of reminder.' She tilted her head to one side, thinking.

'Or?' Harmon prompted.

'Or, she could be worried you'd see through her fabrication.'

'You mean she's deliberately lying?'

'I think that the trauma of losing a child so horribly is liable to send a person reeling from one emotional disaster to another. When did all this start?'

'End of November.'

'Over three weeks. And she hasn't said anything?'

'Except to Shepherd, nothing, apparently.'

Michael and Joseph tumbled into the kitchen.

'Out!'

The boys froze. Joseph stared in mock horror at his feet. He lifted one foot in an exaggerated movement and set it down behind him in the track of his last muddy print.

Michael chortled.

'The prints led to the middle of the room and then . . . vanished!' he said, inventing a story line for Michael to take up.

The younger boy copied his brother's retreat. 'Did they beam aboard the *Enterprise*, Captain?'

'No, Lieutenant Riker. They were eaten alive by the Mummy Monster!'

Michael screamed delightedly and fled through the utility room and then outside, followed by Joseph, growling and gurgling.

Trevor Harmon's eyebrows shot up. 'The Mummy Monster! Could that be a Freudian reference, Dr Harmon?'

'Trevor—' Angie pleaded.

'I'll fetch them,' he said. 'But do you really think she's lying?'

Angie was rummaging in a cupboard. 'Not intentionally. Or at least, not with any malicious intent. Maybe she's just so— Damn!' Something fell from its hook with a clatter, and Angie set it back before continuing '. . . so desperately unhappy that she doesn't know what she's doing.'

Kate read the statement several times, unable to make sense of it.

One thousand five hundred and twenty-five pounds – twenty-five pounds over her credit limit. But she had cleared the balance on her Visa card the previous month. She had only ever used it to pay for the short holidays she took Melanie on – and, of course, for buying Mel's birthday and Christmas presents.

Kate checked the balance again. The figure was unchanged. She searched back through the itemized list, and her stomach lurched.

Toys 'R' Us. Halford's. Tammy Girl. Biker's World. The Disney Store Ltd.

Presents. Presents for Melanie? Darkness began to close in on her, and she felt herself near fainting. She shook her head.

'Stop it,' she said, her voice reverberating in the high, cold silence of the dark hallway. 'Get a grip.' There had to be a mistake. She hadn't bought anything in months. Since Melanie's death there had been no point. She didn't want anything for herself – except the one thing she knew she couldn't have. And, without her little girl, what could she need to spend money on? Why would she want to?

She breathed into the silent, frigid air for some time.

He didn't leave any notes on your e-mail yesterday. She blinked. Her breath steamed in the cold air, but she felt hot, suffocated. Her hand twitched, and the statement fluttered like a broken butterfly to the doormat. She looked down at her numb fingers. A second envelope. *Did you think he would let you be?*

She tore open the second envelope and looked down at the letter. Her breath caught.

'. . . contact us at your earliest convenience regarding this unauthorized overdraft'. She glanced at the letterhead. The bank.

I have to phone them to explain, she thought. She reached for the receiver, then hesitated. Her hand, still hovering over the handset, began to shake. What if he'd had the telephone cut off too? She fumbled the handset from the cradle, hearing the dialling tone with a flood of relief. Steadying her left hand with her right, she set the receiver back on the hook. Eight fifteen. Too early.

Kate stooped to pick up the Visa-card statement. Now take your time, she told herself. Find the bastard. Each transaction bore a reference number. All the posting dates were 15 November. The transaction dates were the day before that. The stores and their locations were listed alongside the transactions. It shouldn't be too hard to trace them. And him. Kate reached for the phone book, her anger keeping her fear in check.

The statement was in her shoulder bag. Laid out in her small, neat hand, an extra column: the telephone number of every retailer on the statement. She went straight to Adam's desk. He looked up from his work, and the pain in his eyes made her wince and look away.

She set some money down on the desk. 'We agreed to go Dutch,' she said quietly.

He glanced down at the money, then back at her face.

She could not look at him. He did not speak to her, and rather than allow the silence to continue she said: 'If it makes you feel any better, you were right.' She turned on her heel, moved swiftly to her own station and started her work with a fierce concentration.

At ten fifteen Kate slipped out to the pay-phone. She heard a footfall behind her, then: 'Right about what?' His voice echoed on the fire-escape stairwell.

Kate closed her eyes. She shrugged. 'About everything. About him not stopping. About going to the police. About my not hearing a word you said at the restaurant. About my patronizing you. About the whole bloody mess.'

She stood, swaying, her eyes closed, sensing him near her, feeling his warmth. She held up the statement, and he took it without a word, scanned it and returned it without comment.

'It isn't the money. I don't care about that. But he took Melanie from me. And that wasn't enough for him. He's back. Manipulating me. And I keep thinking—'

Adam squeezed her shoulder. 'It's okay . . .'

'I keep thinking, what did he do to her? To Mel. An eleven-year-old girl. If he can do this to me – make me feel this way – what could he do to a child? Did he—?' Her hand went to her mouth. 'Did he promise she could go home?'

'Kate,' he said, softly stroking her shoulder, touching her hair lightly, 'it's all right. You don't have to . . .'

'The post-mortem showed that Melanie had been dead less than twenty-four hours when they found her,' she went on, compulsively. 'She'd been with him a whole week. And when I think of what he— I think I'll go mad.' She stopped, her breath hitching. Adam tried to turn her to him, but she broke free.

'No – I can't. I've got to get some air.'

'All right. All right. But take it slowly.' He followed her

down the stairway and out through the foyer on the ground floor.

The mid-morning traffic was heavy. It tainted the high ceiling of the clear, blue winter sky with a dirty smudge of yellow-brown haze. Kate dashed across the road into Albert Square. A car horn blared, making Adam shout in alarm. He waited for a safe gap, then followed her. She was seated on a bench, watching the pigeons peck at the cobblestones beneath the town hall's clock-tower.

'Do you want to get yourself killed?' he yelled, shaken by her near miss. She answered him with a look of such terrible bleakness that he was, for a moment, unable to find words to say to her.

'I'm going to kill him.'

At first he wasn't sure he'd heard right. A look at her face was enough to convince him.

'Kate, you don't—'

'I do. I do mean it.'

'I don't know what to say to you.'

'You don't have to say anything. It's a statement of fact.'

'Kate, you don't want to get anywhere near this guy, believe me.'

Kate levelled her gaze at him; it was Arctic-cold.

'Let's make the calls,' she said.

Moira watched them return, checking the time against the big office clock. Half-hour breaks now, she thought. Kate Pearson thinks she's a law unto herself. She opened the note-book she kept in her desk drawer and jotted down the details. She wouldn't go to Mr Owen just yet. This little peccadillo wasn't substantial enough, but give them enough rope . . .

'You're sure this is it?'

'Seven, Wood Street,' Kate confirmed, adding with a tired

smile, 'After all, fifteen retailers can't be wrong, can they?' All of the orders had been placed by telephone, and all had been directed to the same delivery address. They had made the short walk from Albert Square to the little side street off Deansgate in under ten minutes, despite the streets being solid with Christmas shoppers. 'But why here? Is he trying to tell me something?'

'Have you been here before?'

'Not that I remember. But it must have some significance.'

They both looked up at the painted restaurant sign: Cacciatore's. On either side, in block capitals, ITALIAN FOOD. Kate opened the door and stepped inside, releasing a blast of warm air and chatter into the shadowy street. It followed them back inside as the door closed and they were engulfed by the noise and the smells of pasta and pizza, garlic and herbs.

The restaurant was busy with lunchtime business, and the little Italian proprietor fussed over their holding up his clientele, so that eventually they agreed to sit at a table and order coffee. He came over when he had settled the backlog of customers at their tables, weaving his way through the clutter of tables with the agility and grace of an athlete.

'Sure, I got the kiddie's stuff. All for Mrs Pearson, who, by the way, I don't know. I telephone the people who send these things and they say they got the address right, and I say they don't got it right. And they say, "Sure, Wood Street, Mrs Pearson." I tell them, I don't know this Mrs Pearson, "My name is Cacciatore," I say.' He straightened, proudly, as he spoke his name. 'I don't know nobody call Mrs Pearson.'

'I'm Mrs Pearson.' Kate spoke quietly, but Mr Cacciatore's response was immediate. He opened his eyes wide and raised his shoulders, turning his palms up.

'What do you want to do this to me for? You can't see I'm a busy man?' He gestured to the crowded restaurant. 'Don't

I have troubles enough? You gotta give me some more, with a room full of kiddies' toys and bikes and clothes and everything? What did I ever do to you?'

'Mr Cacciatore, I didn't order any of those things. I don't know who did. Someone's been playing a sick joke on me.'

The little man snorted. 'On you, on me. I tell you,' he tapped the middle of his chest with the tips of his fingers, 'that I am not laughing.'

'What did you do with the stuff? Is it still here?' Adam asked.

'What, you think I got room for these things? I send it back before they come in. I tell them I don't want it.'

'You refused delivery?' Kate felt immensely relieved. 'Thank you, Mr Cacciatore.'

'You want to thank me? You tell them not to send no more things to my restaurant. I got too much to do. I don't want all this aggravation. I work hard. My wife works hard. This is a family business. It's hard enough to make a living without all this.' The little man took a deep breath and stood on tiptoe, bracing himself for another tirade.

'I'll do my best,' said Kate, also standing, anxious to avoid another explosion of words. They had attracted an appreciative audience among the diners, and there was a discernible movement as they all turned their attention to Mr Cacciatore, waiting for his response. It was disappointingly flat.

'You do that,' he said, folding his arms across his chest.

Kate offered to pay for the coffee, but he waved her away angrily. 'Just don't come to my restaurant again, and see that you leave me in peace.'

Kate and Adam exchanged a look. The time had definitely come for them to leave.

'What'll you do now?' asked Adam. They were outside the restaurant, grateful for the comparative quiet and the coolness of the street.

Kate shrugged. 'Make sure the money's credited to my account, then close it, I suppose.'

'What about the bank? You can't do without that so easily.'

'I don't know. They said they'd look into it. The money went out in one lot, but there's no record of a transfer or a cheque or anything. They're trying to find out where the money went. I just can't see how he got all my personal details . . .'

'Banks're easy enough. All you need is access to employee records – and everyone with a PC in our place has, at least in theory, got that. All they do is find the payroll accounts and they've got details of bank accounts, salaries. Even the banks' phone numbers are listed.'

Kate gave Adam a long, slow look that changed from surprise to puzzlement, then to doubt and suspicion. Adam coloured under her stare.

'What's up?' he asked.

'Nothing. Only you seem pretty well up on this stuff.'

Adam shrugged, smiling crookedly. 'Misspent youth,' he said.

Chief Inspector Harmon agreed to see them immediately. He welcomed Kate warmly and offered her a seat. He looked Adam over with a cool, appraising glance, then indicated a chair at the other end of the desk. Adam accepted, reminding himself to keep his hands still, and waited for Kate to begin.

Harmon walked round the desk and rested against its edge, half-turned from Adam. Kate found making a start difficult; the last time she had been in this room was just after they had found Melanie. It was a large, business-like office, but with the odd personal touch – a photograph of Harmon's family, a vibrant abstract in acrylics.

'I hope I haven't interrupted anything important,' Kate said, unable to bring herself at once to the reason for her visit.

'Nothing that won't wait.' Harmon caught Kate's eye and his penetrating gaze held her attention. 'You don't look well, Mrs Pearson.'

This simple observation, made with such kind concern, was almost too much for Kate. She felt tears well up, and she quickly dropped her eyes. There was a silence. Harmon remained still, allowing her time to collect her thoughts.

She was unable to see Adam from where she sat; the Inspector's body interrupted her line of sight. I wish Adam would say something, she thought.

Chief Inspector Harmon glanced at Shepherd. He was staring determinedly at his feet. His hands were clasped in his lap. Harmon recalled the nervous, twitchy gesture he had noted during their first interview and nodded to himself.

'You have been getting messages – electronic mail.' He paused, giving Kate a chance to continue, but she remained silent. Her mouth was clenched in a tight line. He tried again: 'Do you have copies of the messages? It would help if you had saved the messages to disk – it'd give us something to work with.'

'They've been deleted,' Kate said, abruptly.

Harmon was disappointed but said, 'Of course, it's understandable. They would be very upsetting. Disturbing.'

Kate shook her head, impatiently. 'No, I didn't delete them, but they're gone anyway.'

Harmon frowned. 'I think Mr Shepherd said some documents had been altered. Did you perhaps print the documents before you realized they had been tampered with?'

Kate lifted her head. Her mouth opened a fraction, as though she was about to speak, then it snapped shut. She rummaged in her handbag and handed Inspector Harmon the printout of the bulletin she had shown John James.

Unable to bear the silence as he read it, unwilling to recall its contents, and knowing the words would come back if she didn't say something, she blurted out: 'He wiped out my bank account. He's used my credit card, buying things. Children's things.'

'You lost your credit card?'

'No. I have it here.' She half-opened her handbag again, intending to show him the card, but changed her mind and took her cigarettes out instead. She lit up without asking, then shot Harmon a guilty look. He shook his head, accepting her unspoken apology. 'But he— I don't know how he does it. He can get into everything – my bank account, the files at the office, my credit card—'

'He got the credit-card details the same way he got your bank account number.' Adam had spoken.

Katie tried to get a look at him, but the big policeman still blocked her view. She stood, impatiently. 'The payments department don't have that sort of information,' she said, testily.

'I said in the same *way*, not from the same *place*. Maybe he hacked into your credit-card company's records. Maybe he got your details through an insurance company. Are you a member of the NCCSS, Kate?' He had been stung by her impatience and her dismissal of his suggestion, and now he was out to prove a point.

Kate blinked. 'Yes.'

Adam turned to the inspector. 'The National Credit Card Security Service. They indemnify against losses due to theft or credit-card fraud. At least you're covered there, Kate.'

Harmon made no comment. He glanced down at the slip of paper in his hand. 'This e-mail address—' he said, looking over at Adam.

Adam threw Kate a look of shocked disbelief. 'Address?' Then he too was out of his seat and standing next to Harmon.

Harmon raised his eyebrows, inviting an explanation.
'I didn't show it to Adam,' Kate said, a little guilty.
'Shit.'
'Mr Shepherd?'
'It's no damn good,' Adam said, returning to his seat. 'He's used an APS.'
'APS?'
'An Anonymous Posting Service.'
'And that means it's not traceable?'
'It's been redirected via a remailer, and that's a bugger to trace.'
'Is it worth trying?'
'Anything's worth trying to nail the bastard who's doing this to Kate. But you can't trace deleted files.'
'Meaning?'
'Meaning you'd have to try and trace him next time he gets in touch.'
Harmon studied the rather angular features for a few moments, and saw the finger go up, in an unconscious movement, and stroke the eyebrow.
Adam cursed himself, silently.
'Will you?' It was said with a careful deliberateness.
Adam's eyes darted to Kate, then back to Harmon.
'Will I what?'
'Try to trace the next bulletin.'
'Me? How would I know . . . ?' The lie died on his lips.
Harmon's eyes twinkled briefly with what may have been amusement. Adam's hand moved to his face and then, recalling himself, he made it continue, past his eyebrows and over his hair.
'I could give it a go. But no promises, right?'
'Right.'
There was a strange, calculating coldness in Harmon's exchanges with Adam that Kate had never seen before. It

troubled her, and she found herself looking from one to the other, trying to discover the cause of Adam's anxious irritability and Harmon's apparent dislike or distrust. She was unable to decide which it was.

Kate walked away from the police headquarters without looking back.

'What was all that about?'

'What?'

'Harmon. All that talking in code. Why's he got it in for you?'

Adam shrugged. 'Bit of a technophobe, if you ask me.'

A taxi approached and Kate flagged it. 'Want to bunk a ride?'

Adam shook his head. 'Got a bit of Christmas shopping to do.'

Chapter Seven

Kate settled back in the taxi.

Christmas. Kate could not imagine a Christmas without Melanie. For Kate, Christmas *was* Melanie. They had shared its warmth for seven years in happiness, ever since she left David. Melanie was four and a half years old and so excited. Kate had always tried to shield her from her own misery, and in spite of the bruises David had given her in lieu of presents, despite the fact that they had fled with only a bin-bag full of clothes and had only one week's wages to live on, she too was excited. Excited and, for the first time since Melanie's birth, hopeful. They had shared that Christmas with a joy and contentment Kate would never have thought possible.

They had lived in a hostel for a while until Kate found a new job. She was too frightened to go back to her old place because David, of course, knew where she worked. He had told her that if she ever left him, he would find her and kill her, and she believed him.

At the hostel she had been afraid for a lot of the time, but so were the other women, and Kate had gained strength from knowing she wasn't the only one who felt that way and from helping newcomers to find the courage to stay. Some women found it easier to go back and face a beating than to wait for their partner to find them. Kate had almost given in to that herself. It seemed incredible to her now, but she had actually thought of going back to David. It was also instructional, listening to so many of the women blame themselves while barely able to make themselves intelligible through the swelling and bruising on their faces. A lot of them came to the refuge for fear of their children's safety; few came on their own account; always they carried a burden of guilt that Kate slowly realized was undeserved. By them as well as by her.

And then there was Bernie, who ran the hostel. She was dependable. Solid. In the literal as well as the metaphorical sense. Bernie was a small, stockily built woman of mixed Irish and Polish descent. She spoke with a Mancunian accent, although she had been brought up in Preston. She taught women's self-defence classes at the local sports centre as well as running the refuge. She had persuaded Kate to go to her classes, and Kate had been surprised by the confidence the self-defence training and improved fitness had given her.

Bernie seemed to know when someone needed to talk; she had a knack of saying the right thing at the right time; and she knew to keep silent when that was what was needed.

At first Kate thought she must be a trained psychologist, but later, when she got to know Bernie, it became apparent that she understood because she had been through it herself and had learned from her own experience. She said little, but she was a keen and attentive listener, which in itself was a novelty encounter for many of the women who passed through the refuge.

She fought shy of giving direct advice, so it came as a shock when Kate told her she was considering going back to David, that Bernie took her by the shoulders and made her sit, saying: 'I'm going to tell you a few things that you may find hard to accept right now, but, believe me, after a while, perhaps not all at once but gradually, they'll start making sense. You're afraid, right?'

Kate nodded, bowing her head, ashamed.

Bernie put her finger under Kate's chin, gently tilting her head up. 'Good,' she said. 'That's normal, right? Healthy. I want you to remember that, and I want you to think about why you're so afraid.'

Kate looked away.

'If you don't think about it, Kate, you're going to get yourself in a sorry mess all over again. What about the night you came here? He'd gone a bit further than usual, hadn't he?' When Kate did not respond, Bernie went on, 'He didn't just beat you where it didn't show that time. Your face was so bruised you couldn't eat your Christmas turkey, remember? What did he beat you with, Kate?'

Kate was frowning, fighting back tears, but Bernie had persisted. 'Come on, Kate. It's no good trying to forget the bad things until you're free of them. If you're thinking of going back to him, you're not free. You might as well realize what's going to happen when you go back. Tell me why you're frightened of him.'

Kate shook her head.

'Because of the knife he kept hidden under the settee, right?'

Kate nodded.

'He didn't just hit you when he lost his temper, Kate. He sadistically and systematically *terrorized* you by keeping that special knife in that special place where you would see it every time you cleaned, where you would feel its presence every time you went into that room, every time you sat on the settee. You knew it was there, waiting for your first mistake. Remember how he used to fiddle about under the settee, just to tease you, then pretend he'd been looking for an ashtray? What a sense of humour, eh? Right little tinker, wasn't he? He humiliated you so many times you thought you didn't deserve better. Why d'you think he went through the same old rigmarole before he beat the shit out of you? So you'd know it was coming, Kate. So he could feel powerful, seeing the fear in your eyes, watching you shaking and trembling, and listening to you pleading with him.'

'Bitch!' Kate, appalled by the venom in her voice, looked over at Bernie, shocked. But Bernie seemed unaffected. 'I wish I'd never told you,' she said hoarsely.

'So that I could never remind you?' Bernie went on when it became clear that Kate would not reply: 'Go back to him and you'll get all the reminders you'll ever need. It'll be like you've never been out the house – after he's given you a bloody good hiding to let you know who's boss. And then he'll cry, and he'll blame you for making him lose his rag, and you know what? You'll feel sorry for him. You'll feel like it's all your fault. Because that's what you're supposed to feel. That's what he wants you to feel. Shall I tell you why you think you should go back?' Receiving no answer, Bernie persisted, 'You think you should go back because you think you're no good.'

'I don't—'

Bernie interrupted her protestations, her voice hard, unrelenting: 'When you first came here, you were scared for Mel's sake. As the bruises faded, you started thinking, "What if he finds me? He said he'd kill me if he found me." Then you felt bad because when you had that thought, you were scared for yourself – you weren't even *thinking* about Melanie. After all, he didn't threaten to kill her, did he? But what sort of mother thinks like that? So you feel bad and you think he was right all along. He said you were selfish, and he was right. You are a lousy wife and a lousy mother, and you'd best go back and take what's coming to you. Right?'

Kate nodded, chewing at her lip.

'Wrong, Kate.' Bernie took Kate's hands in her own, talking softly now. 'They threaten to kill us if we leave because it means losing control,' she said. 'It's not love that makes them say it. It isn't that they're afraid of losing us, except that they're weak and can't survive without somebody else to organize and drudge for them – and take the blame when they fail.' She paused while Kate wiped her eyes. 'What they're afraid of is what they don't know, what they can't control. That's why they have to check up on everything we do, why they make us do things their way. It gives them control. And when they have control over the little things, it makes them less fearful of the big things – of real life.

'Then what does the bitch go and do? She buggers off in the middle of the night, or day, or whenever she finally discovers she can't take any more. What does that do to him? It leaves him totally without control. The creature he has dominated and bullied and beaten for so long that she thinks it's natural has left. He's not got control over her any more. If he's lost control of *her*, how can he be in control of anything else? His job, his daily routine, his interactions with real people? Because although he lives with her, and has sex with her, and expects her to clean and cook and wash and iron for him – she may even be the mother of his children – he has never before seen her as a real person with feelings and rights and a will of her own. He's even convinced *her* that she doesn't exist outside of his control. Now she's gone. And he's lost that tiny empire where he was god and no one dare disobey him.'

Kate murmured, 'I don't know what to do . . .'

Bernie smiled at her. 'Is that so surprising? You've had some other bugger make all your decisions for you, down to what you should wear, for – how many years?'

'Five,' Kate answered without hesitation.

'It takes time, Kate. Sometimes I think it's a kind of madness that we suffer from. That's what makes so many women go back again and again. We have to regain our sanity before we can be trusted to make the right decisions about our lives.'

'Are you saying you're making the decision for me?' Kate smiled.

The irony was not lost on Bernie, and she smiled back, a little sheepishly. 'If you like. I'd prefer to call it advice. Only I won't beat you with the wooden end of a bread knife if you go against my advice.'

Kate winced, and Bernie stroked her hair. 'I'm sorry, Kate, but that's what he did to you.'

'I feel so ashamed,' Kate whispered.

'I know. We all do. But you've no need. You've done nothing to be ashamed of. He has. You've not.'

Kate had stayed and the madness that Bernie had spoken of lifted, a little at a time. Melanie had helped. She had such confidence, such an open and friendly nature, that Kate found herself making new friends with relative ease, her daughter acting as go-between. The friendships were brief because of the transient nature of the place, but they were healing, and slowly she grew strong.

Chapter Eight

Kate sensed the danger as soon as she saw the parcel. The small package looked odd – sinister. It was wrapped in old brown paper, and it had several stickers placed with careful negligence on its crinkled faces:

HANDLE WITH CARE

and stuck at an angle on its base:

THIS WAY UP*

A third made her stomach turn:

PERISHABLE ITEMS – OPEN IMMEDIATELY!

The package was tied with string and addressed to 'Katie Pearson'. Nobody called her Katie. Not even her mother. She fought with a powerful need to know what was in the package and a strong revulsion: her daughter's murderer may have sent it.

If I don't open it, I'm letting him frighten me into paralysis, she thought. If I *do* open it, I may be playing right into his hands – being the helpless victim he wants me to be.

*

Adam worked on, rarely blinking. His eyes darted from keyboard to screen. He was in an almost trance-like state. His heart rate was up and he was feeling the buzz, the adrenaline surge. Half-smiling, he thought, *you never lose it. And it never lets you go.*

'Talk to me,' he said. As if at his command, characters appeared on screen. 'Real-time comms,' he murmured. 'That's what I've missed . . .'

Sims had once asked him if there were any office perks — he had always been baffled that Adam, who could have made thousands by bending a few rules, had chosen to go straight for so long. Adam had told Sims that endless supplies of pencils and paperclips weren't his idea of a good perk. He thought now that he should have added that almost unlimited access to the Internet more than made up for the lousy salary and a begrudged three-week holiday allowance.

'I would have opened it. But if there are fingerprints . . .'

'You did the right thing, Mrs Pearson,' Harmon reassured her. 'We'll have someone from the fingerprint lab take a look at it right away.'

The man worked with fastidious precision, dusting the outside of the package. There were several prints — Kate's among them. *Mine, because I took it from the postman,* she thought, then backtracked: *the postman's, the sorters', the counter-clerks' . . .* But not, she knew with depressing certainty, the prints of the man who had rigged up the parcel. Melanie's murderer. The technician removed the string and, with gloved hands, carefully lifted a small box from its wrapping. It was a Care Bears gift box.

Kate focused hard on the man's delicate movements to fight off the nausea she felt. He dusted, then gently brushed, the outside of the box. Looking up at Harmon, he shook his head. No prints. Not on the box, nor on the inner layer of the brown-paper wrapping. The technician opened the box with forceps.

Kate cried out. Her hand went to her throat. Harmon took her gently by the elbow and eased her into a chair. The box contained a crumpled, roughly circular band of dark-blue, silky material.

Harmon looked at Kate questioningly.

Kate shook her head.

'What is it?' he asked.

The technician was holding the silk band in one pair of forceps. He pulled at it with a second pair. It was elasticated.

'It's a scrunchy, sir.'

'Melanie's,' Kate said, finding her voice.

'A scrunchy?'

'A pony-tail band.'

Harmon nodded, enlightened. Such things were new to him.

'What makes you think it was Melanie's?' he asked.

'She was wearing it when she left the house. She didn't—' Kate shook her head, swallowing hard. 'Her hair was loose when they – when you found her.'

Harmon placed a reassuring hand on her shoulder. 'Is there any message?' he asked the technician.

'No, sir. I'll check for fingerprints inside the box, but I doubt—'

'Let forensics have a look at that lot when you've finished, would you?'

The technician nodded, instantly absorbed in his work, and Harmon turned his attention to Kate. She was trembling, and all the colour seemed to have washed from her skin.

'Mrs Pearson?'

Kate was staring at the scrunchy, which the technician had placed in a self-sealing bag and labelled with a number and the date.

'I know I can't,' she said. 'I understand why, but I wish . . . I'd like to hold it, once. It was hers and—'

'Kate . . .' The Chief Inspector rarely called her by her first name. He was kind, gentle but always formal. He maintained a proper distance.

She looked up at him, concentrating on the fact that he had called her Kate in order to distract herself from the thoughts that were gathering in a jumble in her mind.

Harmon drew up a chair and sat facing her, taking her hands in his. His hands felt warm and soft to her own thin, icy fingers, and she was struck by the rich darkness of his skin next to her own. She frowned, recalling against her will, despite her careful observation of the reality around her, a far starker reality. The last time – the only other time – he had called her Kate.

The day they had found Melanie.

When, mad with grief and terror and fury, she had fought to go to her little girl. She wanted only to comfort her, to hold her, to wipe away the dirt from her face. To cherish her just once more. To kiss her poor, bruised skin and make everything all right.

Two officers held her back, screaming and crying, struggling to free herself. Only Inspector Harmon's quiet voice, calmly calling her name, had broken through the barrier of grief. She forced herself back to the present, bracing herself for what he was about to say.

'We don't know that the . . . scrunchy' – he felt foolish saying the word – 'is Melanie's.'

'I know,' said Kate, stubbornly.

'We don't know that the person doing these things is the

person who killed Melanie.' He waited for this idea to register in her confused thoughts.

She looked at him, puzzled at first, then angry, and looking away again. '*I* know,' she repeated. 'The scrunchy is Melanie's. And I know he is still out there. I know it's him.'

'If it is, we'll find out, I promise, but it may not be,' he persisted.

'Who else would torture me like this? Who?' Her eyes flashed terror that someone else could want to harm her in this way.

'I don't know. I wish I did. But I can tell you that we're doing all we can to find out. We'll catch him.'

Kate stared into his sad, serious eyes, searching for an answer. 'How can you be so sure? You didn't get him last time. You're not going to get him this time. He's playing games with you. You can't get anywhere near him.'

'I think we can,' said Harmon, with an assurance that exasperated her.

'How?' she asked, desperation creeping into her voice.

'He's getting careless. Yes, he *is* playing a game of cat and mouse, but he seems . . . driven. It's as though he needs to communicate with you—'

'To hurt me,' Kate corrected, angrily.

Harmon drew down the corners of his mouth. 'Perhaps that's the only way he knows how to communicate.'

Closing her eyes, Kate passed a hand over her face. She had read about men like that. It had been something of an obsession after she left David. The need to understand why it was that he felt he had to hurt her. She knew all about men who are so insecure – for whom life is so frighteningly uncertain – that they need to dominate, to have power over people and to hurt.

'Don't ask me to understand him, Mr Harmon,' she said. 'I

just want him caught. He's sick, I know that, but Melanie
didn't hurt him, and she didn't deserve to be hurt by him.'

'Any more than you do, Mrs Pearson.'

Kate glanced up sharply. Harmon's expression was un-
readable.

'Any more than I do,' she agreed.

Chapter Nine

He worked on in contented silence. Like a spider, spinning out the tendrils of his web from his keyboard, his fingers flexing with elegant precision, tapping new commands, weaving each new stage of his perfect construction.

Closing his eyes, he saw the beautifully executed communications – points of contact – shimmering with dewy light, like mist on November webs. He reached out to her across the network, his words disappearing into the void but leaving trails of such ethereal beauty that a dazzling image formed momentarily, real and substantial on his retina: cirrus clouds soaring across an empty sky, catching sunlight in their manes and then vaporizing in an instant.

He manipulated the keyboard, imagining his thoughts reaching out into the cyberdark, dendritic interconnections forming at his command, gossamer-fine, interlacing to perform his own special magic, as silky, as invisible and as deadly as the sticky strands of snare lines in a spider's web.

A laugh escaped him. *Kate has blundered into the World Wide Web, and I am at its centre. Waiting, listening, with arachnid attentiveness.* In that instant he felt his entire body receptive, antenna-like, anticipating the tremors that would signal her capture.

*

Kate downloaded all of her e-mail to floppy disk before reading it. She had promised to deliver the disk to Chief Inspector Harmon on her way home from work.

Adam seemed engrossed in something. Totally absorbed, his eyes flickered from keyboard to screen, unaware that she was watching him.

Seems I'm not the only one losing sleep, Kate thought, noting the dark rings under his eyes. He had barely spoken to her for two days. He had not commented on her late arrival at work, and Harmon had advised her not to tell him about the delivery of Melanie's hair-tie. Oblivious to her, his eyes darted almost feverishly from screen to keyboard. From time to time he would stop and jot something down on a notepad. He looked unshaven, and his hair was more than usually untidy. Kate shrugged. Well, like the man said, you're not the only one with problems, she told herself.

Sighing, she listed her e-mail on screen.

An anonymous posting. She considered Harmon had tried to extract a further promise that she would not read anything suspect. She had agreed to think it over, but the temptation was too great, the need to know too strong.

'I've thought,' she muttered.

She selected the message and then clicked the mouse on 'view'.

Hope you enjoyed the snail mail ;-)
Melanie dropped her scrunchy at my place, but that's OK now you've got it back.
Hope the black bobby didn't waste his time looking for prints :-D

Kate felt sick. She leaned back in her chair, looking away from the screen, back towards the window – catching Adam's eye. He glanced away sharply, then typed something on his keyboard.

The fibres danced to the rhythm of her fear. She is there! Listening. Reading his last creation. The smiley faces had been a chance discovery in a new Internet magazine which provided a glossary of the little sideways faces. They gave his writing new emphasis, an irony that was so difficult to convey in simple lines of text.

I'm laughing at you, Katie. I'm laughing at Harmon :-D *I've got you now. Caught.* He felt the tremors of her emotion and, elated, could not resist the thrill of talking to her directly. He tapped in another line, lightly, with the pads of his fingers, so that the keys barely rustled as each character appeared on screen and sent the message real-time to her station.

Kate was startled by a sharp *bleep* from her system.

Melanie's got more material to send you. Want to see?

Kate stared over at Adam.

'What are you doing?' she asked.

Adam looked up. He seemed dazed, disorientated, as though woken from sleep. 'Kate, are you—'

'Answer the question, Adam. What are you doing?'

He looked quickly at his monitor, then away. He would not meet her eyes. 'Working. I'm working.'

Kate walked to his station, shaking. She swung the monitor round, scanning the lines of programme. Looking at him, then back at the monitor. Unsure. And afraid.

'What is it?' she demanded.

Adam darted a look past her. People were watching.

'None of your damn business.' He leaned forward to press a key, and the screen immediately blanked.

Kate saw a gulf of difference between them in that moment. She turned on her heel and walked straight out of the office without a backward glance.

Moira noted the time, then slipped her notebook back into her desk drawer.

'Kate!'

Kate jumped and then wheeled in the direction of the shout. 'What the hell—?'

'You're a bit jumpy, aren't you?' Bernie moved from the shadows of the covered walkway where she had been talking to what looked like an assortment of carrier bags and blankets tied to a bike. Kate recognized the dosser who appeared and disappeared on a regular basis from the sparse shelter of the office building's overhang. Bernie said a few more words to the man and then strode over to Kate.

'What are you doing here?' Kate asked. 'What have you done to your hair?'

'Nice compliment.'

'No. It suits you.'

'Bollocks! You think it makes me look like a bull dyke, right?'

Kate grimaced. 'The jacket doesn't help—'

'What's wrong with the jacket?' Bernie looked down at the black leather of her coat sleeve. 'Got this half price in a closing-down sale. Who said the Tories never did owt for working-class folk?'

'No,' said Kate, chiding herself for expecting Bernie to adopt her own softer, more feminine style of dress, 'you're right. The jacket is okay, but the hair— Bernie, what possessed you?'

'Okay.' Bernie ran her hand over the spiky new cut. 'It was a mistake. Thought I needed a change.' She smiled sheepishly. 'It looked good on Sinead O'Connor.'

Kate laughed. 'It'll grow.'

'I bloody hope so!' Bernie grinned, elbowing Kate lightly. 'So what are you doing? Playing hookey or what?'

'I could ask you the same thing.'

'Only I'm my own boss, aren't I? I can come and go as I like.'

Kate glanced back into the foyer. Beyond the smoky glass of the door the security guard was watching them.

'I can't talk here,' she said, guiding Bernie from the shadowy front of the building, away from the bundle of rags on a bike, and into Lincoln Square. Ornamental maples, their bark a patchwork of colour, gave an impression of dappled light even at this bleak time of year. Set against taller limes, their branches formed a tracery of shadow over the square.

'So?'

'Long story,' said Kate.

'So I gather. I've been trying to reach you for two days. All I get's some bloke asking what my business is.'

'So you hung up.' This was so typical of her.

'Time was,' Bernie began, 'only doctors' receptionists wanted to know the size and quality of your haemorrhoids before they'd put you through to someone who knew their arse from a hole in the ground—'

Kate laughed. 'Delicately put,' she said.

'Way I work it,' Bernie weighed up the possibilities, 'either you've got promoted, or you're in some kind of bother.'

Kate chewed at her lip.

'It was the police, weren't it?'

Kate looked at her in astonishment.

'Who is it?' Bernie persisted, 'David?' Her eyes searched Kate's. 'Worse? Bloody hell, it is, i'n't it?' She slid one leather-jacketed arm through Kate's. 'Come on.'

'Where are we going?' Kate asked.

'In search of food. Helps me think.'

They strode through the city centre, exciting interest and turning a few heads: a tall, willowy woman in a soft grey wool skirt and short black jacket linking arms with a short, dangerous-looking creature wearing cycle boots and leathers, cropped hair adding to the pugnaciousness of her appearance. They ended up at a café on Deansgate. Kate waited for Bernie to finish eating her cream-cheese-and-ham bagel before lighting a cigarette.

'Since when?' Bernie asked, surprised.

'Since this lot started.'

'Which was?'

'End of November.'

'Wondered why you'd not been in touch.' Bernie waved the waitress across and ordered two more coffees. They sat at the back of the café, out of the glare of the sunshine. Eleven o'clock. A businessman sat at the counter, reading the *Telegraph*. His briefcase leaned against his stool, and from time to time, he would reach down and pat it, like some old and placid dog. Two girls sat at the table behind them, and Kate could see them staring at intervals before resuming a snigger-ing conversation.

Bernie didn't have to say any more. Kate knew she had been upset by this discovery. 'I would've told you, but I thought at first it was just a crank—'

'And now?' Bernie interrupted.

'Now?'

'Well, presumably you don't think it's a crank, since you've got the police involved.' Her grey eyes met Kate's. 'What's he been doing? Sending you hate mail?'

'E-mail,' said Kate. 'And now he's started buggering about with my Visa card and bank account.'

'So what's your excuse now?'

'It's not an excuse, it's a reason,' Kate insisted, annoyed. 'At first the whole thing was just too sordid. Later, when the police got into it, I didn't want to drag you in. You've enough to do without worrying about me.'

'You mean you didn't want to admit you were being abused again.'

Kate was astonished. 'How d'you work that one out?'

'Come on, Kate. First you say you didn't want to talk about it, now you're saying you didn't want to drag me in. Next you'll be saying you were too ashamed.'

Kate flushed angrily. 'You're not talking to one of your battered women now, Bernie.'

'Aren't I?' Bernie's eyes moved swiftly over Kate's face.

'No. And I'm not particularly impressed by your pseudo-psychological insights, so why don't you save the lectures for the women at the refuge?' Kate knew she had gone too far, just as she had done so many times in these last few months. Bernie had been her friend and counsellor through the hardest times. But she couldn't bring herself to apologize, so she slowly raised her eyes to Bernie's, drained of anger and feeling miserable, expecting to see hurt or resentment or rage and instead catching a glimmer of amusement.

'Why don't you blow it out your arse?' Bernie asked pleasantly.

The two girls at the table behind them nearly choked on their coffee, subsiding into coughs and stifled laughter. The businessman turned down a corner of his paper, distracted from his reading by the commotion, and glanced over. He flicked it back up when Bernie caught his eye.

Kate smiled, despite herself. 'Sod you,' she said.

'Anyway,' Bernie was grinning now. 'It isn't so very long since you were greatly impressed by my pseudo-psychology.'

The door swung open, admitting a woman and two small children. A swirl of exhaust fumes followed them, lingering for some moments in the air after the door had closed and abruptly cut off the traffic noise. The children fell to arguing where they would sit and the woman left them to it, balancing one set of carrier bags against another in a heap on the floor as she ordered at the high chrome-and-glass counter.

'Who's on the suspect list?'

Kate shrugged. 'Same as—' She left the rest for Bernie to fill in for herself. Same as last summer. Same as when Melanie was murdered.

Bernie nodded. 'Okay, who do *you* think it is?'

'Me?'

'Well, if they think it's someone they interviewed before . . .'

'But they all had alibis.'

'For Melanie's murder, yes. But . . .' She hesitated. 'This is different, Kate. This is someone taking advantage of your pain. Making you feel worse because they get off on it.'

'No. It's him, Bernie. I'm sure of it.' She picked up her spoon and stirred her coffee unnecessarily. 'This morning he sent me a scrunchy. One of Melanie's.'

'Jesus.' Bernie sat back and the leather of her jacket creaked. 'So you're discounting anyone the police interviewed before?'

Kate had to think about that. 'I've been through them all. They all had good, strong alibis. The police checked.'

'What if one of them was lying? What if the person who gave that guy an alibi was mistaken – or lying?'

Kate shook her head. 'I can't see how any of them could – would want to—'

'Since when has a man needed a motive?' Bernie asked.

'You've just got a downer on men.'

'I'm not into the macho type as much as you are, that's all. They're trouble. Know why?' She didn't wait for a reply, but went on: 'They've got so much to prove and so little wherewithal.'

'Like I said,' Kate smiled. 'And what makes you think I'm into the macho type?'

'David, Bob Newman, Ingrams – sorry, *Dr* Ingrams.' She waggled three fingers at Kate. 'They're all so chock-full of testosterone they can barely walk straight, ne'er mind think.'

Kate knew there was no point in arguing; for one thing, Bernie was probably right. 'Why am I such a lousy judge of character when it comes to men?' she asked.

Bernie's wide mouth drew itself together into a pout. 'They say that little girls fall in love with their fathers, and when they grow up they look for someone to take his place.'

Kate shrugged. She had never really known her father; he had died when she was small.

'Now that young bloke – whatsisname? Shepherd. He's not your usual choice. Nice-looking, but not obsessed with it. Could do with a bit of feeding up, but at least he's possessed of a greater sensitivity than most – am I right?'

Kate winced, remembering their argument in the restaurant. She frowned. 'I'm not sure about him.' She recalled the screen of jumbled symbols and letters, commas, colons and numbers. 'He's been—' She stopped, collecting her thoughts. 'He's trying to be helpful, I suppose. But he takes over sometimes. He went to Harmon without my permission. And he's so secretive – there's a side to him I can't get near.'

'Man with a past?' Bernie ventured.

'There was a bloke called Sims. Adam was visiting him in hospital the day Melanie was abducted. He was a drug addict. Died of hepatitis B or something. Adam won't tell me anything about him, other than that they were mates from way back. I don't know, it makes me uneasy.'

'Want my advice?'

'Do I have a choice?'

'Not much.'

'Go on, then.'

'Trust your instincts.'

'Great,' said Kate, stubbing out one cigarette and lighting another. 'What if my instincts are confused? I like him, but he's a mystery to me. I start to trust him, then he goes and does something that makes me wonder about him.' An image of Adam reaching across to blank the screen flashed across her vision.

'That's a bugger,' Bernie agreed cheerfully. The two girls behind them moved to go. Bernie glanced up briefly as they edged past.

'Dykes,' one girl growled.

Bernie grinned broadly, then, turning away from them, she ran one large hand over the fuzz of dark hair. 'This bloody haircut!' she laughed. 'Case in point: appearances can be deceptive. Now what are you going to do about this crank?'

Kate shrugged. 'What can I do? Harmon's doing all he can.'

'What about you? Are *you* doing all you can?'

'I'm cooperating, yes. What else did you have in mind?'

'You could keep in touch. That'd do for starters. Let me know if anything happens.'

'I will.'

'I wish I could believe that.' She regarded Kate solemnly for some time.

Bernie walked Kate back to the office. 'That bloke,' Kate ventured, her curiosity overcoming her natural inhibition. She nodded towards the bundle of rags next to the bike. 'D'you know him?'

'Ron? Good bloke is Ron. See,' Bernie teased, 'I haven't got a downer on all men.'

'Who is he?'

'He's a bloke who's had a rough time and still manages to show more humanity than most. He used to be an accountant. Lost his job in the Eighties crash. Lost his house, his wife, everything. He's put a few women in touch with the hostel. Keeps an eye out for women with kids. Had kids of his own once.' She glanced at Kate and then back at the man. 'Lost them too.'

Kate nodded thoughtfully. 'You're right,' she said. 'Appearances can be deceptive.'

Chapter Ten

Sergeant Wainwright checked his watch before knocking on DCI Harmon's door. The face had slipped round his wrist and he readjusted it, noting it as another depressing indication of his loss of weight. It was six thirty. He hitched up trousers that were inches too big in the waist and ran his hand through his hair in a vain effort to get it to lie neatly.

'I've drawn up a list of everyone we interviewed in July,' he said.

'Good. See if the ex-boyfriends check out first.' Harmon stood with his back to the window, aware of the traffic noise below and the darkness outside, thinking he should have phoned Angie before now and wondering how Kate Pearson would spend Christmas. Christmas could be a lousy time in his job.

'That shouldn't take long – there's only the two that we know of.' Wainwright fought to keep the tension out of his voice. Jan would be frantic by now. 'Will tomorrow be all right? Only—'

'Tomorrow's fine. Let's take it gently until we know what we're dealing with.' Harmon half sat, resting his buttocks lightly against the windowsill, his long legs stretched out in front of him. 'The university lecturer and the personnel manager, right?'

'Both of them were squeaky-clean last time, so—'

'We were looking for a murderer last time, Sergeant. I want everyone we interviewed about Melanie's disappearance carefully questioned. The man – or woman – we're looking for may have entirely different motives from the murderer's, but it is very likely they know Mrs Pearson personally.'

'You don't think they're one and the same person, sir?'

'It's possible, but I don't like making assumptions. It could be some sick bastard who's seen her name in the papers, or it could be someone who has a grudge against her. Someone from the office maybe. We have her ex-husband's address on file, don't we?'

No reply was expected and none was given. Detective Sergeant Wainwright understood from the question that he was to give priority to interviewing Mr Pearson.

'Do a check on the staff at her office as well, will you? Make it low-key – I don't want to stampede anyone into doing anything rash.'

'What about Shepherd, sir?' Immediately he had said it, he regretted it. The suggestion could easily have waited until the morning, and time was ticking away. Tiredness. Tiredness, always tripping him up, making him say things he didn't mean to say.

Harmon smiled. 'I especially don't want to stampede him. He was on the list last time, wasn't he? Well, we can hardly leave him out. Wouldn't seem fair. He's being very helpful, after all. Let's go ahead on that footing for now. We'll re-evaluate after he's completed the trace for us.'

Wainwright coughed politely, and Harmon glanced at him, his eyebrows raised. 'You're not passing this one on, sir? Only – Inspector Craine expressed an interest.' In normal circumstances, DS Wainwright wouldn't go out of his way to do Craine any favours, but circumstances had been far from normal at home for the past few months. If Craine took the case, Wainwright knew that his services would not be required; he and Craine had never got on. Wainwright was half embarrassed by the proposal, but he needed to spend some time with Jan just now, and this case looked like taking up a lot of time he couldn't spare.

Harmon regarded Wainwright thoughtfully. 'I don't like unsolved crimes, Sergeant Wainwright. I particularly dislike unsolved murders. And when it seems the murderer is continuing his torment of the victim's family—'

'You aren't ruling out the possibility that it is the murderer, then?' Drawn in, despite himself, feeling time running away, wasting.

'We can't be sure who is doing this. It could be a total stranger. Could be someone close to her. Or the murderer. Or' – Harmon paused, considering – 'her ex, punishing Kate for his daughter's death. He wasn't exactly supportive when Melanie disappeared.'

Wainwright nodded. He had interviewed David Pearson himself and had wondered at the time how a woman like Kate could end up with a bloke like Pearson. He had just come from Mrs Pearson's flat. She had quietly, and with dignity, shown them her daughter's room, had tensed when he asked for an item of her daughter's clothing but had gone immediately to the child's bed and handed him Melanie's nightdress, saying in a tight voice that it would carry Mel's scent. Her unquestioning acceptance of the necessity of it somehow made the request seem more sordid.

On his return to the station, Harmon had asked him to sit in on the interview with Pearson. Jesus, that bloke had a foul mouth.

'I'll tell you what I think,' he had said, his eyes narrowing meanly, a snarl on his lips. 'I think she lets Melanie wander off while she was letting some guy sniff her cunt. She was a terrible wife and a worse mother. She should be spayed, like the bitch she is.'

'Yeah,' said Wainwright. 'Bloke like that probably does blame her for Melanie's death.' He grimaced. 'Nasty piece of work.'

'Precisely,' said Harmon, drily. He let Sergeant Wainwright ponder about Pearson for a while, then said, 'Of course, it could be the enigmatic Mr Shepherd.'

'It would be one way of getting her attention,' Wainwright agreed, glancing at the clock on the wall.

'And a blind man in a coal hole could see that he's desperate for that. Or it could be a third party we haven't encountered yet.'

Wainwright checked a smile at the elegant West Indian's use of so blatantly northern an expression, and said, 'Someone from outside the office, for instance.'

Harmon nodded. 'It's possible. But Shepherd said it would be easy for someone *inside* the office to gain access to Mrs Pearson's personal details. Let's go for the probable first — anyone who knows, or knew, her socially, anyone who uses the office network. Then we'll consider the possible.'

'You're the boss.' Wainwright had heard Harmon's advice about the possible and the probable many times before. Usually it had a pleasant rhythm that he found appealing, but now, at close on a quarter to seven, with Jan in all probability near hysteria, it seemed pedantic, unnecessary.

'While you're at it, see if you can get an impression of what Kate Pearson's colleagues think of her. In general, I mean. Is she popular?' He hesitated before adding. 'See if you can find out how much she knows about the Internet.'

Wainwright looked up from his notebook, startled.

Harmon turned down the corners of his mouth. 'Experiences like the one she's been through are apt to change people.' He remembered Angie's distant look of anguish as she said, 'I'm trying to imagine how I would feel if one of the boys . . .' Sometimes his recall of details was a curse. 'I don't think anyone comes through something like that with their sanity completely intact.'

Wainwright put down his notebook, setting the pen next to it. 'Let's get this straight.' He stared pensively at the nib of his pen. 'You're saying that Kate Pearson could be making the whole thing up.' The accusation seemed to him an outrageous cruelty. He felt anger race like fire through his veins, colouring his face and neck. Lay off, he told himself. It's only lack of sleep.

'It's possible,' Harmon said carefully.

'We're talking about Kate Pearson here, sir,' Wainwright heard himself saying. 'The only time I ever saw her break down was when she saw her kid on the slab. And, let me tell you, I found that hard to stomach myself.'

'I know, but a lot has happened since then.'

Wainwright wanted to stop, but he couldn't. 'I interviewed Melanie Pearson's teachers, her classmates. She was a popular, well-balanced kid. If her mother was two players short of a squad, would the kid be so . . .' – he struggled for a suitable adjective – 'so normal?'

'Kate's been through nearly five months on her own. Who knows how it's affected her?'

'Grieving for your kid is a far cry from hoaxing an entire police force.'

'I'm not saying she's hoaxing us, Bill.'

'No?' The use of his name was a deliberate ploy; only rarely did DCI Harmon allow such informality. Wainwright became even more incensed. He didn't want Harmon tiptoeing round him like he was acting unreasonably. He was right in this and Harmon was wrong.

'No,' Harmon reassured him. 'I'm saying we should check all angles.'

Wainwright saw the sense in Harmon's argument, but his anger simmered dangerously close to boiling point for some seconds.

'I'll get Diane Rowson on to it then.'

Harmon studied Wainwright closely. This was not typical of Bill. He was generally tactful, unobtrusive, almost diffident in approach at times. He noticed with a shock that Wainwright's shirt collar was loose at the neck and that the skin around his eyes was bruised and puffy. He observed for the first time how dishevelled the sergeant looked. Wainwright was something of a favourite with the WPCs on account of his athletic build and his pleasant manner. He was careful about his appearance, even a little vain perhaps. Certainly Harmon had never before seen him with his thick thatch of blond hair uncombed and wearing a shirt that had evidently not been ironed.

Wainwright turned to go.

'All right, Bill?'

'No problem.'

'I mean, are you all right?'

Wainwright said nothing, not trusting himself. He clenched his jaw tighter. What would Harmon know, he thought resentfully, with his healthy boys and his elegant, successful professional wife? He had met Dr Angeline Harmon a number of times when he'd had to pick up the DCI from his home. She never had his Jan's harried look. Poised and charming, she always knew the right thing to say.

He nodded, still unable to speak. Not Harmon's fault. Then whose? He returned to the question he had asked himself a thousand times in the last month, and for the thousandth time he came to the same conclusion: children are made in the likeness of their parents. So it came back to them. To him and Jan.

Chapter Eleven

The early sun shone low through the lattice-work of trees at the edge of Victoria Park. Mary's eyes watered as she washed the dishes at the sink, but she kept the curtains open, bathing gratefully in the thin sunshine. She hated the short days.

'Phone her up,' Tony urged.

'I did. Lots of times.'

'That was ages ago.'

Mary rinsed a soapy dish, her eyes screwed up against the glare.

'She knows how I feel.'

'She *knew* how you *felt*. Months ago. This is now.'

Mary began wiping down the work surface. The sun's slanting rays had triggered a headache.

'Don't be so bloody stubborn, Mary. You'd rather be miserable than pick up the phone.'

'I'm not trying to get back at her, if that's what you think.'

'It never crossed my mind.' Tony marvelled at the way his wife's mind worked. 'But you're letting this drag on interminably. What about Jenny? Don't you think she wants to see her Aunty Kate?'

'I don't know. I can hardly get two words out of her since—'

She stopped, feeling the injustice to her child but resenting Jenny's unwillingness to communicate.

Jenny was sitting on the stairs, hearing everything and blaming herself.

'She'd only hang up.'

Tony sensed a bending of Mary's iron resolution. 'Then go and see her.'

Mary considered this, pushing her hair back and leaving suds in her fringe.

'I'll take you.'

'You've got work to do. You've got that OFSTED inspection at the start of next term.'

Tony's stomach did a quick somersault. 'As if I needed reminding,' he said, queasily. 'Look, I can spare a few hours to sort this out.'

'Soon, maybe. Not yet.'

Mary turned into the sunshine. The sunlight danced on the suds, and glinted from the dishes on the draining board, but feebly. It was cold winter sunshine, and it gave her no heart.

Wainwright had not spoken during the short ride to the university engineering department. He'd had plenty of time to regret his flash of temper the previous evening; he'd got less than two hours' sleep.

They stepped out of a hail shower into the wide, arched foyer of the engineering building, and Wainwright pushed open the great wooden door into the main hallway. It was cool, cavernous and oddly curtailed. On either side partitioned offices had been constructed, spoiling the line of the sandstone arches of the entrance hall. Henson checked an incongruously modern-looking plastic noticeboard, and they walked up the central stairway to an office on the first floor.

'Dr Ingrams—?'

Kenneth Ingrams looked up from his AppleMac lap-top, his eyes expressionless, his mind still working on the mathematical problem on the screen. Those eyes had a hypnotic quality. They changed shade with the caprice of a lake that reflects the humour of the day, except that his light came from within; it too was changeable, unpredictable and seductive.

Felicity Burrows was in her usual state of dishevelment, her hair escaping from her pony-tail in mousy wisps, her skirt buckle a little off-centre, not enough to look sluttish, just enough to seem endearingly gauche. Wearing her vulnerability like one of her baggy cardigans. She stood at the entrance to his office, wringing her hands and shuffling from one foot to another.

'What is it, Fliss?' Dr Ingrams was the only member of the department who called her Fliss. She rather liked it but barely noticed in her agitation.

'It's the police,' she whispered.

'Oh, Lord. Has something happened?' He jumped to his feet and was at her side in a moment. 'Are you all right, Fliss?' She blushed at the touch of his hand.

Wainwright showed his warrant card, 'Sergeant Wainwright, Greater Manchester Police. This is Constable Henson.'

Ingrams blanched, his greyish skin washed to a papery pallor. 'Has something happened to Kate? Is she all right?'

'She's fine, sir. This is just a routine inquiry. If we could have a discreet word . . . ?' The sergeant glanced in the direction of the dithering little woman at the door. He had arrived home at ten o'clock the previous night after making all the necessary arrangements for interviews, sorting out the rota and going for a pint that became several pints to give him the courage to face Jan. She had still been crying as he'd left at nine this morning. One neurotic woman was about as much as he could manage in a day.

Ingrams smiled, his composure quickly recovered. 'I wonder, Fliss, if you wouldn't mind making these gentlemen a cup of tea?'

Felicity Burrows brightened immediately, rallying at the thought of doing something to assist the doctor. 'Oh,' she exclaimed, leaving off wringing her hands to clasp them in delight at her bosom, 'yes, it is nearly time for your elevenses anyway, doctor. Tea, gentlemen?' she asked brightly.

'That would be very nice,' Wainwright murmured, nodding at the woman, anxious to be rid of her.

'Your secretary, sir?' he asked, as she closed the door behind her.

'No, no . . .' Ingrams chuckled. 'Alas, no. My humble niche in the hierarchy of academe doesn't warrant my own secretary. No, Felicity is Professor Simon's secretary, but,' he spread his hands, 'she has rather taken me in hand. She thinks I need looking after.'

Wainwright glanced around the orderly office. Its polished wood-and-glass furniture looked in pristine condition and the books and papers were all neatly ranged in clearly labelled ranks. Dr Ingrams was very like this room: glossy, well kept, glowing, a man who took care of himself, who ate well but prudently, always with an eye to the maintenance of his appearance. A man very much like himself before the trouble had started.

'Do you, sir?' he asked, wondering whether a man with Dr Ingrams's grip on life needed a woman to look after him at all.

Ingrams dipped his head. 'Poor Fliss would think any single man in need of female organization.' He smiled. 'It would be cruel to refuse her little kindnesses.' Then, frowning suddenly, 'Is Kate really all right? This is about Kate, isn't it?'

'As a matter of fact – but what made you think—?'

'I've only ever had one brush with the law, Sergeant Wainwright, and that was after the dreadful business with Kate's daughter. I think you interviewed me on that occasion too.'

Wainwright nodded. He had interviewed Dr Ingrams at home, on his return from the States. Ingrams's house was rather like his office, he remembered. Cared-for. Neat. Wainwright looked the doctor over. He wasn't a bad-looking bloke. Nice manners. Bloke like that'd have no trouble finding some nice young woman to clean up after him.

'You haven't heard from Mrs Pearson, then?'

Ingrams sighed. 'I wish I had. Kate and I were once— But you know all that. We had . . . um . . . a tiff, and Katie couldn't forgive me. My own fault entirely.'

'You slapped her.' The statement was intended to provoke, but Ingrams took it mildly.

'To my eternal shame and regret, yes. I ruined a—' He laughed. 'I was about to say a beautiful friendship, but it sounds so terribly corny. Anyway, Bogart had already done that line and in far better style than I could ever attempt.'

Henson stirred beside him, and Wainwright smiled. 'You can put your notebook away, Constable. Dr Ingrams is referring to Humphrey Bogart. In *Casablanca*.'

Henson stared blankly.

Ingrams and Wainwright exchanged a look. Amusement darted from one to the other, but both remained deadpan.

Miss Burrows returned with the tea and Dr Ingrams charmed her, delighting her with compliments as to her indispensability and her long-suffering patience with his quirky ways.

After she had left, Wainwright got down to business. 'Mrs Pearson has been getting some rather unpleasant mail, Dr Ingrams.'

Ingrams frowned. 'I'm sorry to hear that. Of course, one

reads of this sort of thing but' – he shook his head, still frowning – 'I'm surprised it should start now, I mean, so long after . . .' He let silence say the rest.

Wainwright nodded.

'Can't you find out where it was posted? Catch him that way?'

'It's not that sort of mail, sir.'

The frown deepened, then recognition cleared it as though it had never been. Dr Ingrams, the sergeant reflected, had youthful features, although he must be into his forties.

'Oh, I see,' Ingrams exclaimed. 'That's why you're here. It's e-mail, isn't it?'

Wainwright withheld his reply for some moments, watching for signs of discomfort. There was none.

'Yes, Dr Ingrams. It is e-mail. And her bank and credit-card accounts have been tampered with.'

'How distressing. Sounds like you have a hacker. They're like malicious little poltergeists once they get started. Poor Kate. Of course, you're welcome to check out my system if it will help.'

'Just to rule you out of our inquiries, sir. I hope you don't—'

'No, no. No imposition at all. Of course, you must find this fellow. It is likely to be male, by the way. Hackers almost invariably are.'

'So I'm told.'

The computer services department had proved less helpful. They could produce a printout of Dr Ingrams's logins and time spent on the system, but it would take a few days. They had a backlog of work to catch up on after the discovery of a security breach the day before. Someone had been scooping up passwords and hoarding them in a file that had been disguised as a system index file. At the time of discovery there were twenty high-level passwords in the directory and a hundred others, some of which did not belong to the university. All the university users on the list would have to be assigned new logins and passwords.

'So these passwords are no longer valid?' Wainwright talked over the steady hum of the UNIX machines and the computer-controlled air-conditioning of the room that held the university's mainframe computers. The temperature was a little cool for his metabolism, but he supposed the temperature settings were designed for the well-being of the machines and not the human personnel.

The systems manager eyed Sergeant Wainwright suspiciously.

'No. Why?'

'It'd be useful if I could take a copy. Might help us with our inquiries.'

The systems manager looked doubtful. 'I don't see how it could be of interest to you, Sergeant—' He broke off, interrupted by a younger man carrying a clipboard in one hand and the weight of the world on his shoulders. The manager gave him some instructions, which he wrote down with annoying care. Wainwright let his eyes track around the room, trying to distract himself from the technician's dilatory responses. It was lined with computer hardware. Cream and grey. Acres of it. Enough to send him off his rocker. He shivered, reminded suddenly of his son's fascination with computers. He'd developed a real rapport with his DEC*pc*; it was just people he had problems with, Wainwright reflected gloomily.

'You say not all the passwords are from your system.'

'So?'

'So the hacker could've been into other systems elsewhere?'

'More than likely.' The systems manager looked out through the glass panelling on to the network of PCs in the post-grad work area beyond. Ten thirty: early yet. Only two of the keener students were in so far. They'd be scrambling for places by twelve.

'Could be one of those passwords relates to the subject of our inquiry,' Wainwright said.

'Dr Ingrams?'

'No, he's just helping us out.'

The man shrugged. 'I'll have to clear it with the Senate. I'll give you a bell this afternoon.'

'One more thing. Is the hacker someone on your staff? Can you tell?'

The systems manager grimaced. 'Wish I bloody could. It could be anyone. Inside. Outside. Anywhere in the world. It's hard to know where to start with these bastards.'

'Know the feeling,' Wainwright commiserated. 'So who do I ask for?'

The manager returned a blank look.

'In case you're too busy to get back to me,' Wainwright said, sounding more patient than he felt. 'So I'll know who to ask for,' Wainwright repeated. The look of suspicion deepened.

'Ask for Steve. Computer services.'

Spoken like a Good Citizen, Wainwright thought. Christ, whose side does he think he's on?

'No joy?'

'Nor tidings of comfort, Sergeant Wainwright.'

Very seasonal, Wainwright thought, but kept the observation to himself. Harmon was sitting in one of the two easy chairs in his office, sipping tea. He had a way of seeming relaxed in the most frantic situations, a trait Wainwright normally found reassuring but which now irked him, especially since Harmon had not offered him a cup of tea.

'We've had some feedback on the other leads, sir.'
'Oh?'

Newman had opened the door with a smile ready on his lips. It fled when Wainwright showed him his warrant card.

'God,' he said. 'What do you want?'

'Just an informal chat, sir, if I may.'

'I'm busy.' Newman stood with one arm crooked at shoulder height, leaning on a door frame which gleamed, reflecting the golden light of the courtesy lamp above the door on to the smoothness of his freshly shaved skin. He was dressed for company. No tie, but an expensive-looking casual shirt and trousers of the colour Jan called taupe but which Wainwright preferred to call mushroom. Shiny, shiny shoes, he noted – and colour-coordinated.

'It won't take a minute,' Wainwright said, trying to be polite, despite his tiredness. A few more sleepless nights and he'd be climbing the walls.

Newman looked past him, and Wainwright caught a flash of anxiety in his pale-blue eyes. 'I'm expecting a guest,' he said.

Male or female? Wainwright wondered.

'A client,' Newman said, reading his expression, conceding unwillingly to the need for honesty.

'I'll try to keep it brief then.'

Newman uttered a gasp of exasperation, then, after a second's indecision, he flung open the front door.

The stone steps of the portico gave on to a wide hallway. Directly ahead an elegant stairway curved to the upper floors. Newman led him to a large drawing room. Polished wood floor, Bang & Olufsen sound system, diffuse lighting, discreet music.

'Nice place,' Wainwright murmured appreciatively, letting

his gaze move around the room. Soft hide settee, long, low, sensual. Oil paintings, big ones, modern, a style he neither liked nor understood.

Newman watched him, torn between frustration and amusement.

'You said you'd keep it brief, Sergeant,' he prompted.

'It's about Mrs Pearson, sir.' Wainwright's eyes continued to explore his surroundings, absorbing the opulence, the abundance of material comforts, with which Newman surrounded himself. Here, he thought, is a man who believes in the power of money. His exploration came to a halt, finding the computer tucked into an alcove, mounted on a pale oak stand, linked to a printer and what he assumed was a modem. The monitor was black except for a continuous stream of tiny points of light which seemed to streak outwards. It reminded Wainwright of the special effect on *Star Trek*.

'You planning on entertaining your guest with computer games, are you, sir?'

'I'm expecting some e-mail. Is that all right with you, Sergeant?'

'Mrs Pearson has been getting mail via the Internet,' Wainwright said, ignoring the sarcasm. 'Unpleasant mail. Surf the Net, do you, sir?'

'For God's sake! Do I look like a spotty youth with nothing better to do than spend his lonely nights sending dirty messages to women on the Internet?'

No, thought Wainwright. The sunbed tan, the well-toned muscles, the highlighted streaks in the carefully styled hair indicated nights spent in other, more sensual, pursuits.

'I don't suppose you'd let us check through your files—'

'Of course I bloody wouldn't!' The pale eyes protruded slightly.

'It would help us rule you out—'

'Rule me out? She did that well before now.'

Wainwright was startled by the bitterness of this remark, and Newman, sensing his surprise, said, 'We went out for a time. It became . . . tedious.' *For her*, his injured pride screamed. He had waited months, hoping she would change her mind. Had eased off, had given her her head, let her do as she pleased, but she had only grown more distant, even impatient, with him. 'We parted,' he finished, feeling Wainwright's eyes on him. 'But you know all this.'

'We're eager to find out who is sending these messages.' Wainwright watched for Newman's reaction. 'Someone, maybe, who has a grudge against Mrs Pearson.'

Newman flushed slightly. 'Look,' he said, glancing at his watch. 'I'm sorry about the daughter – what happened to her. But it's got nothing to do with me, and it's not right that Kate should be allowed to go on disrupting my schedule – my life—' He corrected himself. 'It was *her* choice that we should split up. She has to accept the consequences.'

'Accept the consequences?' Harmon had listened to Wainwright's account of the interview without interrupting, but this could not pass without comment.

'I got the feeling he thought she'd been besotted with him all along and had only just come to realize it,' Wainwright said.

'And all this is a play for his sympathy? What a monstrously egoistical mind!' Harmon sat in thought for a moment, then asked: 'Could he have meant "consequences" as in "punishment"?'

Wainwright shrugged. 'Dunno, sir. He's obviously carved up at being rejected but – I couldn't say.'

Harmon nodded. 'Did he say anything else of interest?'

'No, I left shortly after that. His guest arrived.' Harmon

caught a glint in the sergeant's eye and wondered how Wainwright had introduced himself to Newman's client.

'You saw Mr Pearson, I believe.'

Wainwright raised his eyebrows. 'It's got round, has it?'

'I've heard he was less than helpful.'

'He was screaming blue murder before I'd finished my introductions.'

'The man has a guilty conscience, Sergeant.'

'Well, if he has, his girlfriend must have one an' all. Thought I'd have to nick her to get her to see reason.'

'She's a rather unstable individual, I seem to remember,' Harmon agreed. 'Does she have a grudge against Kate Pearson?'

'We didn't exactly sit down and talk about it over coffee.' Wainwright heard the edge creeping back into his voice and sneaked a look at his boss. He seemed not to have noticed.

'Pearson?' Harmon asked.

'He's got access to computers through his work. He's a sales manager for Supertech Glazing – one of those smart glass materials, you know, goes dark in bright light, lets in just enough to keep the office comfortable. Anyway he keeps in touch with the various offices and outlets by e-mail. Has a modem in his car, so it seems.'

Harmon nodded. 'What about the others?'

Sergeant Wainwright raised an eyebrow. Apparently DCI Harmon didn't consider Mr Pearson a profitable line of inquiry.

So much for two hours wasted and a lot of needless aggravation from Pearson and his girlfriend. She'd flipped when he'd shown her his warrant card. Just as well he'd thought to take DC Barratt with him; he had remembered Susan Walmsley from last time. She was decidedly unmellowed by age and the experience of the last few months. He had actually ended up feeling sorry for Pearson, who had tried to calm the stupid bitch down and scream police harassment at the same time.

'Mr Owen – that's Kate's boss—' he began.

'I know.' Harmon had noticed his truculence and was playing Wainwright at his own game.

'They don't get on.'

'I know that too.'

A muscle along Wainwright's jawline twitched. 'He's competent with the office network, and he also has a system at home that's linked to the office via the Internet.'

There was a moment of intense concentration, then Harmon said, 'Go on.'

Well, hoo-fucking-ray for Harmon. Wainwright referred to his notebook to hide his annoyance. 'Shepherd's interest in computers got him into a bit of bother a while back—'

'I know Shepherd's record. I meant go on about Owen.'

Wainwright shrugged. 'That's it. What else did you expect?' Sounding belligerent. Not caring.

'His reaction when you asked him his feelings about unsolicited e-mail.'

'That bloke plays everything right down the line. He's not liked for it, mind, but I can't see him getting up to anything even remotely naughty, let alone illegal.'

'Presumably you asked Pearson the same question?'

Wainwright nodded.

'And?'

'As you'd expect. "I'm not talking to you shitheads without my solicitor being present." '

'Go back and see him.'

Wainwright groaned inwardly.

'Tell him we'll haul him in if necessary.'

'Right.' Without enthusiasm.

'Now, Shepherd. Anything new on him?'

Sod it. Wainwright stopped trying to impress. He

shrugged. 'Seems to be playing by the rules. He does have a home system, but it's not networked with the office, although it could be, in theory, if he linked up with the Internet.'

'Does he have a modem?'

Wainwright shrugged again.

'You don't know?'

'He says he doesn't. We didn't search his place, sir. You said you didn't want to spook him—' Wainwright felt his anger surge, and Harmon seemed to sense it.

'Yes. Of course, you're right, Sergeant,' he placated. 'But best not make assumptions, hmm?' Wainwright began to speak, but Harmon interrupted him: 'Do we have anyone who's familiar with the Internet here?'

'There must be someone, sir. We've a few graduates who may've—'

'See if you can find someone, will you? And ask them if it's possible to monitor e-mail going in or out of Mrs Pearson's office. They may need passwords. I don't know. You can talk to Owen about that. We need to trace the anonymous address on the printout Mrs Pearson gave us. No point in relying on the advice of one of our suspects, is there?'

'I thought you'd written Shepherd off as a suspect, sir.'

'I never write anybody off, Sergeant.'

'Not even Mrs Pearson.' Wainwright was unable to conceal his rancour any longer.

'Do you want to tell me what the hell has got into you the last few days?'

'Me?' Wainwright coloured.

'I've got the impression you think I'm going at this arse-about. Now, I'm not particularly sensitive to what other people deem to be flaws in my investigative style, but when it affects our working relationship, it bothers me.'

'It's none of my business what you do, sir. I just follow orders.'

'Bollocks!'

Wainwright blinked. Harmon's repertoire did not usually include the word.

'Come on, Bill. You've been moping about the place, moaning and griping at a bit of legwork, whining about getting off home—'

'Sod this. I don't have to listen to this.' Wainwright headed for the door.

'Yes, you bloody do, Sergeant. Because if you don't, you're heading for a suspension and your arse in a sling.'

Wainwright stopped.

'If you need time off,' Harmon resumed, more gently, 'you're entitled to compassionate leave.'

'How d'you work that one out?' Wainwright bridled. 'Who's been blabbing behind my back?'

'Jesus, Bill. It doesn't take any great powers of deduction. You look like you've lost a stone in weight. You're obviously not sleeping nights. If there's a problem, sort it.'

Wainwright laughed. 'Not that simple, is it?' he said.

'I don't know, since you haven't told me.'

Wainwright bowed his head. 'It's private.'

'It's interfering with your work.'

'I know.'

'So it ceases to be private when it interferes with your work. Take time off and get it sorted.'

What could he say? A million years couldn't sort this problem. 'I will,' he mumbled, 'after we've finished with this one.'

'And in the meantime?'

'I'll manage.'

'But will I?'

When Wainwright finally gathered the courage to look at Harmon, he caught an expression of such bemusement that he smiled. 'I know I'm being a pain in the arse—'

'But it's private.'

'It's – I just don't – I can't – Oh, fuck it. It's not something you can really talk about.'

'Evidently,' said Harmon, drily.

Wainwright thumbed through his notebook to avoid Harmon's eyes. 'Steve . . . Bugger didn't phone back,' he muttered.

'Who?'

'Possible lead. I'll get on to it.'

'Don't neglect Mr Pearson, will you?'

'And I'll try and get to Mr Marchant today. He was on the original list.'

Harmon had not expected a straight answer.

The front of the house faced a mirror-image of modern semis. Front lawn trimmed, candied with a frost that would later crystallize in the air and festoon the winter-black trees. Four o'clock and already it was dark. A thin sliver of moon rose above the chimney pots, and the street was quiet and deserted; even the children had been driven indoors by the intense cold.

Wainwright remembered the place from his previous visit. About this time of day, but on a warm July afternoon, the air fragrant with the honeysuckle that twisted around the cherry tree in the front garden. Then, the street had been busy with mowers, the scent of grass-cutting making him sneeze, kids playing in the roadway, shouts and laughter from the park beyond, summer sounds. His breath froze in a fog around him as he waited on the doorstep.

'Much of a suspect, is he?' Henson asked in a conversational tone.

'What the bloody hell's that supposed to mean?' Wainwright demanded.

Henson shrugged. Wainwright had been in a foul mood

all day. He rang the bell and Wainwright said: 'He's the husband of Mrs Pearson's best friend. He knew Melanie. His daughter and Melanie were practically inseparable.'

'But for the day Melanie was abducted,' Henson said, anxious to show Wainwright that he had read up on the case.

'Aye. And he was meant to meet his wife outside the girls' school that day, some sort of treat for the lasses, but he says he missed them.'

'They say it's the guilty ones as have the best alibis,' Henson observed.

Wainwright grunted, pressing the bell impatiently.

'Happen they're not in,' Henson suggested, but then they heard the unmistakable scrape and crunch of a bin lid being secured. Inside, a child's voiced raised. A few seconds later, hurrying footsteps in the hallway, and then Mrs Marchant answered the door.

'Sorry, I was round the back.' Her smile faltered and faded as Wainwright showed his warrant card.

The door slammed. A familiar thud a moment later told her that Tony had dropped his brief case.

'Tony?'

'Jesus, love, I'm whacked.'

It was a fraction of a second before he noticed her tension, then time raced and he felt his colour go. *Jenny?* But Jenny stared down at him from the top of the stairs, round-eyed and pale. Tony's eyes darted from mother to daughter. 'What's up?'

'Mr Marchant.'

'What do you want?' His voice uncharacteristically hard.

'Sergeant Wainwright, Manchester CID.'

'I know who you are.' Tony glared at the tall, rather gaunt individual standing behind his wife, dwarfing her.

'And this is Detective Constable Henson,' Wainwright continued, unperturbed, indicating a second man behind him. The hall seemed smaller, their presence an invasion.

'You shouldn't have let them in.'

'I couldn't leave them on the doorstep, Tony.'

'We could always interview you at the station, Mr Marchant.'

Tony shrugged off his coat and slung it on the newel of the staircase. 'You'd best come into the lounge. Can't talk out here in the hallway. Go to your room, Jenny,' he called up the stairs.

Jenny stood uncertainly, not understanding this new harshness in her father. Mary took the coat from the newel, smoothing it over her arm, looking at her daughter. 'Do as your dad says, love,' she said kindly. 'It's all right.' And Jenny turned reluctantly. As she hung the coat up in the little cloakroom at the end of the hall, Mary heard the door to Jenny's room close softly.

The two policemen sat in their overcoats, Sergeant Wainwright relaxed in Tony's favourite armchair, DC Henson uneasily at the edge of the sofa. Sergeant Wainwright's eyes rested on a pile of papers Tony had been working on the previous night. Mary felt an urge to sweep them up and take them out of his sight, but that was silly; they were only National Curriculum documents and schemes of work. Still, she felt the outrage at privacy invaded that Tony had experienced earlier in the hallway. She worried that the room looked cold and uninviting with the Christmas tree standing unlit in the curve of the bay, told herself that she was being foolish – these men had no business in their house – but could not quite banish the feeling.

'Been at work, Mr Marchant?' Wainwright asked.

'Yes.'

Wainwright looked him over. Tony Marchant was seething

with resentment. They seemed an ill-matched couple, these two. He was big, tough-looking. Wainwright couldn't imagine the kids giving him much trouble. She, by contrast, was small, soft, a dumpy little matron with her old-fashioned hairstyle and her doughy hands. Hands that did a lot of baking, he would have guessed. Tony's brown eyes stared back at him, raging with hostility. Well, he could hardly match Pearson's ill will. They'd had to take him in to get a statement out of him, and the girlfriend had brought half the street out with her screaming. Marchant dropped his gaze under Wainwright's coolly appraising stare, and the sergeant noticed something the animosity had masked: the guy looked haggard.

Tony rallied under the continued scrutiny of the policeman and lifted his eyes to Wainwright's face once more, surprised to see lines of worry that he recognized as present in his own reflection in the mirror. He looks a bloody mess, Tony thought. Wonder what's causing his sleepless nights?

'I thought schools were on holiday,' Wainwright said. 'Christmas break.'

Tony laughed shortly. 'Teachers *do* work in their holidays, Mr Wainwright.'

'Always on the job, eh?'

Tony met Wainwright's steady gaze. 'Like policemen.' He thought he caught a flicker of a smile on Wainwright's gloomy countenance.

'Blackbrook County Primary, isn't it? Where you work?'

'That's right.'

'On the Internet, are you?'

This time the laughter was full-throated, mirthful. 'We've got three rather elderly BBC Archimedes. They're great for educational software, but we haven't the funding to link them to the Internet. We had a few more, but we've had so many break-ins the LEA won't replace them any more. Got busier than Dixon's down at Blackbrook at one time – all that technology and no hire-purchase to pay. The office has a PC with a modem. Not for the use of teaching staff.'

'Mrs Pearson's been getting anonymous e-mail.'

'Kate?' The three men turned to look at Mary Marchant, Wainwright regretting immediately that he hadn't watched Marchant's reaction to the mention of e-mail.

'Are you still in touch?' he asked.

Mary went over to the window and drew the curtains against the night, turning on the lights of the tree as she did so. 'I've not seen Kate for a few months,' she answered, stationing herself by her husband's chair, one hand resting lightly on his shoulder.

'Oh? Why is that?' Henson asked.

I must be getting old, Mary thought, eyeing the young man. It was the first time the detective constable had spoken, and she had paid him little attention until now. His skin had the clear, almost translucent, quality that only ginger-haired people can boast; it made him look even younger than his years, and the youthful eagerness with which he tried to impress his superior further heightened the impression of youth.

'I don't think that's any of your business,' Mary frowned disapprovingly.

'We're trying to eliminate you from our inquiries,' Henson said, imitating Sergeant Wainwright's successful gambit with Dr Ingrams the previous day. 'It would help us to know.'

'Then you must ask Kate.' Mary's tone left him in no doubt that she considered the matter closed.

'We will,' Wainwright remarked, quietly. Then, lowering his gaze to her husband, he asked, 'Do you have access to the school computers, Mr Marchant?'

'Term-time, yes. But I told you, we're not connected to the Net.'

'Not even the office computer?'

'Like I said – not for staff use. Anyway, the computers are locked away in the strongroom at night.'

'Always?'

'Without fail.'

'Who are the key holders?'

'Mr Atherton, the headmaster, and Pat Stillman, coordinator for IT.'

'IT?' Wainwright asked.

'Information Technology.'

'I see.'

'Is that all? Only I've work to do.'

Wainwright had reached the door when Mary asked, 'Is Kate—?'

The sergeant turned. 'Is she all right?' His look revealed nothing. 'You'll have to ask her that yourself,' he said.

Chapter Twelve

Kate was having trouble sleeping. She had expected that. She would rate going to Harmon as among the most difficult tasks she had ever had to undertake. She had known at the time that it would pull on the barely healing scars of the summer. She had prepared herself for dreams, even nightmares, involving Melanie and a dark figure with no face. What disturbed her – upset her more than she could explain – was that these were not the dreams that wrecked her sleep. Instead she dreamt of David.

David. Her mouth was dry, her tongue so thick it would not allow her to speak. Her mind raced, searching for something to say. Something to do that would calm him, deflect his rage. But it was already too late. She sensed it, despairingly, and her heart hammered in her chest, knowing what would follow, the almost choreographed sequence, anticipating the exchanges and the inevitable conclusion.

'You can't do anything right, can you?' His face was red with fury, but it was his eyes she focused on, his dark, angry eyes, flashing hate.

'I—'

'DON'T!' he screamed, moving towards her. Kate stepped

back, ducking instinctively. He continued in a hoarse whisper. 'Don't give me your fucking whining excuses. It makes me – tired.'

Kate listened, occasionally risking a glance over at Melanie, who lay on the settee, whimpering.

'I said I wanted my suit from the cleaner's. I said I wanted *Match of the Day* taped. And I said I wanted her in bed before I got home.' He jabbed a thumb over his shoulder. Melanie was watching them both solemnly, her eyes huge, her face stippled with tiny red spots. Tears glistened on her cheeks from her last bout of crying.

'I – I think she's got measles. I put her to bed, but she—'

'Don't blame the kid for your incompetence, you hopeless, idle bloody bitch!' He pushed her in the middle of the chest and Kate fell backwards, overturning the telephone table and hitting her head on the wall. Her head boomed. She felt sick, and in the background she could hear that Melanie had started crying again.

'Look what you've done, you stupid cunt!' he raged. 'Tidy it up!'

Kate got to her feet unsteadily, her ears still ringing. She picked up the telephone and set the table right, never taking her eyes off him, waiting for him to lash out with a fist or a foot.

'Three simple instructions. Three clear, straightforward requests. Can she get them right?' he asked an invisible audience. 'Can she *fuck*. I'd do better asking *her* to do them, wouldn't I?' He turned to Melanie.

'I'll put her back to bed,' Kate suggested, anxious to draw his attention away from the crying child. 'I'll put her to bed and then I'll make you some supper, okay?'

David wheeled on Kate, outraged. 'You'll do as you're fucking *told*, that's what you'll do.'

'Yes, yes. I'm sorry—'

'You're sorry now,' he said, softly, 'because you know what you're going to get.' He shook his head. 'But you can't do it right, can you? You can't see the consequences of your actions.' He laughed abruptly. 'Actions. What am I saying? *In*action's what it is. You don't actually *do* fuck-all around here. Look at this place.' He waved a hand at the clutter of talc and cream around the changing mat on the floor.

'I've only just changed her. I was about to—'

'Don't talk back to me,' he warned. 'Get this shit off my floor!' He picked up the wet nappy and threw it at Kate.

She knew better than to try and catch it, letting it strike her face before pulling it away. The ammonia stung her cheek and the stench, added to her nausea from the blow to the back of her head, made her want to retch.

David stared at her for what seemed like an eternity, shaking with fury, then, without turning, he pointed at Melanie and said, 'Get her out of the way. I don't want her to see this.'

Kate went to the screaming child and swept her up, running upstairs with her to the bedroom, lowering her gently into her cot, shushing and soothing her but barely able to contain her own hysteria.

'It's all right . . . All right, darling.' She had dosed Melanie with Calpol an hour before but, after a moment's hesitation, risked a second dose, afraid that her screaming would enrage David further.

Kate closed the door on Melanie's plaintive cries, praying that she would go to sleep, and hurried to the kitchen to dispose of the dirty nappy before returning to the sitting room.

David was watching television, and she crept to the corner to finish tidying away Melanie's things. Perhaps it would be all right. Perhaps he had calmed down.

She chanced a look at her husband. He seemed

engrossed. She tiptoed to the kitchen and prepared him an omelette. She buttered two rounds of bread thickly and set everything on a tray with a mug of tea. This would be the real test.

The mug chinked against the plate as she lifted the tray, so she put it down and moved them apart. It wouldn't do to let him see she was shaking. That only seemed to enrage him further.

Kate balanced the tray on one hand so that she could open the door. He was still sitting on the settee, hunched forward. There was a fury in him that was rarely stilled, even in his concentration there was a kind of rage. She set the tray down on the coffee table and then stood back, wary of the proximity of the mug of hot tea.

David lifted the tray on to his lap and started to eat.

Kate sat in an armchair several feet away from him, tense but allowing herself some cautious optimism. So far it was going well.

For ten minutes he ate steadily, then he pushed the tray on to the coffee table and said, 'Get me a beer.'

She took the tray away and poured him a glass of beer. Not wanting to risk keeping him waiting, she left the dishes and hurried back to the sitting room, pausing only to listen for Melanie. She was snuffling and complaining, but seemed to be settling. She placed the beer on the coffee table, taking care not to spill any.

Suddenly he had her by the hair.

'Did you think I'd forgotten?' he hissed.

'No, David. I—'

'Think you'd got away with it, did you?'

'No.'

'I've been watching this fucking *shit* for half an hour. When I should be watching—?' He jerked Kate's hair, catching her face against the edge of the table. '*Should* be watching—?' he repeated.

'The match. You should be watching the match.'

His hand twisted in her hair, wrapping it round his fingers, forcing her face on to the cool glass of the table. His free hand fished about under the settee.

'No,' she begged. 'Please, David . . .'

'Have you moved it, bitch? Because if you've moved it, I'm going to fucking cripple you.'

'No, I swear. It's there. I haven't . . . I wouldn't . . .'

'So where the fuck is it?'

His grip tightened and Kate whimpered, her hand moving to his.

'Don't you fucking dare!' he warned.

'Stop this, David, please. This is crazy. You've no *right*!'

'No right? No fucking *right*? In my own home?' His hand moved with frantic, jerky actions, trying to retrieve the knife. Kate heard the beer slosh in the glass a little distance from her face, and she prayed he wouldn't decide to use the glass instead. 'I've said it before. You need cutting down to size, you jumped-up little twat. A few A levels and you think you're above everyone else, don't you?'

'No—'

'Ah, here it is.' He brought his hand from under the settee. In it was a bread knife. He held it by the blade and showed her its pliability, its fine balance, the solidness of the handle.

'It's been here a while, hasn't it?' he asked, jerking her head up when she did not respond. 'I said—'

'Yes. *Yes*. It's been there a while. But, David, you don't have to do this . . . I'm sorry about the taping, but Melanie's been so sick. I'm worried—'

'Worried? I hope you *are* fucking worried. I do hope you are, Kate. You see, you've got to get your priorities straight.

121

And being such a numb-cunt, you haven't worked out what those priorities are yet. Have you?'

He brought the handle of the bread knife down hard on the settee next to Kate's head and she cried out.

'It was a mistake. I made a mistake. I won't do it again.'

'You make too many fucking mistakes, Kate. Too many fucking times. And it gets so *fucking* tedious . . .'

'Please, don't hurt me . . .' she whispered. Tears streamed silently down her face.

David sighed and looked over at the television set. Kate felt his grip on her hair slacken. 'I'd like to oblige,' he said.

Kate dared a small movement. Then:

Whack!

The knife handle fell solidly on her elbow. She screamed, trying to pull away, but he held her tightly again.

'I like the feel of this,' David said, flicking the knife backwards and forwards in front of her face. The cheap, thin blade gave the knife a flexibility that seemed to fascinate him. 'It's so satisfyingly . . . *springy.*' He demonstrated with a blow to her shoulder that sounded with a dull thump.

Kate screamed again, twisting in his grasp. This infuriated him, and he rained blows on her shoulders, her back, her arms. When he let go of her to get a better swing, she leapt away to the other side of the room, picking up the telephone table and holding it in front of her.

He lunged at her, grabbing the table and twisting it easily from her grasp. She cried out in pain and he smiled, bringing the knife handle down with a crack on her skull.

Kate collapsed on to her knees and he cracked her again on the head, careful to strike above the hair line. Kate covered her head with her arms as he dealt more blows to her forearms and elbows.

She scurried to a corner, painfully aware of how she appeared to him. Seeing herself as the pathetic, whimpering creature he despised. She wrapped herself in the long, beige curtains at the picture window, babbling at him, begging him to stop.

'You can come out now,' he said at length. 'Sit here.' He patted the settee next to him. His left hand dangled threateningly over the spot where he had just slid the knife.

She sat.

He kissed her on the lips. One hand massaged her breast; the other gripped her bruised arm, above the elbow. Kate gasped in pain, and he moved his hand to her face.

'You see what you make me do?' he whispered.

He cupped her face in both hands and looked into her eyes. He was crying. 'You see? I don't want to hurt you. Look at me,' he sobbed.

'I'm sorry . . .' she said.

'Kate, Kate . . .' he murmured, his hand moving to her thigh, finding her skirt hem, exploring under it.

'Please, I—'

He flung her from him. She arched backwards over the coffee table, clipping the beer glass. It followed her, drenching her skirt as she landed with a thud. She lay dazed for some moments, winded by the fall.

'Two minutes!' he screamed. 'Two *fucking* minutes and you've done it again. You just can't get anything right, can you? Not one thing. Not one' – he slapped her with his open palm, punctuating the sentence – 'sad – sorry – fucking – thing!'

He stood over her. Leaned forward and grabbed her by her hair.

And she woke.

Kate ran to the kitchen, rummaged in the cutlery drawer and pulled out a long, pointed carving knife. She paced the flat, flinging open doors, checking cupboards and wardrobes, knife ready, then returned to the sitting room, shivering with cold. She sat in an armchair, knees drawn up to her chest, arms hugging her knees, the knife a comforting weight in her hand, sensing time pass like a slow freight train, carrying all the memories that pained her. She churned up past events, going over and over them. If she had broken away from her mother sooner . . . if she had stood up to David . . . if she had gone to pick up Melanie herself that day . . .

'Fuck it!' Kate stood impatiently. She walked out into a punishing rain a few minutes later and turned determinedly towards the city centre.

It was an ordinary house in an ordinary street – the sort of house that was often converted into student accommodation except that its three storeys and basement were crammed with up to fifteen families at any time: women and their traumatized children. The original front door, with its ornate leaded glass, had been replaced by a more solid barrier, with a spy hole and a stout chain on the interior. Bernie answered the door dressed in brushed-cotton pyjamas and her black leather jacket. Its buckles jingled tunefully as she took the chain off the door.

Kate was drenched through, her hair plastered to her head and hanging in dark rivulets against her cheeks. Her colour was high and her eyes glittered, whether with fever or rage Bernie could not tell. She stood back wordlessly and Kate stepped into the hallway, dripping, her arms crossed over her chest, the knife gleaming coldly as it caught the icy light of the halogen security lamp at the front of the hostel.

Bernie turned to an anxious huddle of women in the hallway. 'It's okay,' she said quietly. 'This is Kate. She's a friend.'

Satisfied, the knot of women unravelled and they returned

to their rooms, incurious as to Kate's circumstances, having enough horror of their own to cope with and knowing instinctively that this wild-eyed woman's circumstances were as similar and as different as their own.

As she secured the front door, Bernie heard other doors opening; a few of the children were crying, afraid, and their mothers soothed them, telling them it was only someone come to stay. Unconsciously, she counted the clicks as the doors closed and followed Kate through to the kitchen after the last.

The old cooking range gave out a steady, comforting heat. Kate sat before it, shivering, a pool of water collecting at her feet. Bernie had restored the range herself when she had first moved in, keeping the ugly, white electric cooker only until the great enamelled ancient range was back in working order. She opened one of the doors and threw a couple of scoops of coke on to the glowing embers.

Kate heard the familiar crunch of the scoop against the little grey nuggets of fuel, the faint squeak of the hinges and the metallic snap as the door was fastened. She stirred briefly, and blinked, but fell back into her sightless state.

Bernie lifted a kettle from its iron trivet on to one of the smaller rings and then turned to Kate. Her quilted jacket was soaked through, and her jeans were stiff with water and cold. She was shivering violently, droplets of rainwater showering from her face and hair, the knife still gripped in her hand. Bernie crouched in front of her and closed one great paw over Kate's thin fingers, uncurling them, meeting with a slight resistance before Kate relaxed, allowing her to retrieve the knife. She pulled off Kate's jacket and then peeled off her jeans, standing her up and sitting her down, like a child. When Kate was dry and dressed, with her hair wrapped in a towel, Bernie pressed a mug of coffee into her hands, urging her to drink.

Whether it was the warmth, or the smell of the coffee, or Bernie's own reassuring presence, she could not say, but Kate felt herself returning, coming back to herself as one who has been on a long and difficult journey. Bernie saw the change in her and, heaving a sigh of relief, she drew up a chair and sat opposite her friend.

Kate's cigarettes had disintegrated into mush in her coat pocket. Bernie offered her one from a pack on the kitchen table and struck a match. Kate bent to it, concentrating on the flame, but as she pulled away she saw Bernie's grey eyes upon her and, in them, two things: anxiety for her and a question.

'I'm okay,' said Kate and, in answer to the unspoken question, 'I didn't hurt anybody.'

Bernie blew out the match, opening the oven door and throwing it into the now brightly burning flames in one fluid moment. She never used a cloth to pull the catch; the heat didn't seem to bother her.

'And the knife?' she asked.

'I had a dream.'

Bernie nodded. It was enough. She understood. Sometimes – not often but with sufficient frequency to make going to sleep at night an act of bravery – sometimes the dreams were more terrifying than the reality.

She offered Kate a biscuit and took two for herself, sandwiching them, chocolate sides together, to dip into her coffee. 'And nobody's been hurt?' she asked again. 'No blood, no gore, no mess to clear up?'

'I was tempted,' Kate admitted. 'Some bloke asked how much I charged and I threatened to geld him.'

Bernie deliberated. 'A reasonable response,' she said, 'given you had the means at your disposal.'

'I was looking for him.'

Bernie knew immediately who Kate meant.

'He's out there, Bernie. Sometimes it's like he's so close I could touch him.'

Bernie reached across and took her free hand. 'You'll not find him that way, Kate, love,' she said.

'No,' Kate agreed. She sat in silent thought for some minutes, her eyes a deep, impenetrable shade of forest-green. 'I kept wondering,' she began slowly, 'after what you said in the café, whether it could be David, or Kenneth, or Bob. Maybe even Adam – you know they interviewed him when Melanie disappeared?'

'He was at the hospital, wasn't he?' Bernie asked.

Kate nodded. 'With Sims – the one I told you about.'

'Which of them *could* have done it?'

'Do you mean who had the opportunity or which of them is vicious enough, or desperate enough, or crazy enough to abduct a little girl and murder her?'

'I'm sorry, Kate. I know this is a bloody terrible thing to have to contemplate. If it's too painful, we'll leave it.'

Kate shook her head. 'No, you're right. If I want to catch him, I've got to think about things I'd rather not remember.'

'Okay,' said Bernie. 'You might consider another motive while you're at it.'

Kate tilted her head in question.

'Revenge.'

Kate nodded, reluctantly accepting Bernie's suggestion. 'The trouble is,' she said, tapping her cigarette into an ashtray, 'it's like I was saying yesterday, I always seem to end up with men who—' she frowned, losing the thread for a moment.

'Who have more bollocks than brains?' Bernie offered.

'That'll do.'

Bernie whisked her mug away and refilled it, adding a splash of whisky from a bottle hidden in one of the high cupboards. 'Let's start with the easy ones,' she proposed.

'Adam, for instance. Did you row with him, or owt like that, just before Melanie was killed?'

Kate shook her head, warming her hands on the mug and inhaling the sharp heat of the whisky. 'Mary and Tony were going to take the girls to the ice-rink in Warrington so that I could go out with Adam that night. Of course, that was before he got the call from the hospital about Sims.' She shook her head, not allowing herself into the usual loop of recrimination: why hadn't she gone to pick Melanie up herself? If she hadn't delayed going home . . . 'No, we were getting on fine.'

'Okay. What sort of bloke is he? Steady? Well balanced? Flaky? Any weird compulsions or fetishes?'

'Not that I know of. We weren't that close.'

'Right, now David. What about him?'

Kate raised one shoulder. 'He's flaky, weird, with loads of compulsions and a whole sackful of fetishes.' Bernie waited, knowing that there was more to come. 'He tried to make contact the week before. Seven years, he'd done nothing. The divorce settlement stipulated a maintenance allowance. He never paid it and I didn't follow it up. As long as he left me and Melanie alone, I didn't care about the money. Then, suddenly, out of the blue, he wrote me a letter. Said he wanted to see Melanie on her birthday.'

Bernie nodded, remembering. 'You got a restraining order. Did he say anything then – make any threats?'

Kate sighed. 'I tore up the next two letters without reading them. By that time the restraining order had come through and he stopped sending them.'

'Do you think he could have done it?'

Kate reached for another cigarette, and Bernie waited for her to light it. 'When I got the first letter, I was terrified. You see, he'd had it typed. I'd opened it thinking it was a business letter. It was such a shock, for a few minutes I was in a state of terror. I suppose I'd managed to convince myself that he didn't know where we lived. Stupid, really: a man like David would have to know. He couldn't have let it be until he did know. To be honest, I was afraid for myself, not for Melanie. That sounds selfish, I know, but it was because I genuinely didn't think he would hurt her. But I was scared for myself all right. Then I got to thinking, if he was going to do anything, he would have done it years ago, when I first left him – wouldn't he?'

Bernie sipped her coffee and grunted noncommittally.

'I haven't heard from him since,' Kate continued. 'The police warned him off when Melanie was abducted. He sold his story to a tabloid—'

'I read it,' Bernie interrupted. 'Same old shite about him being a model husband and father and you an ungrateful trollop.' She saw a spark of anger in Kate's eyes and added, 'Well, you didn't expect a glowing testimonial, did you?'

Kate set her mug down and began vigorously rubbing her hair. She didn't answer for some time. As she combed out the tangles she conceded, 'Par for the course, I suppose. Attacking me when I'm least able to defend myself.' That had been one of David's specialities when he wanted to get back at her if she had tried to stand up to him: waiting until she had her arms full of shopping or ironing or dirty linen, and then felling her with a blow to the kidneys.

'He's capable of the worst kind of cowardice where I'm concerned, but Melanie?' She thought about it for some time, tilting her head and running her fingers through her hair to dry it. 'I just don't know. He never hurt Melanie when we were together.'

'But he'd threaten to,' Bernie said.

Kate sighed. 'Yes, he'd threaten all right.'

'But it doesn't feel right?' Bernie suggested.

Kate gave her a sheepish look and Bernie answered with

a shrug. 'Don't apologize to me, Kate. Like I said last time we met: go with your instincts.'

Behind them the kitchen door creaked open, letting in a blast of cold air. A girl stood on the red tiles in bare feet, her toes curling up against the cold. She was about six years old, Kate estimated, and had a cap of fine blond, almost white, curls. She was sucking her upper lip, a habit of long standing, judging by the sore red semicircle between nose and lip.

'What's up, Scout?' Bernie asked.

The little girl put one freezing foot on top of the other to warm it. 'There's a man outside.'

Kate was on her feet immediately, but Bernie pressed her gently back on to her chair.

'He's back, is he?' she asked, dropping Kate a solemn wink.

'He's in a car this time,' the little girl embellished.

'Well, let's you and me chase him, shall we?' Bernie scooped up the child, closing her hand around first one foot and then the other. 'Your feet are like ice blocks, Scout, love.'

Scout stared at her with her pale-blue eyes and then she wiped her mouth with the back of her hand. She rested her chin on Bernie's shoulder and gazed longingly at the tin of biscuits on the table.

'I expect you'd be hungry after keeping watch all night, eh, love?'

The child nodded, her little chin creaking twice against the leather of Bernie's jacket.

Kate offered her a biscuit, but she shied away and buried her face against Bernie's shoulder. ''s all right, Scout, this is Kate. She's a friend of mine.' The girl reached up and clasped her arms tightly around Bernie's neck, refusing even to look at Kate.

'Okay,' said Bernie, 'I'll take a biccy for you and we'll go back to your room before your mam misses you.' She carried the child out of the warm kitchen, returning a few minutes later.

'Is she all right?' Kate asked.

'She will be, if her mam stays away from her dad.' Bernie seemed preoccupied.

'What's up?' Kate asked.

'I call her Scout because she's appointed herself look-out for the hostel since she came. They've been here three weeks, and in all that time I've never seen anyone watching the place when I've gone with her to look.'

Kate felt the hairs rise on the back of her neck. 'And this time?'

'Could be summat and nowt, but when I went to the window there was a car just turning out on to the main road.'

Kate ran into the hallway. 'What type of car?'

'Couldn't tell. Dark blue or maybe grey.'

Kate fumbled with the locks on the door.

'He's long gone, Kate.'

She ignored Bernie, slamming back the last bolt and catching the heel of her hand, skinning it. 'Shit!' She flung open the door and ran into the street.

All was quiet. Rainwater gurgled and splashed in the drains and a steady splat of water fell from a broken gutter on to a motor bike parked against the wall of the house next door. She looked up and down the street. One or two windows were lit – students sitting up late or shift workers getting up early – but as yet no one was stirring from the houses. She returned indoors.

Neither spoke for some time. Kate heard the central heating fire up and guessed it must be five o'clock.

'I'd best be going,' she said.

'Stop here and get a bit of rest,' Bernie urged, but she had seen that stubborn look before and knew Kate had made up her mind. She didn't blame her – she felt fairly pissed off herself. 'I know what you're thinking,' she said.

'Bernie,' Kate warned, 'I don't want to talk about it.'

'Aye,' Bernie allowed. 'You're probably right.'

'I'll walk down to the main road,' said Kate. 'Flag a taxi.'

'Don't be daft, Kate. You're in no fit state.' But she had already started for the door. 'Here,' said Bernie, shrugging off her jacket and offering it to her, 'at least it'll keep the rain off.'

Instantly Kate felt mean; Bernie's clothes were mostly cast-offs and charity-shop purchases, but she was really proud of her jacket.

'I can't take your jacket,' she protested.

'It's only on loan,' Bernie replied. 'I can't afford that sort of magnanimous gesture.'

Kate half smiled. 'Sorry. Again. I've no idea why you put up with me.'

'Me neither.' Bernie seized her in a bear hug, then let her go. 'I'll pick it up when I bring your stuff round.'

Kate shrugged into the jacket. She zipped it up to the throat and fastened the buckles to still their musical jingling. 'What do you think?' she asked.

Bernie thought Kate looked a damned sight better in it than she did, but she chose not to say it. 'Just don't get too attached to it,' she warned.

'I can't trace him.'

'Who is it?' Angie was groggy with sleep.

Trevor Harmon cupped his hand over the receiver. 'Shepherd,' he whispered.

'Oh, God. You haven't given him our home number?'

'No,' he said, 'I haven't.' Harmon had heard about people like Shepherd being able to gain access to any information that was electronically stored. Kate Pearson's experience, though disturbing, had not surprised him – it happened. Electronic fraud, hacking, phone phreaking, theft of electronic data, even electronic theft were the crimes of the computer age, but somehow the simple fact that Shepherd was talking to him on his private, ex-directory line was shocking. He felt suddenly vulnerable. It was an invasion of his safe place, his home.

'You still there?' Adam demanded.

Harmon sat up, turning his back to his wife.

'Who gave you my number?' There was a silence, during which Harmon realized he had asked an embarrassing, almost an impertinent, question. 'Has she had another call?' he asked.

'Yeah.'

'Is she all right?'

'She doesn't know yet. I . . . er, dipped into her e-mail, just to check. She's not due in work until nine . . .'

Harmon checked his watch. Seven fifteen. Mr Shepherd seems keen to trace our hacker, he thought.

'He's been very careful to cover his tracks,' Adam continued. 'He's used an APS again, which on its own is hard to crack, but—'

'Anonymous Posting Service?'

'Yeah. Like I said last time, it's a way of keeping your mailing address secret. It's hard to get into, but it can be done. Some APSs still keep a list of their subscribers – a kind of look-up table of anonymous IDs and real addresses. I thought I might gain access to their lists but—'

'You couldn't hack into the system.'

Adam became cagey. 'Let's just say I think he's decided against using the European APSs since the last message.'

'Which implies he *did* use a European posting service for the last message?'

'Based on the return address, yes. But he's not on it now.

I did a trace on the last message. Couldn't get within a mile of him.'

'Where else could he be hiding?'

'There're a number of APSs and remailers. They never send the real address, of course, but some do encrypt the real address and send it with the message—'

'Can you de-encrypt it?' Harmon was finding the cyber-jargon a little wearing.

'Not possible, I'm afraid. But it may be worth considering sending a reply.'

'A reply to an anonymous address?' Harmon was sceptical.

'Most e-mailers copy the message automatically, as part of the reply. It's a kind of protocol – saves time if you don't have to explain what it is you're replying to. The encrypted address is sent as the first part of the reply message, and the APS decrypts it and makes sure it gets to the right node.'

'Node?' Harmon asked, his impatience rising.

'Terminal, computer – whatever.'

There was a pause, then: 'So we could send a message to whoever it is, but we wouldn't know who we were sending it to.'

'That's it.'

'If we contacted the APS, they might agree to help us.'

'They might. But he's routed the mail through a few other addresses, which means he's probably using a stolen login and password in the first place, and just to be sure, he's redirected the mail using a remailer, so the chances are that even if I do trace him, you'll probably end up arresting the wrong guy.'

'You're telling me there's no way to trace him.'

'It's a tough one. The guy's paranoid about being traced – even by hacker standards. He's covered his tracks pretty effectively. He's not going to be easy to catch, but I'll give it some thought.'

'You do that.' Harmon reached across to replace the receiver, then snatched it back. 'Shepherd?'

'I'm here.'

'What was the message?'

' "Prowling the city at three in the morning is a dangerous pursuit for an unchaperoned lady." Seems the hacker is watching Kate.' Adam hung up.

Harmon fumed at being cut off so abruptly. Why hadn't Shepherd told him the content of the message at the start of the conversation? He thought back over the previous few minutes. He'd had plenty of opportunity but had chosen to fog their exchange with a lot of jargon about APSs, nodes and encrypted addresses. And why had Shepherd telephoned him at home? Harmon suspected that he had been extracting a little vengeance. Harmon had, after all, not made things easy for him on the occasions they had met. Shepherd was letting him know that, in his world, the net nerds had the upper hand.

'Lie down, you're letting the cold in.'

'Letting the warmth out,' he corrected grumpily, already planning to contact Kate Pearson before she read her e-mail.

' 'S too early to be scientific.' Angie turned towards him, draping one bare arm across his midriff, kissing him as he raised his arm to encircle her.

'Mm?' Trevor Harmon stared into the middle distance, wondering whether Mrs Pearson needed a police guard, only dimly aware of the pleasurable sensation of Angie's kisses but feeling the vague stirrings of interest.

'For God's sake, Jan!'

'Well, you do something then.' Jan was near tears, shouting over the constant keening of the boy.

'William, come out and eat your breakfast,' he commanded.

The child was suddenly silent. 'Did you hear me?' No reply. Wainwright peered under the kitchen table. William was a sturdy little boy, well proportioned, with creamy skin and large, intelligent brown eyes that always had a far-away look. His mop of blond curls had grown too long again: he always gave Jan such trouble when she tried to cut it. He was playing with one of his toy trains, making it roll along the lines of the kitchen tiles, right to left, up at the corner, on to the next corner, right again, then up and left at the next, making crenellated patterns on the floor.

'William!' He grabbed the child's arm and pulled, and immediately the high, loud screams resumed. William lashed out with the train, catching his father on the forehead. Wainwright jerked back, hitting his head on the table, cursing as he scraped his chair back.

Jan felt an almost uncontrollable urge to laugh. *Serves you right*, she thought. *Serves you bloody well right*. The screams continued as Jan dabbed her husband's head with a piece of damp kitchen roll.

'You've got to do something with him,' Wainwright growled.

'I've got to? Isn't he your son as well?'

'I haven't got time.'

'Then make time, Bill. Dr Fraser won't listen to me. He thinks I'm exaggerating.'

'Is it any bloody wonder?'

'Don't start that again. William's not right. He's not been right for months.'

'It doesn't help, your keeping him here all day. Why can't he go to playschool like—'

'Like what? Like normal kids?'

'I wasn't going to say that.'

'I don't see why not. He isn't normal, Bill.' The screaming had stopped. Jan lifted the tablecloth. William was wordlessly rolling his train along the same predetermined pathways as before. 'That's not normal. You know why I don't take him to playschool any more? They won't have him. They say he can't get on with the other children. He won't play, he gets bouts of screaming, he bites, he won't do as he's told or he deliberately misunderstands what they tell him to do.'

'Christ Almighty! He's four years old. Are you telling me they can't handle a four-year-old child?'

'Can you?' she challenged.

'I'm late for work.' Wainwright hurried to the door, the sound of the toy train's steady progress following him into the hall.

'That's right,' Jan was shouting, near hysteria, 'run away from it. Again. You're going to have to do something, Bill. We can't carry on like this. *He* can't carry on like this.'

Chapter Thirteen

Suzanne Walmsley came in laden with shopping. There was a box of Thornton's Continental on the kitchen table. She dropped the shopping and seized the note propped between the chocolates and the pepper pot.

'ILU – D,' it read. Her heart throbbed in her throat. She gave a little gasp and then looked at the note again, fingering the letters.

'I love you, too,' she whispered. In tiny block capitals at the bottom right-hand corner of the note she saw for the first time *PTO*.

'The bathroom needs cleaning. Change the bed.' Her breathing came fast. She was smiling now. 'I fancy chilli for dinner. Be showered and ready for six. Wear the red.'

She grabbed the mince from the top of one of the bags. How had she guessed? There was a psychic bond between them, she knew it. She just *knew* it.

Suzy flew into the hallway as soon as she heard the latch key. She threw her arms around David and kissed him.

David noted with approval that she tasted of toothpaste and her hair smelt of shampoo. She's wearing Chanel, he thought. Good choice. He would have chosen the same.

'What's this?' he demanded.

Suzy laughed, pulling him into the lounge and through to the dining area. The table was set, and a dozen candles flickered on the table and the sideboard. She pulled off his coat, laughing and panting, and took it with his briefcase into the hallway. She hung the coat up with trembling hands.

David was lying on the settee at the other end of the room when she returned. His eyes were closed. Suzy faltered, then, summoning her courage, she went to the drinks cabinet.

'Drink, Davey?' she asked brightly.

'Vodka tonic.'

She poured the drink, adding ice from the bucket, and then knelt beside him.

'Hard day?' she asked, her stomach churning with writhing maggots of fear. David put out his hand for the drink, eyes still closed, and she gave it to him, kissing his hand as she did so.

'You can serve dinner now,' he said.

Suzy jumped to her feet, her nerves jangling. She shouldn't have rushed him like that. Should have let him come in and relax a bit. Unwind. Stupid. Stupid. She was half way to the kitchen when the music started.

It was their song. 'Lady in Red'.

Suzy's breath caught, and she turned, smile ready. His hand covered her mouth, smearing her lipstick. He pulled her to him, his breathing ragged. Pushing her head back, he kissed her throat, feeling the pulse jump. Then he lifted her on to the dining table, shoving cutlery away with one hand. Her dress rode up and he groaned.

It was foggy when Kate left the police headquarters, the relative warmth of the morning having met with a cold front that swept from the east in the early afternoon. Startling sunshine had given way to mist that by nightfall had become a thick bank of fog. She pulled on her gloves and turned her coat collar up, glancing quickly left and right before stepping out on to the pavement in front of the building.

She hesitated outside the glass doors at the entrance. She had dropped in a copy of her e-mail files, as was her habit, and had been delayed by Harmon's questions about her nocturnal prowling. She had refused a lift home, despite Harmon's exhortations, half hoping that the man who had watched her leave her flat, the man who had sat in his car watching the hostel, the man she knew to be Melanie's murderer, would be watching her now. She carried a small knife in her pocket, and it gave her confidence. Traffic had been snarled earlier in the thickening fog, but now, judging by the relative quiet, there were few cars on the roads. The buses had probably been cancelled. It was already after seven, but she was in no hurry to get home. No hurry at all.

Kate reflected on her conversation with Bernie in the early hours of the morning; their examination of the suspects had not taken them far in their attempt to identify the e-mailer, but they had been interrupted, she recalled, before they'd had a chance to review her relationship with Bob Newman and Kenneth Ingrams. *Dr* Ingrams, Bernie had said at the café. Was Kenneth so puffed up that he would insist on being given his proper title? When they had met, he had introduced himself as Ken. She had been flattered by his solicitous attention. Owen had sent her to the university on a computing course, and Kenneth had been one of the group. He was far too knowledgeable for the level of instruction but had attended the full ten weeks, helping and guiding her in the use of the Internet. He hadn't demanded his title then, but Kate suspected that may have been because he didn't like to admit to any gaps in his own knowledge, given his status.

She turned left, intending to walk home along Chester

Road. She could hear faint sounds of traffic on the road ahead, muffled by the banks of swirling condensation around her. But they were infrequent and dim, almost timid, in the murk of the December fog. The street lighting was lost, adding no more than a tinge of colour to the eddying currents around her. She almost barked her shins on the concrete tubs of dead annuals and half-dead shrubs at the corner of Boyer Street, and, cursing mildly, she felt her way around the remaining tubs and turned left. Even on the main road it was impossible to see more than a few yards ahead.

The fog swirled in currents of coldness. It crept in at her collar and cuffs. The pavement glittered faintly; it was beginning to freeze.

Bernie had proposed vengeance as a motive for the killer. Kate could imagine jealousy spurring Ingrams on – the demise of their relationship had, after all, been caused by his jealousy – but revenge? Had she given him cause to seek revenge? He had called unexpectedly at the office to take her out and had impressed Harry Yates on security with his university staff card. Harry had phoned through to Owen for permission for Kenneth to come up to the office and Owen, scenting a valuable contact, had agreed.

'I'll drop you at home to shower and change, and then the theatre and a meal at my favourite Italian bistro, I think,' he said.

Kate had documents to complete and print before she left, so he had chatted to Owen while she finished up, feeling vaguely irritated by the imposition: she would have to call Mary and ask her to look after Melanie for her.

When they got to the lift, it had started.

'Who's the net nerd?'

'What?'

'The boy who was all over you like a rash.'

141

'You mean Adam,' said Kate, resenting his dismissive tone. 'He isn't a nerd and he certainly isn't a boy.'

She felt Kenneth stiffen beside her. 'You would know, would you?' he asked.

They stepped from the lift into the reception area. Harry sensed the tension between them and refrained from his usual banter with Kate. He watched in silence as they signed out and offered only a polite 'Goodnight' as they left.

'Isn't it rather cheap, throwing yourself at any man who shows an interest?' he asked, walking round to the driver's door. He had parked directly outside the building, narrowing the roadway to a single lane.

'I'm not throwing myself at him,' Kate said. 'And, anyway, surely you don't feel threatened by a mere boy?'

Kenneth left her standing in the cold while he opened his own door, took off his raincoat and folded it, stowing it neatly on the back seat before getting in and opening the passenger door.

'Thanks,' Kate said.

He glanced over, satisfied to some degree by her obvious indignation. 'I don't want you consorting with him.'

'*What?*'

'It's obvious what he wants. He was practically drooling over you.'

Kate laughed suddenly and loudly, making him stare in surprise. 'Are you afraid he's going to seduce me behind the filing cabinets? Steamy sex in a store cupboard – is that it?'

Kenneth lashed out, violently and without warning, then apologized immediately, over and over again. He had reached out to touch the welts that were already coming up, four in a diagonal line from Kate's cheekbone to her mouth. She flinched from him, hissing, 'Get your hands off me, you bastard!'

'Kate—'

'I work with the guy. What he *wants* is a pleasant working relationship. Why is that so intimidating?' She opened the car door and got out. 'I'll get the bus home.' Her face stung as the rain spattered her cheek.

'But what about the theatre? The meal? It's all arranged.'

Kate slammed the door and watched as he screeched away from the kerb, cutting up a van and running a red light.

He had sent flowers the next day, and for the next two weeks. She threw them out. He wrote letters, which she burned. He telephoned her until he got sick of her hanging up. But he had never once threatened her. Actually, she felt sorry for him; if it hadn't been for her experience with David, she might have given him a second chance. It had been months before Melanie's abduction. And he had been in New York when she had disappeared.

She heard a slithering sound behind her and stopped, her eyes trying to penetrate the fog but without success, hearing nothing but the roar of blood in her ears. She walked on, every sense alert, and was startled by the sound of voices nearby.

'Bloody hours I've been waiting!' A woman's voice, angry and frightened.

The man, placating, apologetic. 'I couldn't get away before six, luv. Then I got stuck in the fog. Public transport's chaotic.'

'I bloody know, don't I? How d'you think I got here?'

'Well, if you'd learn to drive—'

'Don't start me!' Her voice was raised almost to screaming pitch. 'Next time you can pick up your own bloody car!'

Kate guessed they must be parked outside the autocentre. It was now closed and invisible in the fog.

'*My* car! I like that!'

She walked on, smiling. They hadn't noticed her and continued their argument.

Her break with Newman had been less dramatic – as

inconsequential, as prosaic, as their affair had been. Superficial and desultory, it had been characterized largely by boredom. Kate wondered whether his proposal had been a listless attempt to vary the dull routine they had fallen into. She snorted, puffing a cloud of vapour into the already saturated air. Proposal! He had said that he wanted her to *belong* to him.

Kate had been unable to rid herself of the perfectly remembered layout of his locked spare room. A room he referred to, with a perfunctory stab at humour, as the 'ladies' room'. A gloomy place, for he kept the curtains closed, it was filled with china dolls. Dolls on the floor, dolls on specially built pedestals, dolls on shelving; tier upon tier of china dolls, each encased in its own glass dome to protect it from dust. Kate could never look at those pink-cheeked porcelain replicas without a nascent feeling of suffocation.

Every so often Bob would take them down and clean every crease with a paintbrush, then lock them away again. Kate had decided she didn't want to become one of Bob Newman's precious possessions. They had drifted along for a month or so after her refusal, but eventually he had stopped calling, and Kate had been secretly relieved.

A shape loomed out of the mist at the periphery of her vision, and her pulse quickened momentarily, then she recognized the bulk of a horse-chestnut tree. She must be passing the roughly reclaimed land at the back of Trafford town hall. A car crawled past at barely walking pace, and Kate edged away from the kerb.

A man's hand clasped over her mouth. He pulled, and she fell backwards over the iron barrier, dropping the knife – she heard it clatter on the concrete a few feet away. Another hand gripped her upper arm. She couldn't breathe.

'*You killed her, you bitch . . .*'

Kate clawed at the man, trying to damage his eyes. She

couldn't turn her head to get a look at him, but she made contact and he let go, shoving her away as he stumbled backwards, swearing. Kate fell to her knees on to rough concrete.

She screamed. Scrambling to her feet, she tripped over the barrier and scraped the palm of one hand. She found a stone and hurled it after her attacker, yelling.

Footsteps. This time from the road. And shouts. A man. And, in the background, a woman.

'All right, love?' A figure stepped forward out of the fog, tentatively, as though anxious not to frighten her. She recognized the voice of the man from the autocentre forecourt.

'Is she all right?' The woman's voice, pitched high, afraid.

Kate looked back over her shoulder into the gloom. 'A man . . . grabbed me. A man . . .' she panted.

'He's gone now, love. You'll be all right with me.' He raised his voice a little as he called to the woman, 'Best come and help me, love. She's had a nasty fright.'

The woman stepped forward, uncertainly. 'You've hurt your knees, love,' she said. Kate looked down at her torn tights and bloody knees and burst into tears. 'Here, come on now, it's okay,' the woman soothed.

'We'll see you home. Or do you want us to take you to th'ospital?'

'No . . . thank you.' Kate was shaking uncontrollably. 'I'll be fine.'

'How about police?'

'No.' Kate couldn't face going back there again, couldn't face Harmon's anger again. Another lecture about safety and avoiding trouble. As though it was her fault.

'Are you in a car, like?' the man asked.

'I was going to walk it,' Kate replied through her tears. 'He – he must've followed me . . .'

'Aye, all right,' the man said, apparently fearful she would start sobbing again. 'Our car's parked at Charlie Brown's. It's only a few yards. D'you think you could walk that far?'

Kate was silent during the car journey home. It was a long ride for a journey that usually took ten minutes by car. The fog was patchy, but in places it was virtually impenetrable, and it was difficult to see turn-offs and road signs. The woman – she introduced herself as Pam – kept patting Kate's hand to reassure her. They pulled up outside the Victorian house with its untidy fence and its broken gate, and Kate felt the woman's pity go out to her.

'I've got it nice inside,' she said, defensively, then smiled, embarrassed. 'Thanks. It was very good of you in this fog. I should give you something for petrol.'

'You'll do no such thing!' Pam insisted.

Kate realized she had offended the couple and began apologizing, but Pam relented, seeing Kate's obvious distress and, exchanging a look with her husband, she said, 'I'll see you inside, shall I? Make you a nice hot cup of tea—'

'No, really. I'm much better now. I'll have a bath and then go and lie down. I've already taken too much of your time.'

'Can we phone anyone for you – to keep you company, like?' Keith, Pam's husband, seemed unwilling to leave her on her own.

'There's no need,' Kate insisted, pulling on the door handle. 'I really am very grateful.'

Pam glanced away, shrugging. 'No more than you'd do for someone yourself, no doubt,' she said, dismissing Kate's thanks as unnecessary. 'Anyhow, we'll wait till we've seen you inside . . .'

Kate smiled her thanks and stepped out of the car, feeling her knees stiffening already. A blast of icy air and fog hit her and she gasped. She made her way up the path, her house key ready in her hand. She fumbled the key in the lock and then turned to wave before going in. The car was no more than a faint shadow at the pavement's edge. Kate couldn't make out the occupants but knew they had seen her wave because Keith tooted his horn briefly, and then they were gone.

Chapter Fourteen

The flat was cold. Kate immediately lit the gas fire and went to run a bath. Her knees were scraped and bruised and she carefully dabbed them clean, then soaked for half an hour. The sitting room was warm when she returned, dressed in a towelling robe and carrying a mug of coffee, with her duvet slung over one shoulder.

She picked up the cassette box that was lying on the table, flipped it open and took out the tape of *River of Dreams* that she had been playing that morning before work. Adam had bought it for her. He knew she liked Billy Joel; it surprised Kate sometimes just how much Adam did seem to know about her.

She drowsed through 'Blonde Over Blue' but jumped up to lower the volume when 'A Minor Variation' began playing – she could do without complaints from Mrs Wilson.

She settled back into her seat, feeling protected by the warmth and the softness of the duvet. She snuggled deep into its folds and wondered . . . Why hadn't she chased after the man who had grabbed her? He had blundered away across the rough land, breaking saplings and stumbling over rocks and debris. If he was Melanie's murderer, she might have – have what? Arrested him? Killed him, as she had fantasized she would do so many times in the past?

Kate shook her head. She had come to think of the killer, the man who was now terrorizing her, as cold, calculating. Somebody who liked to control all the variables. Out there, in the open, what control did he have? Not enough for his needs, she speculated. So someone else must have followed her through the fog. But who?

'Lullaby' had started to play. The lyrics impinged upon her thoughts, and Kate listened to the underlying beat of the song, a rhythm as quiet and regular as the heartbeat of a sleeping child. She wondered whether to get up and turn the tape off, but the gentle, insistent melody carried her with it, and she found herself crying softly.

The singer sang of promises. Promises she had made to Melanie. Promises she had not kept – could not keep – for Melanie had died alone and afraid at the hands of a deranged killer. The tears fell, large and silent, and Kate felt no need to check them. These were tears of sadness, not bitterness. Tears of regret for what she and Melanie had lost. Tears for Melanie's lost chances. Tears of healing.

'Oh, Mel . . .'

'*Mummy . . .*'

Kate froze.

'*Mummy?*'

She looked around the room, her eyes darting wildly. She felt a sudden icy coldness.

'Melanie?'

'*Please . . . I want to come home.*'

'Oh, Jesus, Melanie—' Kate was out of her seat. She ran to the door leading into the little hallway, not feeling the pain in her knees.

'*Mumm-eee.*' The voice came from behind her, in the sitting room.

'No! No!' Kate screamed, staggering to the sound system. She stared up in horror at the speakers.

'*I don't like it here.*' Melanie's voice rose in panic. '*I want to come home—*'

The sound shut off abruptly, and Kate fumbled with the volume control. There was nothing but a faint hiss from the speakers. Kate let out a cry as the music suddenly blasted back, then she was plunged into silence again, flung headlong and with gratitude into darkness.

'Now you begin to understand.' He listened through the earpiece. Hearing the pounding rhythm, and the insistent thud, thud, thud, out of time with the music.

'Now you begin to know what pain is.' And he felt some satisfaction that she was starting to make some recompense for the hurt she had made him suffer.

Pounding from the stereo. Pounding from above. Pounding in her head. Pounding at the front door. Kate stared up at the ceiling. A few flakes of paint fell, spinning lazily down as the pounding continued. She blinked as dusty particles landed on her face. Tranquil, serene amid the noise, she thought: I'm lying on the floor. And it didn't seem to matter.

Then she wondered, in a desultory fashion, why she was lying on the floor. This was a mistake.

Melanie. Kate clamped a hand to her mouth to stifle a scream.

A tinkle of glass and a blast of icy air.

'Mrs Pearson?'

Kate knew the voice but didn't respond.

'She's on the floor,' the voice said. 'I can see her.' He called her again, and Kate answered, surprised that her voice sounded hoarse. She began to get up.

150

'No, lie still,' Wainwright urged. 'We'll be with you in a tick.'

Kate ignored him, edging first into a sitting position and then resting, waiting for her head to steady.

'Melanie,' she mouthed soundlessly.

Mrs Wilson had telephoned the police after hearing Kate's screams. Apparently, the screaming had gone on for five minutes and then stopped abruptly.

'I must've passed out,' Kate whispered, her throat still sore, despite the cup of tea that one of the uniformed policemen had brought her. She sat among police and fingerprint technicians, feeling bewildered by their number.

Wainwright, sensitive to her turmoil, asked the uniformed officers to clear the room. Kate picked up a packet of cigarettes that was lying on the coffee table. Her hands were shaking so badly that Wainwright took the matches from her. She smiled her thanks. He had to steady her hand to light the cigarette and waited until she had taken a drag before asking, 'Feeling better?'

Kate nodded. She sat twirling a lock of her hair compulsively round and round her finger. Wainwright had placed a cardigan around her shoulders, but she continued to shake violently.

'We need you to tell us if anything is missing, or if you think anything has been tampered with.'

Kate turned a troubled face to the sergeant. 'I don't know. The tape – how did he put that on the tape?'

Wainwright shook his head.

'Why is he doing this? Why can't he leave me alone?' She lowered her voice. 'Someone followed me tonight after I left Mr Harmon's office.'

Wainwright's eyes grew wide with alarm. 'Did you get a look at him?'

Kate shrugged. 'The fog was too thick. It was too dark.'

'Is there anyone I can contact? Somebody you would like to be with you? Anyone at all?'

Kate shook her head miserably. It would be unfair to call Bernie away from the hostel, and her bitter recriminations had ruined her friendship with Mary.

'We'll post a WPC with you, but you ought to have someone – a friend – someone you can talk to tonight.'

Kate merely shook her head again.

'Do you have your GP's number?' Wainwright asked.

'I don't want any more pills,' Kate answered wearily. 'It's not a doctor I need, it's peace of mind.'

'Even so—'

'I'd like to go and lie down for a while,' she said.

Wainwright sighed in frustration. He deliberated for some moments. 'I'll get the window boarded up. You rest for a while, then we'll go over the flat together.'

Kate answered with a tired nod. She suddenly felt sick with exhaustion.

From the darkness of her room she could hear the police moving around, snatches of conversation, someone using the telephone. Tense, watchful, she thought it was foolish to leave them out there, dusting every surface for fingerprints, prying into her personal belongings. Except none of it seemed like hers any more. She felt desolate.

Kate was woken by a tentative knock at her door. She started up, clicking on the light by her bed and noting with disbelief that it was nearly midnight. Her heart raced, but she quickly calmed herself and limped to the door. Her knees were stiff with bruising, and the skin around the grazes was tight and tender. Sergeant Wainwright stood outside, looking embarrassed and apologetic.

'DCI Harmon's in the living room,' he began. 'He'd like to speak to you, if you feel up to it.'

Kate tucked her hair behind her ears. 'Must've drifted off,' she said, feeling awkward, even a little guilty.

'Well, when you're ready,' said Wainwright. 'We . . . um . . . the fingerprint guys'd like to—' He peered over her shoulder into her bedroom.

'Oh. Yes. Sorry.' She stepped out into the hallway. 'All yours,' she added, pushing the door wide.

Harmon was in evening dress. His suit looked expensively tailored, his bow-tie immaculate. He looked curiously out of place standing on her hearth rug, waiting for her to speak.

She held his gaze with defensive bravado for a few seconds, knowing at once that he saw through it, that he understood how much she was hurting. Resenting his understanding, but too tired to continue the pretence, she dropped her eyes, folding her arms across her chest, hugging her upper arms.

Harmon reached out, touching her lightly on one hand. Kate jerked away from him. She looked up, her eyes burning with anger. 'At least he's still "communicating", eh, Inspector?' She spat the words out, as though they tasted bitter.

'I'm so sorry, Kate.'

That's the second time he's called me Kate in a matter of days, she thought, and for some reason it made her shudder.

'We'll give you round-the-clock protection,' she heard him say.

'Forgive my cynicism, Inspector, but how long will that last?'

Harmon regarded her steadily. 'As long as it takes,' he said.

A technician handed Harmon the tape in a sealed bag. 'Three sets of prints, sir. We'll check them against records when we get back to the lab.'

Harmon nodded, dismissing the man. 'Where did you get this?' he asked, holding up the tape for Kate to look at.

'It was a present.'

'From whom?'

'Adam Shepherd bought it for me.'

'Have you played it before?'

'Do you think Adam did this? Is that what you're saying?'

Harmon made no reply.

'I've played the tape loads of times. He gave it to me earlier this year, as a birthday present.'

'When would that be?' Harmon asked.

'April.' She watched the chief inspector's expression closely. 'Yes, Inspector. Before Melanie was abducted. Before she was murdered. You're wasting your time on Adam.'

Harmon chose not to answer, but changed the subject by saying, 'You told Sergeant Wainwright that a man followed you tonight.' He checked his watch. 'Last night,' he corrected himself.

Kate nodded, frowning. 'I don't think it's the same man,' she said.

'What makes you think that?' asked Harmon, instantly alert.

'It just doesn't fit. He, the man who is sending the e-mail and now doing . . . this' – she lifted her head, gesturing at the bagged tape – 'he would be more careful. The man who followed me tonight – last night – risked being caught. Some people ran to help me when they heard me scream. And there was something . . .' She drifted away.

The listener adjusted his earpiece. Had she stopped talking, or had he lost the signal?

*

154

'You know him?' Harmon asked.

Kate looked at him, puzzled at first, then the question seemed to register. 'Know him? I'm not sure. He was whispering, but it was like he was trying to disguise his voice.'

Harmon waited, but she shook her head. 'It's no good, I can't remember any more.'

'Perhaps you recognized his voice. Something about his build that was familiar – a smell, perhaps.'

A smell. Kate thought back. When he had grabbed her, she had imagined or felt there was something familiar about him. Was he wearing a cologne? She shuddered, an involuntary movement that somehow dispelled the memory. 'He—' Her voice failed her, and she took a sip of tea. It was cold, and she grimaced. 'He put his hand over my mouth.'

'Did he hurt you? Are you all right?'

'I'm okay.'

'Was he wearing gloves?'

'I think – yes, I think he was. I'm not sure.'

'Perhaps there was a smell on the gloves. Were they leather or made of some artificial fabric?'

Kate shook her head, 'I don't know.' Just thinking about it made her feel suffocated.

'All right,' Harmon reassured her. 'It may come back later, when you've had a chance to rest. Where did it happen?'

'The waste ground on Chester Road, at the back of Trafford town hall.'

'Good God!' the inspector exclaimed. 'That's just around the corner. Why didn't you come and raise the alarm? We might have caught him.'

Kate felt confused. 'You could barely see your hand in front of your face. I didn't see which way he ran. Anyway, I was shaken up – I just wanted to get home. Why are you blaming me?' she shouted suddenly. 'I didn't do anything wrong.'

'No,' Harmon agreed, trying to keep his anger in check. 'But you have to be more careful. If this is the man who murdered Melanie—'

'I told you, the guy who followed me from the station—'

'Was different,' Harmon interjected.

'Yes.'

'And whoever tampered with the tape?'

'Is the murderer.'

'You're sure of that?'

'Depend on it,' Kate said, angrily.

Harmon nodded. 'If he is, then you may be in grave danger.' There was a pause, during which Kate noticed that the police officers and the technicians had fallen silent. It almost seemed that they were holding their breath.

When Harmon spoke again, his voice rang out in the unnaturally still air. 'I really think you should stay with friends tonight, Mrs Pearson.'

Kate shook her head. Bernie had enough to deal with at this time of year.

'The friend who stayed with you at the Midland Hotel – Mrs Marchant, wasn't it?'

'We've sort of lost touch since the summer,' Kate explained, thinking uncomfortably of the row she'd had with Mary. 'It would hardly be fair to call her up at this hour and ask her to take me in. Besides,' she added, 'I don't want to put anyone in danger.'

Alone in his tidy room, the listener smiled. *How noble. How right. This is just between me and you, Katie, my love.*

Wainwright yawned deeply.

'You'd best get off home, Sergeant Wainwright,' Harmon said. 'You look like you need the rest.'

''s all right, sir,' Wainwright said, rubbing a hand over his face. 'I doubt if I'd get any sleep at home anyway.'

They were sitting in Harmon's car outside Kate's flat. Traffic was down to almost nothing now. Just an occasional lorry or taxicab, swishing past in the fog. Harmon had left his flashing light on as a precaution. He looked at Wainwright, but the faint orange glare from the sodium lamp opposite was filtered to almost nothing by the fog, and he reached to switch on the car's interior light.

'You look terrible,' he said.

'I know.'

'What's causing the insomnia?' Harmon stared ahead, seeing his own reflection like a ghost in the windscreen.

'There's nothing wrong with *my* sleep patterns.'

'Then what or who is keeping you awake?' Harmon felt the sergeant stir restlessly beside him. 'Anything I can do?' he asked, unwilling to let the subject drop.

'Not really.' Wainwright had been relieved when the call came through about Kate Pearson. William had been in the middle of one of his tantrums, refusing to go to bed. Jan was shouting at him. Between six, when he had got home, and nine o'clock, when he got the call, William had had four outbursts, one of which had ended up in a mirror being smashed. 'I don't know,' he said, mostly to himself. 'Maybe Jan's right. He should see a specialist.'

'Who?' Harmon had made up his mind that Wainwright was going through marital problems; they were common enough in police families. He had taken the cut on Wainwright's head to be the result of a row. He repeated his question when the sergeant failed to answer.

'What?' He seemed half asleep. 'Oh, William.'

'William? Your boy? Is he sick?'

Wainwright chuckled mirthlessly. 'Not in the usual way.

He—' Wainwright broke off. 'I don't want to bore you with this. What d'you want me to set up for the morning?'

'Nothing until we have the lab results. Tell me about your son.'

Wainwright shrugged. 'Not much to tell. He doesn't sleep, he's badly behaved, he doesn't listen, he won't talk to us unless he wants something—'

'Sounds like a typical teenager.'

'Except William's four years old. He's a total mystery to me. It wouldn't be so bad if he wasn't so violent.' It seemed ludicrous, saying that of a small child. He lapsed into silence.

'The cut on your head?' Harmon asked.

Wainwright fingered the cut absently. 'Among other things . . .'

'If it would help, I could get Angie to set up an appointment – with a paediatrician,' he added hastily, seeing the doubtful look on the sergeant's face.

'Our GP reckons there's nothing wrong with him. Says he's just going through a difficult phase.' He sighed. 'He was always such a good boy. No trouble . . .' He trailed off into reverie.

'Still, best to be sure – get expert advice.'

Wainwright had closed his eyes. For a moment Harmon thought he was asleep.

'He's only four years old, for God's sake!' The exclamation was sudden and explosive.

'Well, perhaps it'd be best to sort it now, while he's still young.'

'Maybe. Let me think about it, okay?'

Harmon knew he would get no further and dropped the subject. He turned off the car's interior light and the flashing light before firing up the engine and pulling out into a fog the consistency of milk.

Chapter Fifteen

There was definitely an atmosphere. Kate had felt it all morning. Mr Owen had come into the office at nine – unusual in itself: he usually preferred to watch his staff from the relative safety of his own glass-fronted office. He cast steely looks from one person to another until, satisfied that they were settled to their work, he returned to his own room. Even so, a restless, inquisitive mood persisted, and Kate wondered if they had heard about her police guard. Mr Owen had necessarily been informed, but it seemed unlike him to discuss the matter with his staff. A detective constable had been placed in the outer office, presumably to avoid unnecessary speculation by the main office staff with whom Kate worked.

She tried to ignore the looks and the snatched, whispered conversations going on around her. She had a job to do. She sat down immediately at her work-station and checked her e-mail. As she had expected, there was an anonymous file. She loaded it but did not read it. Instead she selected the reply option.

You've had it all your own way so far, she thought. Well, not any more. I'm going to hit you right where it hurts, you heartless bastard.

She had thought about it all night, after all but her guard had gone. It was three a.m. by the time the last officer left, and she found herself unable to sleep. She had come to the disturbing conclusion that she had allowed this man to manipulate her. What she planned to do now was to take back some control. He would still be in a more advantageous position, but he would, she hoped, be caught off guard by her actions, and that might make him more careless. Anyway, it would force him to seek direct contact with her instead of scuttling around the Internet in order to maintain his anonymity.

The tape had been the turning point. Melanie's killer, who had so casually taken her daughter's life, had with equal ease taken over her own life, manipulating it to satisfy some weird misogynous fantasy he had invented. It made her seethe with impotent rage that the animal who had taken Melanie had forced her to make the tape. Perhaps he had told her daughter that he had sent it and that Kate had not replied. But she wouldn't think about that. It was enough to know that he had deliberately set about collecting items of Melanie's clothing and had taped recordings of her sounding frightened and despairing – this was enough to build Kate's anger into fury.

Chief Inspector Harmon had given her the idea when he'd said the guy seemed to need to communicate with her. He had exploited her weakness in using Melanie to send messages. Now, thanks to Mr Harmon, she had found the killer's weakness, and she would make sure he knew how it felt to be exploited. She wondered, fleetingly what Bernie would make of it, but Bernie, of course, must not know. She would telephone her later and play down the drama of the previous night.

The anonymous posting waited on screen, but Kate did not read it. She typed a brief message. It took only a few seconds – her touch-typing speed was good – and she willed herself not to look at the monitor. She wouldn't even give him that much control. After sending her reply, she deleted his original message, along with her own reply, then she made a short phone call to the systems manager. He was surprised by her request, but complied when she insisted that the alteration would be only temporary.

Minutes later the phone rang. Kate took a few moments to answer it, gathering her strength and resolve for what was to come, thinking that he had responded faster than she would have predicted. That he must be watching her very closely.

'Kate?'

As she heard the voice, she remembered that her calls were being monitored. He couldn't get in touch that way. At first Kate could not place the voice, although she knew she ought to be able to.

'Are you there?' the woman asked.

'Yes. Who—?' Recognition came a moment later. 'Is that Mary?'

'Are you all right?' She sounded desperately worried.

'I'm fine.' The question puzzled Kate. How could Mary know about what had happened the previous night?

'I tried to phone you at home. I can't believe you're in work. Are you okay?'

'Yes. I said, I'm fine. Really. But – why do you ask?'

'Don't you listen to the radio?'

'Not any more.'

Kate felt Mary's discomfort in the silence that followed and tried to redeem the moment by asking. 'Am I in the news?'

'They said you'd been attacked.'

'Nothing so terrible. I panicked in the fog and fell over,' she lied. 'No big deal.'

'What about the police being called to your flat?'

Kate felt sick. 'What did you say?'

'They interviewed your neighbour – Mrs Wilson?' Kate

had mentioned Mrs Wilson to Mary in less than flattering terms in the past. 'She said she had called the police after hearing screams.'

'Thanks, Mrs Wilson,' Kate muttered. 'Anything else?' Mary did not answer. 'Come on, Mary. I'm bound to hear it sooner or later.'

'They gave the background . . . about Melanie . . . and said the, er . . . the murderer hadn't been caught.'

People find it so hard to say that word, Kate thought, noting Mary's hesitation.

'Thanks for telling me,' she said.

'Kate, are you really all right? I mean, what's going on? Do you want me to come round? I can come over tonight.'

'No, Mary . . . thanks. I think it's best if you don't.'

'Oh, I see . . .'

No, Kate thought, no, you don't. 'Mary, please don't take it badly. I'm really glad you phoned. It's – it's been too long.'

'Hmm.'

'And now I've done it again. I've hurt you, and I don't mean to. It's . . . I can't explain. Look, when this is all over—'

'What?' Mary shouted in exasperation. 'When what's all over? For heaven's sake, Kate, what is going on? Why won't you let me help you?'

'Mary, please try to understand. It's better, much better, if we don't see each other – don't even talk to each other – for a little longer.'

There was an uncomfortable pause, and Kate filled it with the first thing that came into her head. 'How's Jenny?'

The silence continued, and Kate's cheeks burned with the realization that Mary was wondering if Kate still blamed her. 'I'm sorry I didn't send her a birthday card—'

'For God's sake, do you think that matters to us? We miss you. We want you to come and see us, Kate. Tony'll pick you up any time, you know that.'

'Yes, I do. I do know,' Kate said, softly, and Mary subsided for a few moments.

'Jenny sends her love. She misses you, and she misses Melanie so much. Come over. Come for Christmas dinner.'

'No,' Kate said gently. 'Thanks, but no. It's not that I don't want to—'

'Then come!'

Mary sounded tearful, and Kate felt her own control tumbling away. She tightened her grip on the phone and said, 'Maybe at New Year. Maybe then.' She placed the receiver gently back on the cradle.

'Could you put that out?'

Kate looked up, startled. 'What?' she asked.

Moira nodded at Kate's hand, a carefully composed expression of disgust on her face. Smoke curled from a cigarette she had apparently lit while talking on the phone.

Kate walked to the window and opened it, letting in a freezing gust of air, together with the clamour of Christmas noise from the square below. She stared at Moira as she flicked the cigarette out of the window.

Moira gasped. 'That's irresponsible!' she exclaimed.

A faint smile curved Kate's mouth. 'I'd rather be irresponsible than a meddling, insensitive boor,' she observed, just loud enough to be heard.

'That's it. I've had about as much as I can take of this. God knows, I've tried to understand, but you've gone too far this time. I'm complaining of you to Mr Owen.'

'Feel free,' Kate said, unperturbed. 'I'm on extended leave of absence as of today, so I doubt if he'll do anything.'

Moira straightened up. She tried a concerned look but couldn't quite cover the triumph in her expression.

'Well, of course, we know you've been under a strain—'

'Do you, Moira? How perceptive.'

'Perhaps it's best if you take a bit of time off. Christmas is always difficult. I'm sure Mr Owen has your best interests at heart.'

Kate nodded gravely. 'I'm sure he does.' She might have added, but chose to remain silent on the matter, that it was she who had requested a leave of absence.

Moira tried a different tack: 'We've all heard about your . . . trouble last night. Terrible thing. Terrible.'

Kate found herself wondering how much had actually been said in the radio bulletin. Harmon wasn't likely to release details, and Mrs Wilson didn't know so very much. The soft clack of computer keyboards continued but slowed a little, suggesting a mental, if not a physical, leaning across to listen to her response. She was staring, she realized. Moira pressed one palm across her chest and held the file she was carrying at midriff height, as though she felt exposed, naked under her stare.

'Was there anything else, Moira?'

'Just to say if there's anything I can do—'

Like wheedle some facts out of me so you can tell the rest of the staff, Kate thought. 'Yes,' she said, 'as a matter of fact there is.' The keyboard clicking had all but stopped. Many were listening openly now.

Moira flushed with pleasure, moistening her lips in anticipation of the succulent morsel of gossip she was about to hear, and smiled insincerely.

'You can piss off and keep right out of my business.'

Moira's hands flapped and her mouth opened and closed a few times. Fish out of water, Kate thought, watching Moira dive for the safety of Owen's aquarium.

She gave her police escort the slip at lunchtime, and sat in Albert Square. Christmas shoppers hurried with seeming purpose across the cobbles, heading towards the main shopping area, while traffic circled the area, prowling like predatory animals. The fog had dispersed by ten o'clock, leaving a dazzling frost. Looking at it, Kate felt a thrill of optimism. It seemed almost to reflect her own situation. She had been stumbling through a treacherous fog since Melanie had been murdered, but now her way forward seemed clear, there was even a frigid beauty about it. She laughed aloud. 'You always were a sucker for pathetic fallacy,' she told herself.

There was a function at the town hall, and dignitaries began arriving in black cars and dark suits, their wives in hats and bird-bright twin-sets in primary colours. They shivered in the cold, their smiles as brittle as the icicles that hung from the statues in the square. Queen Victoria, taking pride of place in the centre of the assembled figures, looked comical, a frozen, watery spike hanging from her haughty nose. Occasionally tourists would stop and peer up at the giant inflatable Santa clinging to the town-hall clock. Kate's eye was caught by one little boy who was holding his mother's hand and dancing with excitement. He pulled free and ran to chase some pigeons. They flew up as one in a clatter of alarm, their wings whirring in their frantic haste to escape.

His mother ran after him, snatching him back to her crossly. 'Keep hold, I said. The bad man'll get yer.'

'Hold tight. Hold on tightly,' Kate whispered, feeling her loneliness with such force it seemed at that moment that the square was silent and she alone, isolated in a great glass dome, separate – different from other people. Tainted by her experience.

'What're you playing at, Kate?'

'Adam,' Kate answered, making no attempt to explain herself.

He sat beside her.

'Where have you been?' she asked. He had not been at his

desk when she arrived. His absence had puzzled her; he had been there early every morning that week.

'I've been talking to Harmon.'

'About what?'

'About where I was last night.'

'Why?'

'You tell me.'

'Oh,' said Kate. 'They can't think—'

'But they do, Kate. They do – think.' He looked at her questioningly. 'So?' he demanded.

'I – er . . . I had a spot of bother last night.'

'Why didn't you phone me?'

'It was late and—'

'Kate, you've got to stop shutting people out. Don't you realize people *want* to help? What about your girlfriend – Mary, wasn't it? If you won't talk to me, couldn't you talk to her?'

'Funny you should say that. She telephoned earlier.'

Adam raised an eyebrow in question.

'Apparently there was a wildly inaccurate story on the radio news this morning.'

'And?'

'And nothing. We talked.' She shrugged.

Adam sighed, defeated.

'Was Owen all right – about your being late, I mean?'

'He wasn't best pleased.'

'Adam, are *you* all right?'

The question was sudden and startling. For a moment, Adam seemed stunned, then he threw back his head and laughed. It was the first time in months that Kate had heard him laugh out loud and, though perplexed, she was vaguely pleased. He had an unselfconscious, open, deep and masculine laugh.

'Did I say something funny?' she asked.

He shook his head. 'You're followed home and attacked in your own flat,' he said, obviously exasperated by her, 'and you're asking me if I'm all right.'

Kate shrugged again, smiling. Slowly the smile faded and was replaced by a frown. 'I wasn't followed,' she said. 'Not home anyway.'

'Oh.'

'What made you think—?'

Adam looked away. 'Must've got the wrong impression.'

'Why is Mr Harmon so set against you?' she asked.

Adam's expression changed, and he said bitterly, 'Because I made a stupid mistake when I was a kid.'

Kate's frown deepened.

'It's so hard to do something with your life when nobody will give you a chance,' he went on. 'How can you make amends when people won't trust you?'

Kate wanted to ask him more, but she hesitated, and he went on: 'Well, I'm getting out next summer. I've been offered a place at UMIST, and I'm taking it.'

Kate's smile returned. 'That's great,' she said. 'I'm really pleased for you.' She kissed him lightly on the cheek and squeezed his arm.

Adam flushed slightly, adding, 'It's a computing course. I'm interested in neural systems.' His finger went to his eyebrow.

'What?' asked Kate, noting a hesitancy on his part.

'The other day – when you asked me what I was working on—' He stopped.

'Yes?' she prompted cautiously.

'It was a program – they asked me to submit some original work as an entrance requirement.'

'Oh, Adam.' Kate was so relieved she laughed. 'I'm sorry,' she said, choking back a giggle of nervous release. 'I thought—'

'I know what you thought.'

Kate shook her head, still smiling. 'Everyone looking at you and you moonlighting and me accusing you – I'm so sorry,' she repeated.

Adam smiled. 'No harm done,' he said.

'Mrs Pearson!'

Kate squinted up at the young woman standing over them. The low winter sun created a halo around her head, and at first Kate did not recognize her. 'Oh, it's you.' She introduced Adam to her police escort. Slim, attractive, blonde, mid-twenties, she could easily pass for a secretary or computer operator. Inspector Harmon had got her into Technicomm as a temp. Temporary computer operators and filing clerks were a constant feature of the place. If business was good, or if a big account needed speedy attention, Owen might take on three at once, but they rarely stayed more than a few weeks, and permanent staff did not mark their coming or their going.

'Pleased to meet you, Constable Barratt,' said Adam, offering his hand, and looking over her shoulder, down at his feet, anywhere rather than her eyes.

'*Miss* Barratt. You're not supposed to be telling anyone who I am,' she said, dismissing Adam with a perfunctory squeeze of the hand and addressing Kate alone. 'Harmon'll have my guts for garters if he hears about this,' she added hotly.

Kate raised her eyebrows, gently mocking. 'I won't tell if you don't,' she said.

DC Barratt glowered at her and Kate sighed. 'All right,' she said. 'Let's go.'

' "A Trafford woman is said to be badly shaken after an attack in her home last night," ' Moira read. ' "Kate Pearson, whose daughter was murdered in July of this year, has been the subject of various crank calls, according to colleagues. Police have refused to confirm or deny the attack, but it is significant that the investigation is being coordinated by Chief Inspector Harmon, the officer who led the hunt for Melanie Pearson's murderer." ' Someone coughed, and Moira looked up. 'Oh,' she said. 'I thought you'd gone home.' It sounded like an accusation. 'You're in the paper.'

People turned back to their terminals, slowly, carefully, as though trying to escape notice. Kate glanced over at Adam's work-station. It was empty. She walked to Moira's desk.

'Early edition?' she asked.

'Hot off the press.' Moira smiled, her dark little eyes sparkling with spite. 'Says they're still no nearer finding him.'

Kate nodded. Leaning forward, she snatched the paper before Moira could respond and tore it, shredded it, venting her rage and frustration.

Moira stared, open-mouthed. 'You—! You—!' she gasped.

Kate thrust her face into Moira's. 'One word,' she said, 'just one word, and I swear I'll—' A light touch on her shoulder and she spun round, fist bunched.

'Leave it, eh?'

Kate stood for some moments, eye to eye with DC Barratt, her chest heaving and her mind focused on her real and compelling desire to hit Moira.

'Not worth it,' Barratt added, flashing Moira a warning look before taking Kate by the elbow. Kate shrugged her off, but Barratt stood her ground, and at last she turned and walked to her desk.

'Maybe you should go home now,' Constable Barratt suggested. 'I'll square it with your boss.'

'When I've finished this document.'

It was an outline proposal for a new deal to provide hardware and back-up support for a firm that made plastic freezer bags. Owen had been adamant that she finish it before leaving. Kate searched the directory under the date reference, then traced the name via a sub-directory headed 'proposals'. She double-clicked on the file icon to open it and, after checking the heading, skipped to the end of the document.

Melanie stared fearfully out of the screen at her. She had been crying. Strands of hair had come loose and her pony-tail band had slipped to one side. Her uniform blouse was smeared with dirt. Kate reached out and touched the screen, half-expecting the image to vanish. Melanie was wearing the scrunchy that had been sent in the post. Her hands seemed to be pulled behind her, and Kate realized they must be tied. Beneath, a caption:

Say bye-bye to Mummy, Melanie.

Kate was momentarily assailed by the smell of the mortuary – cold air, disinfectant, strong soap and that other, subtle smell: death. She reached out and picked up the phone. John had to ask her to repeat the question. She coughed and spoke again, her voice hoarse: 'Is he here?' she repeated. 'Check if he's in the system.'

She heard, faintly, the sound of John's keyboard. 'I'm not getting anything Kate. What is it?'

'I—' Kate faltered. She was feeling faint. She couldn't make herself say it. She concentrated on regulating her breathing and found the effort almost too much.

'I'm tapping into your terminal,' John told her. Then silence. She knew he had taken over her terminal because the cursor moved, even though both of her hands were gripping the phone.

At length he said, 'Kate?'

She made no reply, but closed her eyes, trying to blot out the terrible image, finding it burned on her retinas. It would not fade.

'Kate, I'm closing down your account now.'

Kate found her voice. 'No!'

'Why not? You asked me to shut it down at five o'clock anyway. What difference will a few hours make?'

'John,' Kate urged. 'You must save all of this, all of the files, to disk. Harmon should see them.'

A pause, then: 'All right. But I want you out of there. Turn off your monitor and leave the rest to me, okay?'

Kate clicked the screen off, feeling almost that she was turning away from her daughter's suffering. 'Done,' she said.

'Now go.'

But Kate did not move. Adam must have noticed something was wrong because he came over and spoke to her. She could make no sense of what he said. All she could see was that dreadful image of Melanie, and she fancied she could hear the words, spoken aloud by some demonic voice:

Say bye-bye to Mummy, Melanie.

Adam reached out and touched her arm and she recoiled, horrified. 'Leave me alone,' she hissed.

He stepped back, shocked, and Constable Barratt, seeing the exchange, hurried over, leaving the mug of coffee she had just poured at the machine.

Owen was standing at the door of his inner sanctum as she passed. 'Get her off my premises,' he muttered, 'before I change my mind about the leave of absence and make it permanent.'

Barratt threw him a withering look. 'You're all heart, Mr Owen,' she said.

Chapter Sixteen

Of course, Harmon wanted to know why she had asked for a leave of absence. Kate was ready for that. She had prepared in her mind what she would say to him.

'You – didn't want to take time off after Melanie's death,' he said.

She had taken three weeks off work in all. If she had stayed home, she would have gone completely, irretrievably mad but few people were able to understand her reasons for returning to work so soon.

'The time you did take was really to avoid further press attention.'

Kate watched him for a full half-minute, then realized she was staring. It was a habit she had got into since Melanie's death; it was so difficult to be sure what people really meant when they said things, who was sincere and who merely curious, and she often found herself studying every feature to try to get at the truth.

'You've seen the files,' she said. 'Isn't that reason enough?'

Harmon gave no answer but continued to watch her.

'I was wrong to refuse help when Melanie was abducted. It was even more stupid to refuse help when my daughter was murdered. An understandable mistake, given the circumstances, I suppose.' She paused for a few moments, began to say something, appeared to change her mind, took a breath, then started again. 'I've been really shaken by what's happened. This guy has got me scared, Mr Harmon. He's – hounded me over these past weeks. He – he taped – my little girl pleading to be allowed to come home. And now he's sending me pictures of her in that terrible place.' She stopped, finding it difficult to breathe.

Harmon made no move but seemed, in his turn, to be studying her. He doesn't believe me, Kate thought. But he *has* to. Sergeant Wainwright, kindly, dependable Sergeant Wainwright, walked over to her and placed one hand on her shoulder. The warmth of this simple human contact and the knowledge that he felt for her gave her the strength to go on. Forcing herself to breathe more slowly, she continued: 'He is monstrous. I can't sit and wait for him to send me more messages. It's destroying me.'

'We're not suggesting you do, Mrs Pearson. We've put a trace on any e-mail messages coming in and a stop on your surface mail. We're monitoring all your phone calls. We've arranged for a female officer to accompany you around the clock.'

'Which is why I'll feel safer at home. Since you're checking my mail, you don't need me to read it. I'm doing no good at work anyway.' She looked Harmon in the eye, willing him to believe her. 'I'm sick of being his victim,' she said, and meant it.

'We're doing all we can,' Harmon answered.

'I know that. I do know that you're trying. But he's clever.' She paused, considering. 'No, not clever – he's cunning. He likes to manipulate. He's used to thinking three steps ahead of everyone else. It's instinctive to him. And I'm afraid I'm not up to playing his mind games.' She shrugged. 'You probably think I'm weak, but—'

Harmon was watching her intently, and she shifted

uncomfortably, thinking that now she knew how Adam felt under his penetrating stare.

'No,' he said, surprising himself, 'I don't think you're weak. I think you are an extremely courageous woman.'

Kate bowed her head, convinced that if she looked at the inspector, he would read her thoughts in her expression.

'But we all have our limits,' he said with quiet emphasis.

'I went beyond mine a long time ago, Mr Harmon.'

Harmon watched Kate go out of the room. He waited for the door to close behind her before asking, 'Who's watching her tonight?'

'Jill Jackson,' Sergeant Wainwright answered promptly.

'Tell her to keep a close eye, will you? There's . . . I don't know.' He fell silent, resuming some moments later. 'There's a recklessness about her, don't you think?'

'No.' Wainwright was taken aback.

'All that guff about feeling safer at home didn't quite ring true. And since when has Kate Pearson admitted to any weakness?' He shook his head, a deep frown creasing his forehead. 'Tell Constable Jackson to watch her very carefully.'

Wainwright left DCI Harmon to his thoughts for a few moments, and then began, 'Er . . .'

'Hmm?' Harmon was still deep in thought.

'The lead I was following up, sir.'

'Any good?'

'The computer services department at the university let me have a list of all the passwords that had been stolen – apparently they'd been salted away in a file somewhere on the mainframe. Kate Pearson's password was on there.'

Harmon looked up sharply. 'I don't suppose they've traced the culprit?' The question was rhetorical.

Wainwright shook his head. 'They say he could be anywhere. It seems they have a constant problem with hackers trying to break in to use their system for storage, number crunching, you name it. They hardly ever track them down.'

Harmon sighed. 'It's an imperfect world, Sergeant. What have you got on the stalker?'

'Not much, I'm afraid. Except it wasn't Shepherd.'

'Oh?'

'He was working on his office computer until 7.40, just after Mrs Pearson was attacked.'

'Got witnesses to that, have we?'

'As good as. He has to log on and off the office system, and the times are recorded. He logged off at 7.40 precisely.'

'Convenient. But what's to stop him leaving his computer switched on and nipping out of the office for half an hour?' Harmon asked.

'A security device. If no operations are performed on a particular computer for five minutes, the system automatically times you out – logs you off,' he added, knowing that Harmon's jargon-tolerance level was low. 'It's to stop people sloping off for a crafty fag when they're working and leaving the system open to abuse. Timing the user out cuts down the chances of anyone else whipping in and using the system for any illegal operations.'

'Can we be sure it was Shepherd on the machine?'

'Everyone has their own login and password, and the night security staff reckon they saw only Shepherd in the office.'

'So, it wasn't Shepherd. What about Mr Pearson?'

'Now, he's more difficult to pin down. He was out visiting clients all day—'

'Where?'

'In and around Manchester.'

Harmon nodded.

'His girlfriend says he was with her from six o'clock.'

'How loyal.'

'He's in interview room two, if you'd like a word, sir.'

Harmon raised an eyebrow.

'He, er, wasn't in a cooperative frame of mind,' Wainwright explained.

'How long's he been here?'

'Since about four. His office said he was out on calls most of the day, and he doesn't always carry his cell phone with him – it puts the clients off – so I sent Tippet and Baines to sit outside his house.'

Harmon nodded. 'I'll see him. But before I do – how did Dr Ingrams check out?'

'Very helpful,' he said. 'Nice bloke, that. First thing he did was ask after Mrs Pearson. Same as last time. He wanted to know if she was all right, like.'

'And where was he last night?' asked Harmon, unimpressed.

'He was delivering a lecture on "The Demise of the Internal Combustion Engine in the Twenty-First Century". He reckons we'll all be battery-powered by 2010. The lecture ran from seven to eight thirty. He says he was in his office from about six until six fifty, and then he went across to the lecture theatre to set up his slides and prepare for the lecture.'

'Was he seen?'

Wainwright nodded. 'The caretaker at the lecture theatre confirms having seen him well before the start of the lecture, although he wasn't too sure about the exact time.' Find fault with that, he thought.

'And Newman? What about him?'

'He's delivering a series of seminars on management restructuring for Bolton Borough Council in a Forte hotel at West-houghton at the minute.'

Harmon drew down the corners of his mouth. 'Not far up the road, then. Go on.'

'His last seminar ended at six, after which he says he went to his room to shower and rest before dinner, but nobody saw him. He could've made it from there to Deansgate by half six, quarter to seven.'

'And Mrs Pearson was attacked between seven fifteen and seven thirty. The fog would've held him up. Do we know how much?'

Wainwright shook his head. 'Depends what route he took.'

'Find out, will you? Traffic division should be able to give us a fairly accurate idea.'

Wainwright nodded. 'My money's on Pearson, though,' he said.

'Why's that?'

'I think you should see him for yourself,' he said, with a grin.

Harmon and Wainwright exchanged glances. 'Nasty set of scratches you've got there, Mr Pearson.'

Pearson snarled, but made no answer. He was in no mood to talk.

'How did you get them?'

'I'm saying nothing till I've seen my solicitor.'

'Duly noted, sir. But it's hardly a cooperative stance to take, is it?'

'I've got clients to see. My office don't know where I am. My girlfriend's in hysterics at home. I've been brought here without explanation and treated like a criminal. Cooperation works both ways, you know?'

'I think they call that a truism, Mr Pearson, but' – Harmon raised his hands, conceding the point – 'you are owed an explanation.' He stood to leave.

'Where the hell d'you think you're going?' Pearson demanded.

Harmon stood with his back to Pearson. 'Let Mr Pearson

call his solicitor, and tell me as soon as he arrives,' he told Wainwright. 'We'll continue the interview at that time.'

'Hey! Hey, hold on!' Pearson protested. 'That could take hours.'

'You are entitled to legal representation, Mr Pearson.'

Pearson looked down at the worn table-top. 'You can ask. I can't say as I'll answer.'

'Seems fair. Let's begin with my original question. How did you come by those scratches?'

'Suzy – my girlfriend. She can be a bit of a cat.'

'Meaning? I'm sorry, you'll have to explain.'

Pearson looked for support from Wainwright and the PC standing by the door. 'A *bit of a cat*, you know.' He made clawing movements with his fingertips.

'You're saying your girlfriend gave you those scratches.'

Pearson tried to stare the inspector down, but couldn't quite swing it. 'Yeah, that's what I'm saying.'

'Where were you between seven fifteen and seven thirty last night?'

Pearsons gaze shifted slightly. 'At home. Suzy will verify that.' He smiled, and the action gave him a dangerous, feral look. 'Has that bitch been spreading malicious lies about me again?'

'I'm afraid you'll have to be more specific, Mr Pearson.'

'Kate. This is about her, isn't it? Look, I don't want anything to do with that fucking bitch. She's been nothing but trouble to me. Melanie goes missing – who gets pulled in? Me. I'm a suspect in my own daughter's *murder*, for Christ's sake. She starts getting a bit of fan mail – who gets the blame? Me. Tell you what,' he said, leaning back in his chair, 'you should be looking for a man with a Labrador and a white stick.'

'Thank you for your advice, Mr Pearson, I'll keep it in mind.' Harmon paused, letting Pearson enjoy his little triumph. 'You're right. This is about your ex-wife. Mrs Pearson has been subjected to sustained and sadistic harassment for several weeks, culminating in an attack last night. I wonder why you immediately spring to mind?'

'It's called victimization,' Pearson replied.

'I'd call it common sense.'

'Now you listen—'

'No, Pearson, you listen.' Harmon thrust his face into Pearson's. 'I intend to put a stop to this.'

Pearson looked away. 'Suzy will tell you, I was home all night.'

'I'm sure she will tell us whatever you want her to,' Harmon said, straightening up and slipping an elegant hand into his trouser pocket, perfectly in control. 'That doesn't make it the truth.'

'I've stayed away from that bitch for this long, why would I suddenly change my mind?'

Harmon shrugged. 'I'm not a psychiatrist, Mr Pearson, but I'd say you had something of a persecution complex. People like you don't always act rationally.'

'People like— Right, that's it. I want my solicitor.'

'Okay.' Harmon had finished anyway. 'When he gets here,' he said, casually, 'tell him we'll need samples for a tissue match with the scrapings we took from under Mrs Pearson's fingernails.'

Pearson laughed suddenly. 'Fine by me,' he said.

Harmon walked to the window and stared out at the city lights below him. 'He's lying through his teeth, Sergeant.'

'What was all that about tissue samples?' Wainwright asked. 'We didn't take any. There was no point – Mrs Pearson was wearing gloves.'

'Yes,' Harmon said, turning back into the room, 'And Pearson seemed pretty sure of himself, didn't he? Why is that?'

'Maybe because he's innocent.'

'Or maybe because he knew I was bluffing, because he knew she was wearing gloves.'

'So where did the scratches come from?'

'They don't look like fingernail marks to me. However, if it *was* him last night, he would have to've run across the rough patch behind Trafford town hall, and over the fence at the edge of the car park—'

'And there's thorn bushes and shrubs both sides,' Wainwright said, picking up the thread.

A silence followed that stretched for several minutes. Harmon slumped into his chair, still managing, somehow, to look elegant, with his long legs stretched out in front of him and his chin on his chest.

'I think we're looking for two men,' he said suddenly.

'What makes you say that, sir?'

Harmon shrugged. 'It seems odd that whoever left the doctored tape for Mrs Pearson would follow her and try to scare the living daylights out of her on the same night. I think she was right about that. Anyway, it's a bit clumsy compared with our man's usual MO.' He breathed a heavy sigh. 'We're missing something. Has Stretton turned up anything on the trace?'

'Not a sausage, sir. Our hacker is too slippery, it seems.'

Harmon sighed again. 'Well, tell him to keep trying. He's bound to make a mistake sooner or later.'

'What about Pearson?'

'The bastard's right, we haven't got anything on him. Let him go, with an apology' – he held a hand up, silencing Wainwright's objections – 'and a discreet tail.'

Wainwright left to arrange Pearson's release and Harmon turned back to the window. The city glittered out of the darkness beyond the window, piercing the reflections from his office lighting like stars through a thin layer of cloud. Somewhere out there was Melanie's killer. And Harmon intended to find him. What worried him was that Kate Pearson might have the same idea – and that she might get there ahead of him.

Chapter Seventeen

He watched the light fade on the shortest day and wondered why they call it nightfall. Night does not fall, he thought. It settles. It insinuates itself, unnoticed, finding the furthest reaches of every cellar, every room and alley and doorway to bed down.

His room was cold, but he barely noticed the chill. Around him the clean, uncluttered surfaces and the carefully arranged bookshelves were comfort enough.

I might have let you share this, he thought, but feeling a simultaneous tightening in his gut. He looked around the room, gaining intense pleasure from the white, unfussy paintwork, tinged mauve for a few minutes in the fading light. He checked with a critical eye the neat array of disks and manuals on the shelves beside his desk, and was satisfied.

He waited for total darkness before switching on his terminal. He was humming a tune. His flat, dead eyes glimmered for a fraction of a second. The monitor and printer lights flashed as they powered up. When the lights steadied, they reflected his eyes: twin oblongs, fixed like shards of green glass, hard and destructive as his intent.

He checked in on his UNIX machine and then reassigned himself to another system. 'Let's go to . . . Glasgow for tonight's performance,' he murmured, tapping in the commands. The scooper program he had been running for the last month raked in over a hundred high-status passwords of university and research laboratory staff in the UK, Cern, NASA and MIT. The university cybercops had got some of them, but they hadn't discovered his smaller, more exclusive cache.

He wondered whether the police were still trying to track him. He chuckled, his breath making light puffs of condensation in the frigid air of the darkened room. The sound of his laughter rattled unmusically, falling flat in the dead, cold air.

He reached further into the darkness of the Web, and his fingers tingled with excitement. First contact since his last missive.

He had intended first to check on Kathy – his chosen name for her today – but, as so often happened, he was diverted and in his peregrinations he found himself somewhere other than he intended. He tapped into the police headquarters and left a message for Harmon, giving the subject as:

Black Bobby's relationship to Melanie

Q: When is a dead girl like a Detective Chief Inspector?
A: When it's Melanin! ('Scuse my spelling)

Geddit? :-D

He exited the police computer system, logging out and then re-entering the Net through a different route, taking no chances of discovery.

He typed a note to Kate:

Did you enjoy the lullaby?
Did you say bye-bye?

And sent the mail. Soon he would cruise her office system. Maybe he would trash a few files, read her mail, add a few lines of his own, perhaps even download another scanned image on to one of her files.

He postponed the pleasure a little longer, closing his eyes and imagining her reading his last message. Still shaking, still hurting from the tape recording he had transferred on to the deck system in her own flat. He could replay the tape he made of Kate as she listened to it – the listening device he had hidden in her flat was worth the expense.

Although he loved the Net, and revelled in the power it afforded him, he found it unsatisfactory in one respect: it lacked the immediacy of direct contact. The quality that had initially attracted him to the Net as a means of contact now frustrated him: anonymity, its greatest asset and its gravest limitation. He wanted, more than anything, to watch her suffer, as she made him suffer. He experienced a god-like strength in striking from the nothingness of cyberspace, out of the ether, so to speak, but it lacked something . . .

He could touch her life outside work only by indirect means – her bank account, her bills – but these things could not perform so . . . intimate a function as the tape he made especially for her – allowing Melanie to speak to her from the grave.

Being in her home, fingering her belongings, breathing her perfume, which lingered in her bedroom, had given him such profound pleasure. Lying on her bed, he had been tempted to wait for her to come home. It wasn't sex, he told himself, but a colossal sense of power . . .

Cruising the Technicomm system, ten minutes later, look-ing for files marked with Kate's tag. Puzzled, he searched again. There was none marked KMP.

He scrolled down the lists of files, and the words snaked slowly up the screen, making the light in his eyes flicker — a facsimile of life. The movements made him dizzy. He logged out, sweating, aware there might be a trace on his activities. Could Manchester University have got closer to him than he gave them credit for? He routed his next login via Liverpool University, gaining access to Katherine's office (Katherine now, rather than Kate, for he was angry with her), using her own login and password, and his puzzlement grew. He was locked out.

He returned to his own system, logging it in under his own name and password, then typed 'elm' at the UNIX prompt to get into his mailbox. His stomach felt hollow. His last letter had been returned; it was there, in the listing:

Mail address unknown.

Below it, another message, addressed via his remailer:

\<From: K. M. Pearson\>

Brief heat flamed in his face, then died. He stared in disbelief. She had closed her account. She must have. He was outraged. This was not expected. This was *not* supposed to happen.

He moved the cursor down, one line at a time, until her message was highlighted, and then tapped the 'enter' key. His original message was there, unaltered, at the top of the screen.

Did you enjoy the lullaby?
Did you say bye-bye?

Below it, her reply:

It's good to keep in touch, but even better to be in control ;-)

I'm off-line now, so send your love letters to oblivion if you like. I won't be there :-D

Dark colour crept into his neck, above his collar.

'Oh, but you will, Katherine, sooner than I'd planned and sooner than you think. But you will be there.' She had tried to out-think him, with her small measure of street cunning and her grammar-school education, but it really wasn't good enough.

'You always did underestimate me,' he murmured.

Chapter Eighteen

The house was dark when he returned; the hall was cold and strangely silent. Suzy usually met him at the front door, talking excitedly, taking his coat, drowning him in kisses. Depressed, Pearson reached out to switch on the hall light.

'They let you go.' Suzy spoke from the shadows on the stairway.

Pearson's hand jerked away from the switch. 'Jesus, you scared the shit out of me!' He flicked the switch and Suzy shielded her eyes, blinking. She had been crying.

'God, you look like a pig,' he said. 'Go and wash your face.' Obediently, Suzy climbed the stairs.

He cast an appraising eye over her when she returned. She'd made a bit of effort, fixing her hair and dabbing some make-up over the worst of the blotches. The only evidence that remained of her crying bout was a heightened colour and a brilliance to her eyes.

'C'm'ere.' He held out an arm and she sat next to him on the settee, still strangely subdued. She looked up at him, her eyes shining, and then buried her face in his chest. At times like this, temper or no, she seemed unbelievably frail and, as a result, overwhelmingly attractive. He held her close, wanting to protect her. They sat like this for some time. Pearson stroked her hair, aware of the soft rise and fall of her breast, feeling the warmth of her breath on his skin.

He lifted his glass to his lips, and ice chinked as he sipped. 'Bastards.' His tone was meditative. Suzy frowned, wondering whether a response was expected.

'Fucking bastards.'

She recognized her cue and asked: 'It's Kate, isn't it?'

'Bitch.'

'I knew it was her.' When he had left her last night, left her without a word, she had known he'd gone to find Kate. She was always there on the edge of their lives, always spoiling things. 'Why's she tormenting you like this?'

He snorted, 'They'll believe any bloody crap she tells them. That black bastard Harmon's probably poking her.'

Suzy giggled and he kissed the top of her head. She smelt of shampoo and talcum powder.

'I've never bothered her. I kept out of her way, like they said. But that's not enough for her. She wants her pound of flesh.'

'Cow,' Suzy said, snuggling closer, then, timidly: 'I thought you weren't coming back, Davey.' Her voice wavered. 'I was so scared . . .'

Pearson hugged her fiercely. 'That's what she wants. Split us up. She's so fucking twisted, she can't get a man. All she's got is that dyke mate of hers, but she's not happy diddling that fat cunt. She wants to ruin it for us an' all.'

Suzy's eyes brimmed with tears. 'I don't know what I'd do without you, Davey. I'd die without you.' Pearson looked down at her pale, little-girl's face, framed with its mass of dark curls. At times like this he felt like a king.

'I'll not let that happen. Never you worry,' he said, tilting her face and planting a kiss on her lips.

*

At home, alone, Moira sorted through the papers. The nationals hadn't got hold of it yet. She'd take care of that tomorrow. The *Manchester Evening News* – a new copy, bought to replace the one Kate had destroyed – was the only one to carry the attack story.

She opened the scrapbook. The last entry was dated 31 August. How quickly the media forget, she thought, disapprovingly. She had kept a detailed journal of events since July – odd remarks and office gossip as well as newspaper clippings. Not morbid curiosity, she told herself, she kept cuttings of anyone she knew. If they got their names in the paper, they deserved a place in her scrapbook. The hobby had started with her mother: she liked Moira to cut out death notices relating to any of her friends or acquaintances. It became something of a habit, and even after she had died, Moira kept it up. It was something to do in the evenings, and she regarded it as a tribute to her mother's memory.

Of course, Kate had her own book, in fact one and a half scrapbooks were dedicated to her, bulging with information, pictures, notes. There had been so much – especially in the early days.

She cut round the article with a craft knife, making precise incisions, using a metal ruler as a guide. Why was Kate so hateful to her? She would never understand. A noise in the street made her look up. Although darkness had come several hours earlier, her curtains stood open and she worked by the light of the street lamp below the window. She liked to watch the comings and goings of the street, sitting at the upstairs window in her mother's room, as she had done when her mother was alive. She would relay details of the goings on, sometimes embellishing for her mother's amusement. Better than telly, her mother would say.

She resumed her cutting, a frown forming and deepening on her forehead. All those cruel things Kate had said – and then to tear up her paper like that. Moira's hand shook, and she nicked herself with the blade. Nothing serious. She watched dark blood bead at the edges of the cut, then pinched the tip of her finger lightly with her thumb and let a drop fall on to the picture of Kate on the newspaper cutting. Moira watched, fascinated, as the blood soaked into the newsprint and wrinkled the photograph. When she had finished mounting the piece, the handle of the knife was smeared with blood. She sucked her finger, waiting for her work to dry.

Tippet and Baines stopped fifty yards down the road from Pearson's house and walked up. They passed an unmarked car on the way. Foster and Lipson looked cold, bored and miserable. Baines tapped at the window.

'Cheer up, you might be seeing some action in a minute or two.'

Foster thanked him kindly and commented that the only action he wanted to see tonight involved a glass of brandy, a couple of mince pies and his wife.

'I'd rather you didn't discuss your perversions with a female officer present,' Baines said.

Tippet grabbed him by the collar. 'Come on, Charlie,' she said, 'you know you're just trying to put off the dreadful moment.'

The house looked newly painted, the garden almost fanatically neat. Few plants were visible, but the borders were hoed and clean of weeds. The frost had settled like a light dusting of icing sugar on the surface of the soil. They stood on the doorstep, stamping their feet in the freezing cold. 'I'm not looking forward to this one little bit,' Baines said.

'You should worry. It's me she went for last time.' Tippet was glad it was Baines who had come with her and not someone else. Although he tipped the scales at sixteen stones and carried rather more fat than was healthy for a man of his age, Baines was as nimble on his feet as he was quick-thinking. Claire Tippet pressed the door bell. There was a pause, then a light came on in the hallway. 'Here we go.'

'Well, *fuck* me if it isn't constables Tipsy and Pains again.' Pearson scowled at them from the doorway.

'Can we come in, sir?' Baines asked.

'No. Next question?'

'I really must insist, sir.' Baines smiled contemptuously, leaving David Pearson in no doubt that he meant business.

'Got a warrant?'

'We could get one. But—' said Baines, putting one meaty hand against the door to prevent Pearson closing it, 'I would advise you not to take that course of action. We're here about nuisance calls.'

Pearson rolled his eyes, 'Change the fucking record, will you? I've not long got back from the station after your last cock-up. I've got nothing to do with the e-mail or whatever the stupid bitch says she's getting. She's probably making it up, any road. Harmon's pissing in the wind.'

'Nevertheless, a series of calls has been made from this address to Mrs Pearson's home number.'

'Bollocks!' Pearson looked from Baines to Tippet. 'This is some kind of joke, right?'

'No joke,' said Tippet. 'I took some of the calls myself.' The lines around her eyes crinkled slightly as she watched Pearson try to work that one out. 'We'll talk inside,' she said. Pearson stepped back as she walked through the door. It was an instinctive reaction. He'd not have budged an inch for a man, and Tippet knew it.

'Hey, I never said—'

'Is Miss Walmsley home, sir?' Tippet pushed open the sitting-room door and saw the little figure immediately. She was curled up on the settee, her eyes large and round. Even in the subdued lighting of the room Tippet could see recent bruising on her neck. Tippet was almost surprised that she wasn't actually sucking her thumb.

'I was frightened, Davey,' she said.

'Shut the fuck up,' he snarled.

'Tell you what, Mr Pearson,' Tippet said, rounding on Pearson, 'why don't *you* shut it? It's Miss Walmsley we've come to see.' She turned back to Suzanne Walmsley. 'You made some calls tonight.' It was a statement.

Suzy nodded. Her eyes were drawn to Pearson. 'I just wanted to tell her to stop. To leave us alone, Davey.'

'How did you get Mrs Pearson's number?' Baines asked.

'It's in the phone book,' said Suzy, puzzled.

They both heard Pearson breathe in sharply.

'It's ex-directory,' said Baines.

'It's in *our* phone book. The address book,' said Suzy, full of nervous impatience.

'How did you get Mrs Pearson's number, sir?' Tippet asked.

'Can't remember.' Pearson shrugged like a petulant child.

'It is an offence to break into the data banks of British Telecom, sir,' she warned.

'What d'you think I am? Some kind of computer freak who spends his nights hacking into confidential files? It's not my idea of erotic fulfilment.'

'No, sir. I can see that,' Tippet poured as much scorn as she could into those words, staring so hard at Pearson's girl-friend as she said them that Suzy caught the collar of her blouse and pulled it closed around her neck.

'So how did you get the number?' Baines asked.

'My solicitor gave it me,' said Pearson, reluctantly.

'He did *what?*'

'Sort of inadvertently. It was in the file on his desk. He left it lying open when he went to photocopy something for me. I wasn't going to use it or anything. I just wanted to have it. In case.'

'In case of what?' Tippet asked. 'In case you wanted to hassle her some time?'

'No!' Pearson thought for a few moments. He didn't want to spend another few wasted hours in the police station, and although he didn't feel he owed these bastards an explanation, they had him cornered. He had promised Suzy that he would keep them together. He'd beat the shit out of the stupid bint after they'd gone, but for now, he had a promise to keep. It was important to him not to fail in this. 'You have to understand that Kate walked out on me, taking our daughter with her. She didn't leave a note or a forwarding address. She didn't even get in touch until I heard from her solicitor that she was filing for divorce. I came home on Christmas Eve and she'd gone. Vanished. She took out an injunction against me, saying I wasn't allowed to see my own kid. I had to know *something*, even if I wasn't allowed to talk to them. I needed some way of getting in touch. I never used it,' he added. 'It was just there – a kind of contact.'

'You finished?' asked Baines.

Pearson flushed angrily. 'It's not a crime to be curious,' he said.

'But it is a crime to make threatening phone calls,' Baines answered. 'Get your coat, love.'

Tippet thought Suzy was going to faint, her skin looked so pale against the dark frame of her hair. Almost like a little china doll, she thought.

'Sit down,' Pearson growled. 'You're not taking her anywhere.'

'See sense, Mr Pearson,' Tippet advised. 'If she comes with us voluntarily, she won't necessarily be charged. We just want to clear up a few points. If we have to get a warrant, it'll put my boss in a bad mood. He might decide he might as well go the whole hog and get a conviction.'

'And think what the papers would make of it,' Baines said.

The sneering smile had reappeared on his lips and Pearson wanted to smash his fist into them. But he heard himself mutter, 'Get your coat.'

Suzy's look of terror nearly killed him.

'Davey—' Her voice rose to a wail.

Baines took Suzy by the elbow, gently encouraging her to her feet. The sight of that great bear's paw on her was more than Pearson could take.

'Get your fucking hands off her!' he yelled.

Baines was not impressed. He raised an eyebrow, amused. 'What is it with you, Pearson? D'you like the station tea or what? Now, either you let us get on with our job, or you come back down the nick with us and I charge you with obstructing police officers in the course of their duties.'

Pearson muttered something and Baines asked with offensive civility, 'What was that, sir? I didn't quite catch that.'

'Mr Pearson said something about this being his ex-wife's fault,' said Tippet, who was standing closer to Pearson.

'Do yourself a favour,' Baines advised with avuncular affability. 'Stay away from your ex-wife. You two are in trouble enough already.'

Pearson fell into a truculent silence. He'd give them trouble. And by the time he'd finished with her, Kate would wish she'd never fucked with him. She'd wish she'd never been born.

Chapter Nineteen

'I'll get it,' Kate called. Someone had knocked at the flat door. Mrs Wilson, probably, wanting the television turned down.

Constable Jackson hurried from the kitchen, where she had been toasting bread, just in time to see her charge disappear into the hallway.

'Mrs Pearson, you're not supposed—' she shouted, running through the dining room into the lounge to catch up with Kate. 'I bloody hate baby-sitting,' she muttered, reaching for the door handle. Her hand, greasy from buttering the toast, slipped, and she swore under her breath.

'Mary.' Kate stared at the woman in the main hall, but did not invite her in.

Constable Jackson appeared in the hallway of the flat a little out of breath. To Kate, she was a looming presence, filling the narrow hallway. The constable sensed an awkwardness and was unsure whether she should retreat.

'Hi,' Mary said. 'I came straight in – the front door was open. I hope you don't mind . . .'

Jill Jackson took the woman in at a glance: five feet four, plump, late – no, early – thirties but with her sandy hair cut in a style that aged her ten years. She wore an unflattering coat, the sort Jill's mum might buy because it was warm and be teased for by the family. She carried no handbag but held a straw shopping-bag hooked over one arm.

Kate lowered her cigarette, almost hiding it behind her back. Constable Jackson noted this and was puzzled.

'It's a bit parky out here,' the woman observed.

'Oh, I'm sorry—' Kate backed up, in order to open the door wider, and trod on Constable Jackson's toes. She apologized again, obviously flustered by Mary's unexpected appearance.

The woman stepped inside, smiling shyly. Kate turned to Constable Jackson, intending to introduce her to her friend, but suddenly she wrinkled her nose.

'Can I smell burning?' she asked.

'Shit! The toast. Sorry.' Kate was unclear which Constable Jackson was apologizing for – her bad language or the fire in Kate's kitchen. She hovered indecisively in the hallway.

'Perhaps you'd better see to it,' Kate suggested mildly.

Constable Jackson glanced down at her hands and then at the door handle, then gripped it with fierce determination and rushed into the now smoky lounge.

Kate pulled the door to after the constable and looked at her hand with distaste when it came away from the door handle covered in grease. She dipped into her trouser pocket and fished out a tissue with her crooked little finger, trying to avoid getting grease inside the pocket. She wiped her hand, grimacing.

'Manchester's finest,' she reflected, jerking her head towards the door.

Mary Marchant shrugged her coat off, laughing. Her laughter was chortling and fruity, and it pulled at Kate in a quite unexpected way. Mary hung her coat on one of the brass hooks next to the door and then clicked the flat door closed.

'I'll be surprised if there's anything left of the place by the time she's finished her shift,' Kate muttered.

Mary smiled and shook her head. 'I don't know why you don't buy yourself a proper toaster.'

'Doesn't taste as good as grilled,' Kate answered, wiping the door handle with the tissue. 'First fingerprint powder, now grease all over everything. Worse than having kids around the place,' she went on, and felt a sudden stab of pain below her heart.

Mary seemed to sense something and reached over to touch Kate's arm. Kate saw her own pain mirrored in Mary's face.

'Oh, Mary, I don't know if I can stand any more.'

Mary put her arms round her friend, hugging her tightly. 'You daft sod,' she said. 'All you need to do is ask. I've been waiting for you to call me since—' She didn't finish, for they both knew since when.

Since they had rowed. Since Kate had accused Mary of being responsible for Melanie's death. Since Kate had left the phone off the hook for a week. Since Kate had hung up on her every time Mary had tried to contact her in work.

'I said some terrible things.'

'Nothing I didn't say to myself.'

Kate broke from the hug and held her friend at arm's length, searching her face, seeing the evidence of suffering in the lines around her mouth and eyes.

'You're not to blame for what happened to Melanie. It wasn't your fault.'

Mary's shoulders slumped. 'I've never stopped blaming myself.'

The door opened and Constable Jackson appeared. 'I've, er, I've opened the back door. The smoke's almost gone now.'

Kate nodded, still looking closely at Mary.

'So' – Constable Jackson wiped the door handle surreptitiously with a cloth – 'I'll, um . . . I'll just go and watch a bit of telly, shall I? That's if you're okay.'

'Fine,' answered Kate, frowning a little in irritation.

'Right.' Constable Jackson disappeared.

The silence between Kate and Mary stretched for some minutes. Both recognized the need for adjusting the positions they had held for some months. Both knew there was much to be done in rebuilding their friendship.

'Mary, I—' Kate's voice caught and she found herself close to tears.

Mary flapped her hand at her friend, eventually catching her breath and laughing through her own tears. 'Look at us!' she said, 'blubbing in the hallway when we could be supping tea and eating burnt toast in the comfort of your kitchen.'

'Mother Malone strikes another blow for common sense.' Kate laughed. 'Come in, Mary.'

Mother Malone had been Mary's nickname at school. Mary was the girl everybody went to if they needed to talk. She was renowned for her matronly concern and her wise saws, gleaned from her Irish mother's admonishments.

Kate followed Mary through the lounge. They edged past the dining table at the far end and into the kitchen. Kate watched her heave the shoulder bag up out of the way of the furniture and was reminded of a day trip in the Fifth Form. All of the other girls had brought duffel bags and haversacks in outrageous colours, stuffed with preposterous quantities of food – mostly junk. Mary had brought a straw shopping-bag, carried in the crook of her arm, which contained tuna sandwiches, an apple and a canned drink.

'You can just see her off t' market with her head scarf and her sensible shoes, can't you?' Joy Sheridan had commented. 'I expect she'll look just like her mam at twenty.'

As for the head scarf, Joy's prediction had proved inaccurate at least in this respect, but Mary did look like her mother at twenty, and nobody thought any less of her because of it.

She had vowed to have at least six children, as her mother had, but an ectopic pregnancy, less than six months after Jenny's birth, had put paid to that particular ambition.

Everyone has their own personal tragedy, Kate reflected, recalling Adam's words to her.

'Holy Mary! It's like a bloody ice-box in here,' Mary exclaimed.

'Sorry,' Jill Jackson's voice, sounding thoroughly miserable, carried through from the lounge. The muffled surge of laughter from a quiz show made Kate think for a moment of Melanie, and then she remembered – it had been one of her favourites.

She closed the back door and returned to the dining area, where it was marginally warmer. 'It'll soon warm up,' she said, feeling sorry for the hapless constable. 'We're going to have a chat. You don't mind if I close the door, do you?' She indicated the sliding glass doors on either side of the square arch that separated the lounge from the dining area.

Jill readily acquiesced. ''Course not. Only be sure and lock the back door, won't you?'

'I'll do it now,' Kate answered, obligingly walking back through the kitchen and turning the key in the lock.

She brewed some tea and they sat opposite each other at the tiny kitchen table. Kate examined her friend's face, seeing the lines of worry and sorrow, and the shadows of sleepless nights under her eyes.

'Mary,' she began, hesitantly, 'what you said earlier, in the hall – do you really still feel that way?'

The smile vanished from Mary's face and she stared down into her tea cup. 'If only I'd seen her . . .'

'It was beyond your control – and mine,' Kate urged. 'I wish I could take them back, all the terrible things I said to you. I never meant them.' She shook her head. 'I – I must have been out of my mind when I said them.'

Mary reached across the table and squeezed Kate's hand. 'Of course you were,' she said. 'Wouldn't anyone be who had a heart? To have your child taken from you in that horrible way . . .'

Kate frowned, remembering. 'It was like I had some infectious disease, you know? Melanie had so many friends. I'd see their mothers shopping, walking the kids to school, whatever. They'd act like they didn't know me.' She turned a puzzled face to Mary.

'That must have hurt so much,' Mary said, gently encouraging her to carry on. It was the first time she had heard Kate speak of her own pain. She had turned obsessively, again and again, to how Melanie must have felt and how her little girl had died alone and afraid, but had never spoken of her own fear or of her own suffering.

'I don't think they meant to be hurtful. I mean, I suppose they didn't know what to say to me.' She stared over Mary's shoulder through the frosted glass of the doors, absently taking in the rapid flashes as scenes or camera angles were changed. The dialogue sounded submerged and distant.

'One of them actually crossed the road when she saw me. I looked at her, right at her, because I wanted to know why. You know what I saw in her eyes? Fear.' Kate shook her head, trying to shake the image from her mind. 'I wanted to scream at her, "It's not contagious, you stupid bitch!" ' She sighed, tapping her cigarette into an ashtray.

'It's not contagious,' Kate repeated, 'but it is like a disease. A cancer that eats at you and spreads until it's everywhere and your whole existence is blighted.' She was quiet for some time, and Mary left her to her thoughts. 'I shouldn't have said those things,' she began again, at length.

'You'd been through a lot.'

'It doesn't excuse what I did, what I said, and to you, of all people. Mary—' She paused, waiting until Mary's blue eyes met her own. She willed her friend to believe what she said, 'It wasn't your fault. None of it was.' She shook her head, staring again at the hypnotic patterns of light through the partition door, 'I suppose – I don't know . . .' Kate struggled for an understanding that had so far eluded her. 'You see, I couldn't stand anyone saying anything against her at first, even trivial things, like how messy she was. I'd want to rave at them. How dared they criticize my little girl? I idealized her, I guess. It wasn't that I was avoiding thinking about the other side of her. It was more that I couldn't remember her having any faults. It seemed like every moment with Melanie had been perfect.' She looked over at Mary, her eyes taking several seconds to focus. 'I know what you're thinking.' She smiled.

'What?'

'That it's not right, thinking like that. After all, nobody's perfect, right?'

Mary shrugged.

'I know,' said Kate. 'I know it now. If she'd never given me any grief – any cause for concern,' she hastily corrected herself, 'it wouldn't be normal, would it? I mean, who wants a *Stepford* kid? No, Melanie was a normal, healthy, demanding, difficult eleven-year-old. I can remember the good and the bad times and I still love her. I always will,' she added softly, 'but I can't get over the guilt.' She frowned away Mary's consoling murmur. 'He knows that. Her killer. The maniac who's been sending the messages and the – the things. He knows it, and he's using it for his own sadistic pleasure. Well,

I don't like being used in that way. Once in a lifetime is quite enough for me.'

'Kate, you're worrying me. If you're thinking of doing something daft—'

'*Don't* worry,' Kate said, laughing. 'All I'm saying is I'll do whatever the police suggest if it'll help catch the bastard.' She grew serious. 'You see why I don't want you involved.'

'Kate!' Mary objected.

'And more especially Jenny,' Kate added.

Mary's hand went to her throat. 'God help us. I hadn't thought—'

Kate tilted her head in apology for the fright she had just given her friend, then she looked into her cup. 'I don't want to put anyone else in danger, Mary.'

Mary considered for some minutes, then she said with quiet determination, 'All right. Until it's over I won't insist on your coming round, and I won't bring Jenny here. But I'm your friend, Kate. I'm your *friend*, and I won't let anyone stop me from seeing you.'

'Mary, you don't understand. He's got eyes and ears everywhere. He's watching me. He could follow you home. I don't want you here until it's over and he's caught.'

Mary's face set in a look that Kate knew well. Tight-lipped, immovable, not to be trifled with.

'Mary, will you see sense?' she said.

Mary said nothing in reply but began clearing away the dishes.

'I'll tell the police to turn you away from the door,' Kate warned. 'I'll refuse your calls.'

Mary went through to the kitchen.

'Mary!' Kate exclaimed in exasperation.

Mary turned on the taps to fill the sink with hot water, squirting Fairy Liquid with suppressed rage. She tidied up while the water rumbled into the sink behind her, picking up the empty bread wrapper Constable Jackson had left on the work surface. She flipped open the bin and exclaimed in surprise as smoke from the charred remains of the toast spilled out.

Kate laughed, despite her concern. 'I really must remember to commend Constable Jackson to Inspector Harmon,' she said. 'I'll empty it. You can do the dishes, if it makes you feel better.'

Mary didn't thaw by one degree. She walked through to the main room without a word. After a few seconds' delay, Kate heard the sliding doors open and then the chink of crockery, together with the muffled thanks of Constable Jackson, as Mary collected her mug and plate.

He fingered the hair-clip in gloved hands, tracing the ridges of gold-embossed decoration, and then moved on, picking up the bright-red gloves, limp and lifeless in his hands. Beneath them, the letters. He selected a few for their poignancy and packed them neatly into the lunch box.

He sat with them in his lap and let his eyes drift to the television screen. A tall man – *Black Bobby* – is standing next to Kate. Her hair is loose and tumbles fabulously over her shoulders. *That hair!* How he loved to touch that hair, to stroke it, smell it, let it fall through his fingers . . .

'No, no,' she is saying, 'she should have been with her friend Jenny – her friend. They were going to have tea together.'

Rewind. Replay. Her eyes are wild with grief. Her skin has taken on a waxy pallor. 'She should have been with her friend – Jenny – her friend – Jenny – her friend Jenny – her friend – Jenny—'

'Jennifer, dear,' he breathed, 'you know, she should have

been with you, and she was with me instead. Jennifer, you did a very bad thing.'

It was cold outside. Bitterly cold. No stars were visible in the orange glare from the main road at the front of the house. Cars swished past less frequently now. It was after seven, and the traffic was down to its nighttime levels.

Kate lifted the bin lid and dropped the bag in. Somewhere a dog barked, an ill-tempered, thin yipping.

A movement. Kate turned.

Pain!

She was on her knees, not knowing how she had got there. Stabs of pain shot from her bruised knees to her thighs, and still she wondered.

A hand twisted in her hair and he pulled her closer. She could smell his cologne. The same cologne she had smelled last night, had remembered from somewhere in her past. And she knew.

'David!'

'You fucking killed her, you bitch.'

Kate's head throbbed, and she felt a warm trickle of blood slide from her forehead to her cheek like a slow teardrop.

'You killed her because you couldn't be bothered to look after her, and now I'm taking the blame. You're not satisfied wrecking your own life – you've got to ruin mine as well.' He was crying.

His face in hers. His breath reeking of whisky. On his knees, like her. One hand in her hair, the other gripping a bottle.

Half empty or half full? Kate wondered idly.

His eyes flashed at her and she knew he had wrought himself up into a fever of hatred. She looked into those eyes and saw also the fear and the pain that had always been there, hidden behind his rage, and she knew that she did not fear him, would not fear him ever again.

'You're talking shit,' she said. 'But old habits are the hardest to break, aren't they?'

His mouth worked soundlessly, then he raised the bottle to hit her.

Kate lunged at him, throwing him off balance. She gouged at his eyes and he fell back, screaming, 'Bitch! Fucking bitch!'

Kate swiped at him with her right hand, discovering that she still held the metal bin-lid only as she hit him across the forehead with a hollow *clunk*.

She panted with fear and, yes, excitement. She had hurt him! And she wished she had done it long ago. She had to hold back from hitting him again and again for all the times that he had hurt her.

'Don't call me a bitch,' she gasped. 'And don't ever come near me again, or I'll finish you once and for all.'

He swung at her with his fist, but she parried the blow and clipped him across the ear with the bin-lid. She carried forward, feeling dizzy and nauseous, losing her balance, falling.

She became dimly aware of screaming in the distance. Someone screaming. She wanted to help them, but she couldn't see. The screaming grew fainter, and it was getting darker now, much darker.

In all this dark I should be seeing stars, she thought, and it seemed uproariously funny.

Chapter Twenty

Angie held the door open. She had a look on her face that could drop a charging bull at fifty paces, but she spoke in her usual pleasant tone. 'Sergeant Wainwright, come in. I expect you'll want to talk to Trevor. He's just putting Michael to bed.'

That evening Michael had positively refused to sleep until Daddy had read him a story. Angie showed Wainwright through to the sitting room. The lighting matched the music: subdued, soothing. She offered him a drink, but he refused. He was agitated, even excited. Trevor was right about how he looked. He had lost a good deal of weight since she had last seen him.

'How's Jan?' she asked.

'Fine. Look, this is really important—'

'He'll be down in a moment.' Angie smiled a cool, will-not-be-hurried smile. 'And William?'

'What?'

'How is William?'

Wainwright searched her face for signs of knowledge, understanding, but Angie Harmon was opaque as far as he was concerned, a middle-class, professional woman trying to put a social inferior at ease.

'Will's fine. Jan's fine. I—' He stood, intending to go and find Harmon, but the door opened before he got to it.

'Stretton's on to something, sir.'

Harmon answered him with a puzzled look. He had just returned from Narnia and hadn't quite made the transition to reality yet.

'He thinks he's traced our hacker.'

'Has he, by God?' Harmon's eyes burned with interest. He'd read the message about Melanin, and he didn't find it funny. It was chilling, getting a message from no one out of nowhere, and he had felt then that he had become a little closer to understanding what Kate Pearson had been put through. But Melanie wasn't his daughter, she was Kate's. If the message had given the name of one of his boys . . . He hadn't told Angie about the bulletin, but he had warned her to keep a close eye on the boys.

He had called Stretton immediately after reading the message, asking him to come in, though he was off duty, and see if he could trace the bastard. Stretton had been kept busy, with Technicomm's system being breached at least half a dozen times in a couple of hours, but until now he had not been able to trace the point of access.

'Where is he?'

'Inspector Davies's office, sir.'

Harmon gave Angie a guilty look.

'Go on,' she said, 'but remember, even supermen need some rest.'

Above, a single star, beautiful in its singularity.

Kate tried to blink, but something prevented her eyelid from closing. Her eye watered with the intensity of the light, and she pulled back, away from the restraining influence, regretting the impulsive action as the dull throb in her head became a searing flash of pain that ripped across her skull.

'Ah,' said a voice behind the light, behind the pain. 'Back with us, are you?' And abruptly the light vanished.

Kate stared into the greenish cloud of semicircular afterglow that it left and blinked to try to see beyond it.

'Kate, are you all right?' Mary's voice.

She tried to answer but her mouth was too dry.

'She's fine.' The first voice had answered for her, gradually resolving into a middle-aged, middle-weight man in a white coat. 'Concussion, a few stitches. Nothing to worry about.'

Kate lay back on the pillows and swallowed. 'I wouldn't mind a tea and a smoke,' she murmured, hopefully.

'This is a non-smoking hospital,' the doctor pointed out, unsympathetically, 'but you might manage a glass of water. We'll have to keep her in overnight,' he added, as Mary poured her a glass of water from the plastic jug on the cabinet by the bed. 'Just for obs.' He wrote something down on her chart, then hooked it over the bed rail. 'I'll pop in and see you first thing.' The doctor disappeared through the door and into the corridor, exchanging a few words with someone unseen outside the door.

Mary helped her to take a sip of water, then Kate relaxed against the pillows. '*Now* do you see why I don't want you involved?'

Mary sat on the bed, next to Kate. 'You've nothing to worry about on that score. The police have caught him. They had two constables following him, but they hadn't come into the garden because they didn't really expect you to go out there on your own.' She made it sound like an accusation.

'Don't start on me, Mary. I'm going to have all this to face when Harmon gets here – or has he already been?'

Mary shook her head. 'He was out on a call.'

'What time is it?'

'Half eight.'

'Hadn't you better get off? Tony'll be worrying.'

'He's taken Jenny bowling. He won't be back till nine.'

'Where is he?'

'He's out bowling,' Mary repeated carefully.

'Not Tony – David. It's all right, Mary. I'm concussed, not totally ga-ga.'

'He's safely in the hands of the police. You've nothing to worry about.'

'He's here, isn't he?'

'Kate—'

'I swiped him with the bin-lid. Twice,' she added, with some satisfaction. 'He *is* here, isn't he?'

'Under police guard.'

Kate smiled. 'You do *worry*, Mary. I'm okay, really. He doesn't frighten me any more.'

'Well, he frightens me. He'd frighten you, too, if you had the sense you were born with. But he's in custody, and he's going to stay in custody.'

'This isn't the end of it, you know.'

Mary looked at her, startled. 'What do you mean?'

'It was David who followed me in the fog, last night. But David didn't send the messages. He didn't make the tape. He didn't murder Melanie.'

Mary was silent.

'He's a wife-beater and a bastard, and I hate him. But he didn't murder his own daughter.'

Mary picked at some fluff on the hospital blanket. She coughed. She looked at Kate and then swiftly away.

'Say it,' said Kate.

Mary shrugged.

'You're thinking that someone as violent as David might be capable of anything.' Kate put her hand over her friend's, stilling her nervous movements. '*Almost* anything, Mary. He might kill me,' she said, so dispassionately that Mary stared at her, shocked. Kate carried on, unaware. 'But not Melanie. He always tried to protect her, in his warped way. He always made me lock Melanie out of the room before he – before he started on me. She never saw him—' Kate broke off, gesturing wildly. Mary half-rose, indecisively. 'I'm going to be sick,' Kate said, and threw up over the side of the bed.

The nurse was efficient but unsympathetic, clearing the vomit from the side of the bed and placing a bowl within arm's reach, with an accusatory look.

'I bloody hate hospitals,' Kate grumbled when the nurse had left.

'Tough,' said Mary. She helped Kate to a few sips of water.

Kate rested for a while, and then tried again. 'I really don't think it was David. He hasn't got the self-discipline to do what this guy has done. Dropping a message here, a trinket there, a tape-recording – God, I could kill for a smoke.'

Mary waited for her to continue, which she did, after another sip of water.

'He's still out there, Mary. And he's angry. He could do anything. You must understand why I don't want you around just now. Please say you understand.'

'I see why you *need* me around,' Mary countered.

Kate sighed. 'You always were a bloody-minded Mick.'

'I get it from me mudther,' said Mary, affecting her mother's West Coast brogue. 'I should be mad at you, letting things come to this and you not askin' for help,' she continued, becoming, for a moment, her bright-eyed, soft-skinned mother, 'but, sure, you're more to be pitied than scolded.'

Kate laughed, then stopped abruptly and moved her hand gingerly to her head.

'Well, now I've made you laugh, I'd better go. I'd like to get back before Tony and Jenny.'

Kate saw a picture of Mary greeting them at the door, tea

on the boil, bread in the toaster, smiling and ready to listen. Always ready to listen . . .

'Kate, are you okay?' Mary's voice had an echoing quality.

'Hmm?' she heard herself say. 'I must've drifted off. I'm so tired . . .'

'There's a policeman outside the door, so you'll be all right.' Kate was aware that Mary had raised her voice, trying to reach her, but she couldn't prevent herself drifting off again.

When she came to, the rubber bulb of the emergency buzzer was in her hand. 'Mary!' she called out, in panic.

Mary returned through the door. 'It's all right, love. Do you want me to stay?'

'No, you should go home. But – how?'

'Is that all? I'm getting a ride home in a police car.'

'What will the neighbours think?' Kate wondered, slurring her words, relaxing because she knew that Mary was safe.

'I expect they'll think still waters run deep. Perhaps they'll think I've been caught shoplifting in Sainsbury's.' Mary's eyes twinkled with wicked humour. 'Imagine what a stir that'd cause.'

Kate shook her head, slowly this time, to save herself from further nausea. 'We got you all wrong at school, Mother Malone,' she said. 'You're more of a closet anarchist than an earth mother.'

Mary smiled. 'There's a bobby outside, so you won't feel anxious.'

'So you say. I hope it's not Constable Jackson.'

'Not fair, Kate. You should never have gone out on your own.'

'Okay, my fault entirely.'

'Be sure and tell Mr Harmon that,' Mary chided. 'The poor girl was terrified of what he was going to say to her.'

'I'll put in a letter of commendation if you want me to,'

Kate said, testily. There was a silence, and then Kate smiled by way of apology.

'He's rather a hunky lad,' Mary said. 'Would you like me to send him in?'

'Not just now. I have a headache.'

Mary laughed and waved as she went through the door.

Kate eased back, feeling suddenly lonely. She was in a side room on her own. A sink stood in one corner, soap dispenser above, bin next to it — a simple metal frame with a yellow bin-bag hanging from it. The walls were painted cream. The floors were tiled in flecked grey. Could be any hospital anywhere, Kate thought, and felt a sudden pang of alarm. She hadn't asked Mary where she was.

A glance down at the sheet reassured her: Royal Manchester Hospital was stencilled in green on its crisply turned edges.

Kate started awake. She listened. Again, a timid knock at the door.

'Come in.' She noted with surprise that she was still slurring her words and wondered whether it was the concussion or perhaps some drug she'd been given while she was asleep.

A uniformed policeman put his head around the door. 'Do you want to see a Mr Shepherd?'

'Adam?' Her thought processes worked sluggishly. And what if it wasn't Adam? 'Could you bring him in, please, Constable?'

Kate let out her breath in a whoosh. 'Thank God,' she exclaimed. 'It's you!'

'Of course it's me. Who else would it be?'

She smiled and shrugged. 'It's all right, Constable, thank you. You can leave us. What time is it?' she asked, when they were alone.

'Eleven o'clock. What happened?'

'David happened.'

'You look awful.'

'Thanks.'

Adam sat in the chair by the bed. 'I thought the police were supposed to be looking after you.'

'Yeah, well, Mary called round and—'

'Mary? Your friend, Mary?' he interrupted.

'The very same.'

He was watching her closely, and for a moment she forgot that she had been speaking.

'I'm sorry,' he said, 'you were saying your friend called round and . . .'

'Oh, yes. I . . .' She was finding it hard to remember. 'I – That's it. My police escort was in the other room, and I went out to empty the bin and—'

'You're crazy! You went outside on your own after all that's happened to you? You could have got yourself killed!'

'But I didn't,' Kate stated firmly. 'I didn't get killed and I am all right, and I stood up to him.' A half-smile flickered around her mouth. Adam exhaled, irritatedly and Kate turned her attention to him. 'Who told you I was here? Harmon?'

'Harmon?'

'Well, how did you know I was here? Didn't Harmon tell you?'

'No. Not Harmon. I got a message – an e-mail from you.' He watched her reaction carefully.

'Not from me,' Kate said, shaking her head, provoking a flash of pain and a surge of nausea that reminded her too late that she shouldn't have bothered.

'That's what I thought,' he said, seeming satisfied with her response. He moved to the edge of his chair and leaned forward. Kate had a sudden urge to touch his hair. Before Melanie's abduction, when things were good between them, she had liked combing her fingers through his hair. She frowned. It's the concussion, she told herself. Adam looked up suddenly, and she blinked. The moment had passed. 'I was working late in the office – Kate, I think I'm getting close to the phantom. I've assigned myself superuser status, which gives me total control over the system.' At Kate's look of concern, he added, 'Only so I can check through everyone's files and stuff, try to trace the bastard. He could be in anyone's account. In fact, he's more likely to be using a high-level status entry point, otherwise he wouldn't have been able to get into your report files and alter them.'

Kate recalled the first message she had found, back in November ('Why did you let him hurt me, Mummy?') on a report she had been writing for Owen. And the one with the picture of Melanie, only yesterday. She nodded.

'Anyway, the phantom breaks in, and he's cruising the directories. So I'm on to him.' Adam's eyes glowed with an excitement Kate had never seen before in him. 'He gets a bit frantic when he realizes your account has vanished off the system—'

'You noticed that.'

'Of course I bloody noticed, Kate. I've rooted through just about every account on the system to try and find the phantom. If a new account appears or an old one disappears – especially if it's yours – I notice.'

He had telephoned John James at home. He had been cruising the system for several hours, dipping into directories and files. The shock he had felt on finding Kate's account closed was almost like a physical blow. He spoke, expecting John to be instantly in tune with his own thoughts. 'What the hell is going on?'

'Well, the girls have just about settled, after three more chapters of *My Best Fiend* than I had originally negotiated,'

he began, pedantically. 'Elspeth's dozing in front of the TV.'
He ignored Adam's attempts to interrupt. 'And I'm standing
in a freezing bloody hallway, taking a meaningless bloody
phone call while a tumbler of good malt is calling to me
from the warmth of my sitting room.'

'Kate's account,' said Adam, taking advantage of John's
pausing for breath.

'You'll have to be more specific, I'm afraid,' said John tiredly.
'At this hour my poor brain isn't in random-access mode.'

'Her account,' Adam repeated, with barely concealed irritation, 'why did you close it?'

'I don't know that it's any business of yours why it's closed,'
said John with sudden warmth. 'And I can't say I approve of
your pratting about with my Server.'

'Come on, John. You know I've always played fair by you
– a favour for a favour. This is important. Someone has just
reopened Kate's account and sent me a message.'

Adam could sense the tension even through the miles of
telephone cable. 'What message?'

Adam hesitated, then said: 'Kate's in hospital.'

'Oh, dear Lord.'

'I'm on my way there now, but I want you to tell me why
she closed her account.'

So John had told him. Filling in the gaps in Adam's knowledge of the more recent messages and adding his own suspicions that Kate had been communicating with the hacker.

'You're bloody mad replying to his messages, Kate. You
know that, don't you?'

'I suppose John told you.'

'For God's sake. You could be dealing with a maniac here. A
murderer. And you're acting like it's a bloody Agatha Christie
mystery or something.'

Kate closed her eyes, too tired to argue or explain. 'You're

215

entitled to your opinion,' was all she said. 'So what did the hacker do when he found me gone?'

Adam regarded her speculatively, then, seeming to decide that the argument could wait, he shrugged. 'He went berserk. He was cruising the directories like a trucking maniac. Then' – he shrugged again – 'he vanished.'

'Did you—?'

Adam shook his head. 'He was on for maybe a few minutes and then gone, like some kind of terrorist. Then, a bit later, the Postmaster got a mail message for you, but it was returned: "User Unknown".'

Kate knew that the Postmaster was a way of addressing mail to someone whose location was known but not their full address.

'You didn't trace that, I suppose.'

'It was an anonymous posting, and it was remailed. The bastard takes no chances.'

'He took one yesterday.'

'How do you mean?'

'The spot of bother I had? The one that Mr Harmon hauled you in for? He broke into my flat and added a message to the tape you bought me for my birthday, the Billy Joel.'

Adam's eyes widened. John had not told him this; perhaps he hadn't known. 'They've got his voice on tape?'

Kate shook her head. 'It was Melanie.'

The silence that followed was broken only by the rattle of the plastic jug against the side of the beaker as Kate poured herself a glass of water. She sipped at it, trying to stave off the sickness that had returned, as Adam paced back and forth on the grey tiles.

'I'm that close to him,' he said, pinching a sliver of air between his thumb and forefinger.

'Adam, can you sit down?' she asked. 'Because you're

making me dizzy, prowling round like that, and I'm feeling queasy as it is.'

Adam complied, muttering under his breath.

'You still haven't told me about the e-mail.'

He stared, uncomprehending, for a few moments, lost in thought, then he came to with a gasp of recognition. 'Oh, yeah. Like I said, his mail was returned. Then he logs on again, as systems manager no less, and reinstates your account. Then he disappears for another few minutes and then logs back on as *you*.'

'So the message was mailed in my name. What did it say?'

'I've got it here.' Adam handed Kate a computer printout.

> **Adam, please come.**
> **I'm so afraid.**
> **Am at Mcr Royal.**
> **I need you.**
> **Kate.**

Kate handed back the sheet, wordlessly, and Adam continued: 'At first I thought it was another hoax, so I called the hospital. When they said you were here, I couldn't believe it.'

'How did he know?' How could he be hacking into Technicomm, logging on and off *and* watching her flat? Kate felt chilled and sick and dizzy. 'They'll never catch him,' she said, weakly.

'I've been trying to get at him through another route. Every time he's logged on, it's been via a university or an academic institution. I'm working with some old Internet buddies. They're going to run a check to see if they can pick up any unusual activities from one of the departments at any of the Manchester universities. You know, late-night activity that isn't the norm, someone logging on and off with unusual frequency—'

He broke off, and they both looked towards the door as a commotion built in the corridor outside. Adam barely had a chance to get up when the door was flung open and three men burst in.

Chapter Twenty-one

They grabbed Adam and forced him, face down, on to the bed, protesting.

Kate's added to the confusion of voices. Outside a nurse was shouting, arguing with the constable on duty outside the room. He was trying to calm the woman, reassuring her that everything was under control.

Then Chief Inspector Harmon walked in, and silence fell.

Adam was handcuffed and set on his feet. He stood between two officers. A welt was beginning to form on his right cheek bone, where his face had smashed into the beaker Kate had been holding.

'What is going on?' Kate asked, her voice wavering.

'Take him outside and read him his rights,' Harmon said.

'Now, wait a minute—' Kate's anger suppressed her nausea just enough to keep it under control, but her gorge rose every time she tried to speak. 'What the—' She swallowed. 'What the hell is going on?'

Adam looked terrified, appearing strangely fragile between the two hefty plain-clothes detectives.

'I'm sorry if we frightened you, Mrs Pearson. I assure you, I would not have caused you this upset if it was avoidable. I believed you to be in danger.'

'In danger? From Adam? Don't be ridiculous!'

Harmon gestured for Adam to be taken out of the room, but Kate again intervened. 'No. Whatever it is, Adam can hear it too.'

Harmon's face was grim. 'Very well. We've just come from Mr Shepherd's flat, Mrs Pearson.'

Adam paled.

'I want you to prepare yourself for a shock.'

Get on with it, Kate thought.

'We found articles of clothing and a lunch box which we believe belonged to your daughter.'

'No!' Adam burst out.

'Also, taped messages and letters.'

Kate looked from the inspector, to Adam and back again.

'Letters?' she asked, in a horrified whisper.

'Written by Melanie.'

'Kate, I don't know anything about this.'

Kate looked down at the counterpane, focusing on a rust-coloured spot that might have been blood. If she hadn't already been lying down, she would have fallen.

'Kate, please look at me.'

Harmon's jaw tightened. 'Take him out,' he said between gritted teeth.

'Kate!' Adam called.

Kate looked up at him with unseeing eyes. *Letters*, she kept thinking. *Letters and tapes* . . .

'Kate, I swear to God I don't know how they got there. I don't know anything about this—'

The two detectives dragged him out of the room, but his voice carried from the corridor.

'Kate, I swear I didn't hurt Melanie. I swear—'

Kate focused her gaze on the counterpane again, frowning. Her hands seemed almost to disappear into the whiteness of the bed sheet.

'It's started,' she murmured.

'What did you say?' Harmon asked, alert, ever watchful.

'I'd like some water, please.'

He retrieved the beaker, which had landed some feet away, then returned to the sink to rinse it out.

Kate's eyes were closed, and she looked deathly white, the rich chestnut of her hair mocking the whiteness of her skin. Harmon touched her arm, struck both by its pallor against his own dark skin and by its coldness.

Kate opened her eyes. 'How did you find out?'

'About Shepherd?'

'Was it a tip-off?'

'Oh,' said Harmon, 'I see. You're thinking, perhaps, that he might have been set up.'

'Was he?'

'One of my men has been trying to find out who has been leaving the messages on your e-mail and altering your files. Your employer, Mr Owen, gave him some top-level passwords to help him out. He discovered that Shepherd has been hacking into the Technicomm system for weeks.'

'You asked him to!' Kate protested.

'Yes, but he's also been hacking *out*, into various universities.'

'He wanted to try and track down the hacker. He said he'd use any means available.'

'He sent you some e-mail.'

'Adam did?'

'It was sent from his e-mail address.'

'My account is closed.'

'Which is why it bounced back to Shepherd's mailbox.'

'Adam knew my account was closed. He just told me. And he reckons the phantom can get into anyone's account at Technicomm.'

'The phantom?'

'That's what Adam calls the hacker.'

'Is that what you call him?'

There was a pause. 'I prefer to call him what he is: a murderer.'

'The evidence we found in his flat—'

'Could have been put there by the murderer. He got into *my* flat, didn't he?'

'We think it was Shepherd who broke into your flat.'

'What?'

'He was absent from the office from twelve until two p.m. on Thursday, the day you were attacked. He would have had ample time to tamper with the tape-recording during that time.'

'But he helped me to track down the credit-card purchases.'

'A good way of throwing suspicion off himself.'

'Why would he be so careless as to send me e-mail without using a remailer? All the e-mail I've had since this started has been sent anonymously via a remailer.'

'He was desperate to get in touch with you. You weren't accessible at the office any more. As I've already said, he seems to need to communicate with you.'

'If it was Adam, all he'd have to do is pick up the phone. He's got my home number. And he knows where I live.'

'He needs to communicate from a position of control,' Mr Harmon expanded.

They regarded each other for some time without speaking.

'What did the message say?'

' "No more games." '

'Is that it?'

Harmon nodded.

Kate sipped at the water. Her head was pounding. 'You interviewed him just after Melanie was found. He was in the clear.'

'We've found . . . discrepancies in the timing of the alibi he gave us.'

'What discrepancies?' Kate demanded.

'Mrs Pearson, I would like to interview Mr Shepherd before I go into any more detail, but I can say that his movements are not fully accounted for, and we now believe he could have abducted Melanie in July.'

'No,' said Kate. 'No, it's not possible.'

'I'm sorry.' Harmon stood by Kate's bed. She had closed her eyes, and he saw that she was exhausted. 'Try to get some rest,' he advised. 'I'm truly sorry about all this.'

Kate made no response and he stood there for some minutes longer, wondering whether to pursue his line of reasoning with her, to tell her that Shepherd had been closer to her than anyone throughout the whole ordeal, which meant he was in a better position than most to set her up. He thought he should tell Kate that the quirky, twitchy hacker had form. He was unstable, by all accounts. That he had coolly manipulated her while playing the part of the outraged protector.

Shepherd had met Melanie on a number of occasions, and the shrinks reckoned the child had probably gone with a man she knew. Harmon could point out that Shepherd had known exactly how the hacker had got Kate's credit-card number. He also had the kind of knowledge of computer systems that could get him access to bank records. He knew the layout of her flat. As for the taped message, Shepherd had provided her with the damned music tape in the first place.

Tonight Shepherd had known to find Kate in the hospital. Would Kate be surprised if Harmon told her that listening equipment had been found in Shepherd's flat? A search of Mrs Pearson's place would, Harmon was confident, turn up some kind of bugging device. But now was not the time to ask for permission to search.

Now was not the time for any of this. Kate was ill, and

the very fact of the existence of the letters and tapes would be about as much as she could deal with at the moment. Harmon reflected that they had handled this badly, allowing Shepherd so much free rein, not having his alibi checked more thoroughly, letting her ex get so damn close . . .

In the corridor Wainwright was waiting.

'How is she?'

'How d'you think?'

'She's taking it hard?'

'She isn't taking it at all, Sergeant. She can't believe that the man she trusted most in the world could be the monster who killed her little girl.'

'Bastard.'

'Where is he?'

'At the nick by now. Shall I get an interview room set up?'

'No. Let him sweat – but make sure he does it safely. I want him handled very carefully. We don't want any mistakes on this one, you understand me?'

Wainwright understood perfectly well. He'd found it hard enough to keep his own hands off the pervert. He wasn't entirely sure if his officers could maintain the same self-control, but he had already warned them of the possible consequences of a lapse of discipline, and he would look over the duty rota carefully when he got back and choose only people he knew he could trust to keep their hands in their pockets if they felt themselves provoked.

Harmon read Wainwright's thoughtful expression but reserved comment. 'Get Craine in, will you?'

'He's on leave for a few days.'

'Even so.'

'Sure, but what for?'

'Didn't you say he'd shown an interest in this case? I'm

going to let him do a warm-up routine on our Mr Shepherd.' Harmon walked off.

'Where are you going, sir?'

'I'm going to get some rest, Sergeant. I suggest you do the same. You're looking a little ragged. The lab results won't be in until tomorrow. There's nothing more to be done tonight. Once you've rearranged the duty rota, the evening is yours. I'll meet you back here at seven thirty in the morning. I should think Mrs Pearson will be awake by then. We'll get her permission to go over her flat again.'

It was already after midnight, and Wainwright would be glad of a few hours' sleep. He wasn't the only one who was bushed, the sergeant thought. Harmon looked like he could do with a few days' leave himself, but he also seemed pretty close to contented, and that was something of a feature.

All hell would break loose within the next twenty-four hours. It was as well that neither of them knew it then.

Chapter Twenty-two

Jenny was dressed for bed when Mary got in.

'How was she?'

'Okay,' said Mary. 'Fine.' Throwing Tony a look that said there was more to tell.

'Is she coming for Christmas dinner?'

'No, Jenny, love.'

'Oh.'

'But she sends her love. And she said to say sorry she didn't send you a card on your birthday.'

Jenny frowned. '*That* doesn't matter,' she said, echoing Mary's earlier conversation with Kate.

'I told her you didn't mind. She's—' Mary gave her husband another signal, 'she's got a few things to sort out, and then she promised she'll come and see us.'

'You said she'd come for Christmas,' Jenny accused.

'I said I'd do my best to get Aunty Kate to come.'

'You promised!'

'Jenny, your mother said no such thing. Now, stop getting yourself into a pet.'

'I'm not! I'm NOT!'

'Jenny, that'll do.'

The girl glared at her mother and father, seething.

'Love, I know you're disappointed, but—'

'I'm not. I hate her. I never want to see her again.' She jumped up and ran out of the room, leaving her parents in baffled silence.

Tony saw Mary's eyes fill with tears. 'She's been on edge all night,' he said.

'Seems like she's been that way ever since it happened,' said Mary. 'I don't know how to get through to her any more. Whatever I do, whatever I say, it's wrong.'

'She's upset, love.'

'So am I.' Mary heard the sharpness in her voice, and began apologizing, but her stricken look was ample apology.

Tony cut in: 'It's okay.' The silence grew uncomfortably long. He asked, 'Did she really say she'd come over on New Year's Day?'

'She said she'd try.'

'Jenny's taking it very hard.'

Mary bit her lip. 'I'm doing all I can, Tony.'

'I know, but—'

'But what? What more can I do? Drag Kate here, kicking and screaming?'

'Hey, hey, come on now.' He put his arms around his wife.

'She – David was there – She went out to empty the bin. The smoke was – Oh, I don't know what I'm saying.' She paused to gather her thoughts, and then began again, 'Kate's in hospital, Tony.'

'Oh, my God. David?'

Mary nodded. 'He was waiting in her garden. He hit her with a *bottle*, for God's sake.'

'Is she all right?'

Mary sighed. 'Concussion. She said she's not afraid of him any more.'

'Where is he? Do they know?'

'They caught him.'

'Just as bloody well.'

'Kate whacked him with a bin-lid.'

It seemed almost comical, but Tony couldn't bring himself to smile. He had met David Pearson only once. He'd come round to the house just after Kate had left him. It was Christmas Eve, and Tony had nipped out to get some replacement bulbs for the fairy lights on the Christmas tree. Pearson had shouldered past Mary into their sitting room. He had threatened to carve her up if she didn't tell him where Kate was.

Tony arrived home to find Mary struggling with Pearson and Jenny screaming hysterically, trying to pull him away from her.

It had ended up with Pearson bleeding on the pavement and Mary pulling Tony off the bastard. Pearson had pressed charges for assault and battery. The case had gone to the Crown Court, and there had been months of worry before it had come up for trial. Tony had been appalled to find himself in the dock, and further outraged that the prosecuting counsel made much of the brutal attack on his client. He had been acquitted, but the episode had left a scar of its own.

'He'll probably sue Kate for assault,' he remarked, bitterly.

Mary bit the side of her mouth and made no reply.

A keening sound, like that of a sick animal, shivered the frozen air and, in a corner of their living room Suzie crouched, wounded and mortally afraid. They had released her without charge, joking that she and David were like Box and Cox. He was under arrest, and she wasn't allowed to speak to him. She was alone, and her solitude was crippling.

Mary tapped lightly at Jenny's door.

'Go away!'

'I can't. I want to talk to you.'

'Well, I don't want to talk to you.'

'Come on now, Jenny—'

'Go away! I hate you!'

'No, you don't.'

'Yes, I do. I hate *her* as well. You promised she'd come.'

'Jenny, your Aunty Kate hasn't been well.'

Silence.

Mary stared at the 'Keep Out' sign trimmed with gold tinsel, thinking, Jenny never used to be like this. God help us all when she hits the hormone hell of the teenage years.

'She really wants to see you.'

'Then why won't she come?'

'I told you, she's got things to do, but she'll try and be here on New Year's Day.'

'She's just saying that to put you off. She won't come on New Year's either.'

'Look, can I come in? I can't have a conversation through a door.'

Mary took the answering silence for an invitation and cautiously opened the door.

Jenny had been crying, she could see that, and she could feel her daughter's anger and frustration like a solid mass between them.

'I wanted Aunty Kate to come too,' Mary ventured.

'Then why didn't you make her come?'

She sat on the end of the bed, uninvited. The dolly-mixture covers had been rejected some months ago as infantile and replaced by peach cotton with ruched edges that were torture to iron.

'You can't make people do things like that, Jenny. They've got to want to.' She thought for a moment, wondering how much to say and how best to put it to her daughter without frightening her. She decided it would be best not to say

229

anything about Kate being in hospital. 'Aunty Kate's still very sad—'

'You mean, she's depressed. You think I'm stupid, but I know people can get depressed. I may be just a kid, but I know that.'

'All right, yes, Aunty Kate is depressed. She's still feeling terrible about what happened to Melanie, and she doesn't think she'd be very good company on Christmas Day.'

'I got her a present and everything.'

'I know. I'm disappointed too. But you can give her your present when she does come.' Mary picked up one of Jenny's soft toys, a white polar bear with cat-soft fur, and began stroking it, wanting to smooth Jenny's hair and knowing she would resent it.

'What if—'

'What, love?'

'What if she never comes?'

'She will, Jen. I'm sure of it.'

'No, she won't.'

'What makes you think that?'

'Because you had a row and she's not your friend any more.'

Jenny had turned away to the wall, moving so that her back didn't touch her mother.

'Don't you ever have arguments with your friends, Jenny?'

'Sometimes.'

'Well, you don't fall out for ever, do you?'

'I'm still not speaking to Penny Barnsley.'

Mary smiled. 'It's only been a week since you fell out with her.'

'But you and Aunty Kate haven't been speaking for ages.'

It was difficult to argue with that, so Mary didn't try. 'That's true, but we made up our differences tonight. We're friends again,' she said.

'Honest?' Jenny turned a hopeful face to her mother.

'Cross my heart.'

'*Best* friends?'

'Like peas in a pod.'

'Only—'

'Yes, love?'

'Penny Barnsley said her mum said how if it was her, she'd never be able to forgive you.'

Mary stiffened. No wonder Jenny had been falling out with her friends if this is what they were saying to her. 'Did she, now?' Jenny nodded. 'You can tell Penny Barnsley that if brains were dynamite, she wouldn't have enough to blow her hat off.'

'I did. Well, sort of.' Jenny blushed, remembering that what she had actually said would not have met with her mother's approval. 'Mum . . .'

Mary sighed, knowing what was coming next. 'What, love?'

'Did Aunty Kate blame you – for not picking up Mel? Is that why you weren't friends any more?'

Mary deliberated. Protecting Jenny from the truth of Kate being in hospital was one thing, but she didn't like telling outright lies. She wasn't much good at it, and anyway Jenny seemed to have a talent for snouting out the truth. 'We rowed about it, yes,' she began. 'Aunty Kate was so upset about Melanie—' Jenny set up a wail that froze Mary to the core. 'Jenny, love, what is it?'

'It's all my fault!' The wail rose to a screech and Mary heard Tony run up the stairs.

'Mary?'

'It's all right, Tony.'

He hesitated outside the door, but she heard him slowly returning to the living room a few moments later.

Jenny was becoming hysterical. Mary took her by the shoulders and shook her. 'Now stop that noise,' she commanded.

Jenny broke down into choking sobs and covered her face with her hands.

'Jenny, what is it? You can tell your mum.'

'It's a-all my f-fault,' she sobbed.

'What is?'

'Melanie-ee.' Jenny flung herself face-down on the bed, weeping uncontrollably, her whole body convulsed.

Mary reached out, almost afraid to touch her, and her own eyes filled with tears. She pulled herself together and tried again: 'Now, you'd better stop this nonsense. It is *not* your fault. Melanie was – was taken by a bad man. It isn't your fault that happened.'

Jenny wiped her nose with her hand, turning her face from her mother. She hitched and coughed until Mary was afraid she would choke, then she managed to cry: 'But it i-is. It's a-all because of m-me . . .'

'Jenny, you're not making sense.' She stroked her daughter's head for a few minutes, and Jenny became a little calmer, eventually sitting up and blowing her nose. 'You'll have to explain to me, love. Mummy doesn't understand.'

Jenny showed her a face of absolute misery. 'O-okay,' she sighed. Mary brushed a stray lock of hair from Jenny's eyes and Jenny began: 'We—' Her eyes filled with tears.

'Go on, love.'

'I can't. Not while you're looking at me.'

'Okay, I'll look at this luscious poster of Gary, or Barry, or Dean, or whatever his name is, shall I?' No smile. Not even a flicker of annoyance that her mother could never remember the name of her current hero. Mary felt a pang of anxiety. She sat by her daughter, one arm around her shoulder. Jenny looked at her hands, compulsively squeezing a tissue in her lap.

'We had an argument,' Jenny said, ''cos I wanted her to invite Liz Turner to her party and she didn't want to and—'

She stopped to wipe away fresh tears. 'And I called her snidey and she said she was going to walk home on her own.' Jenny broke down again, unable to go on.

For a moment Mary was stunned, realizing that all the times she had wondered aloud how Melanie could possibly have got past her had deepened Jenny's feelings of responsibility. Jenny had kept this a secret for so long, blaming herself. Then she hugged Jenny, saying, 'Lots of girls walk home from school alone. You weren't to know—'

'But I knew she was going the long way round, so's you wouldn't see her, but I didn't say—'

'Jenny.' Mary knelt before her daughter, wiping away her tears. 'You can't blame yourself for what happened to Melanie. The only one who's to blame is the man who took Mel away from us.' She smoothed her daughter's hair and eased her into bed.

Jenny was hot with crying and she hiccuped and sobbed miserably, but after a few minutes, she became calmer. Mary crooned and soothed until Jenny lifted her head from the pillow and asked: 'Mum, you won't tell Aunty Kate, will you?'

Mary stopped crooning. 'Why not, love?'

'She already hates me, and if you tell her, she'll hate me for ever.'

'No, love, that isn't true. Your Aunty Kate loves you. She always has and she always will.'

Jenny muttered something Mary didn't catch.

'What was that?'

'I said I wish it'd been me instead of Mel.'

Mary was seized with fear for her daughter. She took her by the shoulders and shouted at her: 'Jenny, you mustn't ever say that. Your dad and me would be lost without you.' Jenny's eyes widened with fear, and Mary eased her grip, talking more gently. 'We love you so much.' She kissed her daughter's hot forehead.

Jenny was crying again. 'I'm sorry, Mummy. I don't really hate you.'

'I know that, Jen.'

'And I don't hate Aunty Kate, even if she does hate me.'

'Which she doesn't. Look, why don't I bring you a nice cup of hot chocolate? You can listen to your radio for half an hour if you like.'

Jenny nodded, recognizing this as a privilege usually reserved for times of sickness. As her mother went to the door, she asked: 'But you won't tell her, will you, Mum?'

He sat outside in the darkness. The education department was tricky; they had mostly closed down for the holidays. But he had found a way in by sheer, dogged determination. Every company, every institution – administrative or academic – had some way in. E-mail provided the easiest trapdoor, for what was the use of being on the Internet if you couldn't exchange mail day and night? So day and night, workdays, weekdays, high days and holidays, he always found an entry route.

Their computerized records had obligingly listed all the girls named Jennifer that attended Trafford Park High School. He eliminated a dozen by their birth date, and that left three in the right year group. Jenny (*her friend Jenny*) would be in year eight now.

He had played back the tape of her conversation with the woman visitor the night before and had picked up several names. Constable Jackson – she was irrelevant – and the name Mary. Mother Malone had cropped up a little later, some facile joke, no doubt. Tony had also been mentioned. The visitor's husband, he surmised. But the most beautiful moment had been when he discovered that this was Jenny's (*her friend Jenny's*) mother. He had almost lost it in the babble of television noise, but it was there. And he had heard it from Kate's own lips. Of course, he would have found her anyway by a simple process of *elimination*. The word intrigued him: it posed other amusing diversions on his route to Katie.

In the event, the eventual location of the child was not as straightforward as he had expected, but this merely added to the *thrill of the trace*. He smiled at his witticism. There was no Jennifer Malone listed. There was a Jennifer Gordon, a Jennifer Marchant and a Jennifer Sheridan. Where, then, was Mother Malone?

It had not taken a great leap of the imagination to deduce that the term was no more than a childish nickname. And, of course, he had the first names of Jenny's parents. Sheridan's parents were listed as Andrew and Gillian, Gordon's as Darren and Michelle. Which left Katherine's good and loyal friend, Mary Elizabeth Marchant, 53, The Leas, Old Trafford, Manchester. A bit up-market from Katie's rather seedy domicile. Well, Mother Marchant, I've found you out.

And here he was, outside their door, and they unaware, inside. He would make his move soon. Christmas Eve held a certain attraction. It would give a dramatic flourish to Kate Pearson's final isolation, he thought.

Chapter Twenty-three

Kate slept badly. The nurses kept coming in every half hour to do her obs, presumably to ensure she didn't sink irretrievably into a coma. The intervals were increased through the night, and she slept undisturbed from four until five, waking abruptly in a sweat. She had followed the man with no face through the woods, hearing Melanie calling to her for help.

She had tracked the man closely, certain that he would lead her to Melanie, but as she had followed, Melanie's voice had grown fainter and fainter, until Kate had become frantic. She ran through the tangle of brambles and ferns, crashing through dense summer growth, tearing her clothing, desperate to reach Melanie before it was too late. And then she remembered that Melanie was dead, and she wept in helpless grief.

In her torment she became confused and lost the trail, wandering for some time along paths that petered out in dead ends, rabbit warrens and fox runs.

Then, impossibly, he was back. The faceless man was watching her, sitting on a boulder beside a stream, and behind the formless mask Kate knew that he was smiling. He sprang to his feet and ran, laughing, into the woods.

Kate found herself in an old house, not knowing how she had arrived. The house was cold, and she was shivering. She tried each door, but the rooms were all empty. Bare floors and white-painted walls, clinically clean.

She made her way, up a winding staircase, to the door of an attic room and was surprised to find that it gave on to an open area that took in the entire top floor of the house. The floor was bare boards, and she thought she could smell the faint after-aroma of varnish.

There were windows on each wall of the room, through which Kate could see wide vistas of the city.

'I can see everything from here,' a voice said. Familiar, yet elusive.

Kate turned sharply and saw, where there had been nothing before, a desk. On the desk, a computer, linked to a printer and modem and, sitting at the desk, the faceless man.

Only he wasn't faceless any more. He wore the face of David.

Kate lay in the orange glow of a night light, orientating herself and focusing on her breathing. Her pulse slowed, heartbeat by heartbeat and the painful hammering in her chest gradually abated.

Why had she dreamt of David as the faceless man? she wondered.

Because Mary had thought him capable of murdering Melanie?

Perhaps.

Because David was a cowardly sadist?

Possibly.

Could it be David?

She made herself consider the possibility seriously. The police were convinced it was someone close to her, and if they hadn't been able to find him, that meant he had covered his tracks very carefully. Or that he was someone she – and they – were unlikely to suspect.

David's work allowed him to travel all over the city and beyond, to Bolton, St Helens, Warrington. He could go where he liked, when he liked, his bosses trusted him, and as long as the sales kept rolling in . . .

He had accused Kate of killing Melanie. That was nothing new. He had often blamed her for his own actions, claiming, 'I wouldn't have done it if you had—'. If she had got the dinner ready on time, if she hadn't said the wrong thing at the wrong moment, if she had been able to convince him that she adored him and hung on his every word, if she had been a better wife/lover/mother, if she had read his mind, submitting always to his will, his judgement, his desires . . .

That she hadn't been able to please him in any of these respects had, naturally, been her fault. And when he beat her and humiliated her, it was, to him, a natural consequence of her own failings.

But Kate sensed that the accusation *You killed her* was different in tone from the usual charge. It did not carry the implication *You made me do it*. He hadn't gone into one of his whinging tirades of *Look what you made me do*.

Anyway, Kate suddenly remembered, Mary had told her he'd been arrested back at her flat. Constable Jackson and two officers who'd been following him had virtually flattened him, she'd said. That meant Adam had received the e-mail telling him that she was in hospital *after* David's arrest. She supposed it was possible to delay the e-mail by re-routing it. And APSs always slowed things down. But Adam hadn't said anything about remailing. He had said that the message had been sent to him from her reinstated account. At that time of night, with so few people using the system, the mail would arrive within minutes. She needed to check times with Adam, but she didn't suppose DCI Harmon would be over-enthusiastic about letting her speak to him. She could ask Harmon when they had traced the other message – the 'No more games' message – but what would that prove? If she could check it against the time of David's arrest, it might put him in the clear. At least on that score.

Kate's head pounded. Why am I trying to find a way out for that bastard? She wondered. Two reasons came to mind, one was that she didn't want to believe that Melanie's own father could have done those terrible things to her, and the other was that she wanted to get the right man. It wouldn't satisfy her that somebody had been punished, that wasn't enough. Unless she could be certain that the man who had hurt Melanie had been caught, she could never rest easy.

Kate was pulled up short by the grim realization that the murderer wouldn't let her rest easy until he was caught. And somehow she didn't think giving himself up was part of his plan.

The other men who knew her all had alibis. It had to be a man, she thought, for what kind of woman would snatch a child and murder her? A woman with a man, maybe, like Hindley and Brady. Kate shivered, remembering that they had buried their victims on the moors not far from Manchester. The idea brought her back to David and his girlfriend. All right, she thought, all right, I won't rule him out.

Bob Newman had been at a conference in Liverpool the day Melanie disappeared. Ingrams had been in America. Adam was at the hospital with his dying friend. All confirmed. But Harmon had said they had discovered 'discrepancies'. What did that mean? And if they were wrong about Adam, could they have been wrong about the others?

Her mind turned to Adam. The police had found evidence in his flat. Kate had trusted Adam more than anyone. Had he been playing with her feelings? Helping, or pretending to help her, so that he could be close to her, watch her going through the nightmare of the last five months? Could he—?

There was, in his past, something he would never talk about, something he had only hinted at. He said he had made a mistake. She felt that Sims was bound up in it in some way. He was an unlikely friend for Adam. Cropped hair, tattoos, more often than not stoned, Sims was a creature who could not be bound by convention or law. He was thick-set and had the air of a belligerent bear, that is, until he got sick. Kate couldn't abide him. His aggression reminded her too much of David's defensive swaggering.

Adam referred to his mistake. What sort of mistake? Harmon was strange with him. It was like he was waiting for Adam to trip up, watching him with the intense concentration of a hunting cat. It made her uncomfortable. The cool detach-ment with which he waited for Adam to lose his footing had brought out the nervous, eyebrow-stroking gesture, which meant that Adam was aware of it too – it wasn't her imagination.

Adam had met Melanie several times. The three of them had even gone roller-skating together. Melanie liked Adam. She said he was a good laugh. High praise indeed.

But Adam?

He had the skills. He knew a lot about computer systems. Although they were employed at the same level, Adam had an affinity, almost a rapport, with computers. He described it as computer logic. When you tuned into it, you could work out just about any problem. Adam rarely referred to program manuals and seemed to take it as a defeat when he was forced to it.

The killer had the same affinity, but—

Kate groaned. 'I can't stand this,' she muttered and reached for the jug of water.

Adam had helped her. He had never pushed, never rushed,

never made her feel any obligation – except that time in the restaurant . . .

But she had been patronizing. He had every right to be angry. Kate's eyes opened. If his anger was justified, wouldn't that give him more excuse to act on his anger? How many other times had she laughed at him, patronized him, made him feel like a naïve kid? She tried hard to remember, frowning a little as she did so. Were they getting on well in the summer, before Melanie was killed? She thought so. She had thought then that she and Adam would become lovers. Kate hadn't felt so good since . . .

She gave up on it. It was painful to think of feeling good when her daughter was dead. Worse than this – it seemed to cheapen Melanie's memory.

The nurse came in and checked Kate's temperature, pulse, blood pressure and pupil dilation, asking her the same pointless questions she had asked on her previous visits. Kate answered mechanically, and then the nurse was gone.

Kate sighed, knowing that her thinking was wrong, convinced as never before by the argument that a time comes when the grieving must be left in the past and the future must be looked to. Conscious that the future she so hungered for was wrapped up in a fantasy of revenge against Melanie's killer, conscious too that this in itself was another kind of wrong-thinking but determined not to let it go.

Adam, she conceded, had had the opportunity, but did he have the motive? Only a weak man would make a motive out of a few jibes and a little loss of face. Was Adam weak? She thought about the sensitive, unassuming man who had, so many times in the previous months, offered himself as a prop, a support in her sorrow. How often she had rebuffed him, and yet he was always there, ready to help whenever he could. Was that weakness?

Nevertheless, the tapes and letters – Kate felt a wave of

nausea, and lay back against the pillows, focusing on her breathing, keeping it even, waiting for the wave to break and recede.

When it finally did, she had come to a decision.

Five thirty. The cell was dark as the pit of hell. Stale urine, stale sweat and the halitotic stench of old vomit breathed from its pores. The combined odours were overlaid with strong disinfectant. Adam could hear a drunk heaving and puking in the next cell.

Kate eased herself out of bed. The pain in her head had receded to a dull throbbing and she stood, taking care not to move too quickly. The bedside cabinet was the most obvious place, she reasoned.

She clicked the cabinet open, anxiously checking the door of her room as she did so, but it remained shut. Faint murmurings and occasional footsteps could be heard outside; she would have to bide her time and choose her moment well. The plastic carrier bag bore the logo 'Manchester Royal Infirmary', and it contained all that Kate needed.

'What've you got for me?'

The man in the lab coat looked tired. His hair stood up in startled tufts, and he had at least a day's growth of stubble.

'Not much. The letters match samples of handwriting we got from her school. The tapes are standard Scotch, normal bias, C90s.'

'You can tell me your life story when I've got a bit more time,' said Wainwright. 'Are there any prints?'

The man in the lab coat shook his head. 'No fingerprints,

no hair, no residue, except for a trace of powder that probably came from the inside of a surgical glove.' He gestured to the various items, bagged and labelled, that had been removed from Shepherd's flat. 'The letters, the tapes, the lunch box – every item has been wiped scrupulously clean. I'd say the guy has a bit of an obsession about it.'

'About what?'

'Cleanliness. These things haven't just been wiped for prints, they've been polished.'

'Polished?'

'Literally. Mr Sheen.'

'Seriously?'

'That's what it smells like to me. You'll have to wait for the test results for confirmation, but—'

'If you say so, that's good enough for me.' Pete's olfactory organ was legendary. He had won innumerable bets, guessing the women clerks' perfumes, and he had once identified seven different types of bottled lager by the aroma alone.

Wainwright rubbed his chin. He'd have to shave before the guv'nor got in. He had gone home, as instructed, but had been unable to rest, expecting William to wake up at any moment and begin his nocturnal prowling. At night, while they slept, William seemed to take special pleasure in destructive exploration. Not enough to find the biscuit tin and gorge; William would empty cornflake packets, flour, jam, butter and milk on the floor. Usually, by the time they had found him, he had moved on to some other form of amuse-ment and seemed to have forgotten what he had done. So Wainwright sat, nursing a glass of beer and watching late-night TV until he couldn't stand it any more, then he had made breakfast and come back into work.

'Thanks, Pete.'

'I know it's not much help,' said the man in the lab coat.

'Yeah, but it helps to have the facts straight before we start the interrogation.'

'I hear Craine's doing a warm-up.'

'News gets around.'

'He called in to find out what the lab results were.'

Wainwright nodded, relaxing. He didn't like gossip; it had a habit of getting round more than just the station. His own problems had, he knew, done the rounds and been distorted by the Chinese whispers of the station grapevine, but if Craine had passed on the information to Pete, it was okay by him.

'Was he disappointed?'

'You know DI Craine. Man of a few words.' Pete chuckled. 'But they were well-chosen ones.'

It hadn't been a surprise, the evidence being clean. There had been no prints on the package sent to Mrs Pearson. It was disappointing, however. The evidence against Shepherd was purely circumstantial, and the absence of fingerprints didn't strengthen it one bit.

'Shouldn't you be watching Mrs Pearson?'

Constable Bingley smiled. It was the smile he reserved for the prettiest girls, and it was effective. Nurse Ford was dazzled.

'I'm only here to reassure her, really,' he explained. 'We've got the bastard who's been after her – pardon my language. But that's what he is. Anyone who can put a girl through all that—'

Nurse Ford warmed to him.

'I expect Harmon'll put us off escort duty tomorrow morning anyway.'

'Harmon?'

'My guv'nor. Good bloke. Black guy,' he said, as though the two made a surprising contradiction.

Nurse Ford raised her eyebrows.

Constable Bingley blushed disarmingly. 'That didn't come out right,' he said.

Kate listened at the door. Muffled conversation. She opened it a crack and peered across to the nurses' station. Light spilled out from it on to the corridor. Inside, her police escort was leaning with his back to the main window. He seemed to be chatting up one of the nurses.

Kate readied herself to creep across to the island station, her shoes in hand. A voice, raised. One of the bays. She had been brought here on the day Melanie's body had been found, so she knew that the hospital wards consisted of a combination of bays and side wards, with a glass box called the nurses' station at the head of each, and with enough space to manoeuvre a trolley-bed around its perimeter.

Kate listened. Someone was being sick, and a nurse was reassuring her. Nice to have a bit of sympathy, she thought, remembering her own bout of vomiting earlier.

Laughter floated through the open door. The nurse was flirting with the policeman. 'No time like the present,' Kate muttered and eased herself through the door.

Just then, a noise. The policeman's voice getting suddenly louder. Kate ducked back inside. She scrambled into bed and pulled the sheets up around her neck as Constable Bingley put his head round the door.

'Asleep,' she heard him whisper to someone outside.

Now what? she asked herself. Kate stepped cautiously on to the cold linoleum tiles, shoes still in her hand, and looked around the room. There were two doors. One led to the corridor, the other to a combined shower and toilet. She checked it, not holding out any hope, and discovered a second door, opposite the one that gave into her room.

Apparently, the facilities were shared with the patients in the bay adjacent to her room.

She slipped the bolt and opened the door a crack. The bay was empty. So near to Christmas, a lot of the non-emergency patients had been sent home. Kate locked the door leading to the side ward and crept out into the bay. She could hear the police escort pacing outside. She moved to the far side of the bay, keeping back from the entrance, out of his line of sight. The nurses' station was empty. If she could get to the far side of it, she would only be a few feet away from the corridor leading to the lifts.

At least she hoped that was where the corridor on the far side of the glass box would lead. When she had been here last, Kate had been taken to the second floor. This floor was somewhere higher in the building – the third, or fourth, she guessed – and if she was going to get out without being seen, it had better be just like the second floor. There was a six-foot gap between the nurses' station and the bay. If she could get to the station, she could keep low and avoid notice.

'Anything I can do?' the policeman asked. He had his back to her.

A nurse's voice carried down the corridor. 'She'll be okay. Hasn't taken the anaesthetic very well, that's all.' Kate heard bed curtains being drawn and took a chance that the constable would still be looking in the direction of all the noise.

She made it to the nurses' station and waited. He hadn't seen her. The nurses' voices became hushed. Move or stay? Kate heard footsteps approaching and that decided her. She made a dash for the walled corridor on the far side of the nurses' station.

As she eased herself down the passage, past the store rooms and showers, she heard the constable resume his pacing, and prayed that he wouldn't check on her again. She wasn't about to wait and find out, however, but made straight for the fire escape and started the dizzying descent to the ground floor.

Six a.m. It would be dark for another two hours. Claustrophobia closed in. Adam watched the hatch of the cell door. It would open in another five minutes and the duty sergeant would check on him. Adam held down the terror he felt by telling himself that soon he would see a brief shaft of light as the hatch opened, and he would have proof that the duty sergeant was still there, that he hadn't been forgotten. He told himself that they would have to let him out soon, if only to interrogate him.

'What the f—' Constable Bingley had followed Nurse Ford into the side ward. Kate Pearson was missing. 'How did she get past me? I've been here. How could she? I checked on her at half five. You saw me, didn't you? You saw me check on her.'

Nurse Ford tried the door to the toilet. It was locked. She banged on the door. 'Mrs Pearson, are you all right?' No answer.

Bingley followed her round into the bay. She opened the door into the toilet. It was empty.

'Oh, shit,' said Bingley. 'My guv'nor's going to hang me by the balls.'

'Breakfast.' The duty sergeant passed a tray through the hatch. Adam's stomach rolled. 'I don't think I can—'

'Try a bit of toast and tea. You're going to need it.'

'Can I see Mr Harmon?'

'Bit early in the day.'

*

'I don't know how she could've got past me, sir,' Bingley protested. Wainwright was giving him the evil eye and he flushed, but his boyish ingenuousness held no fascination for his superior.

'Have you any idea when she left?'

The constable's eyes shifted momentarily to the nurse, who was standing next to Wainwright.

'I last checked her at about ... five thirty or quarter to six, Sarge.'

Wainwright felt, rather than saw, a barely discernible nod of agreement from the nurse.

'When did you do her last obs?' he asked the nurse.

'Five fifteen. We'd had a bit of a crisis in one of the bays, so I was a bit late. Then when I went to check on her at six – well, half past – she was gone. Constable Bingley called the station immediately.'

Sergeant Wainwright checked his watch. It was seven thirty.

'Christ! She could have been gone about two hours.'

'You didn't think to check on her?' Harmon asked Bingley, with dangerous civility.

'Didn't want to disturb her, sir. I mean, she'd only got off at about midnight and, with all the interruptions of the nurses coming and going, I thought—'

'Did you, Constable – think?'

'I was told to check on anyone entering or leaving through that door, sir.' Bingley pointed to the door into the side room. 'And I'll swear no one did.' He showed them the door leading from the shared toilet to the adjoining bay. 'How was I to know that was there—? I mean, nobody said. Nobody told me I had to stop her from getting *out*. I mean, it's not as if she's a criminal or anything—'

'All right, Constable. It looks like she was determined to get out of here unnoticed,' said Harmon. 'Get down to the station and make out a full report. I want it on my desk by nine.'

The strip lighting showed up every ugly feature of the utilitarian room. It was eight forty-five a.m., and Adam hadn't slept. At eight thirty the duty sergeant had brought him to interview room two, and Adam had been waiting since.

The cells had brought back some unpleasant memories, and this room reincarnated a few more. He fought with rising panic, telling himself that he would be able to see Harmon soon and get out of this rat-hole.

'Do you mind?'

Adam glanced up sharply, his eyes questioning in aggressive agitation.

The uniformed officer nodded at Adam's foot. He had been tapping the table leg in a frenzy of nervous energy. He stopped momentarily, then started drumming the table with his fingers. The constable – Adam was later to discover that his name was Ormrod – made an impatient movement, and Adam folded his arms and stared down at the plastic laminate of the table-top. Once patterned in mock leather, it had been worn to a displeasing shade of featureless beige in two equidistant cones, either side of the table, where countless interrogators and their subjects had sat, as he now did, hands clenched, forearms resting at the base of the cone, knuckles at the apex. Set into the wall on his right was a tape-recorder.

The walls of the room had been painted with plain emulsion, probably once cream, he speculated, but now nicotine yellow. The officer stood next to the door, and behind him Adam could see black streaks where a thousand others had rested one foot on the wall while listening to a thousand other interviews.

His eyes travelled up the wall and he noticed patches of dirty staining at shoulder and head height behind his police guard. Ormrod scowled at him. Adam's gaze wandered to the right and up to the ceiling.

The plastic filter of the fluorescent light was thick with the detritus of summers gone, dead flies in stark silhouette against the glare.

Adam let his eyes drop.

'I'd like to speak to Chief Inspector Harmon.'

'I heard you the first time,' Constable Ormrod replied.

'I *have* to talk to him.'

'He's busy.'

'How long are you going to waste my time here?'

'Got better things to do, have you?' sneered the constable.

'I want to see Harmon.'

'Drop it.' Constable Ormrod leaned forward, his hands balled into fists. He had the advantage of both size and weight.

Adam looked down at his hands, then back up to the constable's face. 'Or what?' he asked. Ormrod gave him a warning look. 'Just my luck to be banged up with a Neanderthal.'

'Yeah? Well, I didn't ask for duty watching a fucking pervert.'

Adam laughed. 'Tried and convicted already. I haven't even been charged and I'm a fucking pervert. Who says the legal process is slow?'

The constable curled his lip, looking away from his prisoner. They'd all been warned, Constable Ormrod included: Sergeant Wainwright did not want the pervert touched. All he had to do was keep his cool until DI Craine arrived. Ormrod smiled at the thought. Craine would make the fucking crank shut his beak.

'Where is he?' Adam asked, a knot forming in his stomach

as he saw the barely suppressed rage mounting on the police constable's face. He saw that he was close to pushing the guy over the edge, but he had to speak to Harmon. Had to make him listen. Had to get out of this stinking hole. And if that meant winding this bastard up into belting him, then that's what he would do. He dragged his chair back and swung his feet on to the table. He had been working on the young constable for thirty minutes now, and the wear was beginning to show.

Ormrod gritted his teeth and consoled himself with the thought that Craine would tear the bastard into little pieces.

'You know the difference between a policeman and a Polo mint?' Adam paused, waiting for a response. 'No?' He smiled. 'People *like* Polos.'

The smile never flickered, but Adam fancied it had become more fixed. He thought for a moment about shutting up, but he had to make his move right away. Once Kate got going, he would need to stick close to her. Very close. She had proved a slippery customer, but he thought that now he pretty much had the measure of her. He was on to her all right, and she wasn't going to have it all her way this time. Ormrod was proving a tough nut to crack. Adam thought a spot of whistling might set his nerves on edge.

'Shut it!' Ormrod hissed.

Adam continued.

Constable Ormrod seethed, but somehow managed to keep his station by the door.

And Adam whistled.

Ormrod tried to shut out the sound by reciting all the players of the Manchester United team in his head, forwards and backwards, subs included. The tune filtered through despite his efforts, and suddenly he recognized it. He had been one of the officers called out to Mrs Pearson's flat when she'd heard the taped message from her daughter. She had been listening to the tune Shepherd was whistling just before she heard her daughter's voice, pleading to come home.

Ormrod lunged forward, knocking the table into Shepherd and toppling the chair over. Shepherd lay winded, his breath wheezing painfully, as the constable moved in on him.

'What's going on?'

Shit! thought Ormrod, then, aloud, 'I warned him, sir. Told him he'd come a cropper, balancing the chair on two legs like that.'

'Get him up.'

DI Craine was six feet two and built like a brick shithouse. He could have picked up the pervert one-handed, but Ormrod wasn't about to suggest it. He grabbed Shepherd by the lapels.

'Gently, Constable. You've heard DCI Harmon's instructions *re* this prisoner.'

'I have — haven't been charged,' gasped Adam. 'Charge me or I'll bloody walk!'

Craine raised his eyebrows in what he meant to be gentle irony but looked more like villainous intent from Adam's side of the table.

'All in good time, son. All in good time. As for trying to walk out of here—' He shook his head. 'Wouldn't be advisable.' He bent to pick up a metal ashtray which had fallen to the floor and set it on the table. 'You know,' he resumed, smoothing a moustache as nicotine-stained as his fingers, 'I was not too thrilled by the call from the station. Two in the morning, and I get a call asking me to come in first thing. Now, me and the wife were getting ready for the drive down to Cornwall, to stay with her sister. Early start. Miss the traffic. Let me tell you, if *I* wasn't thrilled, you should have seen the wife.' He smiled humourlessly. 'She'd been looking forward to a few days away, you see.'

It also irked Detective Inspector Craine that he had been

turned down on the case after expressing an interest, and now, having reconciled himself to it, after he had begun looking forward to some time away, Harmon had changed his mind.

'You know why Chief Inspector Harmon asked for me specifically, don't you?' He didn't wait for a response. 'It's because I've got a reputation. Bit of a bastard. Constable Ormrod here'll tell you.'

Ormrod looked away.

Craine was proud of his reputation, and he knew damn well that his first interview with this particular prisoner would also be his last. Since it had also wrecked his Christmas break at his sister-in-law's, who was an exceptional cook, while his wife's cooking was mediocre at best, he intended to make it matter.

Adam shifted in his chair, staring at the worn table top and concentrating on trying to steady his breathing.

'Get Mr Shepherd a glass of water, will you, Ormrod?'

Adam caught the gleam in the constable's eye and, alarmed, tried to protest, but he couldn't get the words out, and Ormrod left the room.

Craine leant across the table and grabbed Adam by the back of the neck with a hand like a baseball glove. He pulled Adam, wheezing and gasping, towards him. He spoke slowly and softly: 'It's unfortunate that Constable Ormrod lost his temper like that. I don't like lapses of discipline. But let me tell you that Constable Ormrod is a kitten compared to me.' His voice hardened as he added, 'So don't try and piss me about!' He shoved Adam back into his chair and waited, watching with benign interest while Adam fought to catch his breath.

Constable Ormrod returned with the water, and Craine set it down in front of him.

'Now then, sir, shall we begin?' He turned on the tape-recorder and gave a time check, stating the names of the three people present in the room.

'I'm not making any statement,' said Adam. 'I've had no sleep. I'm tired. And I want to speak to Mr Harmon.'

'DCI Harmon is not available at this time, sir. He will, no doubt, speak to you in due course.'

'I've *had* this!'

'I must ask you to remain seated, sir.' Craine laid a ham fist on Adam's shoulder. 'Would you like to tell me about the tapes and letters we found at your flat?'

Silence.

'Well, how about the tape-recording that you gave Mrs Pearson?'

'What tape-recording?'

Ormrod stirred, but made no comment.

'The tape of *River of Dreams*, I believe it was. Billy Joel. Not to my taste. Apparently not to yours either. It had been taped over with a message from Melanie Pearson.' Adam shook his head. 'Mr Shepherd is shaking his head,' Craine said, for the official record. 'Your prints were on the tape.'

'It was a present.'

'So you admit to making the tape.'

'No! Jesus, no. I bought the tape for her birthday.'

'Melanie's?' Craine asked, feigning ignorance.

'No, for Kate, not Mel.'

'Mel, is it? Knew the little girl well, did you?'

'Get stuffed.'

'We found the original in your flat.'

Adam looked up. The original what? He had already told the ape: he'd *bought* the tape, from Virgin Megastore.

'The tape with Melanie's voice on it.'

Adam lowered his head again.

'The one where she's pleading to come home.'

Adam closed his eyes. Dear God!

''Course she does that on most of them, so I'm told.' He carefully constructed a silence that made Adam want to blurt everything out, to explain, to make Craine understand. But Craine left the silence a second short. 'There's a bit of an echo on it,' he said. 'Our experts reckon it was taped in a big unfurnished room. Stone walls. Not your flat. We've checked that. Maybe a cellar or a warehouse?' He watched for a reaction. Getting none, he went on, 'The basement of your building is occupied, so that's out an' all. Your neighbour wasn't too pleased when we got him out of bed.'

Adam winced. His neighbour also happened to be his landlord.

'Where was it, Adam?'

Adam shook his head.

'Mr Shepherd is shaking his head,' Craine said again.

'Let me speak to Mr Harmon.'

'I already told you, he's not available.'

'I want a solicitor.'

Craine had been waiting for that one. It had been surprisingly slow in coming. 'We'll see what we can do, sir, but it may be difficult to raise one at this hour of the morning. Do you have someone in particular in mind?'

A muscle twitched convulsively in Adam's cheek.

Craine stopped the tape, noting the time, while Constable Ormrod passed on the message.

They resumed precisely five minutes later.

'Now, these tapes and letters we found. What puzzles me is why you kept them so long without using them. Why wait until – when? – November? Then decide to start sending them to Mrs Pearson.'

'I'm not saying anything more until my solicitor is present.'

'That's your prerogative,' said Craine, thinking, And it's my prerogative to ask you questions. You can answer them or not, as you like. 'What about the e-mail?' he asked with scarcely a pause. 'It's a total bloody mystery to me, I can tell you. Now, me, I've got a theory about the shape of those joysticks, you know. And it doesn't take a degree in psychology to work out that boys are just doing what boys always did, but now they're doing it with a machine.'

'Your kids like it?'

Craine saw the imputation, and said, 'Yeah. But they're twelve and thirteen. The real wankers are the ones who are still doing it into adulthood.'

No response.

'And then there's the perverts.'

A flicker.

'There was a scare not so long ago. Kids calling up porno addresses and getting explicit photos on screen.'

Adam shook his head.

'Mr Shepherd is shaking his head. You go for that sort of thing, Adam?'

Adam glared at DI Craine but made no answer.

'Of course, the Internet's teeming with weirdos,' Craine observed. 'Seems to draw them like flies to shit.' He studied Shepherd closely. 'I believe you like – buzzing around the Net, sir.'

'Surfing.'

'What?'

'It's called *surfing* the Net.'

'As you say,' Craine was beginning to enjoy himself. 'Now the one thing that really pulls my wire is the bastards who get into other people's computers and f— – muck them up. The whatdjamacallits, the hackers. Know anything about them?'

'Let me speak to Harmon, please,' Adam asked, wearily.

'In fact, you're something of an expert in the field of hacking, aren't you, Adam?'

'I don't know what you mean.'

'No? Let me refresh your memory. Nineteen eighty-five. Ring any bells?'

Adam paled.

Craine leaned forward. 'You've got form, Mr Shepherd.'

Adam blinked. 'That has nothing to do with what has been happening—'

'No? Seems to me there's a definite similarity. Computer security breached. Messages left on people's files. E-mail sent to company employees—' he broke off. 'Mr Shepherd is shaking his head. How long did you serve for that? Three years' youth custody, wasn't it?'

'You people make me sick.' There was a stillness in Shepherd that Craine had seen before. He tensed, ready to act.

'MOD, wasn't it? You don't do things by halves, do you?'

'You're making it sound like I stole government secrets. I was a kid. I hacked into the MOD, yeah – big deal. It's not that difficult, you know.'

'You hacked into the MOD,' Craine repeated.

'I didn't steal anything. I didn't leave any viruses. I went in, had a look round and had a chat with their systems manager.'

'And you got caught.'

'I was telling him how to close the trapdoor into the sodding system, right? And he put you bastards on to me.'

'The Crown Prosecution Service considered it a serious enough offence to put you away for three years.'

'Jesus!' Adam slammed the table with his fist. 'Anyone would think I killed someone! I never hurt anybody—'

'Didn't you, sir?'

Chapter Twenty-four

In the near-darkness of the hesitant dawn, a figure passed like the flicker of a shadow in the waking street. Her hair flamed briefly in the sudden flare of a sodium lamp, and then was extinguished as she moved on, shivering in the cold.

Past Victorian houses, once the comfortable tenancies of the middle classes, now broken up into flats and broken down by neglect, Kate Pearson searched for Adam Shepherd's house.

A movement under the porch. She shrank back, wishing for something to cover her hair. The movement gathered form, and someone stepped to the front of the porch. Constable Barratt! She was wearing weatherproofs and gloves but was stamping and shifting, looking cold, almost forlorn in the grey half-light.

Kate was reminded of her own poor state of dress and shivered convulsively. Constable Barratt yawned and turned, and Kate darted into an alleyway, her footsteps echoing back at her a dozen times from the high walls of the terraces on either side, sounding like stones raining into deep water. She turned left at the end of the row and stopped, glancing back around the corner of the wall, but no one was following.

On either side the alleys stretched away, hemmed in by seven-foot-high brick walls. Kate turned left again, breathing shallowly in the fetid air, stepping around dog dirt and detritus, exciting a rabble of barking from the yard-dogs behind the wooden gates. Snouts appeared in the gaps between the steps and the wood, snuffling frantically for her scent, then the irate barking resumed.

One gate had long since disintegrated, and Kate edged past it uncertainly, bracing herself for a sudden attack. None came; she saw only a cracked concrete pathway and raised borders tangled with the remains of last year's rank growth of weeds.

A low growl. She turned in time to see a huge snout snarling at her through the splintered planks of the next gate. Go forward or turn back? If she turned back, she risked being seen, and there could be other dogs waiting like this for her to pass. She moved slowly to the wall opposite the dog. The German Shepherd turned its head sideways and now its whole head was visible. It lunged and snapped, and Kate saw the rotten planking give a little. She inched along the wall, her heart hammering, and the dog stared at her, wild-eyed, baring its fangs and making hoarse, outraged barks.

Abruptly, it pulled its head back in, splintering the wood further, and then hurled itself at the gate baying frantically. Kate broke into a run, turning right at the next alley, emerging into the adjacent street breathless and retching. She threw up in a gutter.

A woman dragged her children across the road to avoid her. Kate ignored them and sat on the low wall of the house by the alley, breathing deeply and trying to steady her head.

She found a tissue in the pocket of her jeans and wiped her mouth. Her hand was shaking, and when she tried to stand up the street seemed to oscillate, so she sat down again, resting her elbows on her knees, and waited for the dizziness to pass.

*

Adam was shaking. Craine had gone into some detail about his conviction, citing his lack of teenage friends as evidence of social maladjustment, recalling the incident at Withenstop Detention Centre in which he'd had to be forcibly restrained after beating up another boy. 'He needed hospital treatment after you'd finished with him.'

'Billy Kinsella was cock of the wing,' said Adam. 'He decided I was fair game. He beat me up a couple of times. Him and a few mates. He got himself switched to garden activities so he could hassle me a bit more. He was always shoving me around, tripping me, digging me in the kidneys while the screws weren't watching. One day he came after me in the showers. Only this time his mates weren't with him. So I took a chance, and it paid off.'

'Two fractured ribs,' Craine read from a sheet. 'A tooth knocked out. Bruised kidneys. Lacerations and contusions to face and body. Says here you kicked him so hard in the bollocks that he walked bow-legged for a week. Some pay-off.' He stared hard at Adam. 'Six months on your sentence, and two weeks' isolation,' he said. 'Was it worth it?'

Adam shrugged. 'He didn't bother me any more. Nobody did.'

'Is that what you do to people who bother you, Adam? Teach them a lesson they won't forget?'

Adam frowned.

'Get them where it really hurts?' Craine chewed on his moustache for a few moments. His eyes never wavered from Adam's face.

Adam felt oppressed by the big man's stare. Of course he knew. It would be in the report. The real reason why he had tried to kill Billy Kinsella. But Adam couldn't help lying about it because he didn't want to believe it had ever really happened to him.

Craine was talking. 'You wait at school gates, don't you?

Aching to touch them, watching them. The way they move, the flick of their skirts as they walk. They're wearing them short again – have you noticed?' A short laugh. 'Silly question.'

Adam looked away.

'It's their skin. It's so . . . smooth, so tight.' He grinned wickedly. 'Makes you wonder what else is tight, eh?'

'For God's sake—'

'Isn't that why you abducted her, Adam? Because you fancied her?'

'No.'

'Why, then?'

'Look, I didn't abduct Melanie.' Adam wanted to tell Craine that he was wrong, but he didn't know how to say it without sounding guilty. He knew he couldn't convince this man.

Craine was speaking, telling the tape-recorder that he was shaking his head. Adam had not been aware of that. Saying something else about Melanie. He tried not to listen.

'Fractured ribs . . .' Craine paused, riffling through the papers in front of him. 'Interesting, that. *Two* fractured ribs.'

I don't want to hear this.

'Rope marks on the wrists and ankles. Marked lividity to—' Stop it.

'Skull fractured by a heavy implement. A rock? Was it a rock, Adam? Or a hammer?'

'*I don't know.*'

'Crushed like an eggshell—'

Dear God. Melanie . . .

'Her brains spilled out on the ground—'

'*Please!*' Adam hid his face in his hands.

'All right, son. Take it easy.' Craine waited. No point in going on until the lad was able to hear what he was saying. 'She was killed in that big, echoey basement, wasn't she? There was a mixture of dirt and whitewash under her finger-

261

nails. Then you took her to the woods and dumped her like some vermin you'd caught in a trap.'

'Stop!' Adam shouted. 'Will you stop this? You're talking about Kate's little girl, for Christ's sake!'

Craine tried persuasiveness, modulating his voice, sympathizing with Adam. 'I'm sorry if this is difficult for you, going through all of it again. I know you have strong feelings for Kate Pearson. It's worse for her, having to think about it. Wondering whether—' He stared sadly at Adam for some moments. 'You know, it would be a kindness if you just admitted to what you did and let her get on with her life – what's left of it. Mr Shepherd is shaking his head.'

Craine watched Shepherd closely. The warning signs were back. His breathing was ragged, and he was close to the point of tears with frustration. Well, let's see how much it'll take, shall we? He set himself the target of five minutes.

'It's not easy for her. Thinking about what you did to her little girl. Leaving her there like that, with her brains leaking out, and her eyes open, and beetles crawling over her face.'

'Oh, Jesus,' Adam moaned. He was feeling sick.

'Kate trusted you. She let you into her home. Into her life. You went bowling together. Roller-skating with her and Melanie. All the time it was there, at the back of your mind. Still, she wasn't interfered with. One small consolation, I suppose.'

Adam closed his eyes tight.

''Course, the shrinks don't think you're a paedophile. They've got this theory.' He waited until Adam opened his eyes. The lad was sweating now. He wiped his face with a shaking hand. 'Impotence,' Craine said, then he drew down the corners of his mouth. 'Shrinks! I suppose it wouldn't be surprising after what they did to you.' He winked. 'I mean at Withenstop.' He leaned forward, breathing coffee and nicotine into Adam's face. 'I mean, Billy Kinsella wasn't called cock of the wing for nothing, was he?' Adam flinched as though he'd been struck. Craine grinned, inviting Adam to share the joke, his moustache splaying to a dirty white fringe on his upper lip. 'Now *me*, I'd like to think you left her – what's the word? – *virgo intacta*, because you were sickened by what you'd done. Was that it, Adam? You saw what you'd done to the little girl, and you felt sick to your stomach.'

A muscle tightened across Adam's jaw line.

Two minutes.

'But the shrinks don't think you've got that kind of compassion in you – empathy, they call it. *They* think it's something else. Something totally different. Who am I to argue? I mean, they're the experts, aren't they? Let me sketch it out for you. You can tell me what you think. They say Kate made you feel that way. Impotent. She made you feel useless. Ignored you. Even when she noticed you it was only to take the piss out of you – belittle you, make you look stupid in front of the others. Oh, yes, we've talked to your colleagues at the office. Kate Pearson has a bit of an acid tongue.'

Adam shrugged.

'Our shrinks say you had the hots for our Kate, but all that constant barracking and bitching – you know what women are like. She made you feel like shit.' He measured these last words carefully, laying them before Shepherd and finishing with a sneer.

Adam stared at the inspector with intense hatred.

'Pretty girl, that Melanie,' Craine said, changing direction abruptly. 'In life, that is. Dark-haired, doe-eyed. Legs right up to her neck. Bit of all right, for a kid. Know what the shrinks reckon? You wanted to poke her mother, but she wouldn't let you near her. So you took her kid. Less of a threat. But you couldn't get it up even for her.'

Adam threw himself at Craine.

The policeman moved with surprising agility, slapping him

away lightly with his left hand. Pain exploded like splintering bone in a radiating band from Adam's nose. He was on the floor and his nose was bleeding.

'Bastard,' he panted. 'Fucking *bastard*. I never touched her.' He was crying. 'You fucking, twisted bastard. I never hurt Melanie. I never hurt anyone.'

Three and a half minutes, thought Inspector Craine, noting the time. Not bad going.

Chapter Twenty-five

'Come *on*, Jenny!'

Mary had called Jenny at least half a dozen times, but the late night and the emotion of the previous evening had left her exhausted.

'Leave her, if she's tired,' said Tony. He reached for the radio, but Mary slapped his hand away.

'I'll never hear the last of it if she doesn't go. Mrs Callaghan's been on at them that it's a great honour being chosen. I dare say she's right—' She broke off. 'Jenn-E E E E!'

'I'm coming.' Jenny's voice sounded muffled and cross.

'You'd better, young lady, else you'll not be going!' Mary warned.

Tony had switched the radio on while she had been at the door, and when Mary came back she hurriedly turned it off. 'The news is on, knuckle-head,' she whispered.

Jenny stumbled into the kitchen five minutes later, looking pale and grumpy.

'D'you want to go or not?' Mary asked.

'Yes!' Jenny sat at the kitchen table, staring with sickly distaste at the sodden cornflakes in her bowl.

'Well, go on,' Mary urged. 'I've got your toast on. Get it down you.'

Jenny pushed her bowl away. 'I'm not so very hungry,' she said. 'I'll just have some tea.'

'You'll do nothing of the sort. You're to have some toast at least. It's freezing outside!'

Jenny rolled her eyes.

Outside, the grey Capri gleamed dully in the grey light of early morning. The engine thrummed quietly and he listened to the radio, switching to Radio Four from Radio Three to try and find some real news.

He'd had little sleep, but he was vibrant with the energy of the plan, his senses awake to the wonderful possibilities of the day.

'Thought for the Day'. He listened to it with a certain indulgence, enjoying its comforting predictability. The opening anecdote. The reading. The prayer. The closing words of wisdom intended to resonate through the actions and interactions of the day.

'In the beginning was the Word,' the reader intoned.

'And the Word was vengeance.' The listener had spoken aloud. He smiled, continuing the theme: 'And the Word became flesh . . .' In the person of a small girl. A daughter. An only child. And he heard the resonance, saw it in the fabric of the air. First Melanie, little Mel – Annie for affectionate moments. Now Jennifer.

The watcher breathed, closing his eyes with pleasure at the aroma of clean upholstery. They are *both* only children, he mused. When this other is taken from you, when your friend rejects you, then you will have nothing, my Katie. And when you have nothing, you will know how it has been for me.

*

'Get him checked out, will you? Who's on duty?'

'Dr Mitra, sir.'

'Call him in.'

Harmon was profoundly depressed. Kate Pearson was God alone knew where, getting up to God knew what, her ex wanted to charge her with assault and Shepherd had a bloody nose.

'Anything yet on Mrs Pearson?'

'No sign at her flat,' Wainwright said. 'I've left Jackson there in case she shows, and a couple of lads are on their way to her office.'

'Tell Jackson to keep a low profile, will you? I don't want her frightened off.'

Wainwright left smartly, leaving a morose DCI Harmon gazing out of the window.

'Morning, Harry.' The security guard looked up from his newspaper.

'Hello, Kate. I thought you were on leave – Bloody hell! What happened to you?'

'Think I'm becoming accident-prone,' said Kate, smiling ruefully. 'Okay if I pop up to the office? I left a few odds and sods in my hurry to get away yesterday.'

'Know the feeling,' Harry smiled, and Kate turned from the reception counter. 'Only you'll have to sign in,' he called.

Kate kept her impatience at bay. Just. 'Sure,' she said, forcing a smile.

'The time is– ' Harry checked his watch, '– eight thirty.'

'I'd better hurry,' said Kate, 'I don't want to bump into the hordes on their way in.'

Harry nodded sympathetically. He wouldn't ask how the investigation was going, because he reckoned it was none of his business, but he felt sorry for the lass.

*

'Nothing much.' Dr Mitra had attended promptly, leaving morning surgery before it had finished. His colleagues had agreed to split the few remaining patients between them. It was unusual that Christmas Eve was so quiet.

'Nosebleed,' he explained. 'Apparently he was prone to them when he was a boy. And his blood pressure's rather high. Wouldn't take much to set one off.' Dr Mitra hesitated. 'There is also some bruising to the cheekbone—'

Harmon nodded. 'It happened during his arrest. An accident. How did he seem?' Harmon was confident that Dr Mitra would have questioned Shepherd to establish the cause of the nosebleed, and he hoped to gain something from the information Mitra had gleaned.

'He'll develop a bit of bruising around the eyes.'

'In himself, I mean.'

Dr Mitra peered at Harmon from behind his spectacles. 'He is very agitated.'

'And?'

Dr Mitra pulled a gleaming white handkerchief from the pocket of his sports jacket and, taking off his glasses, he began polishing them thoughtfully.

'He says that he, um, "went for" Mr Craine.' Dr Mitra abhorred idiomatic English. Brought up with the stylized grammar of Hindi, he shuddered at the vagaries of the English language. Sometimes it seemed to him that English was not one language but a diversity of regional patois. 'He also says that he was provoked.' Harmon nodded. 'He is most anxious to speak with you, Trevor.'

Harmon was aware that the use of his Christian name was a signal, intended to imply that Dr Mitra wanted to say more, but not publicly. In public, the chief inspector and the police surgeon were on formal terms.

'Get Mr Shepherd a cup of tea, and take him back to

the interview room.' Harmon had spoken to Craine, who immediately passed the task on to a WPC.

'Would you like to come through to my office, Sanjit?'

The gesture had been countersigned. They understood each other.

A tray stood on Inspector Harmon's desk. He poured them each a cup of tea and waited until the courtesies had been observed. Then: 'There's something you want to say.' It was a statement.

Dr Mitra peered over the rim of his cup, his eyes sparkling with bright curiosity, and not for the first time Harmon was struck by the youthful inquisitiveness of this middle-aged man.

'You have a quantity of circumstantial evidence against this young man,' Mitra said at length.

'Fairly damning circumstantial evidence,' said Harmon, wincing inwardly at the defensive tone of his reply.

Dr Mitra eyed him seriously. 'He says he didn't murder Melanie Pearson.' He waited a few moments before adding quietly, 'He says he loves Kate Pearson.'

'Do you believe him?'

Dr Mitra sighed. 'I don't know the fellow. He does, however, seem sincere. I think he *believes* that he is speaking the truth.'

He sipped his tea, deep in thought.

'Are you saying he's deluded?' Harmon shrugged. 'Crazy?'

'I have only the undergraduate's training in psychiatry, Trevor,' Dr Mitra reproached.

'Between you and me.'

Sanjit Mitra tilted his head. 'Confidentially?' He considered carefully before answering, 'Strictly off the record, I would say that Mr Shepherd is a rather neurotic individual, nervous of police, somewhat claustrophobic. But not, I think, psychotic.'

'He nearly killed an inmate when he was in Youth Custody.'

'Really? And what was the provocation, I wonder? In such a place a boy like Shepherd would be an easy target for all kinds of abuse.'

Harmon's feelings of depression deepened. Mitra, as always, had seen right to the heart of the matter.

'What would you suggest?' he asked.

'I suggest – nothing. But Mr Shepherd has been asking to speak with you, as a matter of some urgency, ever since his arrest last evening. Perhaps it would be civil to grant him that interview, considering his very fair evaluation of the incident involving your Inspector Craine.' He held up one hand. 'I merely speculate.'

Harmon chuckled. 'I had intended interviewing him this morning, Sanjit.'

Dr Mitra smiled, relieved. 'Good. I should hate to interfere in police business.'

Harmon's chuckle became a laugh.

'You will hear him out?' Dr Mitra added, with an apologetic smile.

Kate sat at her own terminal. No sense in exciting suspicion as well as curiosity. She had already checked Adam's desk, expecting to find nothing; it contained a few pens and a packet of chewing gum. He never left disks accessible. He was too careful for that. But he'd told her he was getting close to the hacker. He must have some record. It had to be somewhere . . .

Probably at home, Kate thought, with sinking heart. And that was out. The police had probably taken away all of his disks anyway. His files on the Technicomm filestore would most likely be a wash-out, but she had to try.

She knew his login, 1stBite – a joke on his name – and

she typed it in confidently. The computer beeped at her, asking her to retype the name, and she frowned at it, puzzled. The protocol was case-sensitive, but she had taken care to use the correct combination of upper- and lower-case characters. She laughed shortly and retyped, with swift, sure movements: '1stByte'. Very funny, Adam.

The screen cleared, then requested a password. This was the hard part. Adam was careful with passwords. He was fond of cyberpunk novels: Gibson's *Neuromancer*, Brunner's *The Shockwave Rider* and Sterling's *Schismatrix* had all been passed on to her. Perhaps he saw himself as a cyberian cowboy, like Case in *Neuromancer*, who regarded cyberspace as 'his distanceless home, his country'.

She typed 'Case' and the computer beeped, indicating that she had entered an incorrect password. Two more incorrect tries and she would be booted off the system, and the account would be suspended until Adam made a trip to the systems manager to get it reinstated. Failure to come up with a satisfactory explanation for the error would result in an investigation.

Bloody hell!

Kate thought back, hurrying now, because she didn't want to be timed out of the system. She should have thought it through before she had tried logging on. Think! Another book Adam had passed on to her was *Cyberpunk*. It was based on the explosion of hacking scares in the Eighties. There was a kid in it who'd written a program with the aim of probing the network security on the Berkeley UNIX machines. It had been planned as an intellectual exercise, a test of his own skill in hacking, and was meant to harm no one. It ended by stalling thousands of computers. Adam said he felt sorry for the guy, whose three-year probation order and $10,000 fine seemed disproportionately severe when compared with Mitnick's one-year custodial sentence. The seventeen-year-old had stolen hundreds of thousands of dollars' worth of software from DEC.

'Robert Morris!' Kate exclaimed triumphantly. That was the name of the boy Adam seemed to identify with so much. He had a favourite login – rtm. Brilliant! She laughed aloud. It so happened that one of Adam's ripostes to lazy operators who asked him stupid questions rather than finding out the answers themselves was 'rtm' – read the manual – an Internet abbreviation.

She typed 'rtm', then tapped the carriage-return key.

The computer beeped. Sod it!

Not rtm – then what? She thought back to the last time she had heard Adam use the term and shook her head impatiently. Not rtm – it was rtfm: read the flaming manual. She tried again, and the computer went into its loading routine.

'Halle-bloody-luja,' Kate muttered.

There was nothing of note on his files. Nothing whatso-ever. He could well have salted away anything important in a hidden file or under his superuser ID. Kate was sweating. A few people had arrived already and were giving her strange looks, not least because of the dressing still taped to her forehead. She was grateful that they apparently thought better of coming to speak to her.

She was about to quit and run for it, when a snatch of conversation came to her. Adam had said he'd asked some Internet friends to find out what they could about the hacker. They would contact him on the Net. And that meant by e-mail. She exited the file manager and typed 'mail' at the prompt.

There were five unread messages. She loaded and printed each of them in turn, hesitated, then deleted the mail files, with a silent apology to Adam.

*

'You've to stay with Mrs Callaghan,' Tony ordered. 'You're not to go anywhere without the rest of the group.'

'Okay, Dad.' Jenny tugged away from him.

'Jenny, I mean it.'

'I know. Look,' she said, trying to be reasonable, 'I'll stand right next to her, okay? And I'll wait with the others till you come and pick me up.'

'I'll be outside the theatre at twelve o'clock sharp, so don't go wandering off.'

'I won't, Dad. Look – they're all going.'

'All right.' Tony kissed her on the cheek, and Jenny escaped, gratefully, into the crowd of schoolchildren. Mrs Callaghan and two other staff lined them up, counting them, and then they left the kerb-side, heading for the pedestrianized area outside the Royal Exchange Theatre.

Tony watched Jenny disappear around the corner with a terrible sense of foreboding.

'You wanted to see me?'

'Have you still got someone watching Kate?'

Harmon did not answer.

'She's in terrible danger.'

'Not any more.'

'He's still out there.'

'Please, Mr Shepherd, spare me the histrionics.'

'*He* planted the stuff in my flat,' Adam insisted.

'I suppose this someone tampered with the tape as well?'

'Yes! Look, where is Kate? She'll believe me. Let me talk to her.'

'Mr Shepherd, your flat is practically stuffed with incriminating evidence.' Harmon had agreed to talk to Shepherd, but that didn't mean he shared Dr Mitra's apparent conviction that he was innocent.

'You had means, motive and opportunity to abduct Melanie Pearson.'

Shepherd seemed nonplussed. 'I knew Melanie, yeah. That's true. But motive? Opportunity?'

'I believe Inspector Craine has already been into possible motives.'

'He's full of it.' Adam glowered at the table-top, his face burning with rage and shame.

'And as for opportunity—'

'I was at the hospital. You've got sworn statements from the nursing staff.'

'Giving arrival and departure times, yes.' Harmon went on, implacably, 'But we've had cause to re-examine those statements since you got careless on the Internet, Mr Shepherd, and since we discovered the . . . trinkets in your flat.' He spoke over Adam's objections, his voice booming angrily. 'The nursing staff cannot confirm that you were in your friend's room for the entire period as originally stated.'

Adam blinked.

'They say that you had visited on a number of occasions and that you tended to the needs of your friend during those visits. They felt it best to leave you alone.'

Adam stroked his eyebrow. Harmon noted it.

'In fact, you could have left the room at any time between two p.m., when Nurse Unsworth brought you a cup of tea, and five forty-five, when Staff Nurse Briggs looked in on you.'

'I was there.'

'Nobody can confirm that you were there when you say you were. You could have left your friend, abducted Melanie, hidden her somewhere and returned to the hospital without anyone knowing.'

'But I *didn't*. Sims had hepatitis. He was dying, for Christ's sake. He was my mate. I wouldn't leave him.' How could he explain to Harmon how important a mate was in prison? Someone you could trust in an atmosphere of brutality and mistrust, someone to watch your back when animals like Kinsella were out to get you. A friend, a confidant. To Harmon, Sims was just another junky who finally injected himself with the kind of poison his body couldn't fight. If it hadn't been hepatitis, it would eventually have been AIDS. But he was a person. He had feelings – rage mostly – but also compassion, and more pain than Harmon could ever imagine.

Harmon went on evenly, 'He was semi-comatose on the day you visited. Drifting in and out of consciousness. The nursing staff were relying on you to notify them of any change.'

Harmon observed that Shepherd seemed to have trouble meeting his eye.

'Yeah? So what?'

'So you didn't. When Sims sank deeper and deeper into a coma, you said nothing. You didn't call anyone. Maybe because you weren't there.'

Adam shook his head, disbelievingly.

'It's a difficult position to be in, Mr Shepherd. On the one hand, you must admit to allowing your friend to die, and on the other, you're facing a charge of murder.'

Harmon watched a stillness come over Shepherd that he had never before seen in the nervy young man. It was the calmness of total defeat. He began quietly, and Harmon had to lean across to hear what he was saying.

'He was dying. He knew it, the nursing staff knew it, although they never said it to him straight. They told me. His liver was too far gone. He – was so sick, you know? Sometimes—' Shepherd stared straight ahead. 'He started having these hallucinations. They said it was the toxins in his blood. He couldn't shift them any more. Your worst nightmares were never as bad as what he went through. It was terrifying, watching him. He said it was like a colossally bad trip.'

Harmon saw that Shepherd had broken out in gooseflesh. 'Staff Nurse Briggs said you'd been called in.'

Shepherd nodded.

'Rather than his family?'

'He named me as next of kin. He had no family. No one that gave a shit anyhow.'

'And you decided not to alert the nursing staff when it was obvious he needed medical attention.'

'Like I said, he was dying. He didn't want to be resuscitated. Didn't want anyone pounding his chest, giving him electric shocks to keep him going for another few days in hell. He—' Shepherd stopped and stared down at the apex of the dingy cone of wear on the table-top. He swallowed. 'Sims asked me to hold his hand until it was over. They didn't expect him to last the night anyway. That's why they called me in from work.'

'So you held his hand and waited nearly four hours for him to die?'

'No.'

Harmon tensed, waiting for an admission. Waiting to hear that Shepherd had not been able to stand it. That he had left his friend and gone for a walk, for a coffee, anything. Once he had admitted that, he would work on Shepherd to admit that he had left the hospital. And from there, he would lead Shepherd to the school. He had gone there without realizing it. He was upset. He just wanted to take a look. Then he had seen Melanie on her own. Had offered to walk her home. It would take time, but he would persuade Shepherd to own up that he had taken the girl on impulse. Perhaps she had panicked and screamed, in turn panicking him. He had put his hand over her mouth to quiet her, and he had known from that point there was no going back.

'No . . .' Harmon prompted gently.

Adam's eyes were deep and wounded. 'No,' repeated Adam. 'It was three and a half hours.' He looked away. 'I, er . . .' His voice was unsteady. 'I promised Sims I'd be sure before—' He coughed. 'Before I told them.' He frowned furiously at his hands, clasped white-knuckled before him, but a tear fell, despite his efforts.

Harmon was aghast. He almost believed it himself.

Chapter Twenty-six

'Kate?' Mary let herself in using the key Kate had given her several years before so that she could prepare tea for Melanie and Jenny when Kate was working late. She hadn't used it since the summer, but even though they had rowed so bitterly, she couldn't bring herself to return it, for that would signal the death of any hope of rekindling the trust that had long been the hallmark of their friendship.

The flat was cold and quiet. It struck Mary that this was how it must be for Kate, returning home to a silence that seemed to reproach laughter. She stood in the hallway trying to recall how it had been, filled with the clamour of the girls, both hungry for food and ravenous for life. If it had been Jenny, she thought, and not Melanie who had been taken . . . She shivered violently, dismissing the idea, and hurried through to the lounge, knowing Kate would not be there.

She let out a shout of surprise on seeing the young woman silhouetted against the brightness of the bay window.

'Mrs Marchant?'

'What on earth are you doing here?' Mary demanded.

Constable Jackson hunched her shoulders. 'Keeping a low profile,' she said gloomily.

The impossibility of the task, given the constable's considerable size, struck Mary as ludicrous, and in the hilarity of released tension she almost let out a laugh but smothered it with seeming annoyance.

'How did you get in?' She frowned angrily at Jackson, who coloured in a guilty flush.

'I, er . . .' Her eyes fluttered towards the door to the kitchen. 'I broke a pane of glass. My sergeant okayed it!' she added, eager to placate the woman. She had misjudged Mrs Marchant on their first meeting, writing her off as the sort of innocuous middle-aged female who escaped responsibility and the difficulties of life in the real world for a comfortable existence as a faceless, colourless housewife. But it had been this same dumpy little woman who had reacted first when Mrs Pearson was attacked. She had rushed, screaming, into the darkness and had thrown herself at her friend's attacker. Mary Marchant had also done her best to mollify DCI Harmon, and for that Jackson had been grateful.

'Where is Mrs Pearson?' Mary asked. Jackson gestured awkwardly but did not reply. 'I take it, from your silence, that you don't know?'

Jackson wondered why all the lousy jobs seemed to come her way. 'She bunked out of hospital this morning—' she began.

'You let a concussed woman just *walk out* of hospital—'

'Hey, slow down a bit! I wasn't even there!' Jackson protested. 'All I know is the nurse went to check on her and she'd gone. Look,' she added, 'don't blame me. I've just been told to watch the flat in case she comes back.'

Mary pursed her lips. 'Of course, you're right. It isn't your fault.'

Jackson, regaining a little confidence, ventured, 'She's taken herself off for reasons best known to herself.'

Mary snorted and Jackson took it for a gesture of contempt. 'I don't know why I bloody bother,' she exclaimed, slumping into an armchair, scowling. 'Doesn't matter what I do, it's bound to be wrong.'

'Cheer up, Constable,' Mary said. 'I was merely observing that Kate's reasons would be better made known to your Chief Inspector than kept to herself. But Kate's not the sort to share confidences easily,' adding with a tinge of bitterness, 'even with an old friend.'

Among the crowd, unnoticed, ordinary, a respectable man, almost invisible in the bustle of Christmas shoppers. He carried two parcels in his gloved hands. One he would have delivered, the other, larger, package would be placed judiciously by himself. Later.

The singing was pleasant and, stepping from the crowd, he stooped to put a coin in the bucket. The wind, catching the hood of his jacket, momentarily scooped it on to his head. A shadow chased across Jenny's face and then was gone as she concentrated on the descant part of 'Deck the Halls'.

The man looked up and smiled into Mrs Callaghan's eyes. She nodded her thanks, though ruffled in an inexplicable way, in a way that would trouble her for the remainder of the morning and only coalesce into meaning in a dream that would disturb the scant sleep that pills would afford her in the early hours of the next day. And the man smiled. He walked away smiling. Biding his time. Biding his time.

'She had her account suspended. She spoke to John, our systems manager. I knew that. Why would I reinstate it just to send myself a bogus message?'

'I don't know, Mr Shepherd. Perhaps you thought it would throw suspicion off you.' Harmon had resumed his interview with Shepherd, determined to make some sense of what was going on.

'Right,' said Adam. 'And then I send a message from my own account to Kate in my own name. That's clever. That'd really throw suspicion off me.'

Harmon had to agree. It didn't seem a logical course of action for the hacker to take. 'We found enough evidence in your flat to get a conviction on circumstantial evidence alone.' He watched Shepherd's reaction closely, alert to any nervous actions or tics. Apparently Shepherd had decided that Harmon was an ally because he dismissed the suggestion with a shrug.

'It was planted,' he said. 'I take it you didn't find my fingerprints on any of the stuff?'

Harmon sucked his teeth. 'And the e-mail?'

'Can be routed wherever you like. A lot of hackers are also phone phreaks. They can dial through the equipment of several long-distance carriers, crossing company boundaries before finally connecting with the target. At each stage false credit-card numbers are used. They're untraceable. They could route it via the PC in your office if they wanted.'

Harmon detected a suggestion of admiration in Shepherd's voice.

'You can't help respecting that kind of talent,' he tried.

'When it's used for the intellectual challenge of breaking into a supposedly secure system, it is kind of thrilling.' Adam saw where Harmon was heading. 'But I never used it to harm people. Not once. Real hackers don't do that kind of thing.'

Harmon laughed. 'First etiquette on the Internet, now you're trying to sell me the hackers' code of honour.'

Adam held his gaze, unsmiling. 'Check it out,' he said. 'I wasn't even in the building when I'm supposed to've sent Kate that message.'

'As you say, messages can be routed from anywhere.'

'You've searched my flat. Did you find a modem? No. How could I have sent the message when I had no access to the Net? I was on my way to the hospital when the threat was sent to Kate.'

'Ah, yes. The e-mail telling you that Mrs Pearson was in hospital. Presumably the, um – what do you call him? – the phantom sent it?' Shepherd's unwavering stare was answer enough: that is what he would have him believe. 'And you went right over there, even though you knew her account had been closed?'

Adam threw him a look of disgust. 'I'm not stupid,' he said. 'I phoned the hospital first.'

'Could we confirm that the message from your terminal to Kate's mailbox was sent after you left the Technicomm building?' Harmon asked.

Adam allowed himself a moment of elation. Harmon was at least considering the possibility that he might be telling the truth.

'I signed out,' he said, trying not to sound too eager, not succeeding. 'You have to sign in and out of the building. The times are entered as well. Security'll confirm it. And the precise time of arrival of each e-mail message is listed.'

Kate sat on a park bench in Piccadilly Gardens. The little oval of cherry trees and flowerbeds was busy with people taking a rest from the rigours of shopping. All around her traffic buzzed and rumbled. Harmon was right. It is possible to be invisible in the centre of things. Nobody bothered her. Nobody even noticed her; they were too preoccupied with the problems and the complexities of their own lives to concern themselves with hers.

She scoured the e-mail messages for information. Adam had some odd friends on the Internet: Anthrax, D-liver, Worf,

Trimorph, Lonny and Zed had all replied. Their messages were short but friendly. Each response pointed towards the same thing.

She had allowed her deliberations to lead her in circles. Hadn't she said often enough that she always seemed to end up with the bastards? Her former lovers were each capable of cruelty of one form or another. Trying to discover which of them was capable of composing the e-mail messages by an analysis of their nature had merely fogged an already cloudy picture. She should have examined their skills. He had the ability – he had *paraded* his expertise before her and she hadn't picked up on it. He had open access to the Internet. He even, she remembered with a jolt, had a fondness for Italian food. The toys he had sent to the Italian restaurant had been a blatant reference to the fact. He had been playing an elaborate game all along. In a moment of weakness, Kate wondered if she should take the information to Inspector Harmon. She waited for a few minutes, watching her breath create a fog around her face, watching it drift and dissipate and form again, and gradually the feeling went away.

A soft *boomph* from the main shopping area behind her was followed by a collective shriek of dismay and fright. For a few seconds there was silence, as though the traffic itself had stopped to listen, then the fire alarms and police sirens began to wail.

The people in the gardens looked at each other in consternation. The sound had been too quiet, too damped, for a bomb. It sounded almost discreet, making no more noise than a dropped bag of flour bursting on the ground. Still, she thought, I am several hundred yards from the source. A column of dark smoke rose from the buildings in the direction of Deansgate, and now the spectators began to move, hesitantly at first but soon becoming determined, even excited, by the prospect of a bomb in the city centre.

Kate stood up and walked away from the crowds. This did not concern her. She had a task to complete, and it was only a matter of time before Harmon would come to the same conclusions she had.

Harmon's office was busy. Two extra phones had been installed and both were ringing. DI Craine was arguing with Harmon. It was more to make a point than from any idea that Harmon would change his mind and let him have another go at Shepherd. He had expected the interview to be a one-off. What really bugged him was that Harmon seemed to be listening to the little perv.

'He's making it up as he goes along,' Craine said.

'I don't think so.' Harmon reached across the desk and answered one of the phones, nodding at Wainwright to answer the other. He talked briefly, then hung up. 'Confirmed,' he said. 'Shepherd left the Technicomm building half an hour before the "no more games" message arrived, according to Stretton.'

'Even so—'

'Sir.' Wainwright had cut in. He pointed to the mouthpiece. 'Jill Jackson. Kate Pearson's had a visitor. Mrs Marchant. She wants to know if it's okay to let her stay.'

Harmon nodded. 'She's less likely to do a runner if she sees a friendly face,' he said. A clerk came in with something for him to sign. Harmon waved to stop Wainwright hanging up. 'Get Jackson to ask if Mrs Marchant has any idea where Kate might go.' He turned his attention to Craine. 'If it'll make you feel any better, Inspector Craine, perhaps you should check with Stretton whether it's possible to delay the sending of an e-mail message. Maybe Shepherd set it up before he left the office, ready to be relayed at a particular time.'

Wainwright found it difficult to cut out the noise around him. He wished to God Craine would stop whining. On the amount of sleep he'd had the last two days, he was finding it hard enough to keep it together without the added annoyance of Craine's constant griping and complaints. He completed the instructions to Jackson and hung up, feeling an irritation with Craine's bluster that was akin to a maddening itch. He had to get out of the office before the urge to scratch it became irresistible.

'Sergeant—'

'Back in a minute, sir.' He did not pause but walked on, out to the elevator and down to the foyer. He jerked back, instantly hitting a button when he saw the throng of newspaper reporters at the entrance. Even as the doors closed they surged forward, shouting questions. The staff canteen was fairly empty and he drank two mugs of coffee, wishing for something stronger, before he had the courage to make the call to Jan and return to Harmon's office.

Harmon had taken another call. It was from Bernie Comiskey, and she was livid. She had just spoken to Mary Marchant after calling round to drop off Kate's clothes. Mary had filled her in on the details of the previous evening and she had come directly to the station but couldn't get past the foyer because of the reporters.

'What sort of protection are you supposed to be giving here?' she demanded, shouting over the noise at the bar of the Trafford Hall Hotel across the road. Some of the media had taken a break and were ordering drinks and talking loudly in foreign-sounding southern accents.

'Ms Comiskey, we have two suspects in custody. We don't believe Mrs Pearson to be in any danger.'

'You've spoken to Mrs Marchant, then.'

Harmon straightened up. 'No.'

Bernie heard the caution in his voice. 'Mary thinks Kate

knows who's been sending the messages. She thinks Kate's gone after him.'

'Does Mrs Marchant know *where* she may have gone?'

'If she did, she wouldn't be sitting on her arse waiting for something to happen, would she?'

'No.' Harmon closed his eyes and pinched the bridge of his nose. 'No, I don't suppose she would.'

'Sir.' The look on Wainwright's face was enough. He put Bernie Comiskey on hold. The two men stared at each other.

'Constable Jackson,' said Wainwright. 'A parcel's just been delivered to the flat.'

'How was it delivered?'

'Motorbike courier. Jackson's got him under arrest.'

Harmon let out a loud exhalation. 'Well, that's a bloody relief.'

'Sir – sorry.' Constable Barratt stood at the door. A WPC had relieved her at Shepherd's flat and she had hot-footed it to where the real action was. 'Press are demanding an interview.' She shrugged apologetically.

'Make sure Jackson gets through without any awkward questions being asked,' he told Wainwright. 'And have the courier put in an interview room as soon as he gets here. Where's Mrs Marchant?'

'Stayed at the flat, sir. In case Mrs Pearson shows up.'

Kate tapped impatiently on the glass screen of the taxi cab. 'What's the hold-up?' she asked. The driver slid back the screen, letting a fug of cigarette smoke into the passenger compartment. Kate inhaled gratefully. She hadn't stopped for cigarettes and wished now that she had.

'City centre's closed,' the driver answered. 'Bomb scare or summat. Bloody bastard animal rights.'

'Can't you skirt round?' Kate asked.

'It'll mean a bit on the fare.'

'Just get me there the quickest way you can,' she said.

The driver swung round in a wide arc, cutting across two lanes of traffic, ignoring the blaring horns and giving a wave of the hand in thanks to the outraged motorists who'd had to stop to let him out. He was smiling to himself.

Harmon watched as the forensics specialist opened the parcel on a plastic sheet, using a scalpel and forceps. He reached inside the box and took out a slip of paper. It was folded in half. Gripping the edges with the tips of the forceps, he opened it out and held it up for Harmon to read.

'My God.' Wainwright had spoken, reading over Harmon's shoulder.

'We'd better get Mr and Mrs Marchant in,' Harmon said.

Chapter Twenty-seven

The interview with the courier was frustrating. He was smoking nervily, sweating in his bike leathers but unwilling to increase his vulnerability by taking off his jacket.

Harmon studied him, unblinking.

'I told you!' the courier insisted. 'I just picked up the parcels and deliver them, right? I don't get told who they're from.'

'Get on to Hermes Courier Service, Constable Barratt. Ask them to confirm Mr Ahmed's story.' He fixed the courier with a baleful eye. 'You picked this one up from the office, yes?'

Ahmed nodded, wiping a drop of sweat from the end of his nose. 'It was just a normal delivery, man. I was supposed to deliver it at twelve o'clock sharp. That's what I did.'

Craine came through the door, looking like he'd been sucking lemons. He jerked his head in the direction of the door.

Harmon stepped outside. 'Is this important, Inspector?' Harmon asked.

'Might be. Stretton says the e-mail could've been delayed if Shepherd had routed it through a remailer to disguise his identity.'

'But he didn't.'

'No.' Craine ground his teeth. 'The message was sent from his terminal to Mrs Pearson's direct.'

'So no time delay. He's in the clear, Inspector.'

Craine shrugged. 'I still say he's fucking weird.'

Harmon raised an eyebrow. 'That,' he said, 'is not yet a crime in this country.' He gripped the handle of the interview room door, and then, with a twinkle of mischief, he said, 'You can break the news to Mr Shepherd and ask him if he wouldn't mind hanging about. We might have need of his computing skills.'

Mary was trembling uncontrollably. Constable Jackson handed her a glass of water. 'It'll be all right, Mrs Marchant,' she said.

'Of course it won't,' Mary spat. 'Don't be so bloody naïve. It wasn't all right for Melanie, was it?'

Harmon drew up a chair and sat opposite Mrs Marchant. 'I know this is difficult for you,' he said, 'but, please, try and think back. Was there anything Mrs Pearson said that might help us?'

'Where's Tony?'

'We're trying to find him. He wasn't at home.'

'He went to pick up Jenny. Oh dear God, he'll be frantic—'

'Mrs Marchant, we'll bring him here as soon as we can. Now, if there's anything . . . It might help us find the man who's taken your daughter.'

'She knew he would do this.'

'What?'

Mary continued, oblivious to the question. Her lips were almost white with shock. 'She told me to stay away until it was over. She said it was dangerous, but I wouldn't listen.'

'Did Mrs Pearson give you any idea who she thought could be sending her the messages?'

Mary frowned, hearing the voice, but the tumult in her head blocked its meaning. 'It isn't over,' she murmured.

'Mrs Marchant?' Harmon prompted.

'That's what Kate said. "It isn't over."'

The taxi was making slow and ill-tempered progress through the Christmas traffic.

'Half the bloody north-west's come to Manchester for their chuffing Christmas shop,' the driver growled. 'At this rate, we'll have to go Stretford way and then up onto the M63.'

'Do whatever you have to,' Kate said. 'I don't care what it costs. And give us one of those fags, will you?'

Harmon asked Constable Jackson to take Mrs Marchant through to the canteen for a cup of tea. He leaned against the edge of his desk, head resting on his chest, and watched her walk down the corridor. She was devastated: shocked to the very core of her being.

'Get word to Jackson, will you? Ask her to find out if Marchant has a lock-up – maybe somewhere off the beaten track.'

'You think it's him, sir?'

Harmon sighed. 'I don't know what to think any more, Bill. I hope for her sake it isn't. Put word out we're looking for him. It may be just as she said – he may be out looking for his daughter.' Kate Pearson had said it once, and she was right. Sometimes it was a lousy, rotten bloody job.

'Where do we start looking? The Arndale Centre?'

'That's the obvious one. It's where the school party's supposed to've been.'

When Wainwright returned a few minutes later, Harmon was standing at the window, listening to the distant roar of the traffic, muted by the double glazing. He turned slowly, feeling the weariness of all the cases and all the misery he had seen over the previous year condensed into that moment.

'What?' he asked, knowing it was more bad news.

'The Arndale Centre's closed. Bomb scare. Incendiary device went off in the foyer of the Royal Exchange Theatre. They're checking the area for other suspect packages now.'

'That could take a few hours at this time of year.' Harmon pressed the heel of his hand into his eye socket in an attempt to silence a stabbing pain that had started up an hour ago. 'The school party?'

'They were split up. The teacher in charge is trying to round them up, but four are still missing.' Wainwright nodded in response to the unspoken question: Jenny Marchant was among the missing.

'Christ! What about her father?'

Wainwright shook his head. 'No sign of him yet.'

The sounds from the office beyond – doors slamming, shouted orders, telephones ringing, bursts of laughter – all were extinguished by a silence which grew loud between them. They stood for some time, motionless, their feeling of impotence paralysing thought and action. The silence was shattered by a telephone ringing on Harmon's desk. They let it ring two, three, four times before the paralysis lifted and they reached for it together.

Harmon got there first. He listened, spoke one word: 'Okay,' and hung up. 'No prints on the note,' he told Wainwright. 'Anything from the couriers yet?'

'I've put Diana Rowson on to it. I'll check if she's heard anything.'

'And get someone over to Mrs Pearson's address as well – a DC. If there are any more deliveries, I don't want them scared off by a uniform.'

*

Kate felt a chill of excitement as they swept off the motorway and into the outskirts of Eccles. The town has been marred by motorways. The M63 runs north–south along its westerly edge, and the M602 runs east–west, bisecting it. They headed for the triangular peninsula, the third side of which was created by the Manchester Ship Canal, on the borders of old Eccles. It was here, among the Victorian merchants' houses, that she expected to find him.

'I've checked with Sergeant Rowson, sir. The parcel was delivered at 10.30 by a short guy, dark hair, glasses.'

Harmon frowned. The description didn't fit any of their suspects. Maybe their man had got an intermediary to take the parcel into the office.

'The instructions were typewritten: it was to be delivered at exactly midday.'

Harmon nodded, thinking. 'It's time we spoke to Mr Shepherd again,' he said.

'I'll set up an interview room,' Wainwright suggested.

'No. DI Craine is entertaining him in the staff canteen. Have him bring Mr Shepherd to my office.' He noted the amused surprise on Wainwright's face. 'Is Stretton about?'

'He's catching up on his off-duty.'

Harmon raised his eyebrows. 'He can do that any time. See if you can rouse him. He might learn something from Shepherd.' He glanced at the computer on his desk.

'Marchant's been found, sir.' Constable Barratt had put her head round the door.

'Where?'

'Arndale Centre. Half-demented. He was looking for his little girl, apparently.'

'Where is he now?'

'On his way. Where d'you want to see him?'

'Interview room, I think. Bring Mrs Marchant in after we've got him settled.'

'Sure. Sir—'

Harmon scowled. 'No press interviews. Not until I know what's going on.'

'No, sir. It's the Comiskey woman on the phone. She says she's coming over, and if she doesn't get an interview with you sharpish, she'll give her own interview to the press.'

'Comiskey.' He'd forgotten her. He wondered how long she'd stayed on hold before losing her temper. It didn't matter much; she would be in no mood for compromise.

'Then I'd better see her, hadn't I? Tell her to come over to the security barrier at the car park. You can meet her yourself. Give me' – he checked his watch – 'five minutes.'

'What about Shepherd, sir?' Wainwright asked.

Harmon rubbed a hand over his head. 'Ask him if he'd like some lunch. You might have some yourself, Sergeant.'

Wainwright was surprised by the suggestion, and even more surprised to find that he actually felt hungry. He hadn't thought about food for a couple of days, getting by on coffee and alcohol. 'I might just do that, sir. Fancy anything yourself?'

Harmon considered a moment. 'A couple of sandwiches, if they're fresh.' He settled himself behind his desk. He knew Bernie Comiskey, both as Kate's friend and as a campaigner for women's rights. She had conducted a few seminars on domestic violence for the Greater Manchester Police and occasionally advised the Domestic Violence Unit on approaches to women whose history of physical abuse was particularly entrenched. He found her belligerent, articulate, difficult, bright. She was passionate about her work, and although she was always willing to hear the other side, it was not guaranteed she would accept what seemed self-evident. She could be fairly brutal in her dismissal of what she considered weak or spurious arguments. He would have to be on his guard.

'Sit down, Ms Comiskey. I'm sorry about the telephone call. We've been rather tied up, I'm afraid.' He didn't think the new hairstyle did much to soften the bull-terrier image of the woman, but his expression betrayed nothing.

'What's going on?' she asked.

They were instinctively wary of each other, Bernie as the representative of a group that had traditionally been ignored by the police, Harmon as the figure of authority, the representative of male decision-makers who reinforced the status quo.

Harmon's feelings were no less complicated. He saw the barrier between them and had some understanding of her reservations, her inability to believe that they both wanted the same thing, but he sensed that this was something he could never convince Comiskey of. Right now, he hadn't the energy to try. He let the silence last a little longer. Comiskey's gaze didn't waver.

'We're doing all we can to find Mrs Pearson,' he said.

'Sure.' The tone was as ambiguous as the word. 'But what's going on?'

Harmon paused, waiting for her to make the next move.

Bernie checked him over. He didn't reveal much: no nervous tics, no defensive body posture, no tell-tale signs. His serious eyes returned her stare, waiting for her to come clean. She shrugged. He held all the cards and seemed intent on playing them close to his chest.

'Your incident room is buzzing, Mr Harmon. The atmosphere is so highly charged I could almost smell the ozone as I walked past the door.'

'We'd like to locate Mrs Pearson soon as possible.' An oblique answer to an oblique question.

'Why?'

Harmon frowned.

'If you've got the right guy, why all the hurry?' Her eyes raked Harmon's, trying to read his thoughts but seeing only tiredness and worry. 'Unless you got the wrong guy.' Her eyes darted away and then back to him. 'She's gone after him, hasn't she?'

'What makes you think that?'

'It's the sort of thing Kate'd do. If you'd got the wrong guy, and she knew the right one. Mary tells me she clobbered her ex last night. She probably thinks she's Captain bloody Scarlet now.'

Harmon puckered his forehead. 'Captain Scarlet?'

'Indestructible,' Bernie explained.

Harmon passed a hand over his face and Bernie saw that she had guessed right. The reality was far more frightening than speculation, and she felt herself grow cold. 'She'll get herself killed,' she murmured.

'We'll find her,' Harmon said, wishing he could believe it.

'I wouldn't bet on it.'

Neither spoke for some time. Then Harmon said, almost apologetically, 'Ms Comiskey, I must get back to work.'

Bernie didn't move. She had been thinking what could happen to Kate if she found the man she was looking for. Now she turned her attention to their conversation in the hostel. She thought hard, trying to remember something that might help, but she couldn't. 'Okay,' she said at last. 'But I'm going to stick around, and I'll make a bloody nuisance of myself until I see something being done about this shambles.'

Harmon didn't doubt it. It seemed to him that Ms Comiskey was the sort of woman whose entire strategy for getting things done was based on making a bloody nuisance of herself.

*

Detached, serene, rising from a garden of closely trained shrubs and dense, green turf, the house gleamed in the greyish light. The scalloped eaves, the window frames and the door were all painted white. The basement windows were barred and shuttered, and these too were glossed – sanded and painted to a glassy white finish.

Harmon had arranged that he would watch Marchant's reactions when he first saw his wife and Wainwright would watch Mrs Marchant. She virtually collapsed into his arms. 'I should've stayed with her. I shouldn't have let her out of my sight,' he said.

'Mr Marchant,' Harmon said, 'where did you arrange to meet your daughter?'

'Outside the Royal Exchange. But they wouldn't let me through. They can't find her, Mary.'

'He's got her, Tony.'

Marchant held his wife at arm's length. 'Mary?' She was unable to explain further, and Harmon spoke:

'There's been a note, Mr Marchant.'

Marchant looked over his wife's head, uncomprehending. 'A note? Who from?'

'We don't know, sir.'

'Kate told me to stay out of it. Oh, God, Tony, it's all my fault.'

Marchant let his wife go. For a moment Harmon thought he would pass out. He looked past his wife, at Harmon, swallowing convulsively. He unzipped his jacket, took a step towards the door, put his hands in his pockets, uncertain what to do, then turned back. 'You have to find her,' he said.

'We're doing all we can, sir.'

Marchant looked down at the floor. He muttered something, then repeated it more loudly: 'I have to go and look for her.' He tried to get past the constable on duty, who held him back. 'She probably got lost,' he said, turning wildly to Harmon. 'She was split up from the rest of the group. Mrs Callaghan may have found her by now.'

'I think she's been abducted, Mr Marchant,' Harmon said quietly.

'No.' Tony Marchant shook his head. This couldn't happen to his little girl. She was with a school party, for Christ's sake. How could this happen? 'No. She's got lost in the crowd. She could be phoning home. Good God, Mary! We should be at home. She might come home and we won't be there.'

Mary took his hand in hers. 'That's what we'll do, Tony. We'll go home now.' She looked to Inspector Harmon for approval.

'That would probably be best. We'll let you know as soon as we hear anything.'

'If that was play-acting, the guy deserves an Oscar,' Wainwright said after they had left.

'Poor bastard,' Harmon agreed. 'Well, we can scrub him from the suspect list. For his wife's sake, I'm glad. Is Shepherd ready? Because as far as I can make out, he's the best chance we have of catching the lunatic who's doing this.'

Chapter Twenty-eight

Harmon got up as Shepherd came into his office. 'Mr Shepherd,' he began, extending a hand.

Adam looked at it. Thrust his hands into his pockets.

'Look, I know we've given you a hard time,' Harmon said. 'You've every right to—'

'No apologies, please. I couldn't take it on a full stomach.' Adam had spent the last half hour eating. Partly because he really was hungry, but mostly as a result of the sense of release he felt on getting out of the reeking cell they had returned him to. The disinfectant smell hung about his clothing; he would like to have showered and changed, to get the stench of imprisonment from his pores. He glanced from Harmon to Wainwright, to Stretton. They were waiting for something, and it seemed that whatever it was depended on him. 'What?' he asked.

Harmon indicated a chair, but Adam remained standing. 'She's vanished,' Harmon said.

Adam swayed on his feet.

'We've got someone at her flat and at yours, but she hasn't shown up.'

'What about her friend's place?' he asked. 'Mary Marchant?' He sensed a tension in the air and although neither of the officers looked at Harmon, he felt their attention directed towards their superior.

'Not there either,' Harmon replied, after a pause; he was unwilling to tell Shepherd too much.

Adam jerked his head towards the computer on Harmon's desk. 'Is that linked to the mainframe?'

Harmon relaxed. Shepherd had done the difficult part for him. 'It's all yours,' he said.

Adam hesitated, momentarily nervous. He touched his eyebrow and then said, 'I'll be performing some dubious procedures.'

'You have my word that nothing will go beyond these four walls.'

'I need a login and a password,' Adam said, sitting down at the terminal. Harmon gave them without hesitation. Adam tapped in commands and within minutes he'd gained access to Technicomm's files. He called up his own mailbox and frowned.

'Problem?' Harmon asked.

'I expected some replies. And what happened to the message I got from Kate to say she was in hospital?'

'*I* didn't wipe it,' Stretton said.

Adam typed a message to the systems manager, who replied within minutes. There had been no changes to files overnight. 'So,' said Adam, 'someone else has wiped it.' He typed a command, calling up Kate's newly reinstated mailbox. This too was empty.

'DC Baines checked with Technicomm security at about nine this morning. He'd just missed Mrs Pearson. Could be she collected her mail and yours, then wiped it,' Stretton suggested.

Adam quit, and then typed a fresh command. 'I'm logging in to Manchester's UNIX system,' he explained.

The phones were ringing off the hook, but he didn't seem

to notice. Harmon sent Wainwright to arrange for some-body to take the calls, and when he turned back, the cursor was flashing next to the UNIX prompt.

Adam typed 'Who' and hit the return key. 'This will tell me who's using the university mainframe at the moment,' he said. A list of userids scrolled up the screen. 'No good. There's no one on-line that I can talk to.' He glanced up briefly at Harmon. 'The guys I need to contact are generally night users.'

'Can't you call them up?'

'What,' Adam asked, 'by phone?' Harmon might have sug-gested sending them a message by carrier pigeon, judging by his astounded reaction. Harmon nodded, and Adam smiled. 'They're not employees or students. In fact, they aren't autho-rized to use the system at all, but,' he shrugged, 'if they only use it off-peak, when other folk don't need it, then they reckon they're doing no harm. I don't know their real names or their whereabouts. They're strictly Net buddies. I'm sorry, all I can do is leave a message for them and hope they read it sooner rather than later.'

'In the meantime,' Harmon told Wainwright, 'I'd like you to organize a sweep of the remaining suspects. Go gently. We just want to know if they've seen Kate Pearson.'

Wainwright left, and Harmon caught Adam Shepherd watching him with some interest. He lifted his eyebrows just discernibly and said: 'Presumably, they're all on the Net?'

Harmon nodded: 'So?'

Adam regarded Harmon with that long, thoughtful look. 'If I knew who the other suspects were . . . I could maybe glean more information than your guy did.'

Stretton shifted uncomfortably.

'Maybe you could, at that,' Harmon replied.

*

Kate walked up the stone steps to the doorway. The brass bell-push had been restored and was polished to gleaming perfection. She rang. And waited.

Harmon had poured himself a cup of tea when Barratt came in. 'You still here?' he asked.

'Frightened of missing out on anything. Just as well, considering Mr and Mrs Marchant are downstairs.' Barratt added, with a grin, 'They've got Jenny with them.'

Adam barely glanced up as the Chief Inspector strode to the door. He was far away surfing the breakers of the Internet, when a small voice next to him made him turn his head away from the monitor.

'Hiya,' it said.

He stared for some moments, taking time to return from virtual space to reality. 'Hiya. Jenny, right?' He had met her several times when he had taken Melanie bowling or roller-skating.

'Yeah,' she said. 'What you doin'?'

'Surfing, man.' They smiled at each other and he moved over so she could get a better look.

'She said they got split up after the fire bomb went off.' Mary Marchant was relaying Jenny's account to DCI Harmon. 'It was right behind them.' A look of pain crossed her face. Tony put his arm around her as she continued. 'They all scattered. Then the place seemed to be full of police and their group was sent off to the other side of the precinct. Jenny got lost in the crowds and she panicked.' Mary lowered her voice. 'She thinks she saw the man who took Melanie away. A man in a hood, she said. He gave Mrs Callaghan some money.'

'Could she give a description?'

Mary shook her head. 'Same as last time. A tall man in a jacket with a hood. That's all she remembers.'

'Why did it take her so long to get home?'

'Traffic. The city centre was closed for a couple of hours. She tried to phone us, but, of course, I was at Kate's and Tony was out looking for her. She didn't know what to do. So she started walking. She took a couple of wrong turns on the way. She was in a terrible state when she got home.'

'The man she saw. Did he try to grab her?'

'No. He just put some money in the bucket and smiled at her.'

'Then why the note?'

Mary shrugged helplessly.

Harmon picked up the internal phone hand set and pressed two digits. 'I'd like a look at the note Mrs Pearson got this morning, please.' He hung up.

Kate walked down the swept alleyway to the back of the house. The back garden was a neat strip of trimmed lawn and no more. The walls were stark, bare, unpainted, unclut-tered by ivy or roses. Devoid of life. The upper panels of the back door were glazed. She looked round for something; a brick or a stone to use. There was none. She turned her face away and gave the glass several sharp blows with her elbow until it shattered. She picked out the larger frag-ments before reaching in and turning the latch.

In her dreams he was always upstairs in the attic room. She moved down the hallway soundlessly, effortlessly, as in her dreams. The banisters gleamed, polished to a warm glow that denied the icy coldness of the house. The walls, painted white, were stained red in a small pool by the dying light that spilled through the little glass rose in the centre of the front door: his one concession to colour. The rest was as antiseptic and impersonal as a doctor's waiting room.

A faint sound from below made her hesitate, but she moved on, trailing her fingers lightly along the stair rail, her footsteps whispering on the carpet. The stairway narrowed and she climbed the last few steps to the attic, pushed open the door, stepped inside. The plain, waxed floorboards, the wide views of the city on two sides, the desk at one window – all were as she remembered them.

'I never expected to see you here again.'

Kate did not turn to the voice, but walked to the desk. 'Is this the computer you used?' she asked.

'That and the one in my office. How did you find me?'

'It really wasn't that difficult.'

Harmon held the note in his hand. It was enclosed in a plastic bag. ' "You see how easy it is?" ' he read, ' "Melanie, Jenny, whoever I like. Whenever I choose." I think we can take it the diversion in the shopping centre was a warning,' he said. 'The man never really intended to take your daughter, Mrs Marchant, but he wants Kate to think he can whenever he wants to.'

'Why would he do that?' Mary asked.

'To punish her. To isolate her. I don't know what motivates that sort of mind.'

The doorbell rang, echoing around the bare walls, reverberating, carrying through the house to the room where they stood. Neither moved. They wanted no interruptions. That was an unspoken agreement between them. They remained in the stillness of the room, motionless. Even their breathing was quiet and shallow. They waited a long time, until they were sure the visitor had gone away.

Kate looked around the room, bare of furniture, barren of pictures or ornaments. The marble fireplace gleamed dully in the mean light of the afternoon. It was cold, bitterly cold, and the wide picture windows admitted a grubby yellow light. It would snow later.

Kate's heart jumped and then fell, a leaden weight in her chest, for Melanie had always wished for snow at Christmas. Once it had come in November, and several times in January, but never at Christmas.

The room reeked of cleanliness. The rigorous sort, performed to hide the smell of decay. The floorboards, freshly sealed and newly waxed, were unblemished by dust or scuff marks. Varnish and paraffin and beeswax mingled with the smell of dust rags, the type her mother would make from old candy-striped sheets. Kate breathed it in like a memory, gagging on the underlying suggestion of rigid control and stiff, unbending coldness.

She felt a kind of torpor, an unwillingness to break the silence. There was a stillness, a fossilized hush of habit and preference that was so complete it was almost tangible. She stood for some time until, far away, echoing in the stillness of the house, a voice came to her. It was Melanie's. She looked round. He had gone. She was alone now. All that remained was the fake tranquillity and Melanie's voice, calling to her. She followed it out of the attic room, with its vertiginous views, down the gleaming stairway into the hall. The door to the basement stood open.

She was being manipulated, she knew. He was drawing her to the quietest, the most secret place in the house, to a place where the bright, cold stillness of the attic room would seem cheerful, even wholesome, by comparison. But she had to see.

Kate's shoes rasped on the stone steps. If he was down here, he must be hiding. Melanie was crying now, begging her to come and take her home. He could be hiding behind any one of a series of stone pillars that bore the weight of the floors above. The centre of the space was lit by neon light, barely penetrating beyond the weights bench with hand weights stacked in a pyramid beside it and, next to it, an exercise cycle. Kate stepped on to the stone flags, feeling the heat drawn from her feet, moving instinctively towards the light.

A figure matched her movements in the darkness beyond the lights. She watched, wary, waiting for him to make his move. The tape-recorder must be near by. The volume had been turned up high and Melanie's voice, distorted and tearful, was begging not to be tied up again.

The figure had stopped. Kate stepped towards it. It took a step forward. She stepped sideways. It moved synchronously. She raised her hand. It mirrored her action. Kate relaxed, walking confidently up to the figure and encountering the smooth, cold surface of a mirror. She wheeled as Melanie's voice was suddenly silenced.

He was behind the light, somewhere in the darkness.

'Are you so in love with yourself that you even have to exercise in front of a mirror?' she asked.

'How does it feel to be alone, Kate?'

Kate, injured, withdrew a fraction, then counter-attacked: 'You ought to know, Kenneth. Haven't you always been alone? I should think you have. Hardly surprising, is it?'

'They say,' he replied, 'that it's often worse to lose something you've had – money, one of the senses, health.' He waited. 'A child.'

'Is that what they say?' Kate paused reflectively. 'Well, they're wrong.'

'Better to have loved and lost?' he taunted.

'Something like that.'

She heard him move to her right and turned in the direction of the sound.

'Your friend Shepherd is under arrest. Your ex-husband too. I don't think your little Irish potato will want to have anything more to do with you after today. You've lost really rather a lot, wouldn't you say, Katya?'

'Harmon's not a fool. He'll soon work out he's got the wrong man. As for David, he's got what's been coming to him for a long time. And Mary—' She shrugged. 'She'll get over it.' Mary would be furious with her for sneaking off without telling her, but it wouldn't break their friendship.

'You set great store by your friend's loyalty.'

Kate smiled. 'I expect you find that hard to understand.'

He did find it puzzling. Surely she couldn't expect her friend to stand by her after the abduction hoax? 'Tell me,' he said, genuinely curious, 'would you risk your child's safety, even for your closest friend?'

Kate paled. 'Jenny?'

Both pleased and intrigued by her reaction, he went on, 'It's always easier to be noble in the abstract.'

'I never meant – I don't want anyone else involved in this. This is between you and me,' Kate said, her voice breathy. She was afraid for the first time.

She can't have seen his note. A pity. But this was far better. She must think he had Melanie's little friend.

'D'you think you'll rescue her, Katie? Did you think you would rescue Melanie?' He repeated the words he had rehearsed so often in his daydreams.

'Yes.' Kate measured her words carefully. 'Yes, I did fantasize that I would find Melanie and take her home. Safe . . .' Her breathing timed the flow of words. 'In my fantasies, I would kill you and take Melanie home.'

He laughed. 'I think that would be extremely unlikely, given your current state of health,' he remarked.

'And what were your fantasies, Kenneth? What did you dream of then? What do you dream of now?'

He remained in the shadows. She would not know his fantasies. How could she presume to understand the complexity of his feelings? The pain she had caused him. The need to cause her pain. He hated her for what she had made him become: an abductor, a murderer, and something more. Something that with half his mind he despised, yet felt the compulsion to gratify again and again.

In his fantasies he always explained why he had been forced to act as he had and the terrible mix-up that had ended in Melanie's death. And she had always seen her own culpability and had wept. Now he knew he could not tell her any of these things. He could only hope to gain some small recompense for what she had made him suffer.

'You never thought beyond causing me pain.'

He was disconcerted by the accuracy of her insight.

'If you had, perhaps Melanie would be alive today.'

'Perhaps.' He shrugged. 'It's possible.'

'Melanie was never the real target,' Kate went on. 'It was me you really wanted to hurt.' She took his silence for acquiescence. 'Where is she?' She could hear his breathing in the darkness, but she could not see him.

'Did you think I would keep her here?'

'Why not? It's where you kept Melanie, isn't it?' Her voice stuttered back at her from the basement walls. They were painted white, like the rest of the house, and in the dim light they threw back from the strip lights over her head she was just beginning to make out his shape.

'Do you see any trace of her, Kathy?' He opened his arms in an expansive invitation to explore.

'Kate,' she said, and the walls repeated it, like a secret disclosed. 'My name is Kate.'

'What's this?' asked Stretton.

'I'm running a password-cracker. It's trawling through dictionary words at the minute,' Adam explained. 'If they've used a dictionary word as a password, it'll find it.' He had found the userid by tapping in to the Finger program. UNIX had obligingly provided him with the name and the userid and now all he needed was a password to break into the files. 'Hah!' he exclaimed, staring into the screen as one looking into someone's eyes to gauge their meaning.

Jenny snatched up a pad and pen from the desk excitedly. 'I've got it!' she told him.

'Good. There'll probably be a few more, so stand by.' A few moments, then: 'We're in,' he called over his shoulder.

Once Kate had taken Melanie to York. They had visited the prison museum. Four of them had volunteered to be locked in the cell that had housed Dick Turpin before he was hanged. As the great oak door swung to, all light, all sound, all sense that life existed beyond this palpable darkness was cut off. Melanie clung to her, and her breathing was like an asthmatic whistle until, after what seemed like hours, the door was opened and daylight flooded in. Kate's throat constricted, not because she was afraid of this dreary, echoing room but because this must have been the last image that Melanie had taken with her into oblivion. This dark and sterile place would be the last thing she saw.

At first she had wanted to feel Melanie's presence, to have some lasting impression, some imprint of her daughter's spirit. There was none. With his compulsive cleaning, he had washed away all trace of Melanie's occupancy. Now it came, unexpectedly, as a kind of relief. Like a slow, incoming tide, the feeling grew deeper and stronger, gaining form. This was no place for Melanie. The walls and floors of this place, even the air, were dead. And Melanie was a living, vibrant force in her memory.

'Phoenix has three different files storing information about Kate,' Adam explained. Jenny had reluctantly gone home with her parents, accompanied by a police escort, so Stretton had taken over as scribe. He kept jotting down points, occasionally laughing with enjoyment at Shepherd's facility with the machine. 'One contains downloads from the Net – bulletin-board stuff – all to do with Melanie's disappearance and murder. The second lists Kate's personal details: address, phone number, bank account, office number. And this one' – he swivelled the monitor for Harmon to see – 'this one clinches it.' The screen showed an e-mail message, one of the mailings the phantom had sent her. 'It's got all the e-mail she ever received from the bastard. Phoenix is the phantom. Ingrams is Phoenix. Ergo, Ingrams is the phantom.'

Harmon straightened up. 'Before we go rushing in,' he said, 'I'd need more proof. He was, after all, in America when Melanie disappeared. He didn't return until after her body was found.'

'Did you talk to him?'

Wainwright spoke up. 'I did. By telephone. I left a message at the hotel reception and he called me back.'

Adam nodded slowly. 'Did anyone check he was actually on the flight out?'

'He checked in and was cleared through customs on the other side.'

'Did anyone actually see him?' Adam insisted. 'I mean, did you get the American police to check him out?'

'The hotel records log meals, telephone calls to and from his room, laundry service—'

'Big hotel, is it?'

'Why do you ask?'

'Bigger hotels are mostly on computer links these days.'

'Are you suggesting that he flew to America, ran up a bill at the New York Waldorf and made several phone calls via the international exchange all from Manchester?'

'I'd lay odds the chambermaid never had to make up the bed with fresh sheets,' Adam speculated. 'The Waldorf? Give me half an hour.' He turned back to the monitor and began tapping in commands.

Wainwright drew Harmon away to the other side of the room. Harmon noticed the sandwiches he had brought from the canteen and picked them up, unwrapping them as they talked.

'He's off his trolley, sir,' Wainwright said.

'I'll reserve judgement on that,' Harmon said, biting into a sandwich. 'Didn't they have anything with salad?'

Wainwright shook his head. 'I've talked to Ingrams several times, sir. I interviewed him just after he got back from New York. He was really upset by the whole thing.'

'If Shepherd can fake a booking, and checking in, then maybe Ingrams could. In which case, we ought to reconsider.'

Wainwright uttered a grunt of disgust.

'Heard anything yet?' Wainwright had asked him to arrange a psychological assessment for William, and Angie had been pulling a few strings.

'After Christmas. The twenty-ninth.'

'Good.' There was an awkward silence, during which they could hear Shepherd tapping away at the keyboard and the occasional exclamation from Stretton.

'How's Jan taking it?' Harmon asked.

Wainwright shrugged. 'Relieved, I suppose. She's said all along there was something wrong. It's just—' He paused. 'A part of me doesn't really want to know. It doesn't make sense, I know that. But it's how I feel.'

'In my experience,' Harmon observed, 'knowledge is preferable to ignorance.'

Wainwright managed a grin. 'Spoken like a true copper,' he said.

Chapter Twenty-nine

'Didn't you ever think that you still had a chance to set things right?' Kate asked. 'Didn't it occur to you to let her go?'

'Would it make you feel better if I did? Wouldn't it complicate your feelings further? That there might have been a moment's hesitation that could have changed everything? Isn't it better – more comforting – to think of me as the evil maniac who cold-bloodedly abducted and murdered your daughter?'

Kate felt an angry flush rise to her face. She was on the balls of her feet and her fists were clenched, ready to fly at him, but the time was not right. So she forced herself to relax, loosening each muscle in turn. She would not act until *she* was ready.

'They're coming for you, Kenneth. It won't be long now. They'll put you away for a long, long time.'

Ingrams felt a sudden shaft of fear, and he shivered, but he made himself smile and stepped into the light. 'I think you're fantasizing again, Katie dear.'

'If you had left it with Melanie's murder, you'd have got away with it.' Kate's eyes roved over his face. 'You couldn't do that for one reason.'

'Oh?' he murmured, his smile growing more fixed. His

muscle tone warned Kate that he too was fighting an inner rage. 'And what reason is that?'

'You're insane,' she said.

Wainwright was shaking his head incredulously.

'Try it,' Adam invited. 'Call the Waldorf and ask them to page me.'

Harmon punched a button for an outside line and dialled direct. He had given orders not to be disturbed unless Kate Pearson had been found.

Shepherd was sitting with his hands behind his head, tilting his chair, looking more relaxed than he had a right to be, and Wainwright had to quell an unreasonable urge to tip him off his chair.

Harmon had read him right. He'd found not knowing what was wrong with William intolerable, so he'd done a few checks of his own. The doctor Angie Harmon had referred them to was a specialist in language and communication problems. Someone had translated that into plain English for him: autism. The name alone so terrified him that he had almost cancelled the appointment, but Jan had insisted. They must go.

'And what if he is autistic?' he had demanded. 'What will we *do*, Jan?'

'We'll deal with it. At least it'll be better than not knowing.' He marvelled that she had been so strong since he'd suggested the consultation with a specialist. It was as if she felt a great burden of guilt lifted from her that their son's abnormal behaviour was not, after all, her fault, that there could be some physiological explanation. She had reassured him. Everything would be okay. They would get by somehow. That was supposed to be his job, reassurance, except he hadn't given her much reassurance in the preceding months.

He felt he'd let her down, and Jan's quiet forgiveness only made it worse.

Harmon was talking into the phone: 'Have him call me back, will you?' He gave his name and details for the receptionist. 'What now?' he asked, hanging up.

'I call the desk and ask if there are any messages for me, and then ring you.'

Wainwright raised his eyebrows. 'Very hi-tech,' he muttered.

Harmon chewed the inside of his mouth.

'I can accept that as far as it goes, but what about the flights? He's logged as a passenger there and back.'

'I flew out last night, on the red-eye flight,' Adam said, smiling crookedly. 'Paid for by a Gold Card I don't have.'

'Of course,' Harmon said queasily, 'I'll have to check that.'

'I've got the airline's number right here,' said Adam, tossing Harmon the notepad.

Moira, like most of the staff at Technicomm, finished early on Christmas Eve. Her leather shoulderbag was crammed even more improbably full than usual. She wasn't expecting to see anyone over Christmas. Friends had rather fallen away after her mother started having her *dos*.

There was a staff party – not at the office, as Mr Owen would never allow that on account of the damage that might be done to the office systems – but Moira had no intention of going. Just a lot of young people making unnecessary noise and drinking too much, using it as an excuse for getting up to no good. Showing off's what her mother would call it. Simon and that tarty new girl, Lynn, were at it already, giggling and laughing over by the photocopier. 'Thought she'd set her cap at Adam Shepherd,' Moira commented to no one in particular.

She'd be better out of it. And she'd plenty to occupy her: her notebooks were packed with news and observations that wanted putting into some kind of order. The police had been again today. And *she*'d been in, although Moira hadn't seen her. She ought not to have been near the place by rights, her being on compassionate leave and all. Mr Owen had told her that – about the compassionate leave. Then there'd been that fire bomb at the Arndale Centre at lunchtime. She'd've been right next to the theatre, only she'd decided to pop into Kendal's on her way down. Fanatics! And at Christmas too. Mr Owen said the police had been in looking for Kate – she could hardly bear to think of the woman. He didn't know what for, though. Moira had her suspicions. Attention-seeking, that's what Kate Pearson was.

She checked around the office once before picking up her shoulderbag and calling goodbye. Nobody replied, or even noticed her leave.

Adam was bewildered by the speed with which things happened after Harmon had made the call to Heathrow.

The uniform division were drafted in to clear the area. A lot of people had been difficult – Christmas Eve and freezing cold made them reluctant to leave the comfort of fireside and television. Harmon checked with two officers who had called at Dr Ingrams's house in Eccles at 2.35 p.m. The house was quiet. They had got no answer, so they tried the university. Dr Ingrams had not been in all day; few staff had.

Operations were moved to the quiet road near the old docks, and Adam was allowed to tag along on condition he stayed out of the way. Two officers – Adam recognized one of them as DC Barratt – were dispatched to suss out the house without causing a panic. While Barratt tried the front door, the beefy guy with her nipped around the back. A glass panel in the back door had been smashed and the door stood open.

'I loved you.' It was an accusation.

'No,' Kate said, 'you didn't. You loved yourself. And you thought you saw yourself in me.'

'You're a spiteful little cat, my Kat. I always said you'd cut yourself one day with that sharp tongue of yours.'

'I'm not a cat. I'm not yours. And I told you, my name is Kate.'

As he moved to her right, Kate had edged to the left. The bench and cycle were still between them, but now she was at the foot of the bench, and the mirror cast tantalizing reflections. She glanced up. A thin bar of uncertain light was just visible at the top of the steps. The basement door was open. Kate wondered whether Chief Inspector Harmon had found Ingrams out yet. The thought brought her mind back to the trip from Manchester to Eccles. Three certainties came to her, like swift strikes of a hammer, sure and true: the bomb scare in the city centre had been Ingrams's doing; Jenny must have been there; the bomb was some sort of diversion.

He moved in a small arc.

'The bomb in Deansgate—'

'Inaccurate reporting. It was actually on the steps of the Royal Exchange. People are always eating lunch there and leaving their detritus behind on the steps. I counted on its being invisible. It was.' He was pleased to have an opportunity to explain his careful planning to her.

'And Jenny?' Kate stepped carefully to her left again.

'She recognized me, I'm sure of it. The teacher too. Jenny, perhaps, more certainly. She looked like she'd seen a ghost.'

'If not a ghost, then a devil.'

He laughed. 'Colourful but rather simplistic, don't you think, Kathy dear?'

'Is Jenny – safe?'

'For now,' he answered, smirking. Thinking it wasn't even necessary to lie to deceive her. Despising her for her gullibility. And moving towards her.

'Safe where?'

'Would you like to see her?'

'Yes.'

'I bet you would.' They were standing close now. The continual circling was dizzying to Kate. Her head pounded unremittingly, and she was feeling faint. They stood opposite each other, with only the narrow width of the weights bench between them. His eyes were hiding something Kate could not read. Had he already harmed Jenny?

'You're lying,' she said. 'She isn't safe.'

He laughed, once. A puff of vapour exploded from his lips. It offended him, being called a liar. She was faced with the truth and couldn't accept it. 'Just like a woman,' he said aloud.

'I want you to tell me where she is,' Kate said. His last remark had sparked a dull glow of anger. It was the sort of remark David had been fond of making. The cut on her head throbbed in time with the viscous coagulation of her rage. She felt it and this time did nothing to quell it.

Ingrams taunted her, flitting, moth-like, in and out of the light. 'Plenty of places to hide a child in the old docks,' he whispered. So many disused buildings, dry docks, warehouses, lots of lonely places. Find a place that's overgrown, grass between the cobblestones and the rail tracks rusted. They're eerie places, Katherine – not like the tarted-up redevelopments nearer the city.'

Kate listened with avid attention. He might give away something, some clue to Jenny's whereabouts.

'They're masterpieces of architecture,' he went on. 'As an engineer I can appreciate the skill that went into their design and construction. Millions of bricks laid with careful precision to make buildings of cathedral beauty. They're surprisingly low-ceilinged. Many of them are groyned – like a catacomb.' He smiled, moving back into the shadows. 'So many floors, Katie. So many dark corners. Upstairs or downstairs or in my lady's chamber. Of course, ladies in those days would never go near a place of such vulgar commerciality. Ironic, isn't it, that the renovated docklands are so attractive to the middle classes?'

'Where—'

'Is she?' His voice, mocking, echoed, shivering the air suspended between walls and ceiling and pillars, making Kate's flesh crawl. 'Quaking in the darkness, trembling and sighing? Listening to the steady drip and splash of seeping walls? Waiting for my return, half in terror that I will come, half in dread that I won't?' He was watching her from the shadows, but Kate could not see him. 'The wind wails like a banshee in those old buildings. And there are rats. God knows what they find to eat—'

'Bastard!' Kate lunged forward, but the weights bench was between them.

'Tut, tut,' Ingrams said. 'You always had a temper, Katie.'

She opened her mouth to speak, but a noise overhead distracted her. She froze. Ingrams stepped into the light and glanced up, then back at Kate. 'Our visitors have returned,' he said. 'The police, no doubt. It seems you are, for once in your sorry existence, right, although I'm loath to believe your friend Black Bobby worked it out all on his own. More likely he simply traced you here.'

'You'll have to tell them where Jenny is now.'

Ingrams smiled. Kate had never seen such cruelty in a smile.

'I'm going to go to prison anyway for Melanie's murder, Katie.' He stopped for a moment and resumed, sounding almost petulant: 'All this is your fault, you know.' Cautious footfalls overhead made him stop. 'Who will it be, do you think?' he asked. 'The unsmiling Sergeant Wainwright? A man with problems, I'd say. Harmon would want to be in on it, of course. I've made such a monkey of our simian detective. Perhaps they've brought in a special operations unit. Is that what they call them? Or perhaps they don't have them out-side London.' He sighed. 'Do you feel the burden of responsi-bility, Katie?'

'How can I feel responsible for your sickness?' she asked.

Ingrams shook his head, weaving into the light like a dream figure to Kate's pain-filled mind. He leant with his knuckles on the weights bench. 'You did this to me, Kate. No one else. When you walked out on me.' He laughed – it was more an angry shout. 'Walked out on me and took up with that twitchy Net nerd. That – freak!' Spittle had col-lected at the corners of his mouth.

'You did all this because you didn't consider Adam a fitting replacement for you?' Kate was appalled by the possibility.

'You don't understand anything, do you?'

'No,' said Kate. 'No, I don't. Explain it to me. I'd like to understand.'

A short, angry laugh again splintered the air. The move-ments above them had stopped, and Kate sensed they were listening. 'For Melanie's sake?' he asked. 'For Jenny's?'

Kate shook her head. 'You need help, Kenneth.' They had come full circle, he with his back to the door, she with her back to the mirror. He snorted and began walking to the steps.

'Where are you going?' she demanded, panic making her voice rise. 'We haven't finished yet.'

He turned slowly. 'We were finished long ago,' he told her. 'I wish I'd realized it then.'

'Wait!' Kate shouted. 'What about Jenny? You have to tell me where she is.'

He could have told her. Let her know the little brat would be safe at home by now, telling her parents of her great adventure. But that would make it too easy for Kate. While he could exercise power over her, he would. She had taken everything from him, and he wanted some recompense.

'You want to understand, Kate? All right. I'll tell you what I'll do for you. I'll let you have a real insight into how I feel. You no doubt think you suffered when you lost Melanie. But did you acknowledge the responsibility? Did you accept the blame? Did you have any idea that it was all your own doing? I went through hell when I killed her. You were right about that too, funnily enough. I never meant to hurt the child. Now you know it's your fault. *You* killed Melanie, just as surely as if you'd done it yourself. Your actions have caused all of this.'

'No.' Kate's hand went to her mouth. 'You can't do this.'

He looked at her, enjoying the exultation of this last brief moment of control over her. 'I'll go to prison for both of them,' he said. 'My life is over anyway.'

'No!'

Kate ran after him and pulled him back. He shrugged her off. She fell against one of the pillars, jarring the base of her spine. He moved on, but she tripped him, scissoring her legs. He toppled, catching his head a glancing blow against the weights bench. Its cushioned edge took most of the force and he recovered quickly, snatching a handful of Kate's hair.

'Bitch,' he growled, raising his fist to strike her. Kate flailed wildly, and her left hand came into contact with something smooth and cold under the bench. She gripped it. With all her force she smashed it into the side of his head.

He fell sideways, bleeding, taking Kate with him, and she cracked her head on the stone floor. A metallic *clunk* followed as she dropped the weight that had been her weapon. Ingrams groaned, putting his hand to his right temple.

Kate fought the now familiar nausea of shock and pain and crawled forward. Drops of blood, almost black in the inadequate light, fell on to the floor, on Ingrams's carefully polished shoes, on his sharply pressed trousers, on his clean white shirt. She grabbed his lapels and hauled him up, face to face with her. Something stung her eye, blotting her vision, and she turned her head sideways, wiping her head on her arm. It came away black and she realized she too was bleeding.

'*Where is she?*' she managed. The room revolved slowly, while Ingrams's face danced in and out of focus. The throbbing in her head seemed to be matched by a dull booming.

Ingrams held her gaze. 'Go to hell,' he said.

Kate brought her fist down with a sick thud on his mouth. Blood spattered on her face and neck. '*Where?*' Tears mixed with his blood and her own, thinning it. Ingrams smiled. Blood on his teeth. Black on white.

She raised her fist again. 'Where?' *Thud*. 'Where?' *Thud*. 'Where? Where? Where?'

'Where?' Kate asked, jolting awake. The room, familiar, yet unfamiliar. The sickness, the dull pounding in her head, as before. A constable – not Barratt or Jackson, someone she'd never seen before – jumped to her feet and left the room. When she returned, Kate had slipped back into unconsciousness. She woke an hour later, with the middle-aged doctor who'd examined her on her previous stay demanding to know if she intended making a career of this.

Kate paid no attention, looking beyond the doctor to the

tall, dark figure behind him. 'Jenny?' she whispered, afraid of the answer.

'She's fine. At home with her parents. She was never in any real danger.'

Kate frowned. 'He said he'd taken her. The bomb scare—'

'A warning. He intended to go on as before. Making your life a misery. I don't think he ever imagined you would find him out. He left a message. You didn't get it.'

'No.' Kate smiled weakly. 'I didn't get it. Not at all.' She brought her hand up to her face, only distantly aware of the cannula and drip attached to it. Gently she probed the bruising on her face. 'Am I under arrest?'

Harmon studied her closely. 'For what?' he asked.

'Ingrams.'

'He's recovering quite well. We expect to be able to charge him later this evening.'

'I thought I'd—'

'The state you were in when we got to you, I doubt you would be able to swat a fly effectively.'

Kate closed her eyes. When she opened them, the doctor and nurse were leaving. Harmon drew up a chair and sat beside her. He said nothing for some time, reluctant to disturb her.

'It's all right,' she said. 'I'm all right.'

There were livid bruises below one eye, as well as faded and fresh bruising around the cut on her forehead. She was pale, sick, unable to lift her head from her pillow, yet she looked strong. 'Yes,' he said, 'I think you are.'

'But—'

Harmon tilted his head. 'But,' he agreed, 'I don't understand why you didn't come to me. Tell me your suspicions.'

'I wanted to talk to him. Would you have let me talk to him?'

'No,' Harmon concurred. 'But what did you hope to gain by talking to him?'

'Understanding. Insight.' She frowned, and then winced with the pain. 'Maybe I wanted to hear him say he regretted what he had done.'

'Does he? Did you get what you wanted?'

'He asked me if I fantasized about rescuing Mel. You do – even though you know it's pointless. It's as if by sheer will you think you can change events.' Her hands fluttered briefly, pale as paper, and then fell to the sheet. 'Of course, it was fruitless. My going there was a stupid delusion. I could never understand him or what he did.'

Harmon nodded.

'He was going to give himself up,' said Kate. 'I thought he had Jenny. He let me believe he was going to leave her to die.' She closed her eyes, swallowing drily. 'I started it.'

Harmon closed one large hand over Kate's. 'No,' he said. 'You didn't start it. But you did finish it.' He patted her hand and stood. 'There's someone here to see you,' he said.

'Mary? Or Bernie?'

'The nursing staff suggested they leave it until morning. And Mrs Marchant's daughter has had quite an ordeal – she needs to spend some time with her mother, I should think. Shepherd,' he said, in answer to her puzzled look. 'We had reason to be thankful for his unique skills tonight.'

'He really gave you a going-over, didn't he?'

'You've looked better yourself,' Kate returned. Adam seemed to have acquired two black eyes in addition to the angry weal her drinking glass had left on his cheek. He touched one puffed eye. 'Got into a disagreement with a brick shithouse, name of Craine,' he said. He sat next to her in the chair Harmon had vacated.

They remained in silence while he took in the drip, the purple bruising, the fresh stitching in her forehead, her painful frailty. He was surprised by tears. 'Christ, Kate!' he said, his voice suddenly hoarse. She took his hand, and he turned it over, stroking it gently as though he was afraid of hurting her.

'I'm surprised you're still talking to me,' she teased, 'after I deleted all your files.'

'What?' he said, wiping his eyes carefully with his free hand. 'And make an enemy of you? I may look daft, but I'm not stupid.'

Jenny insisted on seeing her Aunty Kate on Christmas Day, and although she cried at first, seeing Kate's injuries, both Mary and Tony agreed they had made the right decision. Bernie had shown up later. Subdued. Badly shaken by how close Kate had come to dying.

Despite an aversion to the place, founded on his experience with Sims, Adam visited Kate every day. When she finally took him to bed, two weeks after her release from hospital, it was in his flat. She wept afterwards and he stroked her hair, smoothing it with his fingers until she was calmer. He kissed her and whispered, 'Did I hurt you?'

'No, not you.' She threaded her fingers in his. 'You could never do that. I'm just sad, letting her go, that's all.'

'You won't forget her.'

'I know, but she—' It hurt her to say it. 'Melanie is becoming a part of my past, and it feels like a betrayal.'

He kissed the scar on her forehead. 'Mel was a lively kid. Bursting with energy,' he said. 'She loved people and she loved life.'

Kate struggled on to one elbow. Regular meals and freedom from persecution had rounded her quite pleasantly. Adam stroked the gentle curve of her breast and felt himself stir again. He looked into her eyes. They still sparkled with tears, but he saw something else there. Something that gave him hope. Something akin to affection. 'She wouldn't want your life to end because hers had,' he said.

'No,' Kate agreed, 'that wasn't her style at all.'